THE GOODBYE
COAST

"How the hell do you write a mystery about Philip Marlowe, set it in Los Angeles, and still make it a total gobsmacking original? That's the miracle of Joe Ide's *The Goodbye Coast*. Ide has created a Philip Marlowe for the 2020s. And an LA that he clearly loves and hates."
                                                                    —James Patterson

"The talented Joe Ide manifests Marlowe in the form of a present-day private investigator... The laugh-out-loud dialogue, the vivid similes, the complicated story, and the set-piece subplots are all vintage Chandler. The gripping flashbacks, the adrenaline-pumping action, and the heart-piercing poignance show Mr. Ide at his best. *The Goodbye Coast* delivers the distilled essence of both authors for the price of one."   —Tom Nolan, *Wall Street Journal*

"Every character has great lines, and the descriptions alone make the story worth reading... There is tension, violence, humor, and a bit of sadness, with romance just out of the hero's reach. This one's witty, clever, and fun, and it's worthy of the great Raymond Chandler."
                                            —*Kirkus Reviews* (starred review)

"Raymond Chandler may have inspired him, but this Philip Marlowe is all Joe Ide. I loved this sexy, twisted, complicated Marlowe—he's a perfect match for Ide's sexy, twisted, complicated City of Angels. What a gripping kick-ass book!"   —Rachel Howzell Hall, author of
                                                            These Toxic Things

"Instead of emulating Chandler's stylized first-person point of view, Ide uses his trademark propulsive third-person narrative, entering the heads of multiple characters, including Marlowe's father, Emmet, an aging LAPD officer, and Cody, a client's missing teenage daughter. The prose is pure Ide, infused with whip-smart dialogue and fast-moving scenes throughout iconic Southern California hangouts."

—Naomi Hirahara, *Orange County Register*

"At first I was unsure about Emmet—his character seemed so outside of my idea of Marlowe. But through Emmet Ide offers a thoughtful look at how Marlowe might have come to be the man he is, both in Chandler's books and in this one. It's good to have him back."

—Colette Bancroft, *Tampa Bay Times*

"Sunshine and skulduggery, movie stars and mayhem—Joe Ide brings us a Philip Marlowe who wears our twenty-first century like a well-cut suit."

—Ian Rankin

"Not so much a reimagining of Chandler's world as a reinvigoration. By transplanting Philip Marlowe to 2021 LA, Joe Ide has chiseled off the rust while keeping the soul of one of American fiction's icons. *The Goodbye Coast* is a blast from start to finish."

—Dennis Lehane, author of
Shutter Island and *Mystic River*

"This version of Raymond Chandler's iconic PI patrols the mean streets of contemporary Los Angeles, and while he shares the original's bone-deep iconoclasm, he's distinctly his own man, complete with a rich backstory...The sleuthing here is top-notch, but it's the bantering father-son interplay...that really gives the book its zip. More Marlowe and Emmet would be most welcome."

—Bill Ott, *Booklist* (starred review)

THE GOODBYE
COAST

ALSO BY JOE IDE

IQ
Righteous
Wrecked
Hi Five
Smoke
Fixit

THE GOODBYE COAST

A **PHILIP MARLOWE** NOVEL

JOE IDE

MULHOLLAND BOOKS

Little, Brown and Company
New York Boston London

Copyright © 2022 by Joe Ide and Raymond Chandler Ltd.
Excerpt from *Fixit* copyright © 2023 by Joe Ide

Mulholland Books / Little, Brown and Company
Hachette Book Group
1290 Avenue of the Americas, New York, NY 10104
mulhollandbooks.com

Originally published in hardcover by Mulholland Books, February 2022
First Mulholland Books trade paperback edition, March 2023

Mulholland Books is an imprint of Little, Brown and Company, a division of Hachette Book Group, Inc. The Mulholland Books name and logo are trademarks of Hachette Book Group, Inc.

The Hachette Speakers Bureau provides a wide range of authors for speaking events. To find out more, go to hachettespeakersbureau.com or email hachettespeakers@hbgusa.com.

Little, Brown and Company books may be purchased in bulk for business, educational, or promotional use. For information, please contact your local bookseller or the Hachette Book Group Special Markets Department at special.markets@hbgusa.com.

ISBN 9780316459273 (hc) / 9780316459259 (pb)
LCCN 2021943002

Printing 1, 2022

LSC-C

Printed in the United States of America

To Francis Fukuyama
For his kindness, his generosity, and a whole new life

We all live slapstick lives, under an inexplicable sentence of death.

—Martin Gardner, *The Annotated Alice*

THE GOODBYE
COAST

PROLOGUE

As far back as Marlowe could remember, he'd wanted to be a detective like his dad. He listened intently to the old man's stories about examining the scene, searching for evidence, following leads, questioning witnesses and extracting confessions. It sounded intriguing, exciting, things he wanted to know about, things he wanted to do. He was incensed by the perpetrators. Their cruelty, lack of conscience, lack of decency. He bled for the victims, imagining the undeserved horror the crimes brought down on them.

Marlowe signed up for college courses in law enforcement but almost immediately dropped out. The classes bored the shit out of him but he read the textbooks end to end. A college degree wasn't a requirement to join the LAPD. He applied to the police academy and was accepted. He was nineteen years old. He thought he knew everything. His father worked the homicide table at the Newton Street station.

"You won't make it," Emmet said. "It's your attitude."

"What attitude?" Marlowe said.

"Police departments are paramilitary organizations. You have to follow orders and obey the rules, but you don't like following orders or obeying rules or, for that matter, wearing a uniform, working with a partner or submitting in any way to any kind of authority. *That* attitude."

"You're wrong. That's not me," Marlowe said. "I can do anything I put my mind to." It was one of the rare occasions when Emmet looked at his son with any sort of affection. In this case, it was weary.

"I knew you'd say something like that," Emmet said. "You're hard-headed, son, you don't listen to people who know more than you, another reason why you'll never be a cop." Addie was standing in the doorway. She was holding a mixing bowl in her arms and stirring something with a wooden spoon.

"What about it, Mom?" Marlowe said. "You think I can be a cop, don't you?"

Addie smiled lovingly. "No, sweetheart. You won't last a month."

"Maybe be a plumber, you're good at fixing things," Emmet said.

"Okay, fine," Marlowe said. "When this is over, I'll bring you a spatula to scrape the egg off your face."

Marlowe lasted three weeks. He was discharged from the academy for disrespecting the officer in charge, Cliff Hanson, who oversaw the training division. Hanson was a pompous sort, given to making lengthy, monotonous speeches about serving the community, crime prevention, leadership and being a role model. Marlowe hated the speeches. The whole division had to stand at attention, everybody wishing they could sit the fuck down. Hanson had a long, oblong head, most of which was forehead, a patch of wispy white hair at its apex, bushy eyebrows over a broad nose and an insignificant mouth. Marlowe was enduring yet another speech, this one about patriotism, when he said to a fellow trainee, "You know what? Hanson looks like Howard the Duck." The trainee burst out laughing. Later, he was questioned by the lieutenant and he ratted out Marlowe. After Marlowe's departure, there were further reports about him gambling with the maintenance staff and having sex with a crime scene analyst in the forensics van.

"Didn't I tell you this would happen?" Emmet said gleefully. "Didn't I, hotshot? Are you returning the spatula? Hello? Are you there? Did you want to speak to your mom?"

Marlowe's other career choice was a private investigator. Unfortunately, it involved getting a license. He didn't have the academic requirements, but there was another option. *Applicant has at least three years (2,000 hours each year for a total of 6,000 hours) of compensated experience in the field of investigative work.*

It was the old conundrum. Marlowe needed to work as an investigator, but he couldn't because he didn't have a license to be an investigator. Emmet hooked him up with an old friend and ex-detective, Basilio Ignacia. Basilio agreed to take Marlowe on as an intern. In exchange, he wanted $130 to pay his phone bill and a new set of radial tires for the 1999 Crown Vic he'd bought at a police auction.

They met at Basilio's favorite restaurant, Panda Express on Cahuenga. They sat at a table the size of a school desk eating something called orange chicken with dried-out sticky rice. Marlowe didn't see any Chinese people, they wouldn't recognize the food. Basilio was unshaven, seemingly hungover or maybe that was just how he looked. Bloodhound eyes and Buckwheat hair, hard to do for a Latino man. He wore Bermuda shorts, long white socks and sandals. His T-shirt said VOTE FOR SHANIQUA.

"So tell me, Marlowe," Basilio said, "why do you want to be a PI?"

"I like watching and listening," Marlowe said earnestly. "I like figuring out why people do self-destructive things and why they try to hurt each other. I like watching them trying to walk back their lies."

"Yeah, that's fun," Basilio said.

Marlowe's face hardened, his eyes narrowed. "And I hate it when innocent people get hurt. I want to catch the assholes who hurt them and bring them to their knees."

"Good for you," Basilio said. Not the answer Marlowe was expecting. "I'll tell you, kid, the job isn't exactly like that. I mean the heroic stuff comes up now and then but most of the time, you're looking for a lost horse or working undercover at Burger King or searching a junkyard for an heirloom bedpan." Basilio had ordered broccoli beef along with the orange chicken. He moved the broccoli aside with his plastic fork.

"You're not eating that?" Marlowe said.

"The broccoli? No. It's only there to flavor the meat," Basilio said. He paused. Seemingly his throat was too full to go on eating.

"Remember, you're not a cop," he said with difficulty. "Your main job is looking into things, not catching bad guys."

"No bad guys?" Marlowe said, dismayed.

"No, I didn't mean that. Oh, they're out there. I'm just saying they're not most of the job. Like what I'm working on now. It's a classic. Mrs. Delmonico's husband disappeared two months ago. She's an aggravating cow if I ever saw one. I couldn't stand her, even on the phone. Turns out, Mr. Delmonico is living happily in Boyle Heights with Alejandro, his former golf caddy."

"Have you told Mrs. Delmonico the good news?" Marlowe asked.

"No, it's an ethical thing," Basilio said.

"Isn't fulfilling your contract an ethical thing?"

"Mr. Delmonico left his wife well-off," Basilio said. "And I don't see anything ethical about wrecking the man's life. Besides, I gave the cow a refund." Basilio belched and brushed off the rice kernels clinging to the *q* in *Shaniqua.*

Emmet's having fun with you, Marlowe thought. He hooked you up with a buffoon. Time to cut this short. He started to stand up. "Being a PI is a strange occupation," Basilio continued. He held his plastic fork in the air and struck a philosophical tone. "Reassembling the past, reconstructing relationships, trying to link someone's words with the facts at hand or facts yet to be discovered. You overlay a hundred different constructs over the exact same information and you'll come up with a hundred different theories. Everyone sees, interprets and understands things differently. Everyone has their own aspirations, anxieties and fears. It's what they call human nature." Basilio paused to search his molars with his tongue. "Don't get me wrong, kid. I'm not saying it'll all be mundane. There are things inside people so vicious and depraved you'd think their breath would smell like roadkill. They're out there, Marlowe. Every vile infection, mutant species, every simmering brew of psychopathic evil are waiting for you right outside the door." Basilio unwrapped a toothpick and continued the search. "Sure you're still game?"

That was ten years ago and yes, Marlowe was still game.

CHAPTER ONE
THE CASE

Marlowe drove north on Pacific Coast Highway, heading into Malibu. Eleven thirty in the morning and he was a brick in a brick wall of traffic. It was one of the reasons he almost passed on the meeting. Driving from Hollywood to Malibu and back again was the same as being dead for three hours.

It used to be impossible to get to the beach itself. The big houses were packed in like library books and the wealthy residents blocked access with locked gates and PRIVATE PROPERTY signs. The California Coastal Commission had a difficult time convincing the owners that living on the beach didn't mean they owned the beach itself. For decades, celebrities like Dick Clark, Mel Brooks, Jack Lemmon, Olivia Newton-John and David Geffen fought efforts to let the public use their own beaches. In the end, the public won. Even so, ordinary folks were only seen occasionally. The locals grew azaleas in front of the COASTAL ACCESS signs or blotted out letters so they said COAL ASS.

Marlowe's potential new client was Kendra James, a full-on movie star and all that implied. Homes here and abroad, Bentley and a Prius in the garage, the latter to show her concern for the environment, vacations in Ibiza, on Lake Como and Richard Branson's private island and a personal trainer named Steely Dan who sometimes stayed over. She had a separate closet for her six hundred pairs of shoes. Money will protect you from everything, Marlowe thought, except Mother Nature, love and tragedy. Six weeks ago, Kendra's husband, Terry, was murdered, shot to death on the beach right in front of their home. Terry was forty-three years old.

Marlowe turned off PCH onto Malibu Colony Road. The houses weren't especially impressive from the street, many of them fronted by a bland stucco entry and a driveway. It was deceptive, however. The homes were huge, lavish, median price on the waterfront was almost thirty million. Marlowe had an innate dislike for the wealthy. Their power, privilege, their firewall of conscienceless attorneys, their wretched excess. Marlowe liked nice things but not immoderately, not over-the-top. Somehow, this made him a better person but he wasn't sure how. He passed the public entrance to the beach; a twenty-foot stretch of listing chain link fence. He was surprised it wasn't cloaked in camouflage netting with OPEN SEWER signs next to the gate.

Marlowe arrived at Kendra's place and parked on the road. He hesitated. He didn't want to go in. The idea of meeting a celebrity repelled him. Why? he thought. You don't even know this person. You're being prejudiced, a victim of stereotypes. He'd heard David Beckham was a good guy. Same with Dave Chappelle and Penélope Cruz. Maybe meeting Kendra would be a good experience or, at the very least, interesting. Marlowe waited for his mood to change but the insight made no difference. He didn't want to be here. Reluctantly he got out of the car. "Here we go," he sighed.

Kendra James was sitting on the sand drinking another Bloody Mary. She stared blankly at the flat, gray sea, gray clouds drifting mournfully overhead. The last few weeks had been a terrible ordeal. She was surprised at how much she missed Terry. She'd kicked him out of the house and filed for divorce right after she burned up his clothes and put their wedding pictures in the shredder. She despised him right up to the moment she put a rose on his casket.

She sensed someone was there, like a change in temperature or a breeze through an open window. She turned her head and looked up.

"Hello. I'm Philip Marlowe," he said, a note of regret in his voice. He reached down to shake hands.

"I'm sorry, I don't shake hands. I'm something of a germophobe," she said. "Thank you for schlepping all the way out here. I don't leave the house much these days." She would have made him come out here if she'd been in France. She patted the spot next to her. "Have a seat, Mr. Marlowe. Join me."

"No thank you. I don't want to get sand on my clothes," Marlowe said. He was wearing a dove-gray suit, obviously handmade, black silk tie undone, a milky-white Egyptian cotton shirt, thread count in the 180 to 200 range, and bespoke oxfords, shined but not shiny. Kendra wasn't used to being refused but she'd forgive him this time. She respected nice clothes.

"Let's go up on the deck," she said. Oddly, Marlowe didn't seem the least bit intimidated and people usually were, even if they'd known her for a long time.

As they crossed the sand, she noticed Marlowe was wearing a vintage Patek Philippe Tiffany rectangular watch. Her father had one just like it. The entry gate was held shut with a commercial-grade padlock and a heavy chain. Kendra did the combination, huddling over it as if Marlowe might want to rob the house one day. She led him up the side stairs to the living room. She liked showing the house to newcomers. The great room was an acre of white marble floor, sleek furniture that seemed to defy gravity and art pieces that were hard to differentiate from the furniture. Visitors invariably made a comment. *It's so beautiful! The view is magnificent!* Marlowe said nothing. In fact, he seemed to resent being here.

They went out on the deck and sat at a table shaded by an umbrella. For a moment, neither of them said anything. She gave him one of her favorite looks; a half smile, percipient and slightly amused, as if to say, *I'm way ahead of you, buddy boy.* Marlowe met her gaze and she was instantly uncomfortable. His eyes were the kind that took in everything but gave nothing away, the kind that didn't notice but inhaled; the kind that weren't neutral, but assessed, gleaned and adjudicated. She couldn't help staring. To break the spell she said,

"Would you like something to drink?"

"Black coffee," Marlowe said.

"Lucy, are you there?" she called.

Marlowe had presence, she decided. Surprising for someone who was probably in his early thirties. He was very good-looking, but he wore it differently than the other handsome men she had known. It was as if he was unaware of his appearance and would be surprised if someone remarked on it.

"Lucy, where are you?" Kendra said irritably.

Marlowe was looking off, distracted, as if he was bored and thinking about something other than the A-list celebrity sitting right in front of him. Disrespectful, Kendra thought. She wondered why her father had insisted on him. His quiet intensity was appealing. He reminded her a little of Steve McQueen if Steve McQueen had been a rude, insolent asshole. "Lucy! Are you there?" she called louder.

Marlowe wondered why Kendra didn't walk ten feet to the open door. Moments later, the housekeeper appeared. She was dark, stout, wearing an actual maid's uniform. Black with a white collar, white apron, white cuffs on the sleeves. It was as if a Latina woman had somehow landed a part on *Downton Abbey.* He offered her a friendly smile.

"I'm Philip Marlowe," he said.

"Hello, sir." She was surprised he'd introduced himself.

"I don't know your name."

"Lucy Cabello. Would you like something to drink?"

"Thank you, Lucy. I'll have black coffee."

Lucy nodded and went back inside. Kendra sighed, apparently annoyed by all the civility. She looks like Grace Kelly without the grace, thought Marlowe. Aristocratic features and soft blonde hair, keen blue eyes, her lips artificially plumped, her body teetering between fashionably sexy and she should lose a few pounds. Marlowe took in the view. The sea was the color of mop water, paltry waves lapping, sea gulls fighting over something slimy and covered with sand. An elderly man with a big belly and orange cabana shirt trudged past.

He was talking on the phone and watching his Labradoodle defecate in a tide pool. "The hell I'll give him points," he said heatedly.

"I've heard you can be prickly," Kendra said, as if that were something charming. "May I call you Philip?"

"Call me Marlowe."

"In fact, Marlowe, I've heard you were a rude, impolite boor."

"What's your point?"

"My point?" Kendra said with a laugh. "We're going to be working together and it would be nice if we were at least amicable."

"We'll be working together in the sense that I'm doing the work and you're going about your business," Marlowe said. "This is not a movie project. There will be no meetings, script notes, conference calls or explanatory emails. I do my job and when I'm done, I call you." Now that he'd met her, he almost wanted to get fired.

Kendra glared. Marlowe knew what she was thinking. *Nobody talks to Kendra James that way, not with a billion dollars in ticket sales on her résumé.* She was probably on the verge of saying do you know who I am? Marlowe had seen a video of her saying that to a highway patrolman. It sounded terrible. She might as well have said, *I am a world-famous celebrity and you're a turd on a motorcycle.* Lucy brought their drinks out on a silver tray. Marlowe's coffee and a Bloody Mary for Kendra. She hadn't asked for one. Apparently, it was assumed.

"Thank you, Lucy," Marlowe said.

"Lucy, have you seen Pav?" Kendra asked.

"No, *señora.*"

"He's supposed to take me to a premiere tomorrow night. I have to tell him he's working." She sipped her drink and sighed glumly. "I don't know. I might not go. I wish I had a movie out. What will I talk about?"

Lucy and Marlowe exchanged a glance and she went back inside. Kendra caught it and scowled.

"I can cut this short," Marlowe said. "If you wanted to talk about Terry's case, I can't help you. Your best bet is the police."

"No, this is not about that philandering dimwit, it's about his daughter, Cody. Two weeks ago, she ran away."

"Two weeks," Marlowe said. "The first of the month?"

"I suppose. She stays out overnight but never this long. I've tried to reach her, of course. Phone, email, I left messages. I'm really worried about her."

Marlowe's bullshit detector emitted a loud buzz. Kendra sounded urgent but not sincere.

"How old is Cody?" he asked.

"Seventeen but she comes off as older. I've reported it to the police but they don't look for runaways. It's ridiculous."

"Running away isn't a crime, there's no law to enforce. Do you have a picture?"

Kendra passed him her phone.

"This is pretty recent," she said. Cody was sitting on the hood of a car. She had a boyish figure, pale skin, high cheekbones and green eyes, her expression like a European model, faraway and indifferent. She wore black jeans, Gothy makeup and a T-shirt that said DAS BUNKER. Her hair was styled like a Japanese anime character. Short, dyed black with a purple sheen, jagged layers and jagged bangs angled over her eyebrows.

"I'll email you that one and some others," Kendra said. Somehow, Kendra had finished her drink without him noticing. She put some ice in her mouth and crunched it. She wants another one, Marlowe thought.

"What's Cody like?"

"She's spoiled rotten and not the least bit considerate, I'd like to lock her in the crate my dog used to sleep in."

"Did Cody and Terry get along?"

"Yes, they were very close. They talked about everything together. If I hadn't despised him I would have been jealous." She picked up her glass, tipped it back and drank the pink water at the bottom.

"Smart?"

"Yes, Cody is very smart. She skipped a grade, takes AP classes but she hates school. She can be devious too. I watched her play poker with Terry's friends. She pretended she was a hapless little girl and cleaned them out."

"Any idea where Cody went?" Marlowe asked.

"No. She never said anything about her comings and goings," Kendra said as if the whole topic was boring. "Make an inquiry and Cody would say something vague and perfunctory. She was very secretive."

"Terry have any other kids?"

"Yes, a son. His name is Noah. Cody's opposite." Kendra's whole vibe changed, like she was proud to know him, to show him off. "He was an excellent student, polite and very good-looking," she said. "He's an athlete too. He's playing minor league baseball in Lancaster."

"Was Cody into drugs?" Marlowe asked.

"Weed, alcohol."

"That's all? You're sure."

Kendra huffed. "If it's one thing movie stars know about, it's drugs."

"Did Cody have a boyfriend? Girlfriend?"

"Cody had a fling with a girl but she needs a penis. I never met any of her dates but—oh yes, she did bring a boy here a couple of times. Roy something. What a loser. He was probably pathetic at conception. Noah talked to him. He said Roy was probably giving Cody money. Her allowance is generous but she was always broke."

"Did Noah and Cody get along?"

"No. They were like a reenactment of the war in Vietnam. Fire-fights and bombing runs for years on end."

"Why do you think Cody left?" Marlowe asked.

Kendra shrugged. "Why does a teenage girl do anything?" Kendra slapped her hand on the table and said, "Lucy, *where are you?*" She rose, chair scraping the deck, and marched inside. Marlowe could hear her talking, severe and reproachful. He wanted to drown her in the Labradoodle's tide pool. Kendra came out with a fresh Bloody Mary. Before she sat down, Marlowe said,

"I want to see Cody's room."

They went inside and walked down a long hall. It was lined with movie posters, *Silverlake Story, Love Sucks, Never Say I Do, The*

Coach's Wife, and others. They were all romantic comedies. A couple of years ago, Kendra attempted to escape the tedious but lucrative typecasting by accepting the part of a real serial killer named Donna Ethridge. Ethridge lured seventeen men into her aging Winnebago and cracked their skulls open with an axe handle. The reviewer in the *New York Times* described Kendra's performance as "rather like watching my nine-year-old niece pretending to be a robot."

"How does my father know you?" Kendra asked.

"I'm not saying," Marlowe said. Her famous blue eyes flashed red.

"Why not?"

"For the same reason I won't talk about your case with him."

Cody's room was no more organized than a basket of dirty laundry. Random belongings scattered, stacked and flung everywhere. You could hardly see the floor. "I don't know what you can tell from this mess," Kendra said. Evidently, Cody liked clothes. A fortune's worth were strewn around, enough to wardrobe a movie about Ivanka Trump. Almost everything stupidly expensive. A $4,000 Fendi Peekaboo bag hanging on a chair. Marlowe had recovered one on a robbery case. A box labeled KINGSEAL. Probably sealskin shoes, Marlowe thought. Maybe they were waterproof. A MacBook Pro was stuck in the wastepaper basket, a lone Jimmy Choo waited on the windowsill. Such careless wealth, Marlowe thought. An oddity. A catcher's protective vest half under the bed. Noah played minor league baseball, it was obviously his. Stealing his equipment is a helluva way to punish your brother. The poor guy must have gone crazy looking for it. Kendra was bored. She went into the hall calling for another Bloody Mary.

There were also vintage T-shirts, clunky black Frankenstein shoes and studded belts. There were posters on the wall. Two bands. Rites of Spring and Moss Icon. One was of a sad Batman. The caption: *My parents are dead.* Marlowe looked in the bathroom. It was like the cosmetics counter at Bloomingdale's. A cluster of colored soaps in a silver bowl, the brands imprinted on them. Dior, Côte d'Azur, Elemis and Lava. Lava? There was also a lot of black makeup. Eye shadow, mascara, lipstick. Maybe that explained the Lava.

Kendra returned with another drink. "Christ, I had to go all the way to the kitchen."

"Did Cody have money?" Marlowe asked.

"She took a couple of hundred out of my bag, and maybe three out of my desk drawer," Kendra said. "She also stole Lucy's car."

"Did you replace the car?"

"Yes, I replaced it," Kendra said indignantly, muttering in a lower voice, "with a car of similar value."

"Similar value?" He laughed. "How much did you make on your last movie?"

"Fuck you, Marlowe."

Marlowe didn't like being here. The room was like a Goodwill store in Dubai. If Kendra weren't paying him so much he'd have left right after he met her.

"I have to go," he said.

"What? Why so soon? You've only been here for twenty minutes," Kendra said.

"I have another commitment." Another commitment like playing Hold 'Em at the Bicycle Club or eating a banh mi sandwich at the House of Pho. She trailed him down the hallway.

"When will I hear from you?"

"When I have something to tell you."

"Marlowe, *I want her back!*" she said, adamant. She means it, Marlowe thought, but not out of parental concern. He left her in the great room yelling, "If George hadn't insisted on you, I'd fire you right now!"

Lucy showed him to the door. "She replaced your car with one of similar value?" Marlowe said.

"That *puta* bought a car two years older than my car."

"She must be hell to work for."

"*Sí.* Look at this *estúpida* uniform."

A man in a blue tracksuit came through the door. He was Marlowe's age, in good shape, angled features and obsidian eyes, a calculating, suspicious expression. He might have been an oligarch's chief of security or a stand-in for the craggy guy who played James Bond.

"Philip Marlowe," Marlowe said, extending his hand.

The man brushed past Marlowe and was gone.

"Who's that?"

"Pav is Kendra's bodyguard and he drives her," Lucy said. "He is her slave. She treat him *muy malo*. One day, he will pay her back."

CHAPTER TWO

DAS BUNKER

Marlowe lived on Hollywood Boulevard just off North Ivar, a shabby, sketchy area, a few blocks and a million miles away from the TCL Chinese Theatre, IMAX, the Madame Tussauds wax museum, the El Capitan and the Hollywood and Highland shopping extravaganza. Marlowe's neighbor Mr. Mendoza had told him gentrification was coming here but somebody mugged it along the way.

Marlowe's stretch of the boulevard was littered sidewalks, old men camped out in vestibules and a dreary array of worn-down commercial buildings, their architecture blurred by banners, signs, graffiti, peeling paint and a thick crust of pollution. On street level, there were innumerable small shops that sold clothes, jewelry, mattresses, furniture, toys, shoes, souvenirs and electronics. Some sold all of the above.

Marlowe's home and office was a seemingly derelict two-story building. According to the brass label on the now-defunct coal-fired boiler, it was built in 1936. A heavy security gate guarded the front entrance. The windows were boarded up and plastered with flyers, demolition notices and crude drawings of big dicks.

Marlowe drove his car around the back. A 2008 Mustang GT. He'd always wanted one as a kid and he needed a fast ride from time to time. There were other cars with more horsepower but three hundred and forty-nine was enough for him. The car was devoid of badges, reflectors and chrome strips and painted a dark, flat gray. It suited Marlowe's aesthetic but Emmet said he should take it back to the factory and have them finish it. Marlowe parked and went inside. He turned off the alarm but didn't bother with the light. The first floor was formerly a garage.

There was a nominal office for interviewing gangsters and ex-felons. The usual boxes of stuff you couldn't throw away were stacked on shelves. On Marlowe's twenty-first birthday, Emmet had given him a Remington 870 pump-action shotgun with an eleven-inch barrel. Marlowe didn't have much use for it and he was uncomfortable with guns. He kept it leaning against the wall between a rake and a long pair of pruning shears. He had a 9mm Sig in a covered frying pan on top of the stove. Marlowe went up the narrow stairs, keeping his hands to himself. There was a faint, ragged chalk line on both handrails. An early-warning system. Coming up or going down you'd leave a smear.

Marlowe had restored the hardwood floors. The living room was a rich expanse of umber oak crafted with imperfect boards, the grains and knots nearly artful. New visitors would unfailingly say some variation of "Oh my." The furnishings were minimal. No souvenirs, objets d'art or mementos of his travels. Marlowe didn't need a picture of the Grand Canyon and shiny piece of agate to remind himself he'd been there.

On his way back from Kendra's he picked up some takeout from Sanamluang. He sat at a picnic table, the kind you see in a park with bench seats on either side. He'd sanded it down, stained it and liked the way it looked. He'd always been uncomfortable in dining rooms. He got an Allagash White out of the fridge, drank it with green papaya salad with chicken marinated in soy, sesame oil and coriander root, the chicken infused with a grassy, herbal flavor. He wondered how a small Thai restaurant could make fifty good dishes while Denny's couldn't make one, not even breakfast.

Emmet had sent Marlowe Terry's police file. Marlowe sat down on the Eames easy chair, opened his laptop and started reading. On October thirty-first at approximately twelve midnight, Terry was shot twice in the face with a .45-caliber handgun on the beach about twenty-five yards from Kendra's Malibu home. On occasions when Kendra was away for any length of time, Pav would invite Terry to come over and stay. They were good friends, according to the police. Pav said Terry was living in a "really lousy" apartment in Mar Vista. The temperature was fifty-two degrees, the surf was high and the wind was blowing at seventeen miles an hour. Terry was wearing pajamas and a bathrobe, making it unlikely he came out voluntarily.

Later, the police found that the combination lock on the outside gate had been cut with a bolt cutter. The surveillance camera caught the suspect coming up the side stairs. A male, wearing dark clothes, a cap and a mask. It was too dark to be certain but police thought it was a Jason mask. Height was indeterminate, broad shoulders and back. Police speculated the suspect was strong and athletic. He stumbled twice. His size 10½ shoe prints were found on the stairs. They matched none of the residents or employees.

Surveillance cameras saw Terry arrive at Kendra's at 9:47 p.m. He took Cody to a party on Canaan Road at 10:01 and returned to the house at 10:25. A number of witnesses saw Cody at the party. Nathan Schwartz, a partygoer, age nineteen, wanted to have sex with Cody. He drove her home, arriving there at 2:21 a.m. She was obviously inebriated. Schwartz helped her up the walkway and she shut the door in his face. She wasn't seen leaving the house until the following day. Schwartz was cleared.

Around noon on the thirty-first, Pav drove Kendra to Santa Barbara. She was attending an annual Halloween party and planned to stay with friends for at least a week. They left Malibu at approximately 1:00 in the afternoon. Pav returned from Santa Barbara at approximately 5:30, arriving at his apartment in Santa Monica at approximately 7:30. He said he didn't leave until the following morning when he heard Terry was dead. His story could not be verified. Terry's son, Noah, was in Lancaster playing baseball. His coaches and other players attested to his whereabouts.

Marlowe closed the laptop. He went up on the roof with a

tumbler of Old Forester 1920 Prohibition Style 115-proof bourbon and a package of unfiltered Camels. He didn't drink or smoke very often but when he did, he wanted real liquor and a real cigarette. The atmosphere wasn't exactly pleasant. The air was warm and dirty, Friday night traffic endless in both directions. In this Hollywood there was no romance, no night filled with possibilities, no one was tapped for stardom and life was not an adventure. This Hollywood was workaday and ordinary and a grind.

As a rule, Marlowe kept close track of subcultures, worlds a private investigator might one day need to surveil, search or be a part of. The vintage T-shirts, clunky black Frankenstein shoes, studded belts and black makeup in Cody's room were common to Emos, or "emotional hardcore." They were an offshoot of Goth. Rites of Spring and Moss Icon were Emo bands, their music about painful relationships, emotional anguish and isolation. The T-shirt Cody was wearing in the photo said DAS BUNKER, the name of an Emo and Goth club at Pico and Crenshaw. As good a place to start as any.

The entrance to Das Bunker was like the gate to a medieval prison, the sign overhead in Halloween green. The doorman didn't bother checking his ID. The main room was huge in that clublike way, all red lighting and blinding strobes. It was Friday night, the place packed. There was nothing new here, Marlowe thought. Not the rainbow-colored wigs, zombie makeup, gas masks, eye patches, fishnets, the profusion of buckles and straps and black leather everything. There was a stairway leading up to the simulated S&M room. He stood on the landing and carefully scanned the place. He was good at identifying faces. He didn't see Cody.

The S&M room was as Marlowe thought it would be. Everything painted black, ominous lavender lights, a soundtrack of people screaming for mercy and the usual collection of handcuffs, plastic cat-o'-nine-tails, inexplicable wall racks and harnesses hanging from the black ceiling. A twentysomething guy was kneeling on the spanking bench. "I'm *sorry,* mistress," he said defensively. "I'm really really sorry, *okay?*" He looked ordinary, like the assistant manager at Panda Express.

His mistress was an undernourished young woman, all sinew and elbows, wearing a black leather hood, only her shrewish eyes showing. She was also wearing mommy jeans, a T-shirt that said THE AMERICAN HEART ASSOCIATION and drugstore running shoes, oddly discrepant for a dominatrix. With each whack of the Ping-Pong paddle, she yelled things like, "Submit, or I'll bury your head in Benjamin's sandbox!" and "That's the stupidest haircut I've ever seen!" and "I'm going to burn you with a saucepan!" Abruptly, she stopped, heaved an exasperated sigh and said, "We talked about this, Larry. You're supposed to be screaming, remember?"

Marlowe went back downstairs. He couldn't get over it. Young people imagining what pain would feel like if it were real pain. To feel anything these days you had to join a cult, he thought. It was a little after one, the crowd was thinning, people getting tired of paying $19 for a well drink. Cody was a no-show. Some would go home but that didn't seem to fit Marlowe's idea of Cody. She'd probably go somewhere with friends, have coffee, eat a burger someplace that was open twenty-four hours. He stopped at IHOP, Kitchen 24, Fat Sal's Deli and a few others. Nothing. He was walking back to the car when he stopped, closed his eyes and said, "You're an idiot, Marlowe."

He blamed his mental lapse on fatigue. He looked again at the photo Kendra had emailed him. Cody was sitting on the hood of a car. There was a casual ease about her. She was leaning back against the windshield, something you wouldn't do to a stranger's ride. Cody had left Kendra's two weeks ago, on the first, with around five hundred in cash and Lucy's car, probably abandoned by now. The cheapest motel in Hollywood was a hundred bucks a night. She's broke, Marlowe thought. Someone is supporting her, probably the owner of that car. Was it Roy something, the boy Kendra said was pathetic in the womb? The license plate was legible. He'd do a search in the morning.

Marlowe drove home, climbed the stairs and went into the bedroom. He left the room dark and undressed. A "light painting" hung on the wall opposite the bed. It was created by an artist named Hap

Tivey. It might have been a sixty-inch TV or a super-large monitor. The entire screen was an intense field of saturated light with seemingly infinite depth. Look at it long enough, and the painting began to move, like clouds behind a diaphanous blue curtain. Marlowe stared at it until he became the blue. He relaxed. The whirring images of the day's irritations and activities slowed until his mind was blank. He lay down and fell asleep.

Roy Duncan was the registered owner of a 2010 Nissan Sentra. He was twenty-one years old, 5'11", 145 pounds, no criminal record. His driver's license photo revealed a young man with bad acne, big ears and pink bangs fringing his wide, sweaty forehead. He had a confused expression, like he'd walked into the wrong house. He was an assistant manager at Jiffy Lube. A baby daddy if there ever was one.

Roy lived in a crappy apartment building on South Normandie. Marlowe figured Cody would sleep all day and come out late like a vole or a snake. He went over there around nine thirty and checked the underground garage. Roy's Sentra was there. It was Saturday night. Odds were, a seventeen-year-old Emo with a fake ID and her twenty-one-year-old boyfriend were going out. Marlowe sat in his car, waiting for the Sentra to emerge from the garage. It was nearing ten o'clock when Cody and Roy came out the front door of the building. Are they walking? Marlowe thought. Why not take the car?

Roy was shaped like a stick with two knots that served as his shoulders. He was wearing a long Dracula coat, white makeup, black lipstick, and the unfortunate pink bangs. Convenient for Cody. Roy had his own place, paid the rent, and the possibility of sex, or even affection, was probably enough to keep him subservient. The couple was arguing, Roy pleading and Cody exasperated, her arms folded across her chest. Finally, she looked skyward, conceding. They walked off down the street. The argument was probably about the car, mused Marlowe.

He was about to get out of the Mustang when a man appeared from somewhere behind him and rushed after the kids. It was so abrupt and obvious Marlowe froze. He got out of the car and followed. The man stayed behind the couple and on the other side of the street. Marlowe could only see him from the back. He was of indeterminate age, good build and he moved well. He was wearing dark clothes and a black ski cap. *Uh-oh.* The only people who dressed like that were commandos and criminals. Was the man following Cody or was he going to attack?

Cody and Roy turned on Kenmore, a seedy commercial street. A dry cleaner's, a Persian grocery store, a Korean restaurant, everything closed. Nothing but the same for several blocks. Where are they going? Marlowe wondered. There was some traffic. If the man was going to attack, it wouldn't be here, he thought. The couple stopped at the entrance to an alley. They argued again, Roy explaining, a desperate quality about him, gesturing like the alley would be a better way to go. Cody quarreled, then shook her head wearily and gave in. Roy was paying the rent, after all. They entered the alley, the man not far behind. "Aw hell," Marlowe said. *This is a setup.*

The alley was long, lit only by yellow bulbs over some of the fire exits. The stretch of asphalt went dark-light, dark-light all the way to the end of the block. Broken glass glinted, litter skipped in a light breeze. Cody was walking fast, pissed, Roy trailing, saying things to mollify her. The man quickened his pace. He pulled the ski cap down over his face. A gun had appeared at his side.

"Shit," Marlowe hissed. He went after the man as fast and as quietly as he could. If he was detected too soon, the man would turn and shoot him. Cody and Roy were in a dark patch and so was the man. Marlowe couldn't see either. Instinctively, he shouted, "Cody, RUN!"

The man jerked around and saw Marlowe. He started to shoot but realized his target was getting away. He turned again, the gun rose and the silencer spat three times. But the kids had reached the end of the alley and were turning the corner. The man swung around a second time and fired three more shots, but Marlowe had already darted between two buildings. He ran a bit and hid in a doorway. Was the man following him? No, he'd be focused on getting away.

Pov of Cody

Where did Cody and Roy go? Marlowe thought. When the pair reached the end of the alley, he saw them turning left. They were probably circling around to the apartment and relative safety. Marlowe took off in the other direction. He'd get there ahead of them and wait. He ran easily, his breathing rhythmic and steady. He arrived at the building, stood near the intercom and looked at his phone, an excuse to be anywhere these days.

Minutes later, Cody and Roy arrived, staggering, breathing in heaves and nearly hysterical, Roy fumbling with his keys.

"Hurry up!" Cody said.

"I'm trying!"

Roy finally got the door open. Before it closed, Marlowe slipped in behind them, the kids too distracted to notice. He trailed them down the hall to an apartment. Roy got that door open. The couple went in, Marlowe right behind them. He shoved Cody hard. She bumped into Roy and they both stumbled into the living room and fell to the floor. They were too exhausted to get up.

"Who...are you," Cody said between gasps.

"My name's Marlowe. I'm the guy who saved you from getting shot in the back."

"What...are...you doing here?"

"I'm a private detective, Kendra sent me. She wants you to come home." Cody drew in a sharp breath; her eyes red, wide with anger and fear.

"Oh she does, does she?" she said savagely. "I don't know who you are, asshole, but that's never going to happen!"

"Why not?" Marlowe said. "It'd be better than staying in this dump."

"Do you know what happened to my dad?"

"I know he was murdered."

Cody sneered. "The police don't know who did it but I do."

"Oh really? And who might that be?"

"Kendra. Kendra killed my dad!"

CHAPTER THREE
HANDLE YOUR SHIT, GIRL

Cody was curled up in the passenger seat, arms around herself, her head against the window. Before tonight, the idea of life-threatening danger had seemed adventurous and exciting, even romantic. She'd been so stupid, so naïve. She wanted to smash her face on the dashboard. That unintended consequences thing was no joke. She kept replaying in her mind what happened. Walking with that idiot, Roy, fed up with him—and then that voice, *Cody, RUN!* A gun flashed in the dark, bullets zipping past and then she was running. She saw herself sprawled on the asphalt, life leaking out of the bullet holes in her back. She was almost *killed!* She cried and tried to keep the sniffling down. She hated it when she cried. It made her feel vulnerable, it made her feel weak. She avoided showing her hand to anyone. She glanced at Marlowe. He'd risked his life for her. He didn't have to, he just did.

"Thank you," she whispered.

"You're welcome," he said.

Emmet Marlowe lived in South Central LA, renamed by the city South LA, as if political correctness would make the residents forget about the proliferation of gangs, poverty and drug addiction. It was like naming your attack dog Melissa or Cupcake. Emmet's front yard was overgrown with ferns, agave plants, banana palms and dwarf palmettos. He called it his garden. Marlowe called it laziness. He pushed and ducked his way through the foliage, Cody behind him.

"Who lives here?" Cody said. "Apes?" Marlowe sucked in a deep breath. This was going to be an ordeal. He rang the bell.

"Dad, it's me. Open up." He rang the bell again. "Dad? Open up!"

"Yeah, yeah, I'm coming," Emmet groused. Emmet reminded his son of Harry Dean Stanton. All scrawny and disjointed, like his skeleton had been assembled from leftover parts and not enough screws. The door opened. Emmet was in his boxer shorts, scowling, his legs like hairy chicken bones. For no apparent reason, he was wearing a hideous Hawaiian shirt. It looked like a family of parrots were trying to kill each other.

"Dad," Marlowe said.

"Philip," Emmet said. He always said his son's name like a cuss word. It was the main reason why Marlowe preferred Marlowe. Emmet eyed Cody up and down, his lip curled like he was about to bark. "Who are you?" he said gruffly.

"What's it to you, gramps?" Cody said.

"Gramps? The only way I'd be your gramps is if your mother married a jackass."

"What are you doing here anyway?" Cody retorted. "I thought the Clampetts lived in Beverly Hills."

"Jesus, enough," Marlowe said.

They went inside. Cody looked around, confused and a little dismayed. Except for the dust and dishevelment, the living room was the same as it was thirty-three years ago, when Emmet and Addie first moved in. Same oak-veneer furniture, lacy curtains, lampshades with fringes on them and a thousand knickknacks. It was as if the historical society preserved the place but didn't hire a cleaning lady.

"So what's this about?" Emmet said.

"Her name is Cody, she's Kendra James's stepdaughter," Marlowe explained. "A little while ago somebody tried to kill her. I brought her here for safekeeping."

"*Here?* Christ. Why don't you keep her with you?"

"If the killer finds out she's my client, he'll come to my— Dad, could you please put some pants on?"

"Where's she going to stay?" Emmet said, seemingly outraged.

"Second bedroom."

"You're not eating my food, girlie."

"Food like what?" Cody shot back. "Oatmeal? Ovaltine?" Marlowe sighed. This would be less like an ordeal and more like a cage fight.

Cody dropped her backpack on the floor and sat on the bed. She covered her face with her hands and sobbed, "I'm so fucked." Of all the people who could have rescued her, it was a goddamn private detective! A professional snoop! She was stuck here too. She'd spent the last of Roy's money on a half ounce of Sunset Kush. And the moron kept texting her. *Where are you? Are you okay? Can I pick you up?* Piss off, you mutt. Everything was coming apart and closing in. Panic seized her by the throat. "I've gotta get out of here!" she blurted. She wasn't "allowed" to call Eli. She texted him. *EMERGENCY! EMERGENCY! HAVE TO TALK!* It took him forty-five long minutes to call back.

"Somebody tried to shoot me!" Cody cried.

"What? What are you talking about?" Eli said. She told him about the man in the alley and how Marlowe had saved her. She told him she was safe, a house somewhere in the ghetto. She could feel the change in mood. Eli was paying attention.

"Who was it? The guy with the gun," he said.

"I don't know but he had a silencer," Cody said. Usually Eli had something smartass to say but this time he said nothing. You could feel his alarm escalating through the phone.

"Eli? Are you there?"

"Yeah, I'm here. We might be in trouble."

"*Might?* You've got to be kidding," Cody said.

"Uh, okay, just, uh, sit tight and we'll figure something out."

Eli sounded terrified. He should be, she thought. There was a knock on the door. She jumped.

"Cody, could you come out here, please?" Marlowe said.

"I have to go. I love you," she whispered. Eli ended the call before he could say it back. That hurt.

"Cody?" Marlowe said again.

She took a deep breath. This could unravel everything. She felt her hard self returning. *Handle your shit, girl.* "Coming," she said.

While Cody was cleaning up, Marlowe caught Emmet up on the day's happenings. They worked together on some of Marlowe's cases. Informally. No one was in charge and no one gave orders, each of them independent to do what they thought was best. Emmet had access to police reports and he would send copies to Marlowe. Marlowe would send Emmet his notes. This nonseparation of labor agreement made some of their efforts redundant, but that was understood. Only the narrow focus of the case kept them from having more than words. They both knew where the line was and stayed well away from it.

Marlowe sat at the breakfast table, checking his emails. Emmet was looking in the fridge, nothing in there but a twelve-pack of Coors, two eggs, half a loaf of stale bread and a head of iceberg lettuce the same color as a basketball. Emmet had changed into a pair of stained sweatpants, the crotch sagging nearly to his knees.

"You looked better in the boxer shorts," Cody said as she entered the room. She was wearing jeans and a yellow T-shirt. Her hair was wet, face shiny, no makeup. The Emo girl next door. "Does Grandpa have to be here?" she said.

"It's my goddamn house. I'll be where I want, girlie," Emmet said.

"Could you knock it off with the 'girlie'?"

"Have a seat," Marlowe said.

She sat across from him, drew up her knees and put her arms around them. "Can I have a beer?"

"No, you can't," Emmet said.

"Give her one, Dad. She's been through hell," Marlowe said. Emmet reluctantly took one out of the fridge and set it down in front of her. Marlowe thought she might have asked for a beer to establish herself as an adult, an equal. Emmet refuses, Marlowe consents. He understands. He let her sip her beer and settle in.

"Why do you think Kendra had your father killed?" he asked.

"I have my reasons."

"What reasons?"

"You said Kendra sent you," Cody replied, belligerent. "You're working for her, not me. If I tell you something you might turn around and call her. I'd be trapped here."

"I just saved your life. Why would I want to endanger it?"

"Money trumps everything," she sneered.

"Pretty jaded for a kid," Emmet said. "Yeah, must be hard living out there in Malibu. Walk out your front door and you could get shit on by a sandpiper."

Cody cupped her hand to her ear. "You know, I think I hear them calling you from the senior center, gramps. It's your turn for shuffleboard."

"Okay, that's enough," Marlowe said.

"Look. I'm not saying anything with him here, okay?" Cody said. "Not a word." Emmet got up and abruptly left the room.

"Can we talk now?" Marlowe said.

"No, not really," Cody said. "You're still on Kendra's payroll." Emmet returned and slapped his LAPD badge down on the table.

"Homicide detective for seventeen years. You're gonna talk to us, or I'll drag you down to the station right now. I'll take a statement and put you in a holding cell with girls who will eat you like a raspberry Pop-Tart, so you better start talking or go put your shoes on." Chastened, Cody pursed her lips and tipped her head sideways.

"Who was the man in the alley?" Marlowe asked.

"Pav, Kendra's bodyguard," Cody said.

"How do you know?" Emmet said. "Given your wonderful personality it could have been anybody."

Cody gave him a look. "Kendra had Pav kill Terry and now she wants me dead too."

"Why?" Marlowe said.

"Because I know what they did. I have it on tape," she said, confident now. Father and son exchanged a glance. Cody got out her phone, fiddled with it and played a recording. There was a lot of ambient sound, wind noise, rustling and scraping. "The sound's not too good," she said.

Pav: "Those investigators are...take the blame...your idea."
Kendra: "...be a baby...can't find evidence in...had to kill..."
Pav: "...take the blame...your idea."

Then Pav had a coughing fit; they listened to him hacking and clearing his throat.

Kendra: "Do you have to..."
Pav: "Yes, I have to!"
Kendra: "...glad you killed...little shit."
Pav: "We could still...trouble."
Kendra: "...it's over...they're not going to..."
Pav: "...How...know? You're not..."
Kendra: "How do I...because it's nothing."

There was more ambient noise and the tape ended.
"That's it?" said Emmet.
"Yeah, that's it. Isn't it enough?" Cody said.
"When did you record this?" Marlowe said.
"Two days after Terry was shot," Cody said.
"How did you record it? Why does it keep cutting in and out?"

Cody remembered what happened all too vividly. It was Saturday and Saturdays she had a routine. Her friends would pick her up early, like eleven or noon. No guys. It was a whole different dynamic and they were exhausting. The group would eat somewhere or hang at somebody's house or lie out by the pool, drinking and smoking weed. In the early evening, they'd go home, sleep, do their nails, do nothing, and later on, prepare for a night out.

On that day, Cody had a cold and was pissed about it, spending the whole morning and afternoon thrashing around in bed or watching TV. Her primary occupation was sneezing and blowing her nose. Her nose and upper lip were red. "Very attractive, Cody," she said to the bathroom mirror. She was wearing one of Terry's old sweaters that hung down to her knees and her pajama bottoms, which made her feel worse.

She was hungry. She left her room and slogged down the hallway, wondering if there was anything good left. Noah and Chris had stayed over. They ate like really handsome refugees. She passed through the great room and into the vast open kitchen. She opened the fridge and stopped. Faintly, she could hear Pav and Kendra arguing. She could tell by the tone and the rise and fall of their voices. She loved it when those two assholes went at it. She smiled. She had her phone in the sweater pocket. She could record them. Wouldn't it be cool to play it for them someday? See their faces when they heard themselves being ridiculous? They were out on the deck. No way to do it without being seen.

"Damn," she said. She really wanted to record them. An idea came to her but it would require a lot of effort. Was it really worth the trouble? She felt like shit. But once she decided something she was relentless. Eli said she was part pit bull, part earthmover. She found the blue key in a drawer. She went out the side door and down the stairs that led to the beach. She went around to the opposite side of the house, staying close to the foundation so they wouldn't see her. There was a small door. She opened it with the blue key and entered the crawl space underneath the deck. She had to duck her head. She knew where Kendra and Pav were. Sitting at the table, with a pitcher or two of martinis. She got directly underneath them. She turned on the recording app and held the phone up to the sliver of light between the boards.

They were going back and forth, talking about Pav's screwups. Cody was shocked. "Unbelievable," she whispered. Did they really go that far? She would have stayed longer but her arm was tired and her neck was sore. She brought the phone down—and sneezed.

"Did you hear that?" Kendra said, alarmed.

"Somebody is under the deck," Pav said.

"Well, don't just sit there. Go get him!"

"It's a bum, who cares?" Pav stomped on the boards. "Hey, you! Get out of there or I beat you to shit!" *Get out of here fast, Cody!* She put her phone in her pocket, pulled her head in and headed for the little door. She got the sweater sleeve stuck on a nail.

"I said, go get him," Kendra insisted. "He might have heard us." Pav groaned and got up. *Move your ass, Cody!* She yanked and yanked on the sweater until it came free.

She heard the gate clang. Pav was on the beach.

"Hurry up, Pav, he'll be gone by now," Kendra yelled from the deck. Pav was the length of the house away. Cody had no place to hide, the beach was the beach. *Do something, Cody!* Mrs. Swanson lived next door. Wooden pylons held up their deck. Cody ran over and slipped behind one. It was hardly bigger around than a telephone pole. She couldn't tell if she was completely hidden or not. She heard Pav arrive. A breeze came up. It fluttered her hair. It was coal black with a purple sheen.

Pav was at the little door. He opened it and didn't move for maybe ten seconds and then he walked away. Strange, Cody thought. He didn't call out and he didn't go in. She waited as long as she could stand it, then crossed the sand to the north side of the house. She opened the combination lock, took off the chain. She was too sick to put them on again. She went up the stairs. The side door was glass. Nobody in the great room. She turned the doorknob. *It was locked!* "Oh Christ," she said. Maybe Pav and Kendra had gone out. Cody was feeling feverish and faint. She had her phone but who could she call? Her friends didn't have a key to the house and Lucy had already left.

Cody sat down on the top step and leaned back against the wall. She'd have to wait until someone came home. You could die by then, she thought. She dozed off and when she awoke, there was cloud cover. The temperature had dropped, the breeze had turned into wind. She was freezing, her teeth were chattering and she was already sick. When Kendra and Pav came home, what would she say? They'd know immediately that she was in the crawl space.

She remembered something. The neighbor, Mrs. Swanson, had a key to Kendra's front door in case of an emergency. But the houses on the beach were lined up close together with gates in between. To get to Swanson's front door, she'd have to walk all the way to the public access entrance, a million miles away. In her goddamn bathrobe. In the cold. The air was misting. She was getting damp. She had a sneezing fit. Nothing to wipe the snot off with but her torn sleeve. *To hell with it, Cody. Just sit down and die.* She couldn't let Kendra find out she'd been eavesdropping, not after what she'd heard. It was even colder and windier. She was dizzy. No one around. She'd never make it to the public access entrance. She could feel herself beginning to faint.

She heard a dog barking. A yapper. The kind that didn't stop until you took it to the pound. She looked up. It was Mrs. Swanson's dog, Prim, peering down at her from the deck, flashing its tiny piranha teeth. Mrs. Swanson appeared over the railing. "Cody? Is that you? What in the world are you doing down there?"

Cody left Mrs. Swanson's place with the key to Kendra's house. She went in as quietly as she could. She heard voices. Pav and Kendra were home. Cody went zombielike to her room and collapsed on the bed.

A harsh knock woke her up. "Leave me alone," she said. Kendra came in. She was enraged. She held up the blue key with a trembling hand.

"You left this in the lock," she said. "You were spying on us." There was no defense. Cody said nothing. "What did you hear?" Kendra demanded.

"I didn't hear anything," Cody said. Kendra charged over to the bed and ripped off the covers.

"You little bitch. I asked you what you heard!"

"I didn't hear anything, okay? The wind was too loud!" Cody was frightened, Kendra looked insane.

"You liar!" Kendra screamed. She started hitting her, windmilling overhand punches that landed mostly on the blanket. Cody covered up but got hit in the ear. Shit, that hurt. *That's it, you cunt.* The fever left her. She raised a knee and kicked Kendra in her solar plexus. Kendra grunted, spun and fell into the wall. Cody wasn't done.

She scrambled out of bed, grabbed a bronze paperweight and raised it over her head. "I'll kill you!" she screamed. The paperweight was ripped out of her hands. Pav was there, snarling, his teeth bared. He grabbed her by the arm and with hardly any effort, slung her across the room onto the floor. Pav loomed over her, his dark eyes tunnels with no end, his voice low and gravelly.

"You shut up, do you hear me, Cody? You say nothing or you got problems, you understand?" Kendra dragged herself up, groaning. Pav helped her limp from the room.

"Your life is in the shit can, Cody!" Kendra yelled. "You might as well die!"

Cody finished her story. Emmet exchanged a quick look with Marlowe. The story was plausible. If it weren't, there would have been a different look.

"That's why Kendra wants me dead," Cody said emphatically. "I overheard her and Pav talking about murdering my dad!"

"Okay, let's back up," Marlowe said. "Why would Kendra want to kill Terry in the first place?

"Do you know who Nicole Wyatt is?" Cody said. "She's a movie star, big like Charlize Theron big. Nicole used to do Kendra's hair and makeup. Kendra always thought she looked her best when Nicole had 'done her magic.' Kendra has tons of showbiz friends but she was only close with Nicole. She was like a little sister. I need another beer. My throat is dry." Emmet got her a glass of water. She glared at him and continued.

"Nicole wanted to be an actress and one day she mentioned it to Kendra. Kendra got her a small part in one of her movies. She only had a few scenes but she killed it," Cody said. "Really killed it. It was like when Jessica Chastain played a crazy woman on *ER*. Producers noticed and Nicole got bigger and bigger parts. Kendra was happy for her, told everybody she was Nicole's mentor." Cody huffed. "Typical. Everything was going okay until Nicole got a part Kendra would have been a shoo-in for ten years ago." Cody laughed. "Kendra went berserk! Screaming fits, throwing stuff around, drinking until she blacked out. She fired her agent *and* her manager!" Marlowe thought he'd have to prompt her but her eyes were shining, eager and rancorous.

Cody went on, saying how Nicole kept landing roles Kendra considered hers. Kendra said shitty things about her on Twitter and Facebook, she spread rumors about Nicole being a white nationalist and a drug addict. "Here's the best part," Cody said with a laugh. "Kendra found out Nicole and Terry were having an affair! It had been going on for months. All that time Kendra and Nicole were best buds, Nicole and Terry were meeting at the Four Seasons, fucking and eating room service!" She took a gulp of water. "It was right at Oscar time. Kendra and Nicole went to the same party and they actually got into a fistfight. They had to be pulled apart!" She glanced at Emmet to see if he was listening. He nodded.

"And Nicole didn't get some of Kendra's parts," Cody went on gleefully. "She got *all* of them! Nicole is twenty-seven. Kendra's thirty-eight. Old for romantic comedies and nobody wants her for anything else. She hasn't made a movie in three years! And get this. She's having a big party, invited all her showbiz friends. She wants everybody to know she's still alive."

"Kendra is a loathsome person but I don't believe she's capable of murder," Marlowe said.

"Yeah, everybody thinks Kendra's like the roles she plays," Cody said, shaking her head. "She's nothing like that. Honestly? She's a beast. She's mean, she's hateful and she holds grudges—and vindictive! Oh my God! Kendra has ruined people's careers, got them blackballed for the least little things. Directors, actors, production people. She got a caterer fired because he forgot she doesn't like mayonnaise. Her cockapoo took a dump on her fancy rug and she threw it into the ocean. Lucy had to rescue it. I'm telling you, Kendra's vicious. She hated Terry. I mean she *hated* him." Cody seemed to run out of gas. She slumped, yawned. "I'm wasted, okay? Can we finish this later?"

"Yeah, go on," Marlowe said. She left. They heard her move down the hall and close her door.

Emmet and Marlowe were outside, standing on the front steps. It was a little breezy, Emmet's rain forest shushing and swaying. They knew how to tell if someone was lying. The obvious tells; fidgeting, dry mouth, touching their face, hiding behind a coffee cup and the rest, but there are other indicators too. Liars' stories are simple. They keep to what they saw and what they heard. They lack confidence. They hedge. They say "sort of," "maybe" and "I'm not sure." Ask them for details and their stories fall apart; like they drove their best friend's car but can't recall the color. They're too earnest. They try to convince. Cody's story had none of that. She was eager to tell the tale, and she wasn't trying to sell it. She had fun with it, which said a lot about her personality, thought Marlowe. Then there were the details. The cold and wind, the blue key and small door and hiding behind the pylon, afraid Pav might see her hair. Hard things to ad-lib.

"I like her story," Marlowe said. "The tape is suggestive, but that's all."

Emmet nodded. "I'll look into Pav," he said.

"I'll see if there are any other players," Marlowe said. Just because there was one suspect didn't mean there weren't others.

"How long is the kid gonna be here?" Emmet asked. Marlowe turned to go.

"I don't know, but when I come back I'd like Cody to be alive."

"You're worried about Cody? What about me?"

Marlowe walked to his car. He was excited. He loved the beginning of a case. Resolving it was always gratifying, but the unraveling was what drove you, your brain humming, your practiced eyes gathering the details, finding disparate elements, your hard-won wits seeing patterns and pulling them together. The doing was what mattered. The doing was what you remembered. Talking to Emmet saddened

Marlowe. Their most intimate times were about cases; talking shop in low voices, the words mere leaves floating on the surface, the current beneath them, heavy and dark.

Cody was in the backyard, sometimes pacing, sometimes lying on the chaise. She'd been on the phone for an hour and ten minutes. Had to be her boyfriend, Emmet thought. Occasionally, he heard her muffled voice. Strained, upset, pleading. Emmet went into her room. Her few clothes were in the drawers. He went through them, found nothing. Her backpack was under the bed, pushed all the way to the wall. He noted its exact position, brought it out and set it on the unmade bed. It was empty but there was a Velcro pocket on the inside. The pocket held a box cutter, two joints wrapped in foil and a lighter. Roy's checkbook and Visa card were in a Ziploc bag. Emmet shook his head in wonder and disgust. Roy had to know Cody stole them or maybe he gave them to her.

Emmet's office was small, dim, low ceiling, the desk lamp like a votive candle. The shelves were full of old case files, souvenirs from long-forgotten places, stacks of cassette tapes, books on forensics and stacks of magazines: *Law Enforcement Technology, National Geographic, Bass Angler* and *American Police Beat*. Struggling fish were mounted on plaques. Most of the photos were of Emmet and his friends catching the fish that were presently on the walls. There was one photo of Marlowe, posing in his uniform at the police academy. Emmet left it up just for spite.

In a moment of melancholy, Emmet went to the bookshelves. He moved a bowling trophy aside, revealing a wall safe. The combination was Addie's birthday. He took out her jewelry box. It was a real antique; French, dark wood with a cloisonné lid depicting a horse in a field of grass. Addie loved horses. She had a pony when she was a kid. The jewelry box was an anniversary present and the most expensive thing Emmet had ever bought her. The most expensive thing he'd ever bought. Looking at it was a lance of pain and warm, sad pleasure. He went to the desk, took off the lid and spread Addie's jewelry on the blotter. It was all costume stuff. Inexpensive gemstones set in pewter or brass or 10-carat gold. Addie had an eye, though, Emmet thought with a smile. At first or second blush, the items looked real. There were pearl earrings, beads, a chain bracelet, a necklace, several rings. He looked at them a few moments. Then he put them back in the box and returned the box to the safe.

There were two silver-framed photos on the desk, both of Addie. Their wedding day, holding hands with him. He'd cut himself out of the picture. The other was of Addie sleeping on the couch, her King Charles spaniel dozing beside her. For years, she'd struggled to find a name for the dog but nothing stuck. She ended up calling it D.O.G., which she pronounced Dee-OH-gee. She said it sounded Japanese. Addie was the most beautiful woman Emmet had ever seen. Even when she was bald and shriveled with cancer she was a swan with a minor cold. He wondered if there was any vodka in the freezer.

CHAPTER FOUR
TRUTHINESS

Marlowe drove back to Hollywood from Emmet's place, something on his mind. How did the man in the alley locate Cody in the first place? He was waiting outside Roy's apartment building when Marlowe arrived. Somebody must have tipped him. Marlowe stopped in an alley. He picked up a cardboard box. He put in a few rocks and a tin can, closed the box and got back in the car.

Marlowe banged on the door. "Open up."

"No. Why should I?" said a frightened voice.

"Don't you want to know what happened to Cody? She told me she's worried about you. She gave me some things to give to you."

"She did?" Roy exclaimed. The door opened and stopped against the chain. Roy's face appeared, his eyes hopeful and eager. "What things?"

Marlowe hefted the box, the stuff inside shifted. "Could you open up? This thing is heavy." Roy quickly unlatched the chain and opened the door. Marlowe put the box in his hands and gave him a shove. Roy was propelled backward, dropping the box, tripping over a beanbag chair patched with duct tape. Marlowe closed the door, walked over and put his foot on the kid's chest.

"Who paid you to take Cody into that alley?" Marlowe said.

"Get off me, will you? Nobody paid me to do anything!" Roy said, struggling under the weight.

"Then where were you taking her? That alley doesn't lead anywhere."

"It's a shortcut," Roy croaked.

"A shortcut to where?"

"To, uh...to a new place."

"What kind of new place? Restaurant? Bar? Club?"

Marlowe pressed harder; Roy was writhing, trying to push Marlowe's foot off. "I don't remember, okay? You're breaking my ribs!"

"You nearly got Cody killed," Marlowe said, glaring down at him. "I'll break your ribs, your skull and both your legs if you don't answer me. *Who paid you?*"

"Okay! Okay, I'll tell you!"

Marlowe helped Roy up and sat him down again on the beanbag chair. Roy was whimpering and rubbed his chest. Sweat streamed, snail trails through the white makeup. He was crying, snotlike icicles hanging from his nose, pink bangs stuck to his forehead.

"Who paid you?" Marlowe said.

"I don't know," Roy said. "I was going to my car after work. This guy starts coming toward me, walking fast and waving, you know, like he was a friend." The mystery man told Roy he was a friend of Cody's family. He said Cody's sister was dying and Cody had cut off all communication. "The guy said they had to see each other before it was too late," Roy said. He started to cry. "I didn't know he wanted to shoot her! How could I know that? I love her! I really love her! I wouldn't do anything to hurt her."

"I know you wouldn't," Marlowe said quietly. Poor kid. Dressed up like Dracula because he thought it made him look shocking, a rebel, just the kind of guy Cody would be attracted to.

"I paid for everything," Roy whimpered. "Food, rent, weed, clothes. Everything." He was barely audible. "I thought the man wanted to help her. I would never—"

"What did the man say he wanted?" Marlowe said.

"He wanted me to lead her into the alley," said Roy. "He said it would be harder for her to walk away. He gave me money." He nodded at a coffee table. A thick wad of new twenties. "A thousand dollars," Roy said. "The man said Cody's sister could die at any moment."

"What did this guy look like?" Marlowe asked.

"I don't know, I didn't look at him. It was getting dark and I didn't *want* to look at him. He scared me. I was afraid to say no."

"Height? Weight?" Marlowe said.

"I don't know. He had muscles. I guess he works out."

"His voice. Did he have an accent?"

"I . . . I don't think so," Roy said.

Could be
Noah or Pav

"Did he sound young or old?"

"In between, I guess."

"Hair, eyes, tattoos?"

"I don't remember."

"Clothes? Shoes?"

"I don't remember!" Roy shouted. "The guy was handing me the money! I was looking at that, not him."

"Anything else you can tell me? A detail, anything?" Marlowe asked hopefully. Roy shook his head. "I did everything for her," he said, his voice faraway. "Everything. I spent all my money. I borrowed from my parents. I cooked for her. I didn't care about sex. I just wanted her to be with me." Roy's heartbreak turned to anger. He sat up, face in a snarl.

"I knew she was screwing somebody else. I knew it all along."

"Who? What was his name?" Marlowe said.

"Eli," Roy said bitterly. "I don't know his last name. I saw him with Cody at Das Bunker. They were making out. She thought I was working. Working to make money for her!" He started crying again.

"What did he look like?" Marlowe said.

Roy festered a long moment and screamed, "That bitch! THAT GODDAMN FUCKING BITCH!" The kid has a point, Marlowe thought. Cody was a goddamn bitch. "There's nothing in the box, is there?" Roy said. Marlowe didn't know what to say. He opened the door and left.

Marlowe was on the roof again with his bourbon and cigarette. It was early morning. Beams of golden sunlight reflected off a thousand windows, heralding a miracle that would never come. Even at this hour, a long line of cars waited at the intersection. Marlowe could see the drivers, heads back, blank faces, blank eyes, listening to the news or music or nothing at all. Whoever you were, wherever you were going, you were convinced that if you weren't right here, right now, everything would fall apart. Your unquestioned fate was waiting at a stoplight with your kidney stones, your sick kid and your busted lottery tickets—in a hurry, because you didn't want to be late for a day just like the last one.

Marlowe slept restlessly and woke up early. He had his coffee and thought about last night. He was growing more dubious about Pav. Killing someone is extreme. Kendra ordering him to do it seemed tenuous as a motive, no matter how angry she was. Lucy said Pav was Kendra's slave but was he that beholden? If the price of keeping your job was shooting someone, maybe think about going to college. Emmet said often, "Look at the family first. They're the ones who hate you the most." Kendra said Cody and her brother, Noah, were a reenactment of the war in Vietnam.

Noah played minor league baseball for the Lancaster Hawkeyes. Marlowe called the coach. He used his authoritative, no-time-for-bullshit voice and identified himself as an LAPD detective. He said he needed information about Noah James. No, there was nothing wrong. It was routine, indirectly pertaining to Noah. Specifically, he needed to know if Noah was in Lancaster yesterday night, the fifteenth, when Cody and Roy were attacked.

"I don't know," the coach said. "There was no practice yesterday. Talk to his buddy, Chris Patterson, he probably knows." The coach gave him the number and Marlowe called Patterson. Marlowe introduced himself the same way and asked the same question.

Patterson said. "Yeah, I saw him. There were four or five of us at the bar. We stayed until, I don't know, closing time." Noah had an alibi. Marlowe was glad. Interfamily murder was always unpleasant. Another possibility was that someone else wanted Cody gone. She'd somehow done something so egregious she needed to be assassinated. That seemed unlikely for a seventeen-year-old girl.

More likely it had something to do with Terry, Marlowe thought. He would have more entanglements and there was a lot involved in making a movie. Throughout the day and into the evening he read everything he could find about Terry James. There were numerous articles in *Variety, Hollywood Reporter,* C21Media, CinemaBlend, the gossip mags and public records. Terry got a lot of coverage because he was married to Kendra.

Terry's story was familiar. After he finished film school, he partnered up with a longtime friend, Andy Kirk, and together they became TK Productions. Terry was the talent. Andy produced and handled the money. To make their first movie, they maxed out their credit cards, borrowed from everyone they knew, lived in their parents' basements, sold their cars, ate Spam, bananas and noodles in a cup and worked two jobs. Their movie was called *Remains,* a horror flick with some similarities to *Paranormal Activity.* That film was made for $15,000 and grossed nearly $200 million worldwide. *Remains* didn't do nearly as well but it won at Sundance, got terrific reviews and brought in enough box office to impress the studios.

Suddenly, TK Productions was the flavor on everyone's tongue; there were numerous invitations to premieres, parties, drinks, interviews and what seemed a thousand lunches. Offers came streaming through the transoms. Terry and Andy, like so many before them, went on to make a series of high-budget flops. The phone not only stopped ringing, it was as if it had never been invented. Their agent didn't return their calls. They told themselves it was a slow patch, that it happened to everyone, that the studios were cutting production, never feeling the boot that kicked them off the A, B and C lists or the finger that deleted them out of showbiz.

Marlowe found an interesting article in an online blog called *In Progress,* written by someone named Austin Claremont. It was dated a few months before Terry's death. It said the talented but out-of-favor director was making his comeback. His new movie was close to production. A major star was on board, and funding was in place. Shooting was scheduled to begin on location in Finland.

That made no sense, Marlowe thought. How did Terry land a

"major star," unless it was his wife, and his wife despised him? The average cost of an A-list movie was at least $100 million. No studio, private investors, hedge funds or anybody else would spend that kind of coin on a film written and directed by Terry James. Marlowe wondered why it was announced in an obscure blog and not in the trades. Most worrisome was the money. People get crazy when a hundred mill is involved. They do stupid things. They do risky things. They do bad things.

Emmet checked out Pav. Pavlo Lomos was born in Sofia, Bulgaria. Came to the US as a child, grew up in Glendale, an LA suburb. A sketchy area about forty miles from the city. Pav dropped out of school. He belonged to a street gang, did an eighteen-month stint at YA camp. He joined the army and saw combat in Iraq. After his discharge, he was sporadically employed and arrested a number of times. Drug sales, bar fights, possession of an unlicensed gun. He was suspected of an armed robbery but not charged. He did time at CCI. His uncle, a wealthy man named Petros, owned a company that provided security guards for businesses. Uncle Petros overlooked the bonding requirements and hired his wayward nephew. It was a low-paying job with no access to cash or valuables.

Pav was on his rounds at Costco one night, patrolling the parking lot. He saw a woman being accosted by two men. According to the police report, Pav "subdued the suspects. Both individuals were seriously injured." He was in the newspaper and Uncle Petros rewarded him with a plum assignment. Prime Set Rental in Burbank. Prime was a huge sound stage that housed permanent sets. A courtroom, a bar, an operating room, a corner store, an executive office, and a number of others. Stars, celebrities, directors and producers came in all the time. Is that where Pav met Terry? Emmet thought.

Emmet called Prime and identified himself. He wanted to know if Terry James had ever used their sets and the dates. The woman checked her computer. She said Terry had directed a movie called *The Gavel* and some of the interiors were shot at Prime. Pav's employment at Prime overlapped with Terry's production. Immediately after the movie was completed, Terry hired Pav as a bodyguard.

Something happened at Prime that bonded the director and the security guard. Maybe they were lovers, thought Emmet. Terry cheated on Kendra, maybe he cheated on Pav too. Pav was a soldier, a gangster and a felon and he knew how to use weapons. Maybe shooting Cody wasn't that farfetched.

Emmet was in the kitchen, eating microwaved blintzes, drinking red wine and reading the *L.A. Times*. He didn't like reading from a tablet or a phone. It was like looking at your hand or being in church, reciting something from the Bible. Cody came in wearing full makeup, black jeans and a black T-shirt and carrying a bag covered in colorful beads. Is this how you dress up these days? Emmet thought. What happened to dresses and sweaters and bags that didn't look like a gay Apache's rucksack? Kind of racist

"Got a date?" Emmet said.

"None of your business," she said.

"You shouldn't go out, you know. You're still a target."

"That's truthiness and you know it," she replied. "No one knows I'm here so no one can follow me."

"*Truthiness?* What does that mean?" Emmet said.

"It's like saying something is true when it's not. Look it up. It's in the dictionary."

"Bullshit," Emmet said. But there it was in Webster's dictionary: **Truthiness** *refers to the quality of seeming to be true but not necessarily or actually true according to known facts.*

"It's the end of the world," Emmet said.

"I'm outta here," Cody said.

"Got any money?"

She huffed. "What do you think?"

"Here." He took out his wallet, fat as a phone book, and gave her $47, all he had on him. *Why are you doing this, Emmet?* She stared at the money, puzzled, as if he were offering her an apricot or a small frog. "There's no strings, just take it." Gingerly, she took the money.

She went to the door, started to say something but Emmet cut her off. "Just go on and get out of here." Someone was picking her up, Emmet thought. Maybe he could ID the guy. He went out the door and hurried after Cody. She was heading for the intersection. There were streetlights and Emmet could get a look at the guy. But Cody didn't stop at the intersection. She turned the corner. Emmet cursed, remembering there was a bus stop over there, an easier place for a car to pull over. He reached the corner just as a car sped by. He glimpsed Cody's silhouette but saw nothing of the driver. He got a flash look at the license plate. He closed his eyes. *What was the number, Emmet? Where's that cop's memory you're so proud of?* "*J R R . . . ,*" Emmet said aloud. "No, that wasn't an *R,* it was a *B . . . J R B.*" Then two letters that were the same. *C C?* No. It was a closed letter. "*D D,*" he said. Then a number. He tried to remember the shape. "Eight," he said. "JRBDD48." He smiled. *You've still got it, old man.* He went back to the house and ran a check on the license plate. A seven-year-old Sentra. The registered owner was Roy Duncan, Cody's chump and baby daddy. Emmet was sad for the world. Roy was taking Cody to see her boyfriend.

Emmet went into the kitchen and took the Grey Goose out of the freezer. He poured three fingers into a water glass, sat down at the breakfast table and took a sip. It was really cold and a little syrupy. *Ahh, just right.* The guy who created Grey Goose, François Thibault, said freezing masks subtle scents and flavorings in the vodka. Maybe. But Emmet was not a subtle guy. He finished the drink and poured another. He wished he were on the job. He was a Grade III detective. His chevron had a star in the middle. He had investigated major homicide and robbery cases. He was awarded a Distinguished Service Medal. He had the highest clearance rate in the division.

Emmet began drinking heavily when the doctors told him Addie wouldn't make it. She had ovarian cancer. The treatment was long and seemed more like torture than anything helpful. When Addie died, the drinking accelerated. Emmet thought he hid it pretty well, forgetting that his colleagues were trained detectives. Command put him on medical leave and he was advised to seek treatment. Emmet was sure he wasn't an alcoholic, no matter what his knucklehead son said. The drinking was temporary. Yeah, it had been going on for three years but that wasn't the point. He was grieving. He was coming home to an empty house. In time, he'd quit all by himself.

CHAPTER FIVE
REN

Marlowe drove to USC, the University of Southern California. The campus was located a few miles south of Downtown LA. It was a prestigious school but it had done nothing to uplift the area. More violent crimes were reported in the vicinity than in any other comparable area in LA. Marlowe parked his car and headed across campus to the School of Cinematic Arts, a vast complex, its programs teaching all aspects of film and TV production. The school's founders included Douglas Fairbanks, Charlie Chaplin, Ernst Lubitsch and Darryl Zanuck. Alfred Hitchcock had been a professor there. Buildings were named after Steven Spielberg and George Lucas. They, and others, had contributed hundreds of millions of dollars to the school's endowment. Marlowe wondered why they hadn't contributed a few bucks to the neighborhood.

Austin Claremont wrote the article on Terry and his new production. Austin was an archivist in the school film library. He described himself on Facebook as "a film nut, film historian, collector of vintage movie posters, and gossip hound of all things cinema." Over the phone, Marlowe told Austin that he was a private investigator working on a book about the movie business. A kid at the school's front desk told him Austin was waiting for him in one of the screening rooms.

Austin Claremont sat watching an old movie. The sharp whites and blacks turned his face into a cubist painting. When Marlowe sat down, Austin started, as if he'd been snapped out of a trance. He was wearing a checked shirt and little round glasses.

"Austin, I'm Philip Marlowe, the one who called. I'd like to ask you a few questions. It won't take long."

Austin looked embarrassed. "Um, if you don't mind, I'd like to watch a little more. *To Have and Have Not.* I've seen it a thousand times but it's like an old friend." He looked back at the screen and his eyes brightened. "Oh, this scene is a classic. You've probably seen it before." Marlowe had. Bogart was hurriedly entering his hotel room. Austin smiled. "Only Bogie could get away with a Norwegian sailor's cap and a cravat." Bogart began rifling through his bag. Offscreen, a sultry, husky voice says, "Anybody got a match?" Bogart turned around. He froze, his mouth open. Lauren Bacall was leaning against the doorway, a half smile on her face, skeptical and slightly amused.

Austin was entranced. "Sidney Hickox, the cinematographer, shot her in inverse parabolas of light and shadow. Isn't she magnificent? This was Bacall's first movie, if you can believe it. That voice. It was high and nasal until Howard Hawks hired her a vocal coach." Bacall lit her cigarette. Bogart was mesmerized, the sparks between them palpable. Austin sighed wistfully. "She met Bogart on set. One night, he came into her trailer, lifted her chin and kissed her. Then he wrote his number down on a book of matches. They were married on Louis Bromfield's farm—the Pulitzer Prize winner? They were together until Bogart died in 1957—am I boring you?"

"No, not at all," Marlowe said. It was something he shared with Austin. The love of old movies and the Golden Age of Hollywood. The films were made by filmmakers, not technology wizards who worked on green screen, in special effects labs and in the editing room. The actors acted unaided by space travel, colossal explosions, hip-hop musical scores, super weapons, superheroes, invasions from other planets and more pointless gore and horror than a genocide. There were real movie stars. Charlie Chaplin, Joan Crawford, Marlene Dietrich, Clark Gable, Marilyn Monroe, Fred Astaire and a long list of others. The Marx Brothers, Cary Grant,

Katharine Hepburn, Jimmy Stewart. There were films that were funny without dick jokes, sweeping without bloodshed, romantic without cynicism, scary without zombies and heroic without assault weapons. Television killed the glory days of Hollywood and killed them dead. Marlowe had been in a movie theater once in recent memory. He saw *Sunset Boulevard* at the Cinemark Theatre in Santa Monica.

Marlowe and Austin went to the cafeteria and had coffee.

"I want talk to you about this article you wrote," Marlowe said.

"Ah yes, Terry James," Austin said ruefully. "He might have had a serious career but he made that classic mistake. He equated big budgets with good movies. Sad, the way he died."

"Your article said Terry was about to shoot a movie," Marlowe said. "It says he landed a major star and the funding was in place. You're the only one who reported on it."

Austin smiled, pleased with himself. "Yes, sometimes I'm ahead of the game. My sources are PAs, office staff, makeup artists, costume designers, limo drivers, boyfriends and girlfriends. They know the real dope and the trades don't talk to them. Anyway, the project never got off the ground. I heard Terry bilked his investors for a ton. Lots of people were mad at him."

"Who were the investors?" Marlowe said.

"I don't know, but from what I hear they were shady," Austin said. "They wanted to be in the movie business and were throwing a lot of money around."

"Why shady? Doesn't everybody throw money around?" Marlowe said.

"Yes, but it's who you throw it to. Terry James?" Austin scoffed. "The investors were either ignorant or they had something going."

"Going like what?"

Austin shrugged. "Don't know specifically." Suddenly, his eyes were dinner plates. He gasped and leaned forward. "You don't think Terry's death had anything to do with—"

"No, no, it's nothing like that," Marlowe said, with a comforting smile. "The book is about the underside of the movie business.

Bankruptcies, corruption, blackmail, people who had a promising start and failed."

"Well, there are plenty of those," Austin said. He rose from the table. "I have to go. It was nice meeting you. Call me anytime."

Marlowe returned to his car, started the engine and sat there. He needed to talk to an insider, somebody who knew what the players were up to; what Steve Tisch, Arnon Milchan and Brian Kavanagh were saying over lunch at the Polo Lounge or what the CEOs from LStar, Aperture Media and Deutsche Bank were confiding over drinks at Bar Marmont, or what the entertainment attorneys were whispering to the agents from CAA, ICM and UTA while they smoked cigars in the Grand Havana Room. Marlowe needed someone with the key to the illicit closet and knew where the sins were buried.

Marlowe got a call from Basilio. He wanted to meet. Marlowe could have refused but he still felt indebted to the man who helped him get his start, a card Basilio had played many times.

"Why do you want to meet?" Marlowe said.

"Don't interrogate me," Basilio said.

"I'm not interrogating you. I just asked you why."

"I'm at Panda Express. This is important," Basilio said, and he ended the call.

When Marlowe got there, his unkempt mentor was devouring his favorites, orange chicken, beef with broccoli and a double white rice. His T-shirt said CONGRATULATIONS SHANIQUA. Emmet and Basilio had graduated from the academy in the same class. Marlowe had seen a picture of him. Basilio was a handsome kid, wide shoulders, intelligent eyes, his hair as black as a crow in the sunshine. Unfortunately, time had done to Basilio what it had done to Russell Crowe. Bloated him, added the jowls of a basset hound, bags under his eyes and a beard somewhere between Santa Claus and Grizzly Adams.

Marlowe sat down, sighed deeply. "What is it?" he said.

"I have a new case for you," Basilio replied. Marlowe inhaled a deeper sigh.

"Is that why you dragged me over here? I'm really busy."

Basilio put on his serious face. "You're busy, right, of course, I shouldn't have bothered you in the first place," he said. "I don't know what got into me. I hope you're not offended—"

"I didn't mean it that way, Basilio—"

"It's okay, I'm fine. I'm glad you're doing so well." Basilio paused, frowned, pointed his plastic fork in the air. "You know, something just occurred to me—that guy, I can't remember his name. You know who I'm talking about. That generous soul who hired you so you could get your PI license and didn't end up at the post office selling Kwanzaa stamps or killing termites with poison gas."

"Is there some reason you can't take the case?" Marlowe said.

"I have other matters to attend to," Basilio said. "Remember Mrs. Delmonico? She's suing me after all this time. Can you believe it?" He speared a piece of chicken that looked like a burnt ear.

"Well, what's it about?" Marlowe said.

"Ren will tell you all about it," Basilio said.

"Ren? That's the client's name?"

"Yeah, like Ren and Stimpy," said Basilio, chewing the burnt ear with difficulty. "In case you didn't know, Ren was a psychotic Chihuahua." Basilio glanced at his Bullwinkle watch that never had the right time. "Oh, by the way," he went on. "I set up a meeting at your place in twenty minutes. I'll give you the number. Have you got something to write with?"

"You mean like a pencil? No, but I have my phone," Marlowe said.

"Right, of course," Basilio said. He smiled wistfully. "You youngsters and your newfangled gadgets. Gosh, I'll never keep up."

Marlowe drove back to his place. Basilio had sent clients to him before but this time he was exceptionally coy. That only meant one thing. The client couldn't pay. That was the last thing Marlowe needed. A psychotic Chihuahua with no money.

The doorbell rang and Marlowe went down the stairs. He was irritable. He didn't want another client, especially one that was imposed on him. He also had a meeting with George Bamford, Kendra's father, and didn't want to be late. He crossed the garage and opened the door.

"Hello, Mr. Marlowe," she said. She had an English accent. "I'm Ren Stewart. Thank you for seeing me on such short notice." Marlowe took a moment to gather himself. Ren was about his age. Dark hair, dark eyes, an angular, aristocratic face. A young Charlotte Rampling, Marlowe thought. He liked how she was dressed. A chambray shirt, white sweater draped over her shoulders, jeans and very nice moccasins.

"Just Marlowe is fine. Come on in." He was standing in the doorway, near darkness behind him. Warily, she stepped into the gloom. She looked around as if she were pricing things for auction.

"I see," she said.

"I live upstairs," Marlowe said. As they crossed toward the stairs, he felt exposed, as if his random possessions held deep emotional insights. He started noticing things he hadn't before. A trail bike with flat tires, a broken space heater, a laundry basket full of old shoes, boxes of tax records with no lids and a pink stuffed rhinoceros he won at a fair for a woman he couldn't remember. Ren noted the shotgun. It was in its usual place, leaning against the wall between a rake and the long pruning shears.

"Quite a selection of gardening tools," she observed.

"I grow ammo," Marlowe replied. "The .357s are doing nicely. The .45s won't bloom until next year." Ren didn't laugh and she didn't smile. He covered with a question: "Ever fire a shotgun?"

"When I was a teenager I went grouse hunting with my father," Ren said. "He stopped taking me. I was too quick on the trigger. I fired before I had a shot."

"Nervous?"

"No, I was trying to scare away the birds." She said it with a straight face. Is she messing with you, Marlowe? Her accent sounded proper but not stuck-up, more self-assured, intelligent, capable of wit. They went up the stairs and entered the living room. "Lovely," she said, admiring the floor. "Are you just moving in?"

"No, I've been here for a couple of years now. Why do you ask?"

"This room must be three hundred square meters and there's seating for three."

"Yes, I'm not much for company. Does it bother you?"

"The chairs are very far apart. I'm afraid we'll have to shout at each other." Again, the straight face. He took her to the kitchen area. She blinked twice at the picnic table, put down her things and sat. For a half second, he thought she smiled.

"Would you like something? I have water, coffee, tea."

"Water, please."

He went to the fridge. The smile bothered him. What was so funny about a picnic table? He liked it. He bought it at a yard sale.

Marlowe filled two glasses with filtered tap water. He didn't like drinking from a plastic bottle. The first gulp invariably spurted out and wet your very expensive shirts. He gave her the glass and sat down. Her demeanor had changed. It startled him. She was looking at him frankly, intense, down to business.

"Are you qualified for this kind of work, Mr. Marlowe?" she said. No one had ever asked him that before.

"I think so. I've been a private investigator for a long time and I've handled hundreds of cases." She pondered him a moment as if she were comparing his words with the man sitting in front of her. It made him nervous. He broke the ice before it broke him.

"How did you meet Basilio?"

"I met with a number of private investigators but I couldn't afford any of them," Ren said. "The last one apologetically referred me to Basilio. Basilio was busy. I hardly think so unless he was busy eating grotesque Chinese food."

"Why do you need a private investigator?" Marlowe asked.

"Before we begin, can we discuss fees?" Ren said. "I'm afraid I don't have much money." Bingo, thought Marlowe.

"My fees are based on the situation," he replied. That was true. He charged Kendra three times his normal rate. "Why don't you tell me about the problem."

Ren took a deep breath and began. "I was married to my husband, Fallon, for seven years. We were an unhappy cliché, victims of the insidious whirlwind romance. We argued about everything; whose needs got priority, how the money was spent, who was responsible for what. There were social issues and politics too." She sipped her water and cleared her throat. "Fallon has a very controlling nature. He alone knows the way, the *only* way, to deal with life's ups and downs. My role was to listen and if I really paid attention, perhaps I might learn something. Then there was Jeremy, our son. Child-rearing was always a hot topic. We were a ridiculous couple, really, the type you don't invite to your dinner party." She took another sip and shifted in her seat. Getting to the hard part, Marlowe thought. "On one of Fallon's regular visits, he kidnapped Jeremy," she said. There was a film over her eyes but she didn't cry.

"When was this?" Marlowe said.

"Six weeks ago. I would have come sooner but if I quit my job, I couldn't pay for the trip and I couldn't support Jeremy when I got him back. As you might imagine, I was in terrible straits." Her voice had started to rise. She settled herself. She was shaking. "I notified the MPS, of course, but there was little they could do. Fallon is Jeremy's legal father. Whether or not he broke the terms of the divorce has to be determined by the court. Fallon also took off with our savings. Nine thousand pounds, most of which was mine."

"May I ask what you do for a living?" Marlowe said.

"I teach literature at West London University but I like to call myself a writer." She said it flatly, not embarrassed. "My novels are abstruse and convoluted. I have a small following, which never seems to grow. The most success I've had is with a book of children's poems titled *Urtle the Turtle*. It hasn't done well."

Marlowe was impressed. Most people would offer a more en-couraging assessment of themselves. Ren was direct and unflinching, eliminating one of the most exasperating things about clients. They lie. "I assume you've done a search on Fallon," he said.

"Everything about him is from the UK. His address here is the one he used before he came to England. His mobile was disconnected."

"No contact of any kind?"

"Four or five idiotic emails," she said. "Things like 'don't worry' and 'Jeremy said hello.' They were painful to read and Fallon knew they would be."

"My father is a police officer," Marlowe said. "I'll have him run a check. He may have better luck. Do you have a picture of Fallon?" She took out her phone, scrolled through the photos and showed him. Fallon was standing in front of the Empire Casino in London. He was stylishly thin and very handsome; mischievous eyes, a cheeky smile, a cool unflappable air about him. He was wearing jeans, a white shirt open at the collar, his tie undone, a gray herringbone tam pulled down just enough. A little Jude Law–ish, Marlowe thought.

"Looks aren't everything," Ren lamented. "After we were married, he worked there, at the casino. He dealt cards, stick man at the craps table, everybody loved him. He disdained it, of course. He thought the job was beneath him. He gambled most of his paycheck away."

"Why did Fallon come to LA?" Marlowe asked.

"He was born and raised here. He was on holiday in the UK when I met him. Fallon has a wealthy grandmother, Victoria. I'm sure he went to her for help."

"Did you talk to her?"

"I couldn't get near her," Ren said, exasperated. "She has a circle of sycophants who zealously protect her from the unwashed—like myself, for example. I spoke to her attorney, told him my story but he didn't call back. I have no way of meeting her. All her friends are society people."

"Does Victoria have any activities outside of socializing?" Marlowe asked. "Theater? The arts? Music?"

"Charities," Ren said. "But she only gets involved because she adores celebrities. She'll spend whatever it takes to meet someone famous."

"Is there any other reason Fallon came here?" Marlowe said.

"He wants to be an actor," Ren said, shaking her head. "He went to a few theater auditions in London. He'd read for a minute, no more, and get dismissed. In England, we take our actors seriously."

"If you catch up with Fallon, what will you do?"

"I'll kill him first and then we'll talk."

"I'm going to make some inquiries," Marlowe said. "I'll call you in a couple of days. I have another case to attend to." He got to his feet.

Ren stayed sitting. "Mr. Marlowe, please—" She was trying to keep her expression under control. Her anguish embarrassed her. "If you could give me another minute?" He sat down. She spoke carefully, as if the placement of her words was critical. "This is about my son, Jeremy. I love him like I love nothing else. I can't wait a couple of days." Her voice was trembling, tears spilled. "I know I have no right to ask this, but I want you to do something now." She was helpless and utterly desperate. She said in a whisper, *"Please."* Marlowe was stunned a moment. Ren's love was so pure and crystalline it broke his heart. She brightened, mistaking his hesitation for hope. "You will?" she said.

"I...I can't," Marlowe said. "I'm sorry, Ren. I understand your urgency, I really do, but I have other commitments. I take them as seriously as I take my commitment to you." He thought of Cody, running down the alley, a man trying to shoot her in the back. "I'll call you as soon as I can," he said. It was as if he'd slapped her. She started to reply but didn't. She didn't blink, her mouth open slightly. An awful moment passed.

"Thank you," Ren said, "I'll show myself out." She got up, hurried across the room, her quick footsteps descending the stairs.

CHAPTER SIX
BOTTOMS UP, WEDGE

Bel Air was an extremely wealthy but not very diverse community. Eighty-some percent was white, a smattering of Asians, possibly three or four Latinos, Jay-Z and Magic Johnson. The gate was at Sunset and Bellagio. A guardhouse was there so you'd think you needed a pass to get in. Marlowe was on his way to see George Bamford, Kendra's father. George was a semiretired superagent who only repped a select few A-listers. He knew everybody because everybody wanted to know him. Marlowe met George over a decade ago. George was one of Marlowe's first cases. From this vantage point, it was a fond and amusing memory. Back then it was neither. Back then, it was appalling.

At the time, Marlowe was dating George's sister, Lila. One afternoon, they were lying in bed having just consummated some very good sex. Marlowe was warm and comfortable, eyes closed, drifting, sated. Lila was lying next to him, hopefully asleep. Whenever they met, their hormones did the mambo but otherwise, there wasn't much there for either of them.

Marlowe was just starting to doze off when Lila rolled on her side to face him. She cleared her throat. Inwardly, Marlowe groaned. She sat up.

"I have a brother," Lila said. "His name is George."

"Oh?" he said. He wanted to keep his eyes closed but the urgency in her voice demanded he open them. He was sorry he did. She was tearful, distraught.

"He's done something so stupid I can hardly believe it," Lila went on.

"Oh?"

"George could go to jail, Marlowe!"

"Oh?"

"Will you please stop saying 'oh' and pay attention!" she said. "And sit up for God's sake!"

"I don't want to," Marlowe said.

"Marlowe, this is my *brother*. George could go to prison!" She shook his arm forcefully until he sat up. "This is an emergency," she went on. "You *have* to help him!" Do I? Marlowe wondered. By his estimation, they'd have one more round later this afternoon and another three times before they broke up. He was naked. Lila was naked.

"What's the emergency?" he said wearily.

"It's a story."

At that point in his life, George Bamford was an alcoholic and a struggling director. His filmography consisted of commercials for Dependz Adult Diapers, Chia Pet, El Dorado Dry Cleaners, an energy drink called Adrenalinz, Uncle Buck's Feral Hog and Sweet Potato Dog Food and a few other products with the same prestige. He'd also directed a documentary about catfishing with needle-nose pliers, and another about Mongolians cooking meat by putting it under their saddles. There were several features that never made it into theaters. The best was about a cowboy who finds a Neanderthal baby on a cattle drive. George didn't give up, always lurking on the fringes of the movie business, looking for that one important contact. Unfortunately showbiz folks can smell dejection and failure. They avoid them like gluten, tract houses and commuter hotels.

The actress Bessie from the cowboy movie took George to a party in posh Holmby Hills. When he got there, he discovered the host was Wedge Freeman, the director of the *Sky Man* trilogy, the *Killer Squaw* TV series and other massive hits. In an interview on *Entertainment Tonight,* Wedge said his residual checks were three feet long to accommodate all the zeroes.

Wedge and George had loathed each other in film school. A clash of personalities. Both were smug, egotistical and competitive, each vowing to be the next Scorsese while the other was scraping gum off the bottom of theater seats. George didn't want to see Wedge but they ran into each other at the bar. "Is that you, George?" Wedge said. "It's great to see you." He couldn't hide his smirk or maybe he wasn't trying.

"Yeah, great to see you too," George said.

"How's it going? What are you up to these days?" Wedge said. George tried to keep his composure. *You already know the answer, asshole.*

"Oh, this and that," George said with a wan smile. "I've got a project at Paramount and another at Fox. Stuck in development, you know how it is." They looked at each other, George praying Wedge wouldn't ask for specifics and Wedge considering whether he would.

"I'm leaving for Rome tomorrow," Wedge said casually. "Scouting for locations. I'm shooting the sequel to *Gladiator.* Ridley Scott is producing. Have you met him?"

"Have I met Ridley Scott? No, I haven't," George said as if someday he might.

"Well, I should be mingling," Wedge said with a terrible smile. "Take care, George. Take really good care."

George drank a lot of Wedge's liquor and got sloppy drunk. He was jealous and bitter and feeling sorry for himself. He couldn't find the bathroom and decided he'd pee in a planter or drawer. He wandered around until he found himself in Wedge's colosseum-sized office. George relieved himself in a crystal decanter. The yellow liquid looked a lot like Chartreuse or Strega. *Bottoms up, Wedge.*

Absently, he poked around the office, making faces at Wedge's awards and celebrity photos. He riffled through the papers on the giant rosewood desk. There were legal documents, blueprints for an office building and a contract with Lionsgate studio. Wedge's next film was a movie titled *Rhett Butler,* starring Brad Pitt. George was about to pee on the contract and that was when he saw it. A bronze statuette. It was a woman doing a Spanish dance, her arms up as if to say *olé!* It was a slender thing, a little over a foot in height. It was a dead ringer for a Degas. George had studied art as well as film. He picked it up. Was it real? It looked authentic but you could buy a realistic copy online. But why would Wedge have a copy? He was vain and a show-off. Just like him to have something worth a fortune sitting on his desk like a stapler. On an inebriated impulse, George took the Degas and hid it under his jacket.

When George awoke the next morning, he saw the Degas where he'd dropped it on the linoleum. He was aghast and terrified. It was worth hundreds of thousands of dollars and Degas's dancers were known all over the world. George went to the bathroom and threw up. Fortunately, Wedge was leaving for Rome and wouldn't miss it. Either that or he'd already called the police. George recalled he'd left seven thousand fingerprints in Wedge's office and a quart of his DNA in a crystal decanter.

George had never been in this kind of trouble. Like, prison trouble. He imagined himself sweeping out the cell wearing only an apron and flip-flops. George's new husband, Darnell Vesuvius, liked to call him Melanie. George went back to bed and pulled the covers over his face. He desperately needed help but his friends were as dissolute as he was. There was only his sister, Lila. After yelling at him for fifteen minutes she said she knew someone who could help and his name was Marlowe.

He met George at Panda Express. George also liked orange chicken. It was like a curse. George was sallow, wilted and miserable. He had the Degas wrapped in newspaper. "Please, help me, Mr. Marlowe," he pleaded. "I don't know what to do." Marlowe had surveilled Wedge's house. It looked impregnable. State-of-the-art alarm system, a male house sitter, a yappy little Shih Tzu and private security that patrolled the neighborhood. He didn't like his odds.

"The only way to get in that house is to be invited," Marlowe said. "Describe the office, I want details."

"I was drunk. I'm afraid I didn't notice much," George said.

"Then you'll qualify for Medicare while you're locked up in Folsom."

After leaving George, Marlowe stopped at Ackerman Printing. Doug Ackerman was an ex-client. One night a truck had backed up to the rear door of his shop. Two thieves used a sledgehammer and a crowbar to open the door and carted away a $30,000 IBM InfoPrint 2085 copier. They were gone before the police could respond to the alarm.

Who would need a printer like that? Marlowe wondered. And why that particular one?

The IBM was professional-grade. It could print 105 pages per minute. Who needs speed like that? A big company? Maybe. But why would a big company send two crooks to steal a printer? Could be another print shop, Marlowe thought, one that couldn't afford new equipment. And the thieves were probably local, he mused. They wouldn't have toured the city looking for that particular model. There were eight independent copy shops in greater Hollywood. Marlowe checked them out. He didn't find the IBM but he reasoned the thieves would let some time pass before they installed it. Two weeks later, there it was, in a dingy little shop on Western. Ackerman couldn't afford Marlowe's per diem, so from then on, he printed up anything Marlowe needed. Posters, flyers, notices that looked legal, fake business cards, even counterfeit money.

Ackerman printed up cards with the Lionsgate studio logo. *Philbert Marlowe, Assistant to Jane Windsor, Vice President of Business Affairs* and the general phone number for Lionsgate. Marlowe used a reverse phone service and found Wedge's landline number. He called and got the house sitter.

"Hi, my name is Philbert Marlowe. I work at Lionsgate studio," Marlowe said. "I'm supposed to pick up a contract. I wanted to make sure someone was home." George told him there was a contract on Wedge's desk.

Marlowe met the house sitter at the door. The guy filled up his muscle shirt like too much water in a rubber glove. He had thick hairy arms, a thick gold chain and an expression that suggested a thick, stupid brain. Maybe he's a stunt man, George thought.

"I'm Philbert Marlowe. I called earlier." Marlowe handed him the business card. Stuntman gave it a glance and said, "ID." Marlowe showed him his license. Nobody looked at the name close enough to spell it. They looked at the photo and looked at your face. Stuntman did the same.

"Okay, come in. Did Wedge say where the contract was?"

"No, I'm afraid not," Marlowe said. He wanted Stuntman to answer the question himself.

"Probably in his office," Stuntman said. He assumed the role of prison guard and ushered Marlowe down a hallway. Marlowe had the Degas tucked into his pants and hidden by his coat. They stepped over a turd left by the Shih Tzu and went into the office. The decanter of piss was still there. "I don't like this," Stuntman said, "I'm not supposed to be in here."

"All I know is that Jane told me to pick it up."

"Who's Jane?"

"Jane Windsor, VP of business affairs. It says so on the card." They approached the desk. "Stay back, this stuff is private," Stuntman said. He riffled through the papers. Marlowe had to get closer to the desk. He was sweating and the Degas was slipping through his belt. He took a step forward. Stuntman looked up sharply. "I said *stay back.*" Marlowe stepped back. He was three feet from the desk. He had to get closer. The Degas slipped and fell down Marlowe's pant leg, the dancer's head sticking out of his cuff. *Oh shit, oh shit!* Stuntman had found the contract. He was reading the first page. *You're screwed, Marlowe. You're an idiot.*

"This is it, let's go," Stuntman said. Marlowe bent over, slid the Degas out of his pant leg and stood up.

"Is this supposed to be here?" he said.

"On the floor? I don't think so. Just put it on the desk."

Marlowe left the house and stuck the contract in the mailbox. Lila richly rewarded him but George was broke. They made a deal.

If George ever came into money he'd buy Marlowe a 1928 Patek Philippe Tiffany & Co. Rectangular Platinum watch. George did come into money. He bought the watch for Marlowe and had a copy made for himself.

In the months that followed, George became Bessie's boyfriend and manager. Bessie was bouncy and cute in a corn-fed kind of way, her personality unwaveringly cheerful. George contacted the company that produced the Adrenalinz commercial. Bessie was immediately cast as one of the Adrenalinz Girlz. She wore a bikini or brightly colored spandex and posed with other A Girlz; skateboarding, lying on the beach or dancing at raves with a tall can of the product. She was very popular.

With George's guidance, Bessie developed a very successful career selling everything from virility pills and cat hair removers to laser beam toenail clippers and granola made by Native Americans in Arizona. Other aspiring actors heard about her success and sought George's help. There are no set qualifications for being an agent, except a relentless determination, a dedication to your clients and a willingness to humiliate yourself. The work was ceaseless because it tracked a business that was constantly changing.

George always thought an agent's job was answering the phone and taking ten percent, but it was much more than that. An agent, he discovered, was a facilitator. A hub through which scripts, books, ideas, actors, directors, producers, financiers, networks and studios try to find each other in a vast jumble of disjointed data, rumor, speculation, hearsay, gossip and meeting after endless meeting. An agent had to read. Scripts, articles, books, notes, treatments, pilots, the trades and the newspapers. Who knew what or where the Next Big Thing might be? And what did an agent do with all that random information? George thought it was like looking at the Milky Way. If he selected the right moons, meteors, comets and stars, and could somehow connect them, a new and wonderful world would be created.

George developed an impressive client list. After six years on his own, he was bought out by the Titan Agency. Under his leadership, the company rivaled the mother ship, CAA. In his later years, George only repped top talent.

Marlowe drove the Mustang into George's cobblestone driveway. Marlowe parked near the fountain, a lithe Spanish dancer twirling under a silver spray. Marlowe stopped to admire it a moment, standing there despite the cool mist on his face. The house was modest by Bel Air standards. Two floors, three chimneys and a lush garden worthy of a conservatory. George answered the door himself.

"Hello, Marlowe," he said with a welcoming smile. "Please come in." George had aged handsomely. A warm face made smooth by a facelift, salt-and-pepper hair and broad shoulders. They went into the study and he poured two Old Crows. "To your health," George said, and they raised their glasses. They sat in leather armchairs and sipped their whiskey. "I hear about you from time to time. Some good, some bad. Apparently, you're just as unpleasant as you always were. Is Kendra paying you well?"

"Yes, she is," Marlowe said. "Thank you for introducing me."

"A mixed blessing, I'm sure."

"*Mixed* is the word for it."

"I've been curious," George said. "Why do you want to talk to me about Cody? We barely knew each other."

"I'm actually here about Terry. I want to know what he was up to before his death."

George shook his head ruefully. "I never should have introduced him to Kendra. Terry was a handsome devil and charming too, but as for talent, he was a one-hit wonder. That first movie he made was really good, amazing in fact, but it's like a writer who writes one great book. After that, he's got nothing left to say."

"Did Terry have money problems?" Marlowe asked.

"Indeed. His big movies were flopping and he was spending like he was Elon Musk. Terry had two Ferraris, three assistants, a racehorse, that kind of thing, and he couldn't get a job. Look at

Coppola, one of the best directors in film history. Then *Godfather III* and *Bram Stoker's Dracula* flopped and he doesn't work anymore. Or David Cronenberg. Another great director. *The Fly* and *The Dead Zone* were groundbreaking but *Cosmopolis* and *Maps to the Stars* lost money and he's gone from the scene too. The only way Terry could resurrect himself was to make a comeback movie but he was broke. Pour you another?"

Marlowe loved the feel of George's house. Furniture made from Brazilian rosewood and African blackwood. A sixteenth-century limestone fireplace. Leather-bound books from Gryphon and Easton Press, Isfahan carpets, Steuben wineglasses, oil paintings by Dirck van Baburen and Frans Hals and real art deco wall sconces. You sat in the warmth of wealth, cocooned in a ten-thousand-square-foot house with handmade doorknobs, Winston Churchill's coatrack and bathtubs big enough to raise crocodiles. Marlowe wondered what it was like to never worry about money. He'd spent most of his life in pursuit of it. George never needed to *think* about money. If you were magically a billionaire, what would you do with yourself, Marlowe? If the world was at your feet, where would you go? What would you become? Sadly, he'd never know.

George continued. "The IRS sued Terry for tax evasion. He was fortunate Eric DeSallis negotiated a deal. DeSallis is a tax accountant. He was mine for years but I let him go. He walks a little too close to the line, but he could recite the IRS regulations and ski at the same time. DeSallis could find a deduction if it was hidden in my neighbor's duck pond." George sipped his whiskey.

"Do you think DeSallis would help me out, give me some background on Terry?"

"Terry's dead, so I don't know why not. I'll give him a call," George said.

"Another thing," Marlowe went on. "I found out Terry was going to direct a movie. He was to shoot it in Finland and the funding was in place."

George sighed. "Yeah, I heard that. Terry and that idiot partner of his, Andy, were mixed up with some Armenians."

"Armenians?"

"Yes, and not the good ones. Some kind of gang, I think that was it. The way I heard it, the Armenians were hooked up with the Russian mob," George said.

"What were they up to?"

"Best guess? Money laundering. Washing money through phony production costs is not new." George offered Marlowe another drink.

"I'm good," he said.

"It's simple in theory," George said. "Let's suppose the Russians need to wash a hundred million dollars. They funnel it through Terry's production company. He spends it on an ersatz movie, the money is paid to Russian shell companies until it's gone. Terry gets a cut, declares bankruptcy and that's that."

"You sure about this, George?"

"No," George said. "Anything you hear in this town is automatically suspect. Don't take it on faith."

"Okay, I appreciate that," said Marlowe. "But suppose that's true, about Terry and the Russians. Why would they kill Terry if he was doing the laundering? Do you think he was stealing?"

"I think it's more than possible," George replied. "In fact, I'd be surprised if Terry wasn't stealing. In addition to the taxes, he'd accumulated a lot of debt. Kendra refused to pay for any of it. She made him sign a prenup too. When she kicked him out, he walked away with a dog's breakfast and a good pair of socks."

"Incredible what people will do to be in the movie business."

George smiled, knowing and sad. "The movie business is like Mount Everest. Once you climb to the top of the world, everything else is a molehill. The studios don't remember Terry's hit. They remember the hundreds of millions he lost for them."

"Stealing from the Russian mob is a stupid thing to do on its face," Marlowe said.

"You don't know how stupid you can be until you're desperate," George said. "Until you're eating bakery samples for lunch and buying two gallons of gas at a time and saving your minutes on the cell phone you can't afford." There was a wink in his smile. "Believe me, I should know."

George walked Marlowe out to his car. "I have another favor to ask," Marlowe said.

"Another? You haven't asked for the first one."

"I want to meet Nicole Wyatt."

"Hmm, yeah, that's a tough one," George said. "She and Kendra aren't exactly pals. I'll work on it."

"Thanks, George."

"Nice watch."

"I think so too."

George called Nicole's agent, Nancy Reese. She was a partner at William Morris and they'd done deals together, always amicable, always straightforward. She was smart, capable and attractive. They'd lunched together numerous times, and he'd attended her first and second weddings. George told Nancy he'd hired an investigator to look into Terry's death. The police were making no headway and he was anxious to get it resolved. The investigator wanted to talk to Nicole.

"Mm, I don't know about that," Nancy said. "A lot of emotions involved."

"Look, Terry was my son-in-law," George said. "I'm not proud of that but there's a family connection here. Is there a way to work this?" Nancy thought a moment.

"There might be an angle. Nicole was truly in love with Terry," she said. "Why is a mystery. She's a great girl. She was devastated by his death."

"I'll leave it to you," George said. There was an odd pause.

"Did you know I got divorced again?" Nancy said.

"Really?"

"Really." He could hear her smiling over the phone. He smiled too.

"How do you feel about dinner?" he said.

The Venice Beach boardwalk was crowded with tourists. The smells of popcorn, suntan lotion and hot dog water were cut with a sea breeze.

Marlowe liked visiting places he hadn't seen in a while—to check out the changes, feel the vibe, see if he could spot the sketchy characters, the ones looking too hard at handbags, purses and cash registers.

Marlowe moved past the usual assortment of souvenir stalls, T-shirt shops, tattoo parlors, tables of homemade trinkets and bad art, street performers, food vendors and eccentrics. If you want to roller-skate in a neon thong or dress up like a Bedouin Hells Angel, have at it. Fast-food jobs were never easy, but Marlowe thought the employees at Hot Dog on a Stick had it the worst. That uniform. A short-sleeve shirt and shorts in blaring red, white, blue and canary yellow, and a fez-style hat in the same overbright colors. Hard to say what they looked like. Shriners turned clowns or fraternity pledges in Morocco.

A long list of celebs live or used to live in Venice. Julia Roberts, Kate Beckinsale, Fiona Apple, John Frusciante, Nicolas Cage and a who's who of others. Nicole lived in the canal district. In 1905, a developer named Abbot Kinney built a network of canals in the city. He'd made his fortune in the tobacco business and wanted to create the feel of Venice, Italy, a hard thing to pull off. He ended up with some nice canals, but lack of upkeep turned them into mini swamps and mosquito resorts. It took decades of political wrangling to rehabilitate them. Marlowe loved the place. It was one of the few idyllic areas in LA. Cheerful ducks and burbling grebes cruised stretches of glassy green water, dragonflies skimming the water surface. Palm trees, lush greenery and luxury homes lined the banks. Marlowe stood on a quaint footbridge, taking in the view and appreciating the quiet. He'd once thought of living here, but a one-bedroom, one-bath, five-hundred-square-foot cottage went for two mill.

Nicole lived in a charming Cape Cod with an arbor over the front gate draped with pink bougainvillea. He rang the bell. There was today's *New York Times* on the doorstep. Marlowe had watched one of Nicole's movies. It was silly, but he was impressed with her. She had nuance, grace, a naturalness you couldn't teach. No wonder she took Kendra's parts.

She welcomed him with an easy smile.

"Hello, Mr. Marlowe, please come in."

"If you don't mind, it's just Marlowe."

"Marlowe it is. Would you like water, a beer? I have wine too."

"A beer would be great."

She had freckles, auburn hair and no makeup. She was wearing jeans and a plaid cowboy shirt with pearl buttons. She should be saddling a horse, Marlowe thought, or standing in a field of grass dotted with blue cornflowers.

They went into the kitchen and sat at the center island.

"I'm investigating Terry's death," Marlowe said. "The police have hit a dead end."

"I don't know how I can help," Nicole said. "As they say, I only know what I read in the newspaper."

"I think Terry's death had something to do with his comeback movie. Could you tell me about that?"

She crinkled her forehead and thought for a few seconds. "It was very strange. Terry had been very depressed and he was drinking. I told him to stay at his place until he got himself together. I should have broken up with him well before that—but that's another story. I guess I didn't want to kick him when he was down. And then one day, out of the blue, he comes over and he's absolutely ecstatic. He'd found funding for his movie. He was vague about the investors. He said they were foreign and they wanted to get into the movie business. Right then, I knew something was wrong. There were lots of talented directors around who could have done the job without Terry's baggage."

"Did you see changes in him?" Marlowe said.

"Oh yes. Suddenly, he was chipper. He had money. He bought new clothes and leased a new car. He had a production office. He stopped drinking and worked on his script." She screwed up her face. "I met Andy. A fly-by-night dirtball if there ever was one. He and Terry were longtime partners, so I didn't say anything."

"Did you meet Cody?" Marlowe asked.

"Yes, I did. I think she was a sneaky, hateful little creature long before we met."

"Were there new people in Terry's life?"

"I think so. He talked about his backers but didn't say who they were. He had meetings, he was on the phone a lot." She crinkled her brow again. "There was this odd thing that happened."

"What's that?" Marlowe said.

"I went to the office one day. Terry was so upbeat I thought it would be a good time to break it off. Well, I walked into the reception area and there were two street thugs there. They had the look, the attitude—you know how they are. One of them was smoking, which Terry would never allow, and the other was browbeating the receptionist. He was a scary guy and an ugly slug if I ever saw one. He had an accent. Eastern Europe or thereabouts."

"What did they want?"

"The ugly one kept saying 'Terry wants to see me,'" Nicole said, "and when the receptionist said he'd have to wait a few minutes, the man cursed at her and walked into Terry's office, and the other guy followed him in. He put his cigarette out on the receptionist's desk. I turned around and left."

"Did Terry talk about it?"

"No. I never told him I was there."

Nicole's phone buzzed. She looked at the caller ID. "Excuse me. I have to take this." She left.

Marlowe had researched Nicole. She grew up in Cheyenne, Wyoming, where her family made a living growing and raising hogs. In an interview with *People* magazine, she said her father was abusive and she ran away when she was twelve. The police picked her up and returned her home. Her father "beat me up pretty good, but it wasn't the first time." She ran away again and lived on the streets of Cheyenne. She slept in abandoned buildings with a pack of other runaways. She was always dirty, always hungry. She begged for spare change. She stole food. She ate out of dumpsters. Some of the older boys were addicted to meth. There was always the danger of rape. Wyoming winters are brutal. The kids made garbage-can fires to stay warm. The girls shared blankets and sleeping bags with her. They gave her their extra clothes.

"People were kind to me. I'll never forget that." She said she couldn't take the street life anymore and showed up at her aunt's house. This aunt was elderly, half blind and living on Social Security. "She took me in, can you imagine?" Nicole told the magazine. "She saved my life. She was an angel. God bless you, Auntie Ruth." The teenage Nicole went back to school and worked two jobs. At night, she mopped floors at a supermarket. On weekends, she worked at an industrial laundry.

Marlowe marveled at this. How some kids were destroyed by abuse and poverty. They became junkies or hardened criminals, unfeeling and violent.

Yet others, like Nicole, became good-hearted human beings. How does this happen? Marlowe wondered. Why can some overcome their past and others are slaves to it? Marlowe had met, chased, confronted, fought with, worked for and collaborated with every kind of person imaginable, but human nature was still as elusive as it was mystifying.

There was more to Nicole's story. She was still living with Auntie Ruth when she decided she needed a trade, steady work, something reliable. She went to beauty school. She completed her two thousand hours of training at Dotty's Beauty Salon and got her licenses in cosmetology and esthiology. It cost her seventeen thousand dollars, all the money she had. She worked at Dotty's and joined a theater group, but she was restless. She was ready for a wider world and looked to LA, but was hesitant about going. It was such a cliché. Dotty loved Nicole and knew her ambitions. She gave her a thousand dollars to get out there. "Pay me back when you're rich and famous," Dotty said. Later, after Nicole's third movie, she bought Dotty a house.

Once in California, Nicole worked at Ereganto, a hair salon in Westwood. Her boss was a prim, efficient Japanese woman named Sumiko. Sumiko told *People* magazine that the customers loved

Nicole. Even if they didn't know what they wanted, she gave them exactly what they had in mind.

"I wish she hadn't become a movie star," Sumiko said. "She could have worked here for the rest of her life."

Nicole had been at Ereganto about a year when Sumiko took her to the set of Kendra's movie *The Coach's Wife*. Kendra had already earned a reputation as "the worst diva in Hollywood," unfair because there were others who were more fastidious. Beyoncé demanded red toilet paper, titanium drinking straws and 100 percent cotton clothing for her staff. Kanye West stipulated the carpet in his hotel rooms be ironed.

Kendra had fired a dozen hair and makeup artists before she hired Sumiko. Sumiko later said the star was a terrible person and she wouldn't work for her again, even if they paid her more. Kendra was in the makeup chair, Sumiko just beginning her work. Kendra began yelling—something about her color corrector—loud, shrill and abusive. Sumiko didn't reply. She put on her jacket, picked up her handbag and left the set. Everyone was shocked. Kendra was supposed to shoot a scene running through a crowd at a football game. Fifteen other actors, a production crew of fifty-seven, one insane director, three apoplectic producers, two catatonic studio execs and seven hundred fifty extras were waiting for her in the hot California sun.

Nicole was packing up Sumiko's kit. *"You,"* Kendra said. "Can you finish the job that incompetent bitch started?"

Other people in the room said Nicole was calm, not the least bit intimidated. She replied, "Sumiko isn't a bitch or incompetent, but yes, I can finish the job." Later, her poise was attributed to the life she'd already lived. Hard to intimidate someone who grew up tending hogs and begging on the streets of Cheyenne.

"You fuck this up and you won't get a job putting makeup on dead bodies at a funeral home," Kendra said.

"I don't fuck up," Nicole replied. She delivered. Kendra looked radiant. Some said she looked five years younger. Kendra was startled, pleased and disappointed at the same time. She had no one to yell at.

Kendra had her assistant tip Nicole five hundred dollars. The director hugged her for way too long and offered her a ride home in his Lamborghini. Sumiko wasn't called back for the rest of the twenty-eight-day shoot.

Nicole returned to the kitchen and took her place at the island. "Sorry, Marlowe. That was my agent, Nancy. She really takes care of me."

"Can you tell me about Terry and Pav's relationship?" Marlowe asked.

"Why? Do you think Pav is involved?"

"No, but he's unwilling to speak to me." A lie. He hadn't talked to Pav, but in the words of Chick Hearn, No harm, no foul. "He may know something relevant and not be aware of it."

Pav and Terry were very close, Nicole said. "They met at a sound stage in the Valley. Terry was working on his last big movie and he knew it. The Paramount execs had seen a rough cut and they were less than enthusiastic. Test audiences panned it." She finished her beer. "Terry's career as a film director was over."

There was only some minor editing to do, Nicole went on. As soon as it was done, the studio would take away Terry's entry pass, parking space and privileges. One night, Terry was at the sound stage in Burbank. He was milling around the courtroom set the studio had rented for the movie. He had wanted to do some reshoots but the studio said no. The rent was a lousy four grand a day, but he was already over budget. He felt persecuted. The catering budget was a million and a half dollars. That's what happens when you have a five-hundred-man crew and serve them spice-rubbed char-grilled tri-tip, New Zealand lamb chops with apricot and fresh mint jelly, roasted butternut squash with beet medley and seven different cream options. For the stars? Add on hot towel delivery and a bowl of M&M's.

Terry decided the studio had wronged him. If they'd only let him make the movie he'd wanted to make, things would have turned out fine. Instead, they forced casting on him, cut the budget he'd asked for and made script changes over his objections. It wasn't his fault the movie was shitty, but he'd get all the blame.

"He told me he sat down in the witness chair," Nicole said. "He imagined a jury of his peers, eager to find him guilty, and the judge waiting to sentence him to a life of failure." Terry thought there was no point in going on, Nicole continued. He said he knew she had lost all respect for him. She denied it, but they both knew that wasn't true. The only person left in the world who thought he was worth anything was Cody. Terry had a moment's indecision. Cody would be devastated, but his own pain was overwhelming.

"He thought it was fitting that he was in a courtroom," Nicole said. In the prop room, Terry found a length of rope, a three-foot aluminum stepladder and a crescent wrench. He went back to the courtroom. He tied one end of the rope to the leg of the defense table. It was bolted to the floor. Then he tied the wrench to the other end of the rope and flung it over a rafter. He put the stepladder beneath it and climbed the two steps to the top. The rope dangled about head height. He removed the wrench and tossed it.

Terry didn't know how to tie a hangman's knot so he settled for a bowline, a common knot used to hold things securely. Once it was cinched down, it wouldn't come loose. When he stepped off the ladder, he'd be hanging a few feet from the floor. He hoped Cody wouldn't take it too hard. "I'm sorry, kitten," he whispered.

"Terry said he stood there for a long time," Nicole went on. "Weeping and moaning, his mind filled with regrets, mistakes, foolishness and all the love he had lost." She blew out a sigh and shook her head. "And then, like an idiot, he did it."

Terry stepped off the ladder. His foot was still in midair when he realized he'd made a terrible mistake. As he swung free, he reached up, grabbed the rope with both hands and held on. He knew he couldn't last more than a few seconds. He was out of shape and his hands were slipping.

Later, he told Nicole the last thing he saw before he let go was the hanging scene from the Coen brothers' highly unnecessary film *True Grit*. He was the prisoner in the middle, crying pitiably and lamenting his miserable life.

Pav was the guard on duty that night, sitting at the front desk, playing *Call of Duty* on his laptop. He switched to watching porn and writing emails to his mother and sister. He hadn't seen them in a year. About eleven that evening, Terry had entered the building. Clothes a mess, unshaven, smelling of booze and talking to himself. He showed his ID, signed the clipboard and went in. He didn't say anything and disappeared into the main hallway.

Pav switched from porn to *The Walking Dead*, ate a cold roast beef sandwich he'd bought at Ralphs and drank coffee from a thermos. The next time he looked at his watch it was 2 a.m. Terry still hadn't come out. What was he doing here so late? Pav thought. There was nothing to do, there was no one else around. Pav knew Terry as The Director. Not the down-and-out has-been on his way to the show business slush pile. Maybe he was passed out somewhere. Better go find him, Pav thought.

The twenty-thousand-square-foot sound stage housed a variety of standing sets. Pav didn't know which one was Terry's. He called Terry's name numerous times but got no response. What if it was worse than passing out? What if he'd had a heart attack? *Oh shit.* The Director dying on your shift? You'll get fired, you'll get blamed. Pav ran from set to set and finally saw Terry. He was stupefied. Terry had a rope around his neck and was dangling from a rafter, his hands at his throat, his face purple, a grinding noise coming from his throat.

Pav ran over, grabbed Terry around his waist and lifted him, putting an inch of slack in the rope and saving Terry's life by a millisecond.

"Terry said he was yelling but he couldn't remember what," Nicole said. "It was probably something like, Save me! Dear God, please save me! I've heard him say that before."

Terry's chin was pointed at the ceiling, back arched, hands still clutching the rope. He fumbled with the knot, but it was too tight to loosen. He grabbed the rope again. "More...slack," he gasped.

The stepladder was two feet away. If Pav could move it under Terry, Terry could stand on it. But if he did that, the slack would go out of the rope and Terry's head would explode. Sweat singed Pav's eyes, his teeth clenched so tight he thought they would fracture. He sucked in a huge breath, bent his knees, grunted like a weight lifter and hoisted Terry up, giving him an inch more slack. Pav moved his foot behind one leg of the ladder and jerked it closer.

Every muscle in Pav's body was in flames, his arms were in cinders. He was in agony. He had to let go. He screamed, his arms dropping—and then *the load lightened!* Terry had put one foot on top of the ladder. His hands were still clutching the rope, his chin still pointed at the ceiling. Both men were screaming, their mouths wide open, sweat raining off them. Pav couldn't take it. This was the end. His arms were in ashes. He let go, staggered back and fell to the floor. He looked up at Terry. He looked up at the dead man. Who wasn't dead. Terry had put both feet on the ladder. It wasn't directly underneath him. He was hanging at a slight angle, wobbling, the ladder rattling, his hands still clenching the rope.

"Incredible, under the circumstances," Marlowe said.

"Death is really a motivator," Nicole said.

Terry managed to stand on top of the ladder, his legs not aligned with his body, the tension in his torso twisted and tight, only his hands on the rope holding him upright, his knees giving way, and he was breathing like a Pomeranian in Florida. To untie the bowline, there's a spot on the rope you push through the knot until it comes free. Terry found the spot, pushed it, but it didn't go all the way through. He tried again. And again. Then he collapsed.

Pav was sitting on the floor, too exhausted to move. In slow motion, he saw Terry fall. "NO!" he shouted. The knot held, Terry was going to die—and then it unfurled, the ladder tipped over and Terry went sprawling to the floor.

"Terry said they lay there for a long time," Nicole continued. There was a burn mark around his neck that looked like a red kerchief. I saw it. It made me think, *This man is dumber than the dumbest man in Wyoming, and they've got an unbeatable selection.* Pav took him to his place. He gave him a couple of Vicodin and treated the burn. Pav is a pretty handy guy. They drank some, Terry took more Vicodin and they slept until the next day.

"That's the most amazing thing I've ever heard," Marlowe said.

"Yeah, me too."

"I'm exhausted just hearing about it."

"After that, Terry said he and Pav were blood brothers."

Terry was very grateful, Nicole went on. He asked Pav what he could do in return. He expected Pav to ask for money. But the security guard saw an opportunity. This was The Director. He had power and connections. Pav told Terry he wanted out of his dead-end job. The Director, who had no power or connections, said sure, absolutely. Terry netted a million and a half from his terrible movie. He took Pav on as a driver and bodyguard, though he hardly needed either.

"He told me he was making a statement," Nicole said. "A way of saying to the business, I'm doing fine. I'm still important. Of course, nobody bought it. They thought he was a fool."

Terry bought Pav a new car, new clothes, paid a year's lease on a luxe apartment. They ate out at Spago and Matsuhisa, went to clubs, fancy bars, golf weekends, Vegas weekends. They gambled and hired hookers. He was burning through the money.

"I think Terry was trying to make himself feel better," Nicole said. "He had someone to take care of, someone that looked up to him. And then Kendra found out we'd been having an affair. Somebody had seen us together. It was over by that time, but of course it didn't matter. There was a media war. It was all Kendra. I was at an Oscar party and she attacked me. Did you read about it?"

"Yeah, I did," Marlowe said.

"It was humiliating, more so for her, I think. Us country girls can throw a punch or two." She met Marlowe's gaze.

"I know what you're thinking," she said.

"You do? I hardly know myself."

"You're thinking, why did I get involved with a flake like Terry."

"As a matter of fact—"

"I met him while I was still doing Kendra's hair and makeup," Nicole said. "He was a hot ticket then. Dashing, handsome, funny. Then Kendra got me a part in one of her movies. It was a stinker, but it launched my career. Terry was always around. I wasn't innocent to the ways of the world, but I was to the ways of Hollywood." Nicole looked despondent and breathed a deep sigh. "It was an awful thing I did, taking up with Terry. I'll burn in hell for that one."

"There are worse things," Marlowe said.

Nicole continued. "Even when I knew the relationship was bad for me, I stuck with him, just like my mother stuck with Dad even though he beat her. That was my example of love, I guess."

There was a pause. "Are you hungry?" Nicole said.

"Yeah, I could eat," Marlowe said.

"Do you know how to fry bacon properly?"

"Yes, I do."

"Then I'll leave you to it."

Marlowe looked in the fridge. He was pleased to find bacon from Vande Rose Farms. Slow smoked, thick cut, uncured, from a heritage breed of Duroc hogs. He rarely cooked but when he did he wanted real food. He took a cast-iron pan off the rack, set it on medium-high heat and laid the strips down in an even row. As the bacon began to cook, he moved the strips from inside out. The middle of the pan is hotter and rotating them lets them cook evenly.

"I like your style," Nicole said. When the bacon was nearly done, she got out a skillet, set it on low heat and added a healthy knob of butter. She cracked six eggs in a bowl and whipped them vigorously with a fork. She gently poured the eggs into the pan and didn't stir right away. Marlowe approved. Stir them and you get a bunch of broken-up curds. Marlowe made a fresh pot of coffee, sliced some fresh tomatoes and waited before he put the toast on. Too early and it would be cold when the eggs were done.

The eggs were setting up. Nicole used a spatula and pushed the edges of the curds toward the center of the pan, the liquid egg taking their place. She was patient, folds of egg taking shape in the middle. The egg was still moist when she folded it over on itself. Marlowe smiled. He hated dry eggs. The toast popped up. They plated everything and poured the coffee.

"It's beautiful," Nicole said.

"Yes it is," Marlowe said.

Nicole bowed her head and said grace. She was earnest and sincere, adding warmth to the occasion. They spoke little while they ate. Good food requires respect.

When they finished, she said, "Let's go out on the deck."

A breeze made the willows shimmer. A blue dragonfly skimmed over the golden yarrow. They sat under an umbrella and finished their coffee. There was the faint smell of charcoal. Marlowe noticed some of the wooden siding and part of the deck had been replaced and painted. There'd been a fire here.

"I've heard about you, Marlowe," Nicole said with an amused smile.

"That's regrettable," he said with the same smile.

"You don't seem at all as abrasive and unpleasant as I've heard."

"I'm neither abrasive nor unpleasant. I am as you see me here. Amiable and cordial as you please."

"Is that so?" Nicole said. "A business acquaintance said you returned his retainer because he was, and I quote, 'a festering boil on the rectum of humanity.'"

"Ah yes, him. An exception I can assure you."

"Yesterday, I had lunch with one of your former clients. You told her to get her fallopian tubes filled with cement so her husband's sperm would turn back and her eggs would die. Another exception?"

"I don't remember saying that," Marlowe said.

"You were right about both of them," Nicole said, smiling. She considered him a moment.

"Are you unattached, Marlowe?"

"Yes, I am."

"Maybe we could have a drink sometime."

"I'd like that very much." He had a momentary twinge about Ren. But she'd be back in the UK soon and that would be the end of it. A drink with Nicole would be fine.

CHAPTER SEVEN
CECIL THE BALLS

If your job involved crime in LA, you had to know about gangs. Marlowe studied them, tracked their activities and kept files. George had mentioned an Armenian gang and the only significant outfit in LA was Armenian Power—and they had Russian connections. Armenian Power was formed in the eighties. Their original ambition was similar to the Tiny Rascals gang in Long Beach. To protect their own from the fierce Latino and Black gangs. In the mid-2000s, Mher Darbinyan, aka Capone, aka Hollywood Mike, took over the leadership. He was ruthless, the gang preying on its own people. They robbed, extorted, dealt drugs, kidnapped and murdered, their community frightened into silence.

Under Darbinyan's leadership the gang transitioned to more modern crimes. Credit card fraud, identity theft and mortgage fraud. Medicare paid millions to a clinic controlled by the gang. Darbinyan operated a scam at some of the ninety-nine-cent stores. The credit card scanners were switched out with ones that were trick. Insert your ATM card and the scanner recorded the number. A tiny camera recorded the PIN.

Hollywood Mike and his partners scored big when they forged a strategic relationship with the notoriously violent prison gang the Mexican Mafia, aka La Eme. AP paid "taxes" on its criminal activities and La Eme provided protection for AP members in the joint. By making this alliance, AP had access to the street gangs, gateways to the drug distribution network.

AP was dealt a severe blow when one of their victims came forward, known only as MM. MM had foolishly taken out a loan from the gang. The vig was twenty percent a week and MM soon exhausted himself financially. One month he couldn't come up with the vig. In a recorded call, Darbinyan said, "You are lying. I'll jerk off on the liar's dead mother." One of his associates was recorded saying, "I will skin you if that deposit does not happen by five o'clock." MM couldn't stand it anymore. He went to the FBI and supplied them with inside information. Nearly a thousand officers and agents from the FBI, DEA, LAPD, Customs and Immigration and the US Secret Service conducted a massive early-morning sweep. A hundred AP members and associates were arrested. Darbinyan was eventually convicted on multiple counts under the RICO Act. In 2019, a judge sent Darbinyan to prison for eighteen years. He was forty-four years old.

Marlowe wanted to know what the gang was up to these days. What had happened since Darbinyan was removed? Had the membership been dispersed? Disbanded? Moved locations? Was there a new leader? He was going to see an ex-client named Garik Roben. He lived near Fountain and Normandie, a tidy area of nondescript houses. Garik was one of the many people Marlowe had met through Basilio. Garik ran a small restaurant that served authentic Armenian food. Marlowe's favorites were *manti,* small meat pies, baked and topped with tomato and yogurt sauces. Garik was like the vast majority of people in the Armenian community. Honorable, hardworking folks who tended to their families, paid their taxes and watched *Game of Thrones* like everybody else.

Basilio assigned Marlowe a case involving the theft of family heirlooms. Someone had broken into Garik's house and stolen his collection of Armenian crafts and memorabilia. Armenian hats made by the only hatmaker in Yerevan, carved wooden amulets called *Daghdagh.* A distant relative of Garik's, fleeing the genocide, knelt in his garden and wrapped a handful of dirt in a handkerchief. A piece of his homeland to which he'd never return. And a *mushurba* or "gurgling cup." It was made of copper and shaped more or less like an Egyptian wine jug without the handles. It had been in Garik's family since the Ottoman Empire. The police took a report but that was all.

On that first visit, a decade ago, Marlowe arrived at Garik's house and checked out the surroundings, something he did out of habit. The house next door stood in sharp contrast to Garik's. Ramshackle, flaking paint, a yard of weeds and dirt. An elderly man, as decrepit as the house, was sitting on the porch. He was drinking a bottle of Kilikia and looking at his red iPhone.

Marlowe sat with Garik in the living room. His wife served mulberry wine. Garik was a small man, as well kept as his house. He was distraught. "I am without words," he said. "The collection represents my family. Our struggles, our courage, our history. It is as if someone has stolen our name." Aside from the collection, nothing else was taken, though there were other valuables in the house. Only an Armenian could have recognized the collection for what it was, Marlowe thought. The thief would either keep them or sell them to another Armenian.

Marlowe sat quietly a moment, Garik waited expectantly. "Are you going to gather clues?" he said.

"Who's your neighbor?" Marlowe asked.

Garik scowled. "Farid? He is an idiot. He is from Azerbaijan. We hate each other. Why do you ask?"

"How is it that Farid can afford a brand-new iPhone?" Red was a new color, unavailable until this year. Garik thought a moment.

"I will beat him until he begs for mercy!" he shouted angrily.

"No, you'll get arrested. I have another idea."

A minute later, Marlowe came bursting out of Garik's front door. He charged over to Farid's house. The old man instinctively shriveled and clutched the iPhone to his chest. Marlowe was wearing a suit. He'd just been kicked out of the police academy and still had short hair.

"Detective Marlowe," he barked. "LAPD, Major Crimes Unit. You stole Garik's collection and sold it. Tell me who or I'll arrest you right now." Farid started to speak, but Marlowe cut him off. "Remember, asshole, if you lie, you go straight to jail."

"If I tell you, will you let me go?" Farid said fearfully.

"Depends on what you say."

Farid had sold Garik's collection to his brother, a gold dealer with a shop downtown. Marlowe ordered Farid to call his brother and demand the immediate return of the stolen goods. Refuse, and they'd both go to jail charged with conspiracy, breaking and entering, grand theft and grand larceny. "Tell him the Los Angeles Police Department is waiting for his answer." Garik got everything back, plus a $500 bonus from the gold dealer for stress and inconvenience. He'd treated Marlowe like a favorite son ever since.

Garik's house looked like it did a decade ago. Farid's hovel had been replaced with a small apartment building. Garik met him at the door and greeted him warmly. They sat in the living room and drank tea.

"What can I do for you, my friend?"

"Armenian Power."

"They are scum," Garik said indignantly. "They are a plague on their own community. When I heard of their arrests, my friends and I had a party."

"What happened to AP after that?" Marlowe asked. Garik's restaurant was a meeting place for the locals. An Armenian Starbucks. All the news, gossip and rumors passed through there.

"They have a new leader," Garik said. "An *apush* named Tato Magarian. He is not as smart as Darbinyan, but he's clever and more violent. He renamed the gang Hzoy. He is involved in everything evil. Drugs, guns, sex trafficking, extortion. He is unpredictable and vicious. Everyone is afraid of him."

"Where does he live?" Marlowe asked.

"I can find out for you."

"Do you know where the gang hangs out?"

"Anywhere they want," Garik replied. "They took over my nephew's bar and made everyone leave."

"Anything else you can tell me?" Marlowe said.

"It is not important," Garik said, "but Tato wants to be a rapper. I am embarrassed for his parents." Garik walked Marlowe to the door. "Come to the restaurant, eat with my family. You will have a wonderful time."

Marlowe searched online for photos of Hzoy. There were only a few. The members could easily be mistaken for Latino or white gangsters. There were the ho-hum shaved heads, stringy mustaches, baggy shorts and oversized white T-shirts. Many of them were bare-chested, covered with the equally ho-hum swarm of tats, HZOY the centerpiece scrawled in a confusing Old English font. Armenian crosses and the Virgin Mary were also popular. The rest were the conventional array of skulls, weapons, naked women, gang signs and dead homies. No way to tell Tato from anybody else. Marlowe remembered Garik saying the gang leader wanted to be a rapper.

Marlowe went to YouTube. He found a video titled *Hzoy Emcee Tato*. Tato was dressed in full camo, rapping against a slideshow of grisly photos from the Armenian-Azerbaijani war. The rapping itself was also ho-hum except for the occasional phrase in Armenian.

Tato was chubby, his round eyes peering out of a round head, thick lips and ears like an elephant listening for a mating call. He reminded Marlowe of a younger Lev Parnas, one of the people who brought down Giuliani. Tato wasn't especially expressive when he rapped, but now and then, he'd flash a warped, snarling, near-psychotic face. The idea that this guy was involved with Terry was George's speculation. It would have to be confirmed.

That evening, Marlowe, Emmet and Cody gathered in the kitchen again. Cody looked bored and sullen, slumped in a chair, twiddling a lock of hair. He'd considered taking her back to Kendra but it was too soon, too risky. The payday would have to wait.

"When can I get out of here? There's nothing to do," Cody said.

"You can go home any time you want," Marlowe said. "Kendra will be thrilled." Cody sighed, shifted her position and looked even more sullen.

The interview technique was standard. Go at the suspect as if you already know everything.

"When did you find out Terry was laundering money for the Russians?" Marlowe said.

Cody looked at him, seemingly incredulous.

"What Russians? What money laundering? What are you talking about?"

"The Russians gave Terry money for his comeback movie," Marlowe said. "He got greedy, skimmed some off the top and they sent Hzoy to kill him."

"In the first place," Cody retorted, "Pav killed Terry, and in the second, what's a Hzoy? Is that how you pronounce it?"

"Stop bullshitting," Emmet said. "You knew about the whole thing. You were in on it."

"In on what? What are you talking about?" Cody said.

"Wait, Emmet, back off for a second," Marlowe said, again the voice of reason. "Here's why it matters, Cody. Suppose—just suppose we're right. Terry was laundering money for the Russians."

"He wasn't!"

"It doesn't make any difference, Cody, don't you see that? You were close to Terry. The Russians will think you were involved and they'll send Hzoy after you. That guy in the alley could have been one of them."

"I don't know any Russians and I don't know any whatever the word is. The guy in the alley was Pav!" she insisted.

"Fine, it was Pav," Marlowe said, conceding. "But that doesn't mean Hzoy isn't after you. We have to know more if we're going to protect you."

Cody looked up at the ceiling and groaned, exasperated. "I have no idea what you're talking about! How many times do I have to say it?" Marlowe considered, looked at Emmet. He shrugged.

"Okay, that's it," Marlowe said, seemingly chagrined. "Just following up on a lead that was obviously wrong. Sorry for the bother."

When he wasn't drunk, Emmet's timing was usually impeccable. He let Cody have a moment's relief, waiting until she was halfway out the door.

"Tato gave me a message for you," he said. Cody didn't flinch, hardly reacted at all.

"I'm sorry, what was that?" she said.

"Nothing," Emmet said. Cody looked at him curiously and left.

"She's either really good or we're really stupid," Emmet said.

"It's a toss-up," Marlowe said. "I have my reservations but I'm liking Pav for the shooter in the alley."

"It wasn't Tato, I can tell you that," Emmet said. "He wouldn't have sent a lone gunner. He would have blocked the alley in both directions and shot her fifty times. And that whole thing about giving Roy a thousand dollars is not something Hzoy would do."

"That means they're two discrete episodes," Marlowe said. "Pav shot at Cody in the alley and Hzoy killed Terry for stealing."

"Too much of a coincidence," Emmet said, shaking his head.

"I think so too," Marlowe said. "The two are connected. The question is how."

Marlowe drove home from Emmet's place. He had a beer, made notes about what was said that day and took a shower. He thought about Ren; how she must feel, desperate for her son, waiting for some PI to get off his ass. He called her to apologize.

"Yes?" she said.

"Hi, it's Marlowe. I'm sorry about today. I know it's late but maybe we could—"

She cut him off. "That's all right, you have your priorities and I have mine. I have a lead and I'm going to follow up on it. I'm waiting for an Uber now."

"You're going out? How 'bout I go with you?"

"We'll talk tomorrow. Good night."

The call ended. Shutting him out was like slamming a door. He was worried. An Uber to where? To meet who? He sensed she could take care of herself but this wasn't her city and LA wasn't what you'd call friendly. The Marriott was close by. He parked across the street hoping he wasn't too late. A short while later, a white Hyundai pulled into the lot. Ren came out of her room, looking grim and anxious. She got in the car and spoke to the driver for a moment. They drove off and Marlowe followed.

Downtown LA was comprised of two worlds. The first was the Disney Music Center, the pricy converted lofts, Staples Center, Grand Central Market, L.A. Live, the Grammy Museum and Little Tokyo. The second world was Skid Row, a slum from somewhere not in America; a catch basin for the perpetually impoverished, the hopelessly addicted, the incurably insane and the disabled beyond repair. It was embarrassing, Marlowe thought, that a city of such massive wealth and influence couldn't fix, or even clean up, an area of less than three square miles. There were excuses for third-world ghettos but not for a metropolis full of Kendras and Katzenbergs and Jay-Z's $88-million palace with its bulletproof windows and four swimming pools, and Jay Leno's car collection was worth $150 million. Cars, for Christ's sake.

The vast majority of people in LA, even those from depressed communities, have never seen raw garbage piled up on the street, buzzing with flies and swarming with rats and roaches, or an entire family living under a plastic tarp, or barefoot kids eating out of trash cans or grown men who can't remember the last time they showered, wearing clothes that have never been laundered.

The white Hyundai pulled over in front of the King Eddy Saloon at Fifth and Los Angeles Street, a few blocks away from Skid Row. The bar had been there since 1906, established on the ground floor of the ritzy King Edward Hotel. It was successful for decades but declined in the late forties. Then its lifeline, the electric rail Red Car line, died in favor of freeways. People quit walking and businesses closed at five and Eddy's sank into dive bar status along with the rest of the neighborhood. Marlowe watched Ren get out of the car and without a glance at the surroundings stride into Eddy's.

He parked and entered the bar. It was properly dim, the decor an incongruent mix of Victorian and Old West. Hipsters, musicians, artists, ne'er-do-wells and adventurous office workers gathered at Eddy's, most never realizing that over a hundred years of shootings, stabbings, drug deals, screaming matches and drunken brawls had happened under its historic roof.

There was an oblong bar with stools on one side, bench seats and tables on the other side. The walls were covered with memorabilia. Strings of lights were hung on the ceiling, their glimmer reflecting off the liquor bottles and beer signs, the glow nostalgic and comforting.

Ren and an Asian man were sitting at the far end of the bar. Marlowe got as close as he dared and sat at a table. He could see all of the Asian man's face and part of Ren's. She was talking; serious, plaintive, urgent. The Asian man had a crew cut, nerd glasses and a squished face like someone had stepped on a soda can. He was pretending to listen, nodding, brow furrowed, stealing glances at her body.

Ren finished and waited for an answer. The Asian man leaned toward her as if he had something confidential to say. As he spoke, his expression changed from interested party to slithery creep. Ren reared back, angry and disbelieving. Furious, she hissed something. The Asian man shrugged. Ren stood up and shouldered her way toward the door; she didn't notice Marlowe.

"It's up to you, babe," the Asian man called after her.

Marlowe caught up with her outside. "Ren?" he said. She turned, ready to fight.

"Marlowe? What are you doing here?"

"I was worried about you. I followed you from the Marriott."

"I don't know how I feel about that."

"Who was that guy you were talking with?" Marlowe said.

"Cecil Watanabe." She said the name like a curse. "One of Fallon's old friends. They ran together when they were in college. He was in Fallon's little black book. I called him. I asked if he'd heard from Fallon and did he know anything about Jeremy. He said yes, so I came to meet him."

"But he wouldn't tell you anything unless you had sex with him."

"Yes, the bastard!"

"Hold on a second," Marlowe said. He got on the phone with Emmet. They talked for a minute and the call ended. "My dad will deal with Cecil, but he wants a favor."

Ren took Marlowe's car and followed the GPS to Emmet's house. She made her way through a ridiculous jungle of trees and plants. A skinny girl with black makeup, black hair and suspicious eyes opened the door a crack.

"Yeah?"

"Hi, I'm Ren Stewart. I think Emmet called to say I was coming? You must be Cody." Cody stared a moment, took off the chain and opened the door.

Ren came in and looked around, puzzled. A woman from another generation had furnished the living room. It was quaint and charming, save for the dust and untidiness. The woman must have passed away or moved out.

"Yeah, weird, huh?" Cody said. "Want something to drink? Put your stuff down anywhere."

They went into the kitchen. Ren sat at the breakfast table. Cody got the bottle of Grey Goose out of the freezer. She found water glasses in the cupboard, poured two drinks and pushed one at Ren.

"Thank you," Ren said. Cody sat down. They sipped their drinks, looking at each other appraisingly.

"You're not going to ask me if I'm supposed to be doing this?" Cody said.

"Let's say you're not," Ren said. "What am I going to do about it? Take away your allowance and lock you in your room?" Cody smiled.

"Emmet said you were coming but he didn't say why," she said.

"He implied that you were in danger of some sort," Ren replied. "He said he was more comfortable if someone else was in the house, especially at night."

"Did he say anything about me?"

"No, but I think he likes you." That unsettled Cody for a moment.

"Are you friends with Marlowe?" Cody asked.

"Not friends. Client."

"Troubles, huh?"

"My ex-husband kidnapped my son, Jeremy."

"I hear you. My boyfriend is an asshole too." They smiled and clinked glasses.

"Cheers," Ren said.

Marlowe was leaning on the police cruiser, waiting. Emmet came out of the bar. "Turns out I know the guy," he said.

"You do?"

"Me and Wittig worked out of Central," Emmet said. "We drank at King Eddy's all the time. They call the guy Cecil the Balls."

"Come again?"

"Wittig told me Cecil's ball sack hangs down to his ankles."

"How does Wittig know?"

"Strip-searched him on a drug thing. Wittig couldn't believe it. He said Cecil's scrotum looked like two bowling balls in a burlap bag. The other cons took bets on how much they weighed but they couldn't figure out how to—"

"That's enough, Dad."

They went inside. Cecil was still at the end of the bar. Father and son sat on either side of him.

"Remember me, Cecil? I was Dave Wittig's partner," Emmet said. If Cecil assumed Marlowe was a cop that was on him.

"There's a name I'd like to forget," Cecil said.

"Let's talk about Ren Stewart."

"Who?"

"That's not a good sign, Cecil," Emmet said. "Saying *who* is a dead giveaway. If you ask a normal person if they know someone they'll say, no, I don't or I'm afraid I haven't met him—not *who*. *Who* makes you sound spooked, like you've got something to hide."

"Good to know," Cecil said.

"Ren Stewart is the woman you were talking to a half hour ago," Marlowe said.

"Doesn't ring a bell," Cecil said. He took a sip of his beer.

"She's filed a complaint against you," Marlowe said. "According to her statement, you're withholding information about her kidnapped son. You wanted sex in return."

"That's bullshit. I want to see a lawyer," Cecil said.

"Okay, fine. We were trying to be nice to you," Emmet said.

"This is nice? What would happen if you weren't nice?"

"We'd take you down to the station, make you wait three or four hours in a holding cell before we let you make your call."

Emmet glanced at his watch. "What is it? Nearly midnight? An attorney's not going to show up until morning. You never know. Maybe you're accidentally put on a bus to say, Vacaville over in Solano County. It's a seven-hour drive. The return bus goes out there once a week."

"Aww come on, fellas," Cecil whined. "You're asking me to admit to extortion."

"No, we're not. All we want you to do is answer a couple of questions," Emmet said.

"I'm waiting."

"Have you heard from Fallon Stewart lately?" Marlowe said.

"Fallon? That asshole?" Cecil said. "Not since I caught him screwing my sister in the backseat of my car. That was a long time ago."

"Do you know anything about Fallon's son, Jeremy?" Emmet asked.

"Like I told you, I haven't heard from him so how would I know anything about his son?"

"So you've got nothing," Emmet said.

"I've always got nothing," Cecil said dolefully. "Ren called me, said something about Fallon and looking for her kid. She sounded desperate so I thought…" He shrugged. "Why not?"

"That's low. Even for a cretin like you," Emmet said.

"I saw a chance to get laid so I took it," Cecil said, like he was perfectly justified. "I haven't had sex in two and a half years, okay?"

"The big balls puts 'em off?"

"Does it ever," Cecil said. "This one girl thought they were a two-headed octopus. I thought she'd never stop screaming."

Marlowe got up. "We'll be going now." They went outside. "Thanks, Dad. I appreciate your help." Emmet was already moving for his car.

"Anytime," he said.

Cody was in her room, changing clothes. It was nice chatting with Ren. No condescension. One adult talking to another. Maybe it was for real, or maybe it was Ren's way of being cool with a teenager. She was going to Eli's place, surprise him, fuck him till he begged for mercy. She couldn't wait to get there.

Ren was in the living room, lounging on the sofa and reading the paper.

"I'm going out," Cody said, casually, like to a friend. "Would you mind loaning me your car? I'll be an hour, no more than that."

Ren didn't look up from the newspaper. "No, I don't think so."

"It's cool, Ren. It's only an hour. How about the keys?"

"No."

"I thought we were friends," Cody said, sounding disappointed.

"We're not friends and the car belongs to Marlowe."

"Re-*en,* you're being unreasonable," Cody moaned. "I'm not going to hurt the car. I have a license and it's only for an hour."

"Sorry," Ren said, turning a page.

Cody started to go back to her room but stopped and turned around. It was infuriating, Ren messing up her surprise. Cody could feel her shoulders tighten, her guts churn. She clenched her teeth and growled, *"I want to borrow the car."*

"So you said," Ren replied, still reading. Cody couldn't believe it.

Why does this snooty bitch get to decide where you go? She has no authority over you.

"Well, the hell with you, then," Cody said. The keys were on the coffee table next to Ren's handbag. Cody snatched them up and marched for the door. Ren didn't say a word. *That's what I thought, you pussy.* Cody went outside and started down the walkway, grinning with satisfaction. She heard the door open and footsteps behind her.

"Give me the keys," Ren said. Cody was ready. She whirled around and threw an overhand right just like Eli had taught her. Ren ducked under the looping punch and grabbed Cody around the waist with both arms. That was stupid. Cody turned to the side and got Ren in a headlock.

"Yeah? What now, asshole? Huh? Huh?" Cody said viciously. It was so easy, like Ren had let it happen. Ren had her left arm wrapped around Cody's waist, her right hand holding Cody's knee. "It's over," Cody said. "I'm gonna choke you out." Ren sat down, her left hand pulled, her right hand lifted Cody's leg. Ren rolled over and slammed Cody to the ground; the impact knocked the wind out of her. She grunted and struggled for breath. Ren stood up and dusted herself off.

"I took jujitsu for eight years," Ren said. "Brown belt. Then I had Jeremy and I didn't have time to qualify for the black. You do that again and I'll hurt you."

She picked up the keys and went back into the house. Cody lay there gasping. There was dirt on her face. Pebbles stuck in her hands. Emmet came up the path.

"This doesn't look voluntary. What happened?" he said.

"None of your goddamn business."

"Well, call me if you need something. A tent, a sleeping bag, a first aid kit."

"Piss off, Emmet," Cody said. Emmet shook his head and went inside.

Cody got up, taking a moment to regain her balance. She'd skinned her knee as well. Ren came out, handbag over her shoulder, jingling the keys. She walked past without a word. Cody was still short of breath, a blast of flaming hatred shooting out of her eyes. *I'll get you, you English bitch. I'm going to make you pay.*

Next morning, Marlowe went to his gym, a small place in West Hollywood called Drive. It had a limited clientele and high fees. The trainer was a West African man named Jahno. Jahno was six-three, broad-shouldered, solid as a cement pillar and the handsomest man Marlowe had ever met. Years ago, Jahno had the body of a bulked-up weight lifter. He abandoned the practice, telling Marlowe he wanted to look like he had a life outside the gym.

"Traditional strength training is impractical," Jahno intoned when Marlowe was starting out. "I can bench-press my body weight but when in life do I push something that heavy straight up from my chest?"

"Doesn't it strengthen your shoulders?" Marlowe said.

"Yes, but think about all the other things it *doesn't* do. Think of all the other muscles around the shoulders that are doing nothing." Jahno emphasized coordination and balance. Capabilities, he said, you needed far more than brute strength. In the beginning the exercises were simple; like carrying a forty-pound dumbbell in one hand like a shopping bag while you walked in wide circles. Jahno explained you rarely carried something with your arms full and you had to use your core to stay balanced. Marlowe was surprised how hard it was. He would weave off course, lose his footwork, even stumble. It was embarrassing. It was only forty pounds.

"Strength is not your problem," Jahno said. "It's your brain. It can't compute fast enough to compensate for the asymmetry. That's why the struggle is the exercise, not the completion. Your brain will learn to respond faster. The neural pathways will open."

Another task was standing on two balance boards, a foot on each. It was like standing on two surfboards with springs beneath them. While you boxed. Marlowe had to stay upright and throw punches while Jahno moved the focus pads at different angles. Marlowe knew well that street fighting was awkward and didn't happen under ideal conditions. He couldn't remember a single instance where he'd hit someone from a stationary boxing stance.

Marlowe had to stand on one foot, do curls with one weight and lateral raises with the other. Jahno said if you fall, it's almost always on one foot and your arms have to move independently. Jahno had dozens of these exercises. After months of hard work, Marlowe was exceptionally agile, quick, and almost impossible to knock down. He had trained his brain, his neural pathways were wide open. His hands, legs and feet could move independently, his strengthened core the center of gravity.

Marlowe was behind a stout woman on an elevator. She slipped and fell backward. In an instant, he knelt to cushion her weight, caught her in the crook of his arm and grabbed her flying Maltese with his off hand. He was chasing an assault suspect across the UCLA campus. The suspect was a varsity tennis player, fast and athletic. He was also graceful and slender and looked like Leslie Howard. He did *not* want prison time. He raced into a building, Marlowe seconds behind him. The hallway was full of students. The suspect deked and darted through the crowd, slipping between two massive jocks. Offended, one of the jocks said, "Hey. What the—"

The jocks saw Marlowe coming and closed ranks. Marlowe tried to cut around them but one jock grabbed him by the arm and slung him. Marlowe knocked over two students, tripped, hit the wall, ricocheted off, collided with another student, spun, staggered but stayed upright. The suspect got away. Marlowe had to pay for a damaged phone, a broken set of headphones and two tall mocha cappuccinos, and the jock who grabbed him filed suit. Marlowe remembered the incident with some pride. He'd kept his feet. *Thank you, Jahno.*

* * *

Some months back, Jahno had asked for help. His fifteen-year-old daughter, Amanda, was an honors student, captain of the swim team, volunteered at the children's hospital, scholarship bound. A sweeter, smarter girl you will never meet, said her father. Amanda had become completely infatuated with a kid who called himself Thor. He was seventeen, tall, good-looking and cocky. "He is a so-called bad boy," Jahno scoffed in his precise African accent. "I know some bad boys in Ghana who would cut off his hands and feed them to the jackals." Since Amanda had hooked up with Thor, her grades had dropped, she'd quit the swim team, and she came home smelling like alcohol and marijuana. Jahno believed the couple were having unprotected sex.

"I want to kill him but apparently, it is against the law."

Marlowe waited across the street from the school. The bell rang and a short while later, Amanda appeared. She came out to the curb, clutching her notebooks to her chest and looking down the street. Thor made her wait fifteen minutes before pulling up in a powder-blue Civic, gold rims, add-on chin spoiler, the car lowered nearly to the ground. The exhaust so loud it nearly drowned out the rap music. Marlowe wondered why Thor's brain wasn't sonically obliterated or maybe it was.

Amanda took a quick glance around. She saw two girls she knew, an envious air to their waves. Amanda brightened, smiling, waving like she was on a cruise liner saying goodbye to her kids. She got in, laughed and looked at Thor adoringly, happy to be with a hot guy, an older guy, a guy with a car. Thor seemed not to notice her presence. Another human anomaly, Marlowe noted. Some perfectly reasonable, intelligent girls were irresistibly drawn to tall Alpha males with symmetrical features and a commanding, even obnoxious personality. Marlowe was familiar because he'd been one. There were parallels in the animal world but that was about instinct. Lions and wildebeest didn't apply logic, make thoughtful observations or assess the pros and cons. Amanda could do all those things but she picked a guy you knew at a glance was a prick.

*   *   *

Marlowe followed the couple to a strip mall parking lot. A group of kids were hanging out, rap music pumping from their car speakers. There were a group of girls, a group of boys and a few mixed clusters. Everyone was laughing like they were privy to a series of private jokes. Marlowe remembered himself in high school, laughing to ease his nervousness, laughing to show he was in.

Thor joined a cluster of guys, smiles all around, fist pounds, shoulder bumps, the Alpha had arrived. The kids looked like seniors, Amanda was a freshman. She didn't seem to know anybody so she stuck with Thor. He dominated the conversation and got most of the laughs. He paid no attention to his supposed girlfriend and introduced her to no one. Amanda pretended to be interested, waiting for a nod or a smile or some acknowledgment of her existence. She gave up, leaned against a car, retreating to the safety of her phone. She settled for so little, Marlowe thought. The only moment of pleasure he saw was when she waved to her friends as she got into Thor's car. The ideal situation was a mutual breakup, Marlowe mused. A perfect job for Emmet.

The following afternoon, Emmet and Marlowe followed Thor's car in the police cruiser. There were no obvious destinations. Thor was probably taking Amanda to his place. Emmet took huge risks when he did things like this. Even having Marlowe in the car was a violation but predatory assholes enraged him. Emmet waited until they were on an isolated street. He flipped on the dash light, gave the siren a whoop and pulled Thor over. Marlowe watched his father get out of the car in that slow, calculated way cops have. He walked up to the driver's-side window.

"License and registration, please," said Emmet.

Thor was instantly combative. "What? What'd I do? You can't pull me over for nothing!" He's showing off for Amanda, Marlowe thought. He's in for it now.

"I *said* license and registration," Emmet growled.

"What are you talking about? I didn't *do* anything!" Emmet opened his sport coat, revealing his badge and gun.

"Do you really want to argue with me, kid?"

"Get the registration out of the glove box," Thor ordered Amanda. "Hurry up." She was terrified, breathless, eyes big as Oreos, fumbling and finally getting the document. Thor gave his license to Emmet.

"This is bullshit," Thor went on. "I was driving the speed limit and there's nothing wrong with my car." The kid better shut up, thought Marlowe. Emmet's patience was thin bordering on see-through. "Don't you have something else to do?" Thor said. "God, what an asshole!" Emmet stopped and dropped the license and registration on the ground. Uh-oh, thought Marlowe. *Here we go.*

"All right, cowboy, get out of the car!" Emmet bellowed. "I SAID GET OUT OF THE GODDAMN CAR!" Shaken, Thor got out. Emmet jerked him around, got him in an arm lock, pushed him down on the hood of the car and kicked his feet apart.

"Move and I'll cuff you," he snarled.

The Alpha Dog wasn't Alpha anymore. He was frightened, his face was red, his zits were brighter. "Hey, I'm sorry, okay? I didn't mean it!"

Marlowe was waiting, you had to time this right. He rapped on Amanda's window. "Out of the car, miss." She did as she was told.

"Anything in your pockets?" Marlowe asked.

"No," she whimpered.

"Empty your bag on the hood of the car. Do it *now.*" She obeyed, bobbling things, hands shaking. Marlowe had positioned her so she was directly across from Thor. She could see him and he could see her.

Emmet was frisking Thor, whacking him more than searching. "Anything in your pockets that could injure me? Any drugs?"

"No, there's nothing," Thor said in a strangled voice. "Really, Officer, I'm sorry for what I said, okay? Sir? You don't have to do this."

Emmet found a baggie of marijuana in Thor's pocket and tossed it on the hood. Seemingly outraged, he applied more pressure on the arm lock until Thor's cheek was smashed against the hood. He yodeled in pain.

"Oww shit, that hurts!"

"Didn't you just say you didn't have drugs on you?" Emmet said.

"It's just weed!"

"You're not twenty-one. That's a violation. Do you have a prescription? No? Another violation."

"Come on, Officer, gimme a break, please?" Thor wailed. He looked like a little kid who'd fallen off his bike. "Please, sir? It's not even mine!"

"Lying to a police officer is another charge, you moron."

Amanda had emptied her handbag on the hood. Marlowe went through every item, inspecting them as if each were a heroin stash.

"There's no drugs or anything!" she cried.

"Don't talk. You'll just get yourself in more trouble. You're only fifteen and drugs were found in the vehicle. I'm going to call your parents."

"Oh no. Please, please, *pleeease* don't call my dad!"

She glared at Thor, his cheek still smashed against the hood, drool dripping on the cold metal. "This is your fault!" she cried. "You screwed up my whole life!"

"Don't take me to jail, Officer," Thor pleaded. "I'll do anything you want."

"Tell that to the other convicts," Emmet said. "Stand still, I'm gonna cuff you."

"No, please, don't!" Thor wailed.

Time to shut this down, Marlowe thought. There was no third act to this play. He pretended to hear something on his imaginary collar mike. "This is twenty-three," he said. "We're on McDougal south of Fairfax…two eleven, copy that." He turned to Emmet. "Robbery in progress. Let's go." They unceremoniously left their suspects, got in the cruiser and drove away. Marlowe looked back. Amanda was yelling at Thor. He was dolefully picking his license off the ground. Seeing your hot boyfriend reduced to a craven little snot takes the romance right out of things, thought Marlowe. And if you're the hot boyfriend? Who wants to be reminded of your humiliation every time you see your girlfriend? Two days later, Jahno reported Amanda had broken up with Thor, blocking his email and phone and deleting his name from her contact list.

"What can I pay you, my friend?" Jahno said.

"Easier workouts."

CHAPTER EIGHT
COOL HAND LUKE

Emmet was uneasy but he wasn't sure about what. Well, that wasn't true. It was Cody. She was on his mind way too much. He didn't really understand why, or why he was even thinking about why. Maybe it was something obvious. The girl was in danger and he was worried for her safety. No, this was different, he thought. Emmet had protected a lot of witnesses, even innocent ones, but he'd never felt this...this...he didn't know the word for it or why he was feeling anything at all. Marlowe called.

"Sorry to say this, Dad, but I think Cody should stay with you," Marlowe said.

"Might as well," Emmet said. "Moving her will be like taking a wolverine to the dentist." He was glad Cody was staying but he had no idea why.

"Well, if that's the case, maybe be a little nicer to her," Marlowe said. "She might be easier to talk to if you turned down the hostility."

"We don't like each other. What'd you expect?" Emmet said. He heard Cody coming down the hall. He turned the speakerphone on and talked a little louder.

"The kid doesn't read the newspaper, doesn't play chess, she can't cook and she's never heard of Kurosawa, David Lean, Preston Sturges or anybody else. Can you believe it?"

"Dad, she's from a different generation."

"And get this," Emmet went on. "I asked her who Jimmy Stewart was and she said he was the president who had a peanut farm."

"Why are you complaining?" Cody said as she came in. "I have to deal with you all day. By the way, don't you have any clothes without crumbs, gravy stains and crud on them?"

"Ohhkay," Marlowe said brightly. "I'll be going now."

"Fine, who needs you," Emmet said.

"Haven't you got another father?" Cody said.

The call ended. Emmet and Cody were alone in the living room. There was yet another long silence, filled with sighs and awkwardness, their eyes roaming around like they were looking for butterflies, none of which were landing on the other.

"Well, looks like we're in for another evening of mirth and merriment," Emmet sighed.

"I'd ask you what mirth means but I'm afraid it's something old," Cody said. She started to leave but stopped. "Can we go out? I've been stuck here in the retirement home for a month."

"It's been eight days."

"Eight days?" Cody was incredulous. "You've done something with how time passes, haven't you, gramps? You've gummed it up with that oatmeal on your shirt."

"Do you want to watch *Arsenic and Old Lace*?"

Emmet was in his office, adding material to the murder book. Cody came in.

"What now?" Emmet said accusingly.

"I'm bored, okay?" Cody said. "I'm a teenager, we like to do stuff. You know, see people, party, enjoy ourselves." Emmet went back to the murder book. Cody meandered around, looking at things, making him nervous. She looked at a trophy fish mounted on the wall.

"Why would anybody want to keep a stuffed barracuda?" she said.

"It's not a barracuda, it's a largemouth bass, and it's not the fish, it's the memory."

"The memory of catching a fish?" Cody huffed. "What about Italy or sex or someone you love."

"You can leave now."

Cody continued her tour unheeded, stopping to scowl, squint, sniff or shake her head. She paused at the bookshelves. All alone on a middle shelf stood a small pink figurine. It was a baby girl in diapers. She was midstride, looking over her shoulder with a winsome, mischievous smile. On the base of the figurine, there was a name. Cody picked it up.

"Susan," she read. "What's all this about?"

Emmet wanted to snatch it from her but he'd give himself away. Without looking up he said, "Put it down." She did so, then came around behind him and looked over his shoulder. Emmet immediately closed the murder book. "Don't you need to tweak somebody?" he said.

"You mean tweet? Not at the moment." Cody said. She nodded at the photos of Addie.

"That's your wife, huh?"

"Yeah, that's my wife. Could you go away now, girlie?"

"She's beautiful, Emmet." That stopped his heart a moment. Cody turned to go, then turned back again. She put her hands together and looked at him beseechingly. She looked like Oliver Twist with a hole in his bowl.

"Please, sir, can we go out?" she begged. "Please? I don't care where we go! You can show me how to drive your stagecoach. We can go to the cemetery and dig up your friends! I don't care! Let's go out!"

"Fine, fine, whatever you say. Just stop talking," Emmet groused. He went into the bedroom and changed into his "going out" clothes. A green-and-yellow hula dancer shirt, a brown corduroy sport coat Addie had patched a hundred times, and old desert boots, similar to the ones Werner Herzog wore. Herzog had promised to eat the boots if Errol Morris ever completed his film *Gates of Heaven*. The meal was made into a short film. It was unwatchable. To top off Emmet's ensemble, he sported a dark gray fedora, the same kind Bogart wore in *Casablanca*. Ingrid Bergman wore one too.

When Emmet met Cody in the living room, she looked at him, blinked twice and said,

"Jesus."

"Turn around," Emmet said.

"What for?"

"Just turn around." Cody turned around. Emmet hastily grabbed his gun and badge from under the cushion of an antique armchair. It had a needlepoint seat cover with a bluebird on it. Addie made it. No one ever sat there. Emmet's badge was a fake, slightly smaller than the real thing, but otherwise indistinguishable. He'd lost his real badge. He was drunk and left it somewhere. That earned him a shitstorm from the captain, a shitload of paperwork and a shitty departmental fine. Emmet kept his new badge inside a frozen turkey. The bird had been in the freezer since Thanksgiving, seven years ago.

They decided on a movie, Cody's choice. *Spider-Man.* Emmet parked in the lot behind Musso & Frank. He was hungry and wanted to come back for dinner. They went west on Hollywood Boulevard and walked the Walk of Fame.

"Who are these people?" she asked as she trampled over Art Carney, Ingrid Bergman, Hal Roach and Edgar Bergen.

"You don't know any of them?" Emmet said.

"No, I don't."

"Not a one?"

"I missed the class on Famous People Who Are Dead, okay?"

"How about this guy?" Emmet said, looking down at a tile. "Thomas Edison. Ever heard of him?"

Grauman's Chinese Theatre was a Hollywood institution and some moron had renamed it the TCL Chinese Theatre. Contemptible, Emmet thought. What's a TCL? A news channel? An ointment for hemorrhoids? "They broke ground in January 1926," Emmet said as they approached the famous pagoda. "Mary Pickford and Douglas Fairbanks were part owners." Cody looked at him. "They were like the Angelina Jolly and the Bryan Pitt of their day," Emmet added.

"It's not Jolly, it's Jolie, and it's Brad Pitt."

"Yeah, there's a big difference." He looked at the pagoda and nodded nostalgically. "The very first movie was shown here in 1927. Cecil B. DeMille's *The King of Kings*."

"They had movies in 1927?"

They walked through the forecourt looking at the handprints. Bogart's inscription said, *Sid may you never die till I kill you.*

"Who's Sid?" Cody asked.

"Sid Grauman," Emmet said.

"Who's Sid?"

Kirk Douglas made a print with his chin. Emmet explained that a workman thought it was a mistake and troweled over it. John Barrymore, "the Great Profile," stuck his face in the wet cement. Mel Brooks wore a prosthetic sixth finger.

Cody stopped and frowned. "Say, gramps, was Edgar Bergen a baby?"

"No. Bergen was a ventriloquist, girlie. Those are his dummy's footprints, Charlie McCarthy."

"What's the circle thing?" Cody asked.

"His monocle," Emmet said. She gave him a long, blank look and moved on.

Cody was getting into it. Robert Pattinson, Leonardo DiCaprio and Charlize Theron. The names meant nothing to Emmet. Some of the prints pissed him off. Why were Trigger's hoofprints here? Why Herbie the Goddamn Love Bug? This wasn't a pasture or a goddamn parking lot. This was a memorial to glamour, excitement and real filmmaking. It was a tribute to the actors and directors who made Hollywood Hollywood.

Fortunately, TCL had left the main theater alone. It was still grand and glorious. Emmet loved the place. From the stunning art deco ceiling to the lush crimson stage curtains, to the imposing Egyptian-like colonnade. The palm trees between the massive pillars were painted by Xavier Cugat. He mentioned that to Cody and she said,

"That's great. I like Mexican food."

They watched the movie. Emmet was stupefied. "Spidey" was a scrawny little asshole in red spandex who crawled up walls, hung from the ceiling and bounced around from one building to another. You wanted to grab him by his neck and feed him to a tarantula. Emmet felt himself getting angrier and angrier. What sent him over the top was Jake Gyllenhaal. Emmet had seen him in *End of Watch*. The guy was a decent actor but here he was, in this colossal pile of cinematic guano, wearing a black plastic body suit, calling himself Mysterio and making an inspirational speech about somebody named Edith. Emmet couldn't take it. He stood up and bellowed, "WHERE'S MY HAT?" and tromped out of the theater.

They were on the sidewalk, Emmet muttering to himself about Gyllenhaal, Cody exasperated.

"Can we eat? I'm hangry," she said. Emmet closed his eyes.

"Hangry?"

"That's when you're so hungry you're pissed off. Look it up, it's in the dictionary."

"No, I don't think so. If I do I might kill myself."

Emmet's favorite restaurant was Musso & Frank. The legendary eatery served its first meal in 1919 and had remained essentially the same since then. Red leather booths, white tablecloths, saloon chandeliers and dark wood paneling. Emmet and Cody came in the back way and took a booth. Cody looked around skeptically and said, "It looks like a restaurant in an Al Capone movie."

"You're not far from the truth," Emmet said. "Bugsy Siegel drank here. Mickey Cohen too. Cohen got beat up in prison and the waiters put hot towels on his knees. They used to have a back room for celebrities. Dashiell Hammett, F. Scott Fitzgerald, William Faulkner."

Cody rolled her eyes. "Did anybody famous come in here that wasn't born during the Bronze Age?"

"Hmm, let me see. There's Keith Richards and George Clooney."

"Now you're talking," Cody said.

"Michael Connelly loves the place," Emmet went on. "Says the martinis are the best."

"Who's Michael Connelly?"

Emmet ordered a double vodka on the rocks and a Coke for Cody. They looked at the menus. She was frowning, dismayed.

"Any place that serves smoked beef tongue and lamb kidneys is not for me," she said.

"You ever eat a steak? Like a real steak?" Emmet said.

"Kendra's a vegetarian but I've had steak and eggs at Denny's."

"I'll order for you."

Emmet ordered Cody a bone-in rib eye, medium rare with peppercorn sauce, mashed potatoes and creamed spinach. He ordered the same for himself. The overladen plates of food arrived. Cody stared at the steak like it was a smoked tongue still in the cow's mouth.

"Eat up, Cody," Emmet said.

Tentatively, Cody cut a piece off the meat and chewed it slowly. It was like she was afraid she might bite into a pebble or a lamb kidney. "Oh my God," she said. She ate a second piece and looked at Emmet in amazement. "Holy shit, this is good!" They ate with gusto. Emmet ordered another double vodka. "This creamed spinach is killer," Cody said.

"You can make anything taste good if you add something that's bad for your heart," she said. She was enjoying herself and for some reason, Emmet felt vindicated. She'd stopped calling him gramps and he'd stopped calling her girlie. He had another double before they finished their meal. Cody didn't seem to notice. These days, drinking yourself blind was like eating a Snickers bar. It was after closing when they left.

Cody had to help Emmet out to the parking lot. It was deserted, only the cars of the kitchen help. He was very drunk. "How about we take an Uber?" Cody said. "You're wasted, dude." She heard something. A man came rushing out of the dark, ski mask, gun held at his side. "Oh shit!" she shouted. Emmet pushed her down between two cars. He fumbled around, trying to find his gun. She could see it in the side holster. "Emmet, it's right there!" The man kept coming. If she ran she'd be in the open. Emmet finally got the gun out.

"Police officer," he shouted drunkenly. "Drop your weapon!" The man turned and ran. Emmet went staggering after him.

"Emmet, don't!" Cody cried.

The man raced across the lot, tripped on a parking block and fell hard. "Police officer," Emmet said. He could hardly stay standing. "Drop your..." Emmet retched, dropping his weapon. The man scrambled to his feet. Emmet lunged at him, vomit spilling out of him. He got his arms around the man, slipping down to his knees. The man raised the butt of his gun, about to bring it down—Cody hit the man in the temple, leaving her feet, her body weight behind the blow. Eli called it the Superman punch. The man cried out, fell against a dumpster and stumbled away.

Emmet was on the ground, groaning, covered in his own puke. Cody helped him to his feet, got him in the car and drove home. Emmet was semiconscious, babbling about his watch commander and where's my son and Addie should be here. For a moment, he opened his eyes. "You know what? I lost my goddamn hat." And he closed them again.

It took a while to get him in the house. She put him in bed and took off his shoes. He looked at her, his eyes glassy, half shut and unseeing. A few seconds later he was snoring. Cody was badly shaken. Her instincts had told her to run but for some unheard-of reason, she'd risked getting shot and hit the guy. She hadn't done something that selfless since—well, ever. She couldn't believe it. Twice now, someone had tried to kill her. *Kill her.* The only good thing that came out of it was the attacker's gun. She'd picked it up after he ran away.

She went into the kitchen, got the vodka out of the freezer. She poured herself a drink and tossed it back. She dropped the glass and threw up in the sink, her half of a hundred-and-eighty-dollar meal splattering into the garbage disposal. The heaving stopped. She drank a bottle of water and took three Advil. She got in the shower with her clothes on. She sat in a corner and hugged her knees, the closeness of the walls an illusory defense. The fear was crushing. Every single one of her plans had exploded to a fiery nothing. Tato terrified her. He'd have Dima flail her skin to shreds, then hand her over to the others. She was so pathetic she couldn't stand herself. She screamed until she'd burned up her throat. Silence. She regained her breath. She felt her hard self returning.

All her life she'd been prone to sudden acts of violence. She was easily frustrated. Her friends said she was a quick burn. She couldn't help it. Sometimes people were so fucking stupid it made you crazy. Literally. Crazy. Terry asked her where her temper came from. Nothing in her privileged childhood would explain it. Shit like this happened all the time, Cody thought. Mom and Dad wondering how their kid ended up eating memory foam or slashing themselves to shit with a boning knife. Good parenting and lots of love sometimes equaled despair.

Cody was ten. She and a bunch of other kids were swimming in a neighbor's pool. The adults were sitting under umbrellas gabbing and having drinks. Cody was dog-paddling and reached the end of the pool. A kid named Gary Marx snuck up behind her and bounced a beach ball off her head. The other boys thought this was hilarious. Gary did this twice more, Cody telling him repeatedly to please stop. He did it again. Cody felt the burn. She got out of the pool, went in the house and found a snow globe. It was heavy. She got back in the water and stayed in the shallow end with her back turned. As soon as she felt the ball bump off her head, she turned and threw the globe as hard as she could. Gary was laughing, his mouth open. The globe hit him in the face. He screamed, blood spurting. Terry went nuts, Noah went nuts, everybody else was shocked. Gary's parents were furious. Terry paid the medical bill, yelled at Cody for days and took away her privileges. She tried to look sorry. But she wasn't.

Terry sent her to a child psychologist, a motherly woman who liked red pantsuits, had big breasts and an enormous engagement ring. Even at ten years old, Cody knew she had to end this shit or it would go on for months. For the first two sessions, she was withdrawn and hardly spoke. On the third session, she broke down sobbing. She said she desperately missed her mom, who she couldn't actually remember, and that the psychologist was the only one she could talk to. Four more sessions of revelation and insight and she was a happy, well-adjusted girl.

Cody recalled another incident. She was at a club called Bar Sinister, sitting in a booth, waiting for Eli to arrive. A Black girl with a big Afro and her two big friends wanted her to leave. Afro Girl leaned over, glaring with her eyes wide open, yelling in Cody's face and ticktocking her head. Cody was scared and started to get up, suddenly realizing she wanted that booth. She wanted to sit there with Eli and have a drink and grope each other and forget the rest of her complicated, fucked-up life. At that moment, the booth was the most important thing in the world. Like if she gave it up, she'd give up everything. Afro Girl wouldn't stop yelling. Cody felt the burn. She put a clawed hand over the girl's face, squeezed and shoved her back. Then she slid out of the booth and threw a punch, getting her hips into it, just the way Eli had taught her. Man, the look on the girl's face was worth the beating she took from the others. There was blood all over the dance floor. The bouncers threw everybody out. She didn't keep the booth but the girls didn't get it either. She felt that way now. Fear and circumstance had destroyed her plans but she wasn't going to quit. Just like she told Afro Girl, *No, no, no, bitch. I'm not giving up shit.*

The morning after Musso's, Emmet was hungover, sitting at the breakfast table, holding a beer in both hands and staring at the floor. He was bruised all over from the tussle with the mystery gunman. Cody was sitting across from him, Marlowe leaning against the doorframe.

"How did the guy know you were at Musso's, Dad?" Marlowe said.

"I don't know," Emmet mumbled. "Maybe I was followed. I wasn't looking for a tail."

"Can you describe him?" Marlowe said.

"Later, okay?" Emmet breathed. He looked like he was going to retch.

"What about you, Cody?" Marlowe said. "Any ideas? Can you remember anything about the guy?"

"Wake up and smell the bullshit, will you?" she said. "It was Pav. How much proof do you need? There isn't anybody else!" She looked at Marlowe and huffed. "You know why you don't have anything to say? Because you don't have anything to say!" The kid's got a point, thought Marlowe. He turned to Emmet.

"Dad? Do you think the guy at Musso's could have been Pav? Do you remember his height? Weight? Anything?"

"Why are you asking him?" Cody said. "The great homicide detective was busy barfing his guts out. He can't tell you shit." Emmet said nothing. He got up and left the room.

Marlowe glared at Cody. "If you ever say anything like that to Emmet again I'll drive you over to Kendra's and dump you on the front lawn."

Marlowe came out of the house, Emmet walking in circles. "I screwed up, okay? I nearly got the kid killed," he shouted. "I should turn in my badge right now! Go ahead, say it! You're ashamed of me! Go on, I don't give a shit! What do you want me to do, shoot myself?"

"I'm worried about you, that's all," Marlowe said evenly. There was a lot more to say that would never be said.

Emmet found the hose, turned it on and held it over his head. "Ohh man, ohh man," he blubbered as the water cascaded over him. He turned off the water and wiped off his face with his hands. Then he slogged into the garage and brought back a sickle. He started slashing at the palm fronds, tree trunks and branches, stopping several times because he'd lost his equilibrium. When he was done, he looked like Paul Newman after George Kennedy beat him to shit in *Cool Hand Luke*.

"If Addie were here she'd worry about you too," Marlowe said. "She said you were the best, most decent, most courageous man she'd ever known. She'd have something to say if she saw you now." Emmet stepped close to his son, the curved blade clenched in his fist.

"Don't you throw that in my face! I don't need you telling me about my dead wife!"

"And my dead mother," Marlowe said. His anger was contained but just as molten, just as long-standing.

"You don't know anything. You don't know one goddamn thing!" Emmet shouted.

"I know everything, Dad."

Emmet's rage exploded out of him. He hit Marlowe with a hard, two-handed shove, square in the chest. Marlowe stumbled back but stayed standing. He looked at Emmet, their eyes like meteors crashing in midair.

"Get outta here!" Emmet roared. "Get off my goddamn property!" Marlowe turned and walked out of the gate.

Emmet went back inside and dried himself off with dish towels. He imagined Addie sitting at the breakfast table with her whole wheat toast, black coffee and a poached egg nestled in a little cup. She'd have a book in a bookstand, reading about art in ancient Mexico or a day in the life of a sea otter or the biography of a woman who'd done something heroic. Addie didn't preach or punish and she didn't add her two cents on top of your ten-dollar guilt. Her rehab program was kindness. That was all. Kindness. If she were here, she'd say something like, You're dehydrated, Emmet. Can I get you a glass of orange juice? Maybe rest awhile longer, darling. I'll come in and check on you. Emmet poured himself a vodka. He took a huge gulp and immediately spat it out. Self-loathing had poisoned the poison. For the first time since Addie died, he started to cry.

Marlowe went home, frustrated and furious. The encounter would stay in the ether with the rest of their grievances. It would never be spoken of, a de facto rule. What would be the point? There were those adages about clearing the air and putting your cards on the table but old anger was as heated as new. You're more likely to foul the air and set the table on fire. He'd seen people try to exculpate their pasts, the confrontation ending in bitterness, acrimony and hyperbolic shaming. Using a counselor or a psychologist to temper the process was distasteful, intrusive, like inviting a stranger to watch you masturbate.

Marlowe was in the shower when his mind started to work again. Terry had been stealing from the Russians and Hzoy killed him. But where was the money? Did the Russians get it back? If they didn't, they'd send Tato after it. The obvious suspects were Andy, DeSallis and Cody. Despite the girl's denials, she had to know about it. More likely, she was in on it. If Tato caught up to her she'd meet her father's fate. If she was to be truly safe, Marlowe had to find out more. And the person he'd ask was the hustler and finance man, Andy.

CHAPTER NINE
DONKEYVILLE, OKLAHOMA

Marlowe and Ren were on their way to Kendra's. Marlowe wanted to see Andy right away but Ren called him three times. She wanted action. They were early so they stopped for lunch at the Reel Inn. A small, funky seafood restaurant on PCH that served fresh fish and good French fries.

"In the fifties this place was either called Marino's or the Zoo, depending on who you talk to," Marlowe said. "Back then it was a Mexican restaurant run by a gay couple. Then this thug shows up, a retired wrestler named Fat Jack McGurk. He bullied the gay couple out and renamed it El Gordo, appropriate since Fat Jack was six-three, three hundred pounds. Sometime later, he was killed right up the road at Big Rock but no one can remember how. The place went through a couple more owners and a fire but here it stands."

"How do you know this?" Ren said.

"One of the old bartenders. A friend of Emmet's."

There were picnic tables covered with red-and-white-checked tablecloths. The menu was on chalkboards. Marlowe ordered rockfish. Ren ordered the combo plate; fried fish, shrimp and calamari.

"Yes, I know, I have a thing about fried foods," she said. "I'd live on fish and chips if I weren't afraid of getting scurvy."

"I hate to bring this up again but there's no point in your going," Marlowe said. "Kendra won't talk to you."

"I can plead my own case," Ren argued. "I'm looking for my son. Isn't that enough to get her attention?"

"That's exactly the wrong thing to do. If you ask for something without leverage she'll immediately turn you down."

"Even if it's for a good cause?"

"*Especially* if it's for a good cause."

They finished their meal and drove to Kendra's. Party preparations were in progress. Delivery trucks jammed in the driveway. MALIBU CATERING, CELEBRITY PARTY PLANNING, SU CASA FURNITURE RENTAL. People with trays of glasses, barstools and decorations were going in and out, a blond woman in nice clothes was studying a clipboard.

"What's the occasion?" Ren asked.

"The party's for industry people," Marlowe said. "Kendra wants them to know she's still alive and wonderful. Stay in the car."

"I could speak to her like one human being to another," Ren insisted.

"That would work if Kendra were human."

"Doesn't she love her children?"

"Not really. They're more like fashion accessories. This shouldn't take long."

Lucy let him in. "How is she?" Marlowe said.

"The same *puta* she was before. I want to poison her food but I don't think she would die."

"You know, I think you'd like my dad a lot."

Kendra was on the deck talking with two young men. She was laughing, animated, incandescent with pride. "Marlowe, this is my stepson, Noah, and his friend Chris."

"Nice to meet you, sir," Noah said. Noah was a young Adonis, blond, buff, brilliant smile. Chris was like a younger Mahershala Ali. A stately presence, graceful, intelligent eyes.

"Noah and Chris play baseball for the Lancaster Hawkeyes," Kendra said, beaming.

"That's great, congratulations," Marlowe said. "Noah, I'd like to talk to you about Cody sometime."

"Sure, happy to," Noah said. "You know we didn't get along, right?"

"I heard. Will you be around?"

"Yeah, I think so. We're going to an infield camp—when was it, Chris?"

"Ten days—no, nine," Chris said with precision. "Then we'll be skiing in Utah for a couple of weeks." He exchanged a smile with Noah. "After that, we'll make it up as we go along." Marlowe wondered what it would be like to be young, rich and beautiful.

"That's enough," Kendra said brusquely. "They have better things to do." Noah and Chris sheepishly said their goodbyes and left.

"They're very much in love," Kendra said, envy in her voice. "They share a house in Lancaster. A terrible place, really. What do they do out there besides skinning rabbits and digging for water?"

"Beats me," Marlowe said.

"Noah and Chris want to get married but they're not sure how it will play in the locker room," Kendra said. "It's a shame, really. Those kinds of prejudices are so destructive." Marlowe was surprised. That was the first humane thing he'd heard Kendra say. An instant later, she was irate. "I've received your invoice, Marlowe. It's laughable! There are no billable hours or a description of your activities, assuming there were any. It's a piece of paper with numbers on it! I wouldn't pay you a Somalian nickel but George said he'd cut me out of his will."

"Your concern for Cody is very touching," Marlowe said. "I had no idea you two were so close."

"I loathe you, Marlowe. If you were a flea I'd kill the dog."

"I have a favor to ask."

She snorted. "A favor from *me*? A washed-up movie actress who makes silly romantic comedies?"

"I never said that," Marlowe said.

"No, but you thought it and you're thinking it now."

"Yes, that's true, but what do you care? You hate me."

"Also true," Kendra sighed. "You were saying something about a favor?"

"Your party," Marlowe said. "I'd like to attend with two guests. It's for another case. A seven-year-old boy has been kidnapped."

"Then his mother should fire the babysitter," Kendra said. "And my party is for my friends and colleagues, not for some hooligan friends of yours."

"I've located Cody," Marlowe said.

"What? Why didn't you tell me?" Kendra exclaimed. She actually put her drink down. Bringing Cody home was more urgent than Marlowe had thought.

"I just found this out," he went on. "She's in Oregon, in a town called Pad Thai. A bunch of kids have a group house. I don't have the exact location. I'll have to figure it out when I get there."

"Well, go get her and bring her back!" Kendra said.

"I can't do it until next week."

"No, not next week! Drop your other cases, I'll pay you double!" He didn't tell her she was already paying triple. It startled him. It was more than urgency, she was desperate.

"It's not about the money," he said.

"It's *always* about the money," Kendra said. "I know, what if we trade? You get Cody and I'll give you Taylor Swift's phone number." She waited for a response. He gave her a wry look. The famous blue eyes flared.

"You're a tapeworm, Marlowe. You're eating my guts out. Fine! You win! But if you want your so-called *guests* to attend my party, I have conditions."

"Yes?"

"Don't bring some yokels here from Donkeyville, Oklahoma, playing their harmonicas and scratching their ass cracks, and they are not to talk about boll weevil season or how they eat roosters for breakfast or that they only wear shoes at funerals and hayrides. And remember. I don't like germs. If your hayseeds bring some mutant strain of hoof-and-mouth into my beautiful home, you won't get a job finding dead flies on a windowsill."

"Yes, I'll remember that," Marlowe said.

"One more thing and if you cross me, I'll toss them out."

"Let's hear it."

"They must look like they belong," Kendra said, "and that means you and your illiterate clodhoppers must wear decent clothes. Nothing from a mall, a discount store, a department store or any of those places where they sell horrible clothes. The Gap, Old Navy, J.Crew, Abercrombie & Fitch, Anne Klein—Nordstrom's is on the borderline. Don't think you can fool me and I don't bluff. If I spot an off brand, cheap shoes or polyester of any kind, two former agents from Mossad will take you and your friends down to the surf and bury you under a sand castle."

Marlowe stood and gave her an unwanted hug. "Thanks, Kendra. You're a peach."

"Stop groping me, Marlowe!" she cried. "Who knows what's on your hands. Hooker juice? Beggar sweat? I'll have to go buy some cootie soap! Are you still here? Get out!"

Lucy appeared. "Phone for you, Kendra. It's Steely Dan."

"Oh dear God."

Ren was elated at the news. "Kendra's inviting Victoria too?"

"Yeah, she is."

"How marvelous! You are a wonder, Marlowe."

"Occasionally but not often."

"Oh my God," she laughed. "Victoria might have actual information!" She put her head back, smiled and breathed deeply. "Who will be at this party? Anybody I would know?"

"Kendra's not a star anymore, she's a celebrity," Marlowe said. "The second tier will come but that's all." Ren sensed his hesitation.

"What is it?"

Be diplomatic, Marlowe. "The other partygoers are used to luxury and luxurious people," he began.

Intuitively, she snapped, "What's wrong with my clothes?"

"How did you know—uh, nothing is wrong with them."

"Except?"

"Except they're not expensive. They're fine for everyday knocking around but—"

"Yes, yes, you needn't go into it," she said impatiently. "It hardly matters. I can't afford new clothes."

"I'll buy them for you."

"That's ridiculous. I'd never let you buy me clothes. Why in the world would you say that? And by the way, we still haven't discussed your fees."

Marlowe shrugged. "If that's what you want to know." He told her his per diem.

"That's an absurd amount of money!" she exclaimed. "It's nearly pornographic. Why didn't you say something before? My entire extended family couldn't pay you back."

"Realistically, what are you going to do?" Marlowe said. "This isn't about what you can afford. It's not even about principle. It's about getting your son back." She folded her arms across her chest and fumed a moment.

"But really, Marlowe, I just met you and you're offering to buy me clothes? It's indecent. I'm reluctant to ask you this but—do you have some other agenda? I hope you're not expecting anything untoward." Chagrined, she added quickly, "Forgive me, I didn't mean that. I know you're an honorable gentleman and I'm a good judge of character."

"You mean like when you married Fallon?" Marlowe said.

"Everyone makes missteps and you've made a few yourself."

"Oh really? Like what?"

"You're friends with Basilio for one," Ren said. "I'm wondering whether your other friends are equally lazy and dissolute or perhaps he's your shining role model—and speaking of missteps, why is a reasonably affluent man like you living in a seedy old warehouse? Is that some sort of misguided version of hip? And your living room. The floor is beautiful. Unfortunately, it's in an unheated space too big for anything but storing pianos, and something else I've been meaning to ask you. How do you explain that bizarre picnic table? You adore picnics? You have an aversion to ants so you brought that silly thing indoors? Or perhaps it's de rigueur for the iconoclastic detective who seeks justice for the needy, the downtrodden and the fabulously wealthy. I'm surprised you're not wearing a raincoat with the collar turned up or you don't have an old dog named Bukowski or Diogenes."

"Never mind. I'm sorry I said anything."

He took her to Lyceum, a shop that sold top-tier designer labels. Eyeless, bald-headed mannequins watched over racks of overpriced, mostly black clothes, with an occasional white item for color. A huge monitor dominated one wall, a fashion show on the screen, women who looked like humorless antelopes prancing up and down the runway.

A young woman approached them. She was sleek, tiger-eyed, her nails painted aquamarine.

"Hello. My name is Aisha. Is there something I can help you with?"

"Jeans," Marlowe said. He looked at Ren. "What are you, an eight?"

"A six," she said, a little miffed. Marlowe and Aisha went through stacks of jeans. She held a pair up. "How about these? Alexander McQueen. They're a nice cut for you."

Ren looked at the price tag. "Seven hundred and fifty dollars? I'd rather make three car payments."

"Try them on," Marlowe said. Marlowe was as flush as he'd ever been. His last few clients were wealthy, his excessive per diem no more bothersome than buying a new nine iron, and they paid huge bonuses. Buying clothes for Ren was somewhat embarrassing, showing off his largesse in such an obvious way. There was something creepy about paying for things. He consoled himself, deciding there's a little creep in all of us.

"Are these pants supposed to be this tight?" Ren said as she came out of the dressing room. "It was like pulling a condom over my feet." She looked in the mirror, aghast.

"They look amazing," Aisha said, Marlowe nodding his approval.

"Thank you," Ren replied, "but I'm a little uncomfortable displaying my pudenda in bas-relief."

To complete the ensemble, Marlowe and Aisha chose Christian Louboutin suede ankle boots in fawn, a simple Brunello Cucinelli white blouse cut like a man's shirt and a thin gold chain. Ren stood in front of the mirror.

"I must admit, I look spectacular," she said. Aisha and Marlowe were quite pleased with themselves.

"You need hair and makeup," said Aisha. "I'll give Tristan a call. He's a friend."

Tristan gave Ren a beautiful cut and the makeup looked remarkably natural.

"I can't believe it," Ren said. "Every yawning pore, unsightly blemish and ominous dark spot is gone."

"You look great, Ren," Marlowe said, meaning it. "You were attractive before but now—"

"Thank you," she said, and she kissed him on the cheek.

Cody was pissed. Emmet made her watch the first seventeen hours of *Gone with the Wind.* Not only was it about the Civil War, it was about a fantasy Civil War where there weren't any slaves working in the scorching Georgia sun all day or getting the shit beat out of them by some white man in filthy coveralls with a cat-o'-nine-tails. Scarlett O'Hara was a spoiled, arrogant bitch, not unlike Kendra. Clark Gable should have punched her in the face and kicked her down those stairs. And the worst line in the history of movies? There's Scarlett standing on a hill with blood and bodies everywhere, soldiers crying for help and the whole fucking city on fire and what does she say? "As God is my witness, I'll never be hungry again!" *I'll never be hungry again?* Cody couldn't believe it. How about, I'm gonna help the guy bleeding to death right in front of me, or, I'm going to kill every Yankee in America? Or, I'll get a bucket and help put out the fire.

"All right already! It's a shitty line, okay?" Emmet said. He reminded Cody of that grouchy character on *Sesame Street.* The one that looks like a green mop with a mouth on it. When they were kids, her brother Noah made her watch the show. According to him, he was "in charge of the remote." That asshole actually sang along with a bunch of stupid puppets. He sang "Rubber Duckie" so much she wanted to stuff and spit-roast every duck in the Malibu bird sanctuary.

Kendra adored Noah. He was "my stepson." You were "Terry's daughter." Noah was Terry's favorite too. They were "pals" and did all that father-and-son bullshit together. Camping, baseball, tree houses, collecting baseball cards, whatever. You were Terry's—what would you call it? Robin to his Batman except Robin was usually in charge. Terry's backbone had dissolved right along with his career. He was lucky you were there. Sometimes she missed him but mostly she was angry. None of what happened had to happen.

Eli said she should be nicer to Emmet, make friends even. She told him he had no idea what it was like living with a man so old he cut his meat with a rock. Eli said they might need him.

"Need him?" Cody said. "How? For what?"

"I mean, use him," Eli said. "You never know what's going to happen. If he likes you, it will be easier for us. Don't be so emotional, Cody. You get caught up in it and you stop thinking." She hated it when he scolded her but he was usually right.

"When can we see each other?" she asked.

"I have to go," he said, and abruptly the call ended. Did he really have to go? Cody fumed. Why? Did his other girlfriend call him? Did Eli have something more important to do, like play *Grand Theft Auto*? She decided she'd cut him some slack. She had problems but not nearly as serious as his. His were dangerous. His were life-threatening, and without him, her dreams were done.

Marlowe didn't believe in most maxims but he liked Sun Tzu's: *Know thy enemy and know yourself; in a hundred battles, you will never be defeated.* Most people didn't know the rest of the quote. *If you know yourself but not the enemy, for every victory gained you will also suffer a defeat. If you know neither the enemy nor yourself, you will succumb in every battle.* It was the know thyself part that was hard, especially when you were divining someone's character. Like Cody. You could hardly look at her and not be pissed off. "You can't control the character of a client," his mother used to say. "You can only control how you react to them." She was right, of course. Anger and impatience almost never helped. Watchfulness, observation and careful notes almost always did. Nevertheless, Marlowe wanted to tie the kid up with baling wire and put her on a bus to Jupiter.

Marlowe knew very little about Tato except what Garik had told him. It was time to get the measure of the man. Tato was living in a small house near Sunset and Vermont. Unremarkable except for the shiny black Escalade parked in the driveway. Marlowe started his stakeout around noon, gangsters not known as early risers. Eventually, there was activity. Three members of Hzoy arrived. Common thugs. One of them had something coiled around his shoulder. What is that? A hose? A lariat? A little later, a young man arrived in a sports car. He looked nervous and reluctant, drawing a deep sigh before he went into the house. A few minutes. Tato and the others came out, piled into the Escalade and drove away. Tato was uglier in person.

Marlowe followed them to a café on the outskirts of Little Armenia. It was dark and small and the awning was sagging. The Escalade parked in front, idled there a few moments. Suddenly, the whole crew got out and strode quickly inside, the young man reluctantly bringing up the rear. Five seconds later three customers hurried out, one of them still holding a fork. This is bad, thought Marlowe. Loan sharking, Tato coming to collect his vig. Either that or to administer a beating. Marlowe put on a baseball cap and dark glasses, got out of the car and walked to the entrance. The dining room was empty. No server. No one at the cash register. He heard a loud conversation in the back, one of the voices high and pleading.

They were in the kitchen. Tato was yelling at an elderly Greek woman named Rhea. She was tiny and gray. She wore a dirty apron, a man's gym socks and clogs.

"I don't have it," she said in a tremulous voice. "I'm very sorry but business is bad." Tato was glaring at her, seemingly unaware that Rhea was elderly, tiny and gray. Eli watched passively. *God, what a bore.* The crew was as indifferent as he was, waiting for this to be over.

"You told me this last week," Tato said disgustedly. He mocked her voice, *"Don't worry, Tato, I'll have it ready for you. I promise!"*

"I thought I could do it but no one came in," the woman said. Her veined hands like birds at a window, trying to escape.

"Lock her in the fridge, Eli," Tato said. There was a walk-in cooler with a heavy door and a rusty door handle.

Eli scoffed. "Are you kidding, Tato? That old bitch could freeze to death."

"It's not that cold," Dima said, yawning. "It's for vegetables." The woman's mouth was open, like she wanted to cry but couldn't find the sound. Her cheeks were concave, layers of dark skin like a wattle beneath her chin. Eli didn't care about her, but this was impractical. "Tato, come on," he said. "You're going to take a murder charge because some old woman didn't pay you the vig?" To the woman, Eli said, "How much do you owe?"

"Three hundred dollars," she croaked.

Eli was incredulous. "Don't do this, Tato. You can't kill somebody for a lousy three hundred." Tato hated being challenged. His big ears turning red, his forehead pinching the black marble eyes together. God, he was ugly, Eli thought. Tato had always been jealous of his looks.

"If you don't know already, little brother," Tato said, "you don't tell me my business." Eli was tired of being belittled, tired of being oppressed. Tired of suppressing his resentment.

"Somebody should tell you," he said flippantly. "This is crazy." Eli braced himself. He'd come to blows with his brother many times before. He'd always lost.

"You're talking back to me, little brother? *Me?*" Tato said, striding forward, bristling, his body coiled, ready to throw a punch. *Duck under it, Eli. Make him miss.* Tato feigned an overhand right, Eli ducked—and got a knee to the chin. His jaws slammed together. He bit his tongue and howled, waves of pain filling his head. He staggered and fell to the floor. He sat there, bleeding and stunned,

Tato taunting him, the crew laughing boisterously. It was worse than the pain. He couldn't give up now. There was so much blood in his mouth he could hardly speak.

"Everybody knows you're a badass, Tato," he said, red froth dripping from his lips. "You don't have to prove anything, okay? Your reputation is safe with me."

Tato snarled, grabbed Eli by his shirt collar, yanked him to his feet and walked him over to the stove. Two burners were on. Tato pushed Eli's head down with one hand, the other pressing into his back, holding him fast, Eli's screams fluttering the scorching blue flames.

"Tato, no, please! Don't, I beg you! My face is burning!" Tato let go of him and shoved him against the wall. Eli gasped for breath; the tips of his hair were burnt and frizzled. He could smell them through the sweat and blood.

"Put the woman in the fridge," Tato said. Eli staggered over to her. She was cowering in the corner, too terrified to scream. He grabbed her by her matchstick arm, lifted her up, opened the cooler door and shoved her in.

"Lock it," Tato said. There was no lock. Eli found a long rolling pin and stuck it through the door handle. Eli kept his hand there to hold himself upright. Tato stood in front of him. "Look at me," he said. Eli raised his head, blood still dripping from his lips, his face hot like a sunburn.

"You dropped out of school," Tato said. *Oh shit, Eli. You're screwed.* "You tell me you are going. You tell me your grades are excellent. You take my money but you don't go. You pretend you are a playboy, you screw girls, you spend money on clubs and drinking. How can you lie to me, Eli? I take care of you and this is what you do? You sneak around? You make a fool of me?"

"I'm sorry, Tato. I just, uh, couldn't take it," Eli said. "I'll enroll in the new semester, I promise."

"No more school," Tato said. "You will work for your money."

"Work? Work how?" Eli said, alarmed.

"You will be part of the gang."

"What? I can't be—" Eli stopped. He didn't want to get hit again.

"And you will live with me," Tato added. The crew laughed, big joke.

"Tato, please—"

"Saturday," Tato said. "If you don't show up, Dima will find you. Let's go." The crew laughed, Dima shoving Eli through the exit, the others following behind.

Marlowe slipped into the kitchen. He heard the woman, opened the cooler door and let her out. She was hysterical. Her whole body was shaking. He helped her into the dining room and sat her down. He went back into the kitchen and brought her a glass of water.

"Hear those sirens?" Marlowe said. "The police are coming and so are the paramedics. They'll take good care of you." He waited until they were right outside. Then he patted the woman on the hand and slipped out the back door. He returned to his car and sat there a moment. There's Tato in a nutshell, he thought. He locks little ol' ladies in refrigerators and burns his brother's face. Cody was in more trouble than she knew.

Eli drove home. He was as enraged as he was frightened. There was no possible way he could move in with Tato, into an atmosphere of violence and threat, where any suggestion of fear or vulnerability would earn you a beating. Eli was tough and ruthless, but *live* like a gangster? Grub around in the sewer with Tato's moronic crew? Those assholes had no ambition to be anything else. If they had all the money in the world, they'd live in the same place, play the same video games, hang in the same stupid places and wear the same shitty clothes. Cody was right. He needed a bigger life.

When Eli enrolled in law school, Tato was proud of his sibling, actually comparing him to the Tom Hagen character in *The Godfather*. But as Eli grew more independent and less tolerant of Tato's lifestyle, he came to represent the straight world that Tato ostensibly held in contempt. That was bullshit, like so much of his brother's bravado.

If Tato could have gone legit, he would have, thought Eli. No one is proud of being a criminal. No matter how much money you make, you're still a winner in a game of losers, and what passes for respect is really intimidation. Yes, there were reasons why Tato was the way he was. A beggar at age six, homeless and starving, he worked the streets of Nor Hachn, a rural town in Kotayk, one of the poorest regions in a poor country, where corruption was a career path and violent crime was as common as doing the laundry. That kind of childhood leaves a mark.

Ironically, the more Eli slogged through law school, the more the outlaw life appealed to him. The straight and narrow, he discovered, went up a very steep hill. He was sitting in Property Law, listening to the professor drone on about the roles of the various parties in a multiple ownership conveyance, when he realized this shit was boring. No chance he could study ten hours a day for another three years. It was ridiculous, and seriously, why flop at something you hated?

Like everybody else Eli knew, he needed something cool to do, but starting your own record label or mining for Bitcoin seemed a little strenuous. The trick, Eli decided, was looking legit. To have something going that gave you the patina of respectability while your money came from something else happening under the table. The best scenario was to have a shitload of money in the first place. Then you could tell people whatever you wanted. You financed the *Fast & Furious* movies. You designed the Xbox. You bought Berkshire Hathaway at six thousand a share and people said you were crazy. *What's the price today? Let me check. At the closing bell, you could buy a share of Berkshire for a mere $438,638.38.* It was that part about having money in the first place that was always the sticking point. But one way or another, Eli knew, he couldn't stay in school.

Tato was paying for Eli's ersatz education. To keep him on the hook, Eli did a number of things. He'd buy law school term papers online, put his name on them and email the papers to Tato. He treated official-looking documents with the university's logo and fake exam results. He'd explain to his brother how the bell curve worked and say a little ruefully, "I'm only in the ninetieth percentile, Tato. But I'm working hard. I'll make you proud yet."

Whenever Eli was around his brother, he wore school T-shirts, hats and hoodies. He had school stickers on his bumper. He made a fake parking pass and hung it on his mirror. If he needed some extra cash there were a variety of tactics. He'd say his Mac Pro crashed and he needed another one. "Sorry, Tato, but it's—I'm afraid to say it. Four grand." "Sorry, Tato, but the textbooks this year are three thousand dollars." He could have kept the scam going indefinitely but somehow, Tato discovered he'd left school. Somebody probably saw him at Das Bunker three nights in a row or drunk out of his mind at two in the morning.

As shitty as that problem was, it was spare change compared to the other one. The Russian money. What a colossal mistake, thought Eli. It was Cody's fault. She was too devious and impulsive, too willing to take enormous risks. One thing he knew for certain. If by some miracle they got their hands on that money, Cody would end up in a ditch and he'd be on a plane to Rio.

Eli met her at the club. It was the weekend, the place so crowded you could hardly move. The tables and booths were full, barely anywhere to stand, even on the dance floor. Eli was known here, especially with the ladies. He dressed well, not the usual muscle shirt with gold chains or black shirt with gold chains or shirt open down to your belly button with gold chains.

Eli wore a real Gucci suit he bought at a luxury consignment store. Have José tailor it for a song and he looked like a million bucks. At some point, he'd hang the jacket over the back of a chair with the label showing or look for something in the inside pocket and flash the one-piece silk lining. He knew he was hot. As handsome as Tato was ugly. Eli was tall, fashionably thin, a devilish smile he practiced in the mirror. He had a V-shaped face and high cheekbones, more

Eastern European than Armenian, with the darker skin and white teeth. The girls thought he looked amazing. He did too.

Eli told everybody he was M. Night Shyamalan's son. They'd immediately search the name. When they saw the director's long list of credits they were instantly overawed. LA was crazy that way. A connection to someone famous was an opportunity, a magic gateway to money and the exclusive club of celebrity. The guys were unimpressed. *Nothing like nepotism. Nice. Being rich and doing shit-all.* A no-neck jock said to him, "If you're that guy's son, what are you doing in a place like this? Why aren't you in Beverly Hills or Malibu?"

"I'm scouting locations," he said, unfazed. The jock huffed, his girlfriend offered up a glittering smile.

One night, Eli was at his place on the bar, leaning back, a drink in one hand, ankles crossed, looking off like he was thinking about something way more hip than you. His favorite pose. The bitches were eyeing him like they usually did. He was wondering which one he would bag when he saw Cody. She stood out because she was leaning against a pillar in *the exact same pose.* She was hot. Wearing all black, Emoish but not extreme. He nodded to himself. She's the one. She looked—what? Different? Unusual? Didn't matter. He was intrigued.

He would introduce himself, smile that smile, flatter her, make her laugh, tell her they had a connection and didn't she feel it too? And somewhere during the conversation he'd casually mention he was Shyamalan's son. He loved to watch the girl's dazed eyes while he talked about premieres, Oscar parties, lunching at the Ivy, production deals, playing golf with Tiger Woods and renting Johnny Depp's villa in the South of France.

Then he'd tell the girl he was waiting for his little sister. She'd stood him up, just like a kid. Then he'd ask the girl if she'd like to get out of this dump. Have a drink at the legendary Roosevelt Hotel, where he happened to have a room he'd reserved on Orbitz at a reduced price. He had it choreographed, step by step, like the dancing in *La La Land.*

The girl in black was still there. Eli put on his busta move face and started his approach, walking directly toward her, looking directly at her, as if to say, *Here I come, sweetheart, and I'm the real thing.* To his surprise, she returned the look, hers saying, *Bring it, sonny boy, let's see what you've got.* Her gaze was steady, not intimidated, impressed, nervous or anything else. It was a little off-putting. Eli wound his way through the crowd, losing sight of her and then seeing her again. Now she was looking away, like she'd lost interest but he knew that bullshit. When she checked him out and heard his game, she'd thaw, bend and think heaven had done an all-day sucker. He was in the clear now. The girl looked bored, indifferent, like she was anticipating yet another loser asshole with another lame pickup line. Eli stayed steady. *You wanna play it that way, baby? Okay with me. We'll see who controls the next fifteen minutes. We'll see who controls the night.*

He neared her, smiled, leaned forward and said into her ear, "My name is—" She cut him off.

"I know you," she said. That pleased him. She knew his name.

He shrugged modestly. "Yeah, I get around."

"No. I mean I know who you are." She wasn't bored anymore. She looked serious, deliberate, like she was telling him the score.

"You mean my dad?" he replied. "Yeah, I'm more like his partner. We work on his projects together. On his last movie I was—"

"You're not getting it," she said impatiently. "I know *what* you are."

He was suddenly angry. No bitch in the world was going to define him, disrespect him. He got in her face. "Okay, whoever you are, *what am I?*" He expected a series of put-downs but instead she said,

"You're like me."

They didn't go to the Roosevelt Hotel. They went to Denny's, the one at Sunset and Van Ness where Eli went all the time. They both ordered the Lumberjack Slam, enough food there to feed the lumberjack's entire neighborhood. They gorged themselves and it eased the tension.

"What did you mean, you're like me?" Eli said.

"I mean, we're both sleazeballs," Cody said, stuffing a pancake in her mouth.

Eli snorted. "Oh really? Well, *you* might be but I'm—" She cut him off.

"What? You're going to tell me you're not?" she said, amused. "You tell those humongous lies so you can fuck girls. Are you telling me that's not sleazy? And by the way, Shyamalan has three daughters. You better change your cover story."

"They're not lies," he said with a shrug. "I mean, not everything."

Cody laughed. "Come on, Eli. Do you know how lame you sound? You can't bullshit a bullshitter, don't you know that?" He wasn't liking this, some Emo girl with an anime haircut trying to put him in his place.

"You know, I don't like people insulting me while I'm eating breakfast," Eli said. "It kind of pisses me off. Maybe get to the point."

Cody lowered her voice. "I've been watching you, Eli, and not because you're hot. Hot guys in LA are like Teslas. They're everywhere."

"Very observant," he said dryly. "Why were you watching me?" He dipped a sausage in maple syrup. The sweet and saltiness went good together.

"I was looking for a kindred spirit," she said.

He chuckled. "That's crazy. Why would you even think that?"

"Hard to describe but—" She drew a breath. "It was the way you moved, your attitude, all the posing, the fake smile, the practiced lines—let me finish. I'm not criticizing, okay?"

"No shit? Then please don't start."

"I saw that look in your eyes," Cody said. "I don't know what to call it. A yearning, maybe, a desperation, like you're trying to find something that isn't there."

"Trying to find something—what are you talking about, dude?" Eli said, exasperated. He pushed his plate away. "That makes no sense."

"You're being too literal," she said irritably. "Don't you get it?"

"Don't I get it?" Eli said. He was angry now. "Check yourself,

Cody. You condescend to me and I'm leaving." That gave her pause. She took a deep breath and blew it out again.

"I'm sorry. I get ahead of myself. I didn't mean anything by it."

Eli shrugged. "Whatever. Just get on with it, will you?" He'd have left already but he wanted a shot at getting her naked.

"What I was trying to say, was that I see in you what I see in myself," Cody said.

"How about you talk about yourself and leave me out of it," Eli said.

"Okay, I will. There I am at the club, pretending to be a player. Like, look, everybody! I do cool things with cool people! I'm only here because I'm bored!" She sipped her coffee and shook her head. "When I go home? The biggest thing I feel is relief. I can put down my five-hundred-pound bag of bullshit and relax." How does she know this stuff? wondered Eli. He felt exactly the same way.

"Then I get frustrated and pissed off," Cody went on. "I think to myself, You shouldn't be here. You're bigger than this, you need a bigger life. You have great things inside you but they're suffocating because they've got no place to go." She paused to slather a ridiculous amount of butter on her pancakes. "I know I'm special," she continued, "but it doesn't matter because I can't get the real me out there in the real world." She's not close to the bone, she's deep in the marrow, thought Eli. Maybe they really were kindred spirits.

"I'll do anything to get out of here—like *anything*," Cody said, "and I don't care who I hurt while I'm doing it."

Another bull's-eye. Eli would drop-kick his mother into a landfill to get away from Tato. He didn't know what to say so he didn't say anything.

"That's why I think we should partner up," Cody said. The idea startled him but he didn't let on. He was good at that. She was looking directly at him. The chick had cool eyes, he thought. Green and hard like an emerald, the message clear. *What about it? Are you up for this?*

Eli met her gaze but he felt unsteady. "Who said I wanted to be your partner?"

"Don't, then," she replied. "But you don't have money and neither do I."

Still he resisted. "I have money."

"I'm not talking about paying for drinks at Das Bunker," she said. "I'm talking about *owning* Das Bunker. I'm talking about enough cash to get out of here and do whatever you want."

That was Eli's wish too. He thought about it all the time. He tried to look blasé, as if he were deciding whether to give the kid a break. "You need an opportunity, the Big Score," he said. "That shit is hard to find." She smiled like he'd made a concession. He hated that.

"My stepmom is Kendra James and you're hooked up with Hzoy," Cody said. "It's common knowledge."

"What about it? We were talking about finding an opportunity," he said.

"We still are," she said, a glint in her eyes. "You look in your world, Eli, and I'll look in mine."

Cody caught an Uber home. Eli went back to his car, thinking about what she'd said. It was a long shot, pulling off something as epic as that. He was not optimistic, but for the sake of argument, let's say they got lucky and somehow made off with a bag full of money. Eli wasn't into sharing. Why settle for half when you could take the whole thing?

Marlowe drove to Andy's place. He wasn't hopeful. The guy would probably stonewall but that could be informative too. Andy's real name was Andov Kerkorian, the Armenian connection. Emmet had checked him out. Andy grew up with Terry and went to the same Culver City high school. They were best buds according to their senior yearbook. After graduation, Terry enrolled in film school. Andy went to LA Community College, majoring in business. He had a part-time job as stage manager in a small theater. He was eventually fired for stealing klieg lights and blackout curtains. He was caught trying to sell them to another theater. Andy dropped out of college and petty crime became his new career. Writing bad checks, B&E, insurance fraud, telemarketing scams. This was his fate until he reunited with Terry to make *Remains* and the flops that followed.

Andy lived with his sister, Racine, age forty-seven. She was an attendant at a retirement home. She was also on probation for a series of shoplifting charges. Her husband, Branko Murik, was fifty-five, an unemployed welder, currently on disability. During the Bosnian War thirty years ago, Branko served in a paramilitary unit known as Arkan's Tigers, responsible for killing, torturing and raping thousands of Muslims. No one in the unit, including their leader, Arkan, was ever prosecuted for their crimes.

The car in the driveway was covered with a new car cover, the tires glossy black, the rims shiny. The doorbell didn't ring, it shrieked like a howler monkey. Two more shrieks and Racine appeared. Her wide face was flushed and scowling, her mostly gray hair was matted. She had on a skimpy bathrobe, buttons were undone, unpleasant nakedness beneath. An ankle monitor was strapped just above her bare, ape-sized foot. She didn't look like Andy. She didn't look like anybody.

"Hello. I'm Philip Marlowe."

"What do you want?" Racine said sharply. "Can't you see I'm busy here? Branko wants to do it all the time."

"I'm a private investigator," Marlowe said. "I'm looking into Terry James's death on behalf of his family. I'd like to talk to Andy if he's around."

"He probably won't say anything," Racine replied. "I went to the morgue to identify the body and he ignored me completely."

"Andy's dead?" Marlowe said. He'd half expected it. When you disappear after a Russian oligarch gives you a hundred and fifty mill, you're in the ocean sharing a gunnysack with an anvil.

"Yeah, he wasn't much to look at," Racine said. "I only saw his head. I don't know what happened to the rest of him." Decapitated? Marlowe thought. Had to be Tato's doing.

Branko appeared behind her. He was big and jowly, black curly chest hair, a towel wrapped around his expansive gut. He was wearing black socks and an enormous gold Rolex.

"Who's this guy?" Branko said.

"He's a PI," Racine said. "He wants to know about Andy."

"Well, that's too bad," Branko said. "Get off my porch."

"It's only a few questions," Marlowe said. Branko pushed Racine aside and stepped into Marlowe's space. He had a torturer's eyes and yellow teeth all the way back to his molars.

"GET OFF MY PORCH!" he roared. Marlowe put his palms up and backed away. As the happy couple went inside, Branko said,

"How about this, Racine? This time you stand on a chair."

"Oh for God's sake."

CHAPTER TEN
NATIONAL VELVET

Marlowe and Ren rolled along the Pacific Coast Highway heading for Kendra's party. Hopefully, Ren would speak to Victoria and get some info about Jeremy. *You never know,* thought Marlowe. Maybe the woman would be sympathetic or maybe she didn't know Ren hadn't given her permission to take the boy. A mother trying desperately to find her seven-year-old was hard to turn away from. Marlowe was unusually tense. He wanted to be done with Ren's case but there was something else too. Something urgent and unabated. He blurted out, "I'm very attracted to you." Ren looked at him, startled. She frowned.

"Well, that's not a good idea."

"When is it ever?" Marlowe said.

"Yes, that's a point," she said with a sigh. Marlowe waited but there was no hint of reciprocity. *Too soon, you rushed it, moron.*

"Why is it so hard to find someone, Marlowe?" Ren said at last. "To be happy, or even content?"

"Why is it so hard?" Marlowe looked through the windshield at his befuddled past with women. "Because no one knows what they're doing." They drove on, the ocean view changing at Las Tunas Beach to houses, condos, fences and small businesses. This continued all the way to Malibu, which was more of the same except for the unremarkable pier.

"*This* is Malibu?" Ren said.

"Malibu is the beach. The rest of it could be anywhere. Are you nervous?"

"About the party?" Ren said. "Certainly not. As far as I can tell, the rich are as tormented and ludicrous as everyone else." Marlowe was liking her more and more. "I really want to thank Kendra," Ren said. "This was so kind of her."

"I wouldn't do that," Marlowe said.

"Why?"

"Wait till you meet her. And don't shake hands. She's a germophobe."

"I'm so excited, Marlowe," Ren said. "Maybe Victoria will help."

Kendra was pissed. Apparently, the A-listers had better things to do. Clooney wasn't coming and neither was his Amazonian wife. They were probably busy with their *causes,* feeding the blind or saving Guatemala. You know who else wasn't coming? Kendra couldn't believe it. That bald-headed weight lifter Dwayne Johnson. Who told that behemoth he could act? He should be in a cave somewhere gnawing on a brontosaurus. There was no Tom Hanks or Jennifer Lawrence and no Matt Damon either. They exchanged Christmas cards, for Christ's sake. Jessica Alba didn't show. Imagine calling your company "Honest." You might as well call it "High-Minded" or "Conscientious." Will and Jada begged off. Another disappointment. Kendra was hoping for a little diversity. The best she could do was a cheerful Chinese guy who made kung fu movies. That wicked bitch Ellen DeMiserly hadn't even bothered to RSVP and she lived down the road. Kendra would never say so but she'd have treated the production staff the same way. Cheaper is cheaper. Not that it mattered. DeMiserly was TV.

Aside from that, things were going smoothly, the guests laughing and chatting while they sipped Veuve Clicquot and snacked on Nobu's hors d'oeuvres. Practically everyone commented on how wonderful and vivacious she looked. She saw Marlowe and said, "Oh Christ." She was surprised. She thought he'd show up with a stripper but the woman looked decent and she was properly dressed.

*   *   *

"Is that her?" Ren whispered as they approached. "She's much shorter in person."

"Kendra James, this is Ren Stewart," Marlowe said. Kendra studied Ren as if she were a scratch on the Bentley or a flaw in her engagement ring.

"Hello," Ren said, smiling warmly. "It's a pleasure to meet you, Kendra. And thank you for inviting me. It's extremely nice of you."

"I should say so," Kendra said. She shot a glare at Marlowe, turned and disappeared into a crowd of guests.

"I should have listened to you," Ren said.

"Have you seen Victoria?" Marlowe said.

"Yes. She's over by that horrible painting talking to someone."

Victoria fell into the "ladies who lunch" category. A nest of them at the Polo Lounge, clucking over an $18 wedge of iceberg lettuce and a $40 six-inch piece of salmon. Victoria was midsixties, pixie-cut hair dyed blond, her face smooth as the surface of a trampoline. Her wide eyes through the sparkly glasses made her look like a scuba diver checking out a sea cave. She was talking nonstop to some poor bastard in Bermuda shorts and a polo shirt, obviously boring the shit out of him. He waved at someone who wasn't there and hastily moved off.

"Wish me luck," Ren said, breathless. She stepped forward, Marlowe behind her. She was so hopeful. He should have said to lower her expectations. Life almost always disappointed. "Excuse me, Victoria. I'm Ren Stewart, your grandson's ex-wife. I'm wondering if I could speak with you a minute. It won't take long."

"What is this about?" Victoria said stiffly.

"I'd like to talk about our son, Jeremy," she said. Her voice quavered. "Please." Seemingly offended, Victoria drew herself up.

"No, not now. You might not have noticed but this is a party. How did you get in here anyway? Now if you'll excuse me—"

Marlowe stepped in. "My name is Philip Marlowe. I got you invited to this party so you and Ren could talk."

"*You* got me—?"

"Did you think Kendra invited you because you're a friend?" Marlowe continued. "A relative? A fellow celebrity? No. You're a rich lady with no job and a lot of jewelry. I convinced her to invite you and I could just as easily have you kicked out. How about we go someplace where we can chat?"

"All right," Victoria said indignantly, "but it had better be brief." She led the way toward a side door, a vapor of perfume in her wake. Marlowe was sensitive to fragrances. He liked flowers but this smelled like a field of blooming gardenias. They came out on the landing. "Before you ask, yes, Fallon came to visit me," Victoria said. "He wanted a loan, of course. He thought he could get by with his savings but—"

Ren restrained her vitriol and said, "Please, Victoria, if you could tell me about Jeremy."

"Fallon was always frugal with money," Victoria went on. "I understand you were quite the spendthrift, Ren. Maxing out the credit cards, buying things you couldn't afford."

"Please, Victoria. How was Jeremy?"

"Quite well. He's a charming child," Victoria said. "He played with his Legos, having a wonderful time. The pieces nearly covered the floor in the den! Delightful, really." She sounds genuine, Marlowe thought. She liked the kid. Victoria went on, "The boy was handling the move quite well, given the circumstances. Odd, don't you think? That Jeremy wasn't more upset? You're his mother, after all."

"You're being deliberately cruel," Ren said. "Don't you understand? I'm trying to find my baby!"

"I'm being no such thing," Victoria said. "I'm simply trying to tell you how things stand." Marlowe resisted the urge to push the old bitch down the stairs.

"Did you give Fallon the loan?" he asked.

"I did. It wasn't much," Victoria said. "I wanted to help the child, of course, and I felt sorry for Fallon. He put on a brave face but I could tell he was miserable. The stress, I imagine. Not surprising, given what you put him through—"

"Fine," Ren said, trying to be patient. "Think whatever you wish. But please, *I have to find my son.* Don't you understand?"

Victoria sighed and tapped her foot. "Was there anything else?"

"Did Fallon say where they were living?" Marlowe asked.

"I don't think so—no, wait, he said they were living near the Miracle Mile," Victoria said. "I'm sure that was it."

"The address?"

"I don't have the address and I'm not sure I'd give it to you if I did."

"Do you have a number for Fallon?" Marlowe said.

"I'm afraid not," Victoria lamented. "To be honest, I didn't want Fallon's number. I didn't want to encourage him. If I called, he would probably ask me for another loan." That's bullshit, thought Marlowe. If she didn't have his number how did they communicate?

Marlowe struggled to maintain his composure. "Do you know if he was working?"

"Yes, as a matter of fact," Victoria said with some pride. "Fallon was quite pleased with himself. He said he'd landed an agent and he'd already gotten a part in a movie! I'm so proud of him," she prattled on. "I always knew he was special. I'm so happy he's getting his life together."

"Victoria, please," Ren whispered. It was dawning on her that Victoria wasn't going to help. Marlowe was torn between hugging her and punching Victoria in the face.

"Did Fallon say what movie?" he said.

"Oh, let me see," Victoria said, her brow furrowed. Ren tried to speak, her mouth open, unable to find words to penetrate the wall of indifference. "I seem to recall it was a Western," Victoria went on. "I hate Westerns, all those cowboy hats and cows. Poor Fallon said he was exhausted from sitting on a horse for hours at a time."

"Victoria," Ren breathed, hands clasped as if it were a prayer. "Please. If you know something..." Marlowe wanted to take her pain, be her pain, lift it off her shoulders and fly away.

Victoria was looking at a compact, checking her hair. "Well, if that's everything..." She snapped it shut.

"No, it's not everything," Marlowe said. His eyes narrowed. He was angry.

"This is LA. Thousands of legit actors who are trying to land an agent, but along comes a card dealer from the UK with no connections who not only hooks up with an agent but gets a part in a movie? Didn't happen."

Victoria huffed. "Oh really? And how would you know?"

"You tell me," Marlowe replied. "Who would cast a pale, skinny guy like Fallon for a Western? What part was he playing? The sheriff? The outlaw? The cook? And whatever he was doing, he wasn't saddled up. Studios don't let anyone ride a horse. You have to be trained and experienced. Fallon lives in the Miracle Mile? One-bedroom apartments go for twenty-five hundred to three grand a month. You only said that because you remembered the name. Now quit obfuscating, Victoria. *Where is Fallon?*" Victoria had no reply. She drew herself up again.

"I'll be going now," she said. She opened the glass door and went in. The two former Mossad agents in dark suits were waiting for Marlowe's signal. He nodded. They converged on the terrified Victoria, took her by the elbows and escorted her out. Ren was stricken, tearful, leaning back against the railing with her hand over her mouth.

"I don't believe it. How could anyone be like that?"

They got in the car. Marlowe started the engine and turned the air conditioning up and drove off. Victoria said the Legos had nearly covered the floor in her den. Safe to say, she had a spacious den, thought Marlowe. Did Fallon bring those hundreds of pieces with him? No. She bought them. She liked Jeremy. It was quid pro quo. Small loans in exchange for bringing the boy to visit. He didn't tell Ren. Why add to her misery? She was staring straight ahead, her face puffy and streaked with tears.

"We'll find him," Marlowe said.

"How can you say that?" Ren said bitterly. "If Fallon has money he could be anywhere."

"It will take some doing but we'll find him," he said firmly. Ren tipped her head back and closed her eyes. It felt good saying that but Marlowe had no idea of what he'd do next. *You better think of something, asshole, or you'll break her heart.*

* * *

Marlowe dropped Ren off at the Marriott. She said she was going to check out more names in Fallon's little black book.

"I'll let you know if I find something."

"Please do," Marlowe said. "And remember one thing."

"What's that?" Ren said.

"Cecil the Balls."

"Funny."

Eric DeSallis, the accountant, had a small office in Burbank. It was situated in a strip mall, between a dry cleaner's and a shop that sold off-brand cosmetics. The blinds were shut. Emmet turned the door-knob and it opened. Hundreds of manila folders and thousands of documents were scattered on the floor. The furniture was slashed, file cabinets and desk upturned, holes smashed in the drywall, floorboards pried up, the air conditioner and fluorescent lights dis-mantled. At least there was no blood or DeSallis's head stapled to a doorframe.

DeSallis's house had a FOR SALE sign on the lawn. The grass hadn't been cut in a while, there were flyers stuck in the screen door. Emmet rang the bell five times, knocked loudly. No answer. He went around to the rear of the house and put on latex gloves. The back door had been kicked down. He entered the kitchen. Like the office, everything was torn apart. Cupboards, drawers, the pantry, the stove was in pieces. Every single food item was cut or smashed open, everything in the fridge and on the shelves was ravaged, even sticks of butter, a watermelon and a sixteen-ounce can of plum tomatoes.

Emmet meandered around. The baby grand piano was in pieces. Photos were torn from their frames and scattered on the carpet. Family pictures, relatives, holidays. Emmet had never seen DeSallis before. There was a photo of him wearing skis, standing in front of a cabin, snow on the railing. He was spindly, no shoulders, the same haircut as Moe in the Three Stooges. Emmet had a trick for matching a name with a face. He likened the person to a character in a movie.

DeSallis's eyes were far apart, large nostrils, a wide space between his nostrils and his overbite. The closest Emmet could come was the horse Elizabeth Taylor rode in *National Velvet*. DeSallis's study was the same story. Everything destroyed. Even a big trout mounted on a wall plaque had been gutted.

In another photo, DeSallis, his wife and daughter were in a restaurant mugging for the camera. They were in a corner booth, menus in front of them that said OHANAS 395. The window looked out onto a sunny day, mountains in the distance. DeSallis's wife was large, bovine and sunburned. The daughter was wearing a bikini top. Her face was remarkably foal-like. All she needed was a tail and a bag of oats, thought Marlowe.

Emmet did a search for Ohanas 395 and found it in June Lake, a tourist town. Elevation 7,800 feet. Great skiing in the winter, and in the summer, an ideal spot to get sunburned, wear your bikini, and catch a big trout. He went to Target and bought Bermuda shorts, a T-shirt with a leaping trout embroidered on the pocket, oversized aviator sunglasses and a cap that said THE MAGIC KINGDOM. He changed in the car. If you want to go unnoticed, look like everybody else. He got his duty belt out of the cruiser, put it in a shopping bag, and caught an Uber to Hertz and rented a car.

Google Maps said June Lake was a five-hour drive. Emmet didn't mind. As a patrol officer and then a detective, he'd driven a million miles and enjoyed most of it. You weren't just puttering along gazing at the scenery, you were alert, watchful, looking for anything that might suggest a crime, be a crime or the aftermath of a crime. One night, Emmet was on patrol with a rookie. The kid was twenty, twenty-one, had a college degree. He'd convinced himself he was smarter than his cranky blue-collar training officer.

It was forty degrees, arctic weather in LA. They were driving down Vermont. They saw a kid, seventeen-eighteen years old, walking quickly, hands in his pockets, hunched over. To Emmet's eye, he looked furtive. "I think we need to talk to him," he said.

"Why?" the rookie said. He sounded indignant. "I don't see anything wrong."

"He's wearing a T-shirt," Emmet said.

The rookie shrugged. "Maybe he forgot his coat or doesn't mind the cold."

"Yeah, but there's another possibility."

"What's that?"

"He left somewhere in a hurry."

They stopped him. The kid had blood on his shoes. His friend had been stabbed, and the kid had fled the apartment without his hoodie. The rookie didn't speak for the rest of the shift. Emmet loved being a cop. Sometimes, you were the smartest guy in the room even if you weren't.

Emmet stopped for gas in Bishop and paid cash. He reached June Lake in the afternoon and parked in a grocery store parking lot. He'd done a name search. There was no DeSallis in the white pages. He walked a half mile to Ohanas 395. He looked through the window. There was a host and several waitstaff. Maybe they knew DeSallis but the likelihood they knew where he lived was minimal. There was probably a surveillance camera too.

He went back to his car, ate a stale energy bar, drank a half bottle of Gatorade. In the skiing picture of DeSallis, there was a cabin in the background. There was no point looking for it. There were dozens of cabins scattered around the area. What Emmet needed was a local that knew everybody and knew where they lived; someone who was approachable and somewhere with no cameras. He peed in a coffee can he used on stakeouts and let his cop's brain hum and macerate. Emmet grinned and then laughed. "You still got it, old man."

The post office was on Boulder Drive, the main thoroughfare through town. It was a federal facility, there might be a camera inside. Emmet pulled his cap low. He stuck his head in the door and asked the guy at the counter if the mail had gone out for delivery yet. "I'm waiting for a check," Emmet said.

"Not yet. The truck will leave in a half hour or so." Emmet returned to his car. Twenty-five minutes later, a mail van left the post office. Emmet followed it into a residential area, where it stopped at every house. He parked behind it, walked hurriedly and caught up with it. He didn't want the mail carrier to see the rental car. "Excuse me?" Emmet said. He tried to look harried and out of breath. "I'm sorry to bother you."

"No worries. What can I do for you?" she said, smiling, glad to help.

"My brother-in-law, Eric DeSallis? I'm supposed to spend the week at his place but I lost the address and he's not answering his phone. I've been driving around for hours. The grandkids are going berserk. Can you help me out?"

"That's easy," the mail carrier said. "Go back to Boulder Drive, turn left, follow it for three miles, make a right on Caisson Drive and go another mile or so. You'll see the DeSallis place on your right. It's all by itself, you can't miss it." Emmet thanked her. He waited for the truck to leave before returning to his car. He followed the directions, slowing down when he got to Caisson. He saw the cabin. It was isolated, just like the mail carrier had said. In the classifieds, it would be described as a fixer-upper. There was no movement. Hard to tell if the lights were on. A station wagon was parked next to the cabin. Emmet drove past the place, turned onto a dirt road and parked. He was above and behind the cabin.

Emmet took the duty belt out of the shopping bag. It held his gun and holster, three extra magazines, two pairs of cuffs, flashlight, Taser, baton, keys, folding knife, latex gloves, utility tool, microrecorder, pager, pepper spray, a pen and a notepad. It weighed twenty pounds. He took the pepper spray and the utility tool. He put on latex gloves and left the rest.

There was a trail that led through pine trees. It was a ten-minute walk to the cabin. The station wagon was covered with dust and pine needles. A bad sign, Emmet thought. He crept up the steps to the back door. It was open. The smell hit him and he stepped back.

Take a rotten pork roast, stuff it with a decaying fish, baste it with a whore's perfume and that was close. DeSallis was dead.

Emmet knew this might happen, that was why he'd taken precautions. He didn't want the mail carrier giving the local police an accurate description of the man who inquired about a murder victim. She would remember aviators and the Magic Kingdom cap. Just another tourist.

Emmet went to the living room and stopped at the door. DeSallis was tied to a chair. He was naked, horribly bruised, his eyes wide open, his tongue black. Dried blood was splattered on the floor, a lot of footprints tracking through it. Emmet took a picture with his phone. He went back the way he came and drove for home, stopping in Santa Clarita. He changed his clothes. The tourist outfit went in a dumpster. He called the June Lake police department from his burner. He told the operator about DeSallis. She asked his name and he hung up.

Marlowe was at Emmet's house, babysitting Cody. Emmet had bought her a PlayStation so she'd have something to do besides complain. She was in the living room, playing *Manhunt 2*. The main character, Danny Lamb, was escaping from a dungeon. He killed a guard with a sledgehammer and chopped another one in half with an axe. Then he beat two cops to death with a caveman club and stabbed two nurses to death with a giant hypodermic, one of them repeatedly in the crotch. From there, Danny got in a shoot-out, his enemies dying out like birthday candles, a blood-fest, the screaming like real screaming. Marlowe watched Cody. She played with intensity, expertly maneuvering the controls, grinning when she made a kill. Her focus was so complete, her pleasure so self-evident it alarmed him. It was as if she wanted to *be* the character, to kill and annihilate without restraint.

When she tired of the game, she whined. She was bored, could she borrow his car, could she have friends over, did he have any weed and if he didn't, could he go get some.

"Watch something on Netflix," Marlowe said wearily.

"No, there's nothing bingeable."

"Bingeable?"

"It means good for binge-watching."

"Did you make that up?" Marlowe said.

"God, you're just like Emmet," she said. "It's in the dictionary, look it up." Marlowe didn't believe her. Webster's definition: *having multiple episodes or parts that can be watched in rapid succession: suitable for binge-watching.*

"It's the end of the world," Marlowe said. He agreed to take her to Starbucks.

"I can't wait," she gushed. "I haven't had a cup of coffee in years."

They sat on stools facing the window, sipping their lattes and watching the traffic go by. "Do you have any aspirations?" Marlowe said.

"What kind of question is that?" she said. "No, I don't have any aspirations and please don't tell me to follow my dreams or you can do anything you put your mind to."

"I wasn't going to say that. It's not true, for one thing. Let me put it another way. What would be your ideal life?"

She thought for a moment. "I'd like to be famous."

"Famous for what?"

She shrugged. "I don't know."

"Modeling? Acting? Fashion?"

"No, there's too many dues to pay. Internships, school, all that bullshit," she said thoughtfully. "God, it could take years and it might not even happen." She sipped her latte. "Maybe...maybe like the Kardashians. They have no talent, but they're celebs, they have big companies and they give each other Cartier watches and Lamborghinis as birthday presents." Yet another deluded teenager with big ambitions and no way to achieve them, thought Marlowe. No skills, competence or education and no desire to acquire them. All you have to be is hot, the thinking goes. Be in the right place at the right time, you'll be discovered and you're in!

"When Kanye asked Kim to marry him, he rented out the AT&T stadium," Cody went on. "He hired a fifty-piece orchestra and put the proposal on the Jumbotron. Is that cool or what?" The Kardashians have ruined America, Marlowe thought.

"How did you meet Andy?" he asked.

"Oh God, do we have to talk about him?" Cody groaned.

"He was your dad's partner. What was your first impression?"

"My first impression was that Andy was a conniving weasel," Cody said. "I didn't like him and he didn't like me. I met his girlfriend too. Zoya. Another winner. They belonged together." Cody finished her latte and crumpled the cup in her hand. "Can I have another latte?" she said.

"In a minute," Marlowe replied. "I'm only halfway done with mine."

"So what's Emmet's story?" Cody asked. "Why is he pissed off all the time? Why does he drink so much?"

"His wife, Addie, died three years ago. He never got over it," Marlowe said. "You know, there's something else I've been wanting to ask you."

"Yeah, what?" Cody said.

"Why are you such an asshole?"

Cody was indignant. "I'm not an asshole, I just look out for myself. There's nothing wrong with that, is there? I want things my own way. It's the same as you. It's the same as everybody."

Marlowe had come across a quote by a writer named John Rogers. It went: "You don't really understand an antagonist until you understand why he's a protagonist in his own version of the world." That was Cody. A protagonist in her own version of the world.

"Andy's dead," Marlowe said. Cody reacted, not horrified, more like she'd been caught unaware. Not by Andy's death, but that Marlowe had said it.

A moment too late she said, "I don't believe you."

"Got his head cut off. I was just talking to his sister, Racine. It was Hzoy," Marlowe said. "That gang you know nothing about?" Cody was silent, eyes darting back and forth, you almost heard her gears whirring.

"Oh my God," she managed. "That's horrible."

"Terry was stealing from the Russians," Marlowe said. "The Russians sent Hzoy to get the money back but Terry didn't have it."

"How do you know?" Cody said.

"Because they killed Andy. They're looking for the money, Cody. Maybe they find DeSallis next or maybe they find you. If I don't know what's going on I can't protect you."

"I don't know anything *about* the money and I don't *have* the money," Cody insisted. The last part was true, thought Marlowe. Cody didn't know where the money was or she'd have fled by now. He kept pressing, hoping to squeeze out a lead, something she hadn't thought of.

"Have you done anything about Pav?" she asked.

"No. I have nothing to go on and no way to put him in that alley with you and Roy, or at Musso's," Marlowe said.

"Well, it was him both times," Cody said, adamant. "I said this before. There's no one else who has it out for me but Kendra and Pav." Marlowe nodded. An acknowledgment, not a concession. "I want another latte," she said.

Emmet got home from June Lake late in the evening. Marlowe was sitting on the stoop, smoking a cigarette and drinking Emmet's vodka.

"How was your day?" Emmet said.

"Tip-top," Marlowe said.

"Get anywhere with Cody?" Emmet asked.

"No. She's still stonewalling."

"Well, she won't like this news," Emmet said. "DeSallis is dead. Tied to a chair and beaten to death—by more than one guy. I'm thinking Tato and his crew."

"Do you think DeSallis gave them the money?" Marlowe said.

"No. If he did, they'd have shot him and left," Emmet said. "They took their time."

"What do we do?" Marlowe said.

Emmet yawned. "Find the money and give it back to the Russians."

"That sounds easy."

*　*　*

Cody lay on her bed with the lights off, her headphones on, Cam'ron rapping about playing razor tag. She knew Andy was going to be killed well before this. When Eli heard Tato was planning it, he warned her. That was when she fled to Roy's. What a dumpster fire that was. Eli hadn't called. He hadn't answered her texts or her voice mails. Something was up. She wished he were here, tearing her clothes off. She'd never been nostalgic about anything and she couldn't recall any good ol' days—except with Eli. She thought about meeting him at Das Bunker and eating pancakes at Denny's and realizing they were kindred spirits, and talking about the Big Score. "You look in your world," she'd told him, "and I'll look in mine."

Even early in their partnership, a sexual vibe was always there. Why not? He was hot, she was hot. She obliged him one night and she wasn't even high. They were watching a movie at his place, sitting almost on top of each other, his arm around her, his hand on her thigh. The movie went by like a cement wall taking a walk. The tension got so extreme she couldn't stand it. *Damn*, he was hot and *damn*, she wanted him naked. *What's wrong with him? What's he waiting for?* She regretted saying there'd be no sex. "It screws up everything," she'd told him. He had on sweatpants and she could see the outline of his boner. He was being respectful in spite of his condition. Another reason to like him.

"To hell with it," she said. Eli looked at her.

"What?"

Eli was a triple gold medalist in bed. He took charge, the way she liked her sex. He had stamina, technique, sensitivity, he knew when to speed up, slow down, stop. He had a gift for talking dirty. He let you know how you were doing too. She jumped him whenever they had ten minutes together. Their relationship was intense but liberating. They told each other everything. People say that but they really did. They talked about people they'd screwed and screwed over, and what they really thought about their friends, their families, the importance of greed and ruthlessness, about hurting people and feeling nothing that resembled guilt. About who they'd like to kill. Cody thought Eli was trying too hard, always talking iron will, his fearlessness, his do-or-die attitude about freeing himself from Tato.

One afternoon, they were at his house, sprawled on the bed, listening to Fall Out Boy and smoking some very good bud.

"You know, I tried to kill Tato once," Eli said.

"You what?" she said.

"With a sniper rifle." Eli began a long tale about Tato and the crew frequenting an outdoor bar called the Place. They were there nearly every Friday night. Tato tipped extravagantly and always got his favorite table; on the railing so he could see the world go by.

"Yeah, but what *happened*," Cody said, impatiently. This had to be bullshit.

"There was a building under construction two blocks away," Eli said. "The view from the roof was perfect." He said he took a rifle from the gang's armory, a TAC, something with a complicated scope. He started explaining some crap about one click was a quarter of an inch at a hundred yards.

"*Eli—*" she said.

"Let me tell it my way, okay?" he said. He told her he'd cut the lock on the security fence with a bolt cutter and got up on the roof. "It was a perfect shot. I could see the bar, no problem," he continued. "I looked through the scope and there was Tato, holding court as usual, the crew pretending he was funny. What a bunch of suck-ups." Eli said he rested the rifle on the balustrade and got comfortable. He checked the windage. There was a slight breeze out of the west and—

"Yeah, but what *happened*?" Cody said.

"I had Tato all lined up," Eli went on. "I couldn't wait to see him die. I exhaled just like you're supposed to and pulled the trigger."

"I'm guessing you missed," Cody said.

"Yeah, twice," Eli sighed. "I'd smoked a blunt and adjusted the scope wrong."

"How come no one heard it?" Cody said.

"I had a noise suppressor," Eli said. "Tato didn't even know someone had shot at him." Cody closed her eyes. What a load of horseshit. He was trying to impress her and it fell flat. He'd made the whole thing up. "You don't believe me, do you?" he said.

"Yes, I believe you. Do you want to fuck or not?"

Later, it bothered her. They'd talked about being honest and here Eli tells a whopper and not even a good one. She wanted to throw it in his face. She went online and did a search of the Place. There were some lifestyle articles in the throwaway papers but that was all.

"I knew it," she muttered. As an afterthought, she searched *The Place + shooting*. "Holy shit," she said. There was an article in an Armenian paper titled BULLET HOLES DISCOVERED AT LOCAL BAR. A maintenance man was on a ladder cleaning windows. He found two bullet holes high on a wall overlooking the bar. The holes were large, police speculating the shots might have come from a rifle. They interviewed staff and witnesses who were there that night but no one remembered two shots being fired. Cody couldn't believe it. Eli was more than slick, calculating and great in bed. The boy had some evil in him. She thought she was falling in love.

When the Russian money started rolling in, the partners were thrilled, joyful, their dreams were in reach. She was definitely in love. In a way, it was embarrassing. Giving a man the power to control your emotions. She never thought it was possible. But here she was in Emmet's second bedroom, waiting like an acolyte for the Holy Word. The balance of power had shifted without her knowing it. Eli was capable of betrayal and she was dependent on him. The idea turned her stomach.

Cody got out of bed, went to the window and stared out at Emmet's dismal backyard. A showcase for dead plants and dried-up bushes. Her phone buzzed. *Eli!*

"Oh my God, where've you been? I've been going crazy waiting for you."

"Everything is going wrong. Everything!" Eli was wrung out and scared. She'd never heard him like this.

"What are you talking about?" she said.

"Tato found out I dropped out of school," Eli said. "I have to move in with him. Everything's gone to shit. All our plans are over!"

"No, no, they're not!" Cody said. "We'll find a way. We have to! I can't stay at Kendra's and you can't be a gangster."

"What are we going to do without money?" he retorted. "Sell our asses on Hollywood Boulevard? I don't show up at Tato's I'm dead! Is that what you want me to do? Have Dima whip me until I'm a bloody mess?" Eli had never yelled at her before.

In a low steady voice Cody said, "I'm not giving up. I can't and you can't either." She knew she sounded corny but she went on anyway. "Maybe we don't know what to do right now, but we will. We love each other and we'll find a way." He didn't say anything. He hated it when she got "inspirational" but maybe this time he was listening. Maybe what he needed was hope.

"I have to go," he said, and he ended the call. She sat there a moment, angry and terribly hurt—but she wouldn't give up. Not after all the harrowing bullshit she'd been through. She felt her hard self returning. She would find that money and strangle whoever had it.

Marlowe was at home, brooding. After all his bravado about finding Jeremy, he was stuck. He didn't know what he'd say to Ren. He'd tried reading one of her novels but it was so densely written, so thick with allegory and metaphor, he'd need a team of coal miners to uncover its meaning. There were passages that intrigued him. A girl had gone on a picnic and lost sight of her friends.

> It was dusk, the hour Rose hungered for. She took a steep trail, climbing through the dense, wooded glen, dripping and glistening from the rain. She wondered if she was lost. She wondered if she was trying to be or whether it mattered at all. She'd always felt like this. Separate and uncertain, drawn away from her friends and drawn back again without knowing why. She wondered what happened between those two impulses, whether she willed them into being or they willed her.

Marlowe wondered how the thoughts occurred to her and where they came from. He wondered how she'd put the words together in a way that made you feel something even if you didn't know what it was. The phone buzzed. It was Ren. He didn't want to answer it. He'd done what he could but had made no progress.

"How are you doing with Fallon's black book?" Marlowe said.

"It's frustrating. Most of the numbers are disconnected," Ren said. "I got through to a few people who all had bad things to say about Fallon. He owed them money, stole their girlfriends, or cheated them at gambling. I hate to ask this but have you made any progress?"

"No, I haven't. I'm sorry, Ren," Marlowe said. "I can't find a way in. I called Victoria a few times, but of course she didn't answer. Her attorney called me and told me I was stalking her. I checked out some of her friends but that was a nonstarter. Emmet checked Fallon's credit card purchases. They're mostly in the Valley, not the Miracle Mile. I used those locations as starting points and checked out the private schools in the area. No Jeremy Stewart."

"Don't those places have privacy rules?" Ren said.

"I take a kid's sweater to the front desk," Marlowe explained. "I tell the person there to give the sweater to Jeremy Stewart. I act like I'm in a hurry and I leave before they can say anything. By the time I reach the front gate, somebody catches up with me and says Jeremy is not a student there."

"That's clever," Ren said.

"But fruitless," Marlowe said. "I was at Victoria's last night. I put a GPS unit on her car but I'm not hopeful. If anything, Fallon would come to her." There was an awful pause. "That doesn't mean I'm giving up," Marlowe added.

"I appreciate this, Marlowe. I really do," Ren said. "I have some more calls to make."

"Can you come by later?" he said. "We can talk. Maybe we'll come up with something."

"Okay. I will."

The call ended and Marlowe went back to reading Emmet's notes about Musso's. Despite his drunkenness, Emmet did remember a few things. The attacker at Musso's ran stiffly. He didn't seem to see the parking block and tripped over it. When Emmet lunged and grabbed the attacker around the waist, he was surprised he could hold on as long as he did. The man had a slender build and wasn't especially strong. Marlowe thought a moment. His shoulders slumped, sad and disbelieving. "Aw hell," he breathed.

Marlowe drove into the lot and lined the car up with one of the bays. A young man with a SUPERVISOR patch on his gray uniform approached. "Good morning, sir. Welcome to Jiffy Lube," he said. Marlowe rolled down his window. Roy recoiled. He looked broken and exhausted. The pink bangs were gone, crudely cut off with a hatchet or a hacksaw.

"Let's talk," Marlowe said.

"I can't. I'm working," Roy said.

"You're the supervisor. Get in."

Marlowe backed out of the bay and parked nearby. Roy was sweating and rumpled. His right cheek swollen where Cody had hit him.

"She's a whore!" Roy said. "I knew about Eli the whole time."

"Who's Eli?" Marlowe said.

"Her boyfriend! I knew about that son of a bitch!" He pounded on the dash in time with his words. "I drove her to his house. How could I do that? God, I'm so stupid!" He looked blindly into his psyche. "I stayed there, you know," he went on. "Yeah, I looked in the window. I couldn't see her but I could hear her, she was an animal. Oh Eli! Oh Eli! Fuck me harder!"

"How did you know Cody was at my dad's house?" Marlowe asked.

"I was across the street in my car. Cody took an Uber home and I followed her." He started to cry. "Yes, I want to kill her!" he shouted. "You know what she did? She liked to walk around the apartment naked to tease me. She'd take the food I made her and dump it down the garbage disposal. She opened the shower door and laughed at my cock!" He wept.

This wasn't new to Marlowe. Someone humiliated, their dignity shorn down to the skin, knowing they'd volunteered to be a boot-licker, realizing too late that the one they loved didn't have the capacity to love them back. Roy would bear the burden of Cody's cruelty for the rest of his life. It would shape him, diminish him, cripple his ability to love. It amazed him. How can you hurt someone so deeply without firing a shot? Still weeping, Roy got out of the car and walked off down the street. Another human shipwreck, Marlowe thought. They're around us every day; unseen and sinking, never missed, even when they're gone from sight.

Cody was in the backyard, sitting yoga-style on the chaise, painting her fingernails black. Emmet came out. "Marlowe called," said Emmet. "The guy at Musso's? It was Roy." Cody didn't look up.

"Roy? You're kidding," she said. "Why would he want to shoot me?"

"Oh, I don't know," Emmet said, looking at the empty birdbath. "When you treat somebody like shit when all they've been is decent, sometimes they get mad."

"I didn't treat him like shit," Cody said. She seemed truly puzzled.

"Is that so," Emmet said. "You mean opening the shower door and making fun of Roy's cock was—what? A joke?"

She shrugged. "It was nothing and it was only one time."

"That's all it takes," Emmet said. He walked away.

"That's all it takes—to do what?" Cody called after him.

Emmet went into his study. He must be insane, protecting Cody or even having her in his house. To ease his mind, he watched the six o'clock news on NBC. He preferred his mayhem in measured chunks. Cable was a ceaseless conga line of carnage in third-grade classrooms, huge turnouts for gangster politicians, immortal viruses, the extinction of oxygen, CEOs screwing anything mammalian, plastic bags suffocating sea turtles and women beheaded for driving to the mall. Emmet hated weathercasters. They'd give you the local temperatures, followed by "Later in the show, I'll tell you when to expect Hurricane Earl!" This wasn't doing anything to improve his mood.

He turned off the TV and made notes about DeSallis in the murder book. He finished and went into the kitchen for a drink. DeSallis stuck in his mind. It wasn't the gore, it was separate from all that. A weird thing to land on, Emmet thought. He trusted his instincts. He went back to his study, feeling a sense of urgency. What the hell did DeSallis have to do with anything? He was dead. Emmet looked at his notes again.

The first time the accountant's name came up was at the meeting between Marlowe and George Bamford. Emmet found Marlowe's original notes. There was a lot of shorthand but nothing stood out. His eyes landed on a notation that read, *GB > DS AFH*. George Bamford was going to call DeSallis and ask him to help Marlowe. So what? His mind drifted back to the murder scene. He visualized Tato and his boys beating the life out of DeSallis, demanding to know where the Russian money was hidden. And what would DeSallis say as the blows landed one after the other? Cody has the money. And where was Cody? Tato would ask. Emmet jolted to his feet. *She's with Marlowe.*

Emmet furiously patted his pockets. "Where's my goddamn phone?" he said. He charged into the bedroom, rifled his clothes and the hamper. He checked the living room, bathroom and kitchen. Nothing. "WHERE'S MY GODDAMN PHONE!" he roared.

Cody came in. "Here. You dropped it while you were drunk," she said, tossing him the phone. "Christ I thought you were dying."

Marlowe went to Jahno's again. He came home and parked behind the building. His phone buzzed. It was Emmet. He'd let it go for the moment and call Emmet when he went upstairs. Marlowe went inside and shut off the alarm. He didn't bother turning on the light. He crossed the cement floor and started up the stairs. He stopped. The chalk line on the railing to his left was smudged. Most people are right-handed. When they come down steep stairs, they usually put their dominant hand on the railing to steady themselves. Someone had gotten in, maybe through a second-story window. No alarm up there. Whoever it was came down the stairs and was presently behind him, out there amid the shelves of junk. Marlowe heard footsteps but couldn't turn around fast enough.

"You try anything, I shoot you," the man said. Marlowe felt a gun barrel pressed into his back. As soon as he entered the living room, he saw two men, one of them in motion, his hand raised, his wrist curled back. Before Marlowe could think, he was lashed with a whip. It came so suddenly he didn't see it coming. CRACK! Blistering pain exploded across his shoulder. He screamed, fell to the floor and curled up in a ball, another CRACK! barely missing him.

"That's only a sample," one of the men said. It was Tato. Marlowe recognized his voice from the rapping video. "Get him up," the gang leader said. Marlowe was lifted to his feet, dragged across the room and slung into his office chair. Shards of pain cut his senses to pieces, he could feel the welt rising, pulsing red. He rocked back and forth, groaning. He heard the men talking in Armenian, the guy with the whip laughing. The men were wearing ski masks and latex gloves.

Tato chuckled. "Your friends are such fools. Did they think they could steal from the Russians? They know everything. It took time, lots of bills and accounts and other things I don't know. Two million missing. They want it back." Marlowe could only grunt. "Where is Cody?" Tato went on. "Lie to me and Dima will whip you to death."

As a warning, Dima flipped his wrist. A hump of energy traveled through heavy plaited leather down to the narrow end and a thin ribbon of leather. Knotted to that was the cracker, a braided length of Kevlar thread, loose strands at the end. The cracker moved so fast it broke the sound barrier, creating that bone-chilling snap beloved by torturers and cattle ranchers all over the world.

"Answer me, Marlowe," Tato snarled. *"Where is Cody?"* Marlowe's next move came to him, but Emmet would have to intuit the plan.

"Cody's with . . . my friend . . . Lucas," he gasped.

"Where is this Lucas?" Tato said.

"I have to take you there. Don't have . . . his address."

"You don't know your friend's address? Bullshit!" Tato said. Dima rolled his wrist forward and then back, the eight-foot whip uncoiling behind him. "Are you sure you don't remember?" Tato said. Marlowe nodded at Dima and croaked,

"Do you know this asshole's street address?"

Tato stewed a moment. "Give him a burner. Call your Lucas on speaker. Make a mistake and Dima will take your eyes out one at a time." Marlowe was in so much pain he misdialed twice. "Hurry, you clumsy piece of shit!" Tato shouted. "Sound normal." Emmet's phone was ringing. *Come on, Dad. Don't be drunk!*

"Yeah?" said Emmet in his usual gruff way.

Marlowe used a lower register and said, "Lucas? It's Marlowe. Cody left her coat in my car." *Come on, Dad, come on, Dad, pick up on it!* Cody didn't have a coat. There was the slight hesitation and Emmet said, irritably,

"All she does is complain about it—'Hey, Cody! Turn that god-damn music down!'"

"I'll bring it over. I need your street address," Marlowe said.

"What for?" Emmet said.

"I got lost the last time. I had to use my GPS."

"Seven ninety-five East Adams, right off San Pedro Street," Emmet said.

"Okay, see you…," Marlowe said. The call ended. The two other men yanked him to his feet. The pain was excruciating. He moaned.

"Shut up," Tato said.

They lifted Marlowe by his elbows and ushered him across the room. Emmet gave them his real address. When Tato and his crew got to his place, the tactical squad and a horde of armed officers would descend upon them. Marlowe nearly smiled. Except for the pain, this was working out fine. Tato led the way down the stairs. Dima behind him, then Marlowe, then a third man with a gun. Marlowe knew he'd never get to pay back Dima and it pissed him off. They reached the ground floor. It was nearly dark, slits of street light around the edges of the boarded-up windows.

"To your left," the third man said. They went left, toward the exit, and heard one of the scariest sounds ever created by man. CLACK CLACK! Racking the slide on a pump-action shotgun.

"Don't you move," Ren said. She didn't sound like an English literature teacher, she sounded like Ben Kingsley in *Sexy Beast.*

Everyone stopped. "Drop your guns and raise your hands," she growled. The gangsters didn't comply. It went quiet, nothing but the sound of their breathing and the swish of cars. A tense two seconds passed and then three. *"I said, drop the weapons and raise your hands!"* Ren repeated. She was standing in a crease of light holding the shotgun at her hip. The men could see her clearly, she was seeing shadows.

"Step out of the light," Marlowe said. All at once, the third man raised his gun, Tato and Dima going for theirs. "Get down, Ren!" Marlowe shouted. Turning quickly, Marlowe head-butted the third man, his shot going wide. He knew Tato and Dima were about to shoot, but there was nothing he could do. In that same instant, Ren fired. BOOM! CLACK CLACK BOOM! A dragon's breath erupting out of the barrel. CLACK CLACK BOOM! CLACK CLACK BOOM! The men scrambled to find cover. Tato stopped to shoot but it was like aiming into cannon fire. CLACK CLACK BOOM! The twelve-gauge double-aught rounds obliterating a thirteen-hundred-dollar trail bike, boxes of tax records, the basket of old shoes and the stuffed rhinoceros. CLACK CLACK BOOM! It was chaos, the men darting slapdash through clouds of smoke and shredded 1099s.

Marlowe was on the floor, crawling toward Ren. He watched the shotgun blasts puncture holes in the washing machine and snap the neck off his very rare 1965 Fender Stratocaster. He cried out as a basketball signed by the LA Lakers three-peat championship team vanished like a popped balloon. CLACK CLACK BOOM! Marlowe was behind Ren now. He stood up as the men scurried for the exit. Marlowe grabbed the gun, racked the slide and fired, BOOM! Hitting Dima in the ass. He screamed stumbling forward, the back of his pants smoldering as he went through the door.

The quiet was a freeze-frame, the smoke dissolving into spiraling tendrils, the smell like a conveyor belt in a bomb factory. Marlowe was relieved but frustrated. A prime opportunity to bust Tato and maybe end this mess was gone. He looked around at the wreckage. Ren was grinning, pleased with herself.

"I'd say that was a proper day's work," she said. "Aren't you going to thank me?"

The police and a forensic team arrived. A detective interviewed Ren. The second detective, Dave Wittig, was Emmet's former partner. They'd both worked the homicide table in downtown LA. A paramedic dressed Marlowe's wound while he talked to Wittig. He said the men were covered up and he couldn't identify them.

"Have any idea who they were?" Wittig asked.

"Hzoy," Marlowe said.

"Why Hzoy?"

"I tangled with them before. I guess they didn't like it," Marlowe said. He had to keep Cody out of it. "Who's their shot caller?" he asked.

"Tater or Taco or something like that," Wittig said. "I'll pay him a visit." Marlowe wanted Tato on defense, keep him from bringing the gang back.

"How's your dad? I heard he's not doing so good," Wittig said.

Marlowe shrugged. "Hard to say if he's improving."

"Your dad is a bad dude," Wittig said with an admiring smile. "Tell him I said hello."

Marlowe was in the emergency room. The doctor cleaned up the welt, applied a topical treatment. She gave him a shot of anesthetic and gave him some pain pills.

Ren took Marlowe back to his place.

"Do you mind getting me a drink?" he said. "The bourbon's on the kitchen counter."

"Coming right up." She disappeared into the kitchen, returning with a bourbon for her and club soda for him.

"You just had a shot of Demerol. No alcohol for you."

She didn't think he should climb another flight of stairs but he insisted. They went up to the roof, leaned on the balustrade, side by side. It was another warm night, the same city smells, sounds, the same stream of headlights creeping along the boulevard. He told her what happened.

"I guess my shotgun escapade foiled your plan," Ren said.

"No, you did fine, and you probably saved my life," Marlowe replied. "Thank you, by the way. That was very brave of you."

"Not really, I just imagined they were grouse." They smiled and he sipped her drink. He could feel her shift from interest to urgency. "Tell me the truth, Marlowe. Do you think we'll find Jeremy?" The drugs made him slow. He didn't know what to say. A film of tears slipped over her eyes.

"I have to go back to London," she said. "The new semester starts soon."

"I don't want you to leave," Marlowe said.

There was an empty moment, as if the air had been drawn out of the world. Ren took her arm from his, her hand lingering a moment before pulling away.

"I swear, of all the bent sons of bitches I've met in my life, you get the crown, girlie!" Emmet yelled. "You knew the first time you walked in here that Tato was looking for you but do you say anything? Hell no! Why inform the people who are trying to protect you that your danger is their danger!" They were in the kitchen. Cody was leaning back against the fridge, staring down at her $200 sneakers and frowning. Emmet rapped his knuckles on the side of his head. "Hello? Anybody in there? My son got hit with a goddamn bullwhip because of you! He's lucky they didn't kill him!" Cody sighed and looked at the floor. "Don't you have anything to say or is that too much effort for Princess Malibu?"

"Can't you say something that doesn't make me feel like shit?" Cody said. She walked out. She might have been crying. Emmet felt bad but wondered why he should. The girl was a goddamn menace. He went outside with a double vodka neat and lay down on the chaise. Addie would do this in the evening except she'd drink this awful tea someone made from stems and acorns. Emmet was rarely conflicted. You either turned left, turned right or you ran into a wall. You never just braked at the intersection and parked there like a dummy. With Cody, Emmet didn't know whether left and right were actual directions or whether the wall might be one too. He sipped his vodka. A mosquito bit him in the arm. He dipped his finger in his drink and rubbed it on the bump.

Cody had planted herself in the kitchen. She was fiddling with her phone when Emmet came in.

"Wanna beer?" he said.

"K," she said. He couldn't believe it. Kids these days were so god-damn lazy that they couldn't bother to say the *O*. He thought he'd yelled at her enough for one night and let it pass. He took two beers out of the fridge and plunked one down in front of her.

"Thanks," she said. Emmet leaned back against the counter and drank his beer. Cody ignored him. After a while, his swallowing seemed really loud. He could hear her fingers typing on the screen. What do you say to a kid like this? You're a detective, Emmet thought. Get her talking, see what's going on.

"What are you doing?" he asked.

"Twitter," she said. "I'm going to take a wild guess and say that you have no social media."

"No, I don't."

"And a good thing too, I can't even think about what you'd post."

"You know what I wouldn't post?" Emmet said.

"What's that?"

Emmet took a moment to organize his thoughts. "First of all, cats. Goddamn cats. What makes these people think that any-body wants to see one more photo of Fuzzy coughing up a hair ball or licking its own patootie? Everybody's seen that crap a million times! At some point in their lives, everybody's *owned* a goddamn cat. I really don't get these people. I mean, what are they thinking? That their cat is special? Oh really? Special how? The cat plays softball? The cat shits in the toilet? The cat has a graduate degree from the University of Meow Mix? I've got news for these folks. Nobody, not your family, your relatives, your coworkers or anybody else wants to see your ordinary, common-as-weeds kitty cat whether it's making its own litter box or doing the mambo!"

"I think I get it, Emmet."

"And you know what else people shouldn't be posting?" Emmet went on. "Food." His voice went up an octave. "Oh look, everybody! I'm in a restaurant! Isn't that amazing! And how 'bout those Brussels sprouts! They came from a farm! I'm the one wearing the apron that says I POST PICTURES OF MY GODDAMN CAT!"

"Emmet, really, you don't have to—"

"I saw a video of a guy making a sandwich!" Emmet exclaimed. "I couldn't believe it. This asshole's criteria for entertainment was so low he videoed himself sticking a slice of baloney between two slices of bread! His secret ingredient was, get this—*jalapeños!* And you know what's even more frightening? There were sixty-one views! Sixty-one people took time out of their day to watch some half-wit make a baloney sandwich!"

"Message received, Emmet. You hate social media."

"I almost forgot," Emmet went on. "*Movie stars.* I love how they support each other, no matter what the hell it's for. I support Charlize and her battle against eating toilet paper! I support Denzel in his stand against burning garbage on Columbus Day! I support Meryl's fight to give away both her kidneys!"

"Emmet, could you stop already?"

"You know what else I don't understand?" Emmet continued. "People posting pictures of their families on every meaningless, made-up occasion. Who really cares about Father's Day? Father doesn't. He'd rather be fishing or lying in a hammock smoking a cigar. And it's the same goddamn shot every time! There you are, in your shorts, sandals and oversized T-shirts, smiling like everybody farted at the same time: Mom, Dad, the kids, your deadbeat brother-in-law, his wife, the kickboxer, and your neighbor, Mr. Cranberry, who spends his whole life fertilizing his goddamn lawn, and then there's Cousin Sheila who wears a maternity dress rain or shine, and of course Grandpa, who doesn't know where the camera is because he's looking at the goddamn sky!"

"Emmet, I'm trying to text, okay?"

"What? Oh yeah, sorry," Emmet said. He suddenly realized he'd been doing all the talking. "What do you do for fun?" he asked. Cody shot him a look, got up from the table and left.

"Nice talkin' to you," Emmet said, adding in a low voice, "Shit, I hate kids."

Cody went to her room and leaned against the windowsill. She thought about Eli. She loved him but there was nothing she could do for him. He was moving into Tato's place soon. Scratch Eli until further notice. There were more important things to ponder, like staying alive and getting the hell out of here. No. She wouldn't leave. She had vowed to make the future of her dreams and she would. No quitting, no backing down, all or nothing.

The Russian money. Andy was the last one who had it. He couldn't possibly have misplaced two million bucks. Somebody took it from him. It had to be someone close, somebody who would know what he was up to. Cody smiled and gave a little laugh. "Gotcha, bitch." She slipped out of the back door and went into the gardening shed. Roy's gun was in a Ziploc bag, hidden underneath a thirty-pound bag of manure. She'd scooped the gun up after the fight. It was small, a .32, short barrel, five-shot capacity. That should be plenty for what she had in mind.

When she first hooked up with Eli, he'd taken her to the Angeles Shooting Range in Sylmar. Nothing much to it. A long corrugated metal roof over shooting stands a few feet apart. It was surrounded by foothills so you wouldn't kill somebody in Sylmar sitting down for a bowl of oatmeal. The police and the FBI practiced there. Eli taught her the basics. How to stand, aim, load the gun. As usual, he went into all kinds of detail that drove her crazy. The pistol targets were only seven yards away. She laughed when she saw them. "Are you kidding?" She fired three times and missed. She couldn't believe it. They were right there in front of her. She emptied the magazine, inserted a new one, emptied that and hit the target twice.

"This is bullshit," she said.

"It's normal," Eli said. "The gun has a short barrel. If your aim is off a half an inch you'll—"

"Okay, okay, you said that." She was pissed. She blasted away. An attendant stopped her, saying rapid firing wasn't allowed. You had to wait a second in between each shot. That was stupid. She kept shooting. If she hit the target, it seemed random, like an accident. "What's wrong with this stupid thing?" she said, glaring at the gun.

"Okay, stop," Eli said. "You're just shooting, Cody. You're not thinking—no, let me finish. Your stance is all wrong, you're not even bothering to aim. You get too emotional." She hated it when he said that. "Think of it as a real-life situation," he went on. "It's not a paper target, it's a guy with a knife and he wants to rape you. If you don't kill him with one shot, you're finished."

That changed everything. The paper target was Gary Marx, Noah, Kendra, Roy, Pav and the three Black girls at Bar Sinister who tried to take the booth. Her percentage went up. Four out of ten. Five. Six was her high score. Her hands were sore, her arm was tired, her ears were numb despite the noise-canceling headphones.

"We've been here half the day. Let's go," Eli said.

"I want to hit it ten out of ten," she said.

"You'll *never* hit ten out of ten. In the first place, you don't have the discipline. In the second, you don't have the aptitude." That pissed her off. She was tired of Eli lording it over her. She slapped another magazine into the gun.

"Okay, cowboy, let's see you do better," she said. She realized she'd made a mistake when he smiled at her. Eli calmly took the gun, got into his stance and hit the target ten out of ten times. Two were bull's-eyes, the rest close by.

"Tato taught me how to shoot," he said. "I've been doing this since I was a kid." Cody sulked all the way home.

Cody left her room. She put on one of Emmet's baseball caps and his rain jacket with the sleeves rolled up. The jacket went down nearly to her knees, but the pockets were deep and she could keep her hand on the .32. This was some scary shit, robbing somebody at gunpoint, but she wasn't going to back off now. Wouldn't Eli be surprised when she called and said, "Hey, hotshot, guess who's got the money?" The thought inspired her.

Let's go, girl. It's time to ransack and remove.

Tato was at his mother's place in the hills. He wanted to get away from the others and think in private. He was used to trouble but this had no solution. He was supposed to watch the Russian money and make sure everything with Terry and the others went smoothly. The Russians didn't trust the Americans because they didn't trust anybody. They had their own security systems in place but they still had reservations. Tato told them his brother Eli would personally oversee the operation. Eli was smart. He had a college degree and he was a number one student. He was going to be Tato's consigliere. But $2 million had been stolen and Tato would be held responsible.

The vig alone was impossible. If the Russians gave you the family rate at say, ten percent a week, you'd owe them $180,000 by Friday. A year would be…Tato was good at calculating numbers in his head…somewhere around, oh, call it $286 million. There were dangers no matter what Tato did but leaving town was the only option. Even then you weren't safe. The mob was like Putin. They had long memories. One day, you and your family would be drinking tea they'd spiked with radium and you'd all die with your cups in your hands.

Tato needed the two million if he wanted to leave and not come back. What bothered him was Eli. If he was overseeing things, why hadn't he spotted the stealing? He said he checked everything several times a day and that nothing would get by him. The truth came slow, then fast like a fist to the face, smashing everything he believed about his family. *Eli?* His own brother stabbed him in the back? *Why?* Why would he do it? He loves you, respects you, Tato, he said so a thousand times. You always tried to help him, didn't you? You gave him money for his school, house, car, everything. You did all these things and this is your reward? Betrayal was an everyday thing but Tato never expected this. He shouted at his mother to bring him another drink.

Tato spent most of every day being angry. Anger helped him survive the loneliness and danger that had been his life. Anger was his daily bread, home base, the size and heat of it dominating every other emotion. Whether he was sad, disgusted, optimistic, afraid or even happy, he would always return to the reassurance of temper and violence. It was like the Russian-made T-54 tank his father crewed during the war. An iron fortress that could defend and attack at the same time.

This anger was something else. It was hatred. He would kill Eli with pain. That was all. Just pain. His little brother didn't have the *huevos* to do this alone, Tato thought. The girl, Cody, she'd led him into betrayal by his dick. Tato punched his fist into his palm. The cunt would die the same way. Grabbing up Eli would be easy. He'd have to set a trap for Cody. Marlowe too. Make him plead and beg, make him do things with the girl before he died.

His mother returned. She looked frightened.

"What is it?"

"*Neghut'yun.*" Trouble.

Two men were leaning against a black Mercedes sedan. Late thirties, early forties, big shoulders, thick necks, their muscles sliding into fat. They wore cheap clothes, leather jackets, gold chains. They looked more dangerous than the younger guys, like they had experience, like they'd seen everything, like there was nothing you could do to get away.

His mother whispered, "*Bravta.*" The Russian mob. Tato knew they'd show up but didn't know when. A third man was standing in the yard, smoking. He was wearing a rumpled suit that needed dry cleaning and dusty loafers with tassels on them. Tato waited. Speaking would be disrespectful. The man turned around. Sixties, balding, his eyes watery, his face soft, sagging like a weary businessman. He could have sold scrap metal or owned an appliance store.

"Send your mother into the house," the man said. She protested in Armenian, gesturing as if the man were a pest and it was time for him to go. The man's soft face went taut so quickly you could almost hear it snap, his eyes glittering and fierce.

"Go into the house, old woman, or my men will drown you in the bathtub." When the door closed behind her, he said, "My name is Grigory. The Americans stole two million dollars. Have you found it?"

"No."

"You know it's your responsibility to pay it back."

"Yes, I know."

"Get in the car."

Tato sat in the back with Grigory, the two thugs in front. They drove down the hill in silence, Grigory handling it differently than Tato would have. He would have beaten the guy in his own front yard, let his mother watch him be humiliated. Grigory was letting the tension build, your mind dreaming up the worst. Just as effective, Tato thought. His insides were doing somersaults. He wished there were a way to stop sweating.

"Tell me everything you know," Grigory said. "Leave out nothing. I want names, places, everything. I want details, no matter how minor." Tato nodded yes. "Are you ready?" Grigory said to the thug in the passenger seat.

"Yes, boss."

"He remembers everything," Grigory said. "Start talking, Tato."

CHAPTER ELEVEN
KOMODO DRAGON

Ren was in her room at the Marriott feeling frustrated and angry. She had to *do* something. The thought of going home without Jeremy was too painful to contemplate. She couldn't sit around while Fallon did who knows what with her son. There were a thousand ways he could corrupt an innocent boy. Marlowe was hurt, which slowed things down even more. No, she wouldn't wait. She had Fallon's little black book. He'd left it behind when he'd fled the UK. Pages were smudged, stained, torn from the binder. Most of the names were women. Ren had been cold-calling but realized it was a mistake. She should be calling the people that Fallon mentioned or reminisced about. Cecil the Balls was one of them. Another was someone called Zorro, no last name. She called.

"Hello. My name is Ren Stewart. I'd like to speak to Zorro, please."

"Sorry, wrong number," a man's voice said. He sounded wary. He sounded like he was lying.

"I'm Fallon Stewart's ex-wife. Was Zorro a former tenant there? I really need to speak to him. It's rather urgent." There was a pause. The man was apparently thinking it over.

"You're Fallon's old lady?"

"Former. Is this Zorro? I'm really not calling about you. It's Fallon. I have to locate him, just to talk, that's all. I mean him no harm." Another pause, then,

"Yeah, this is Zorro. What can I do for you?"

Ren gave Zorro a truncated version of her situation with Fallon and her desperate need to find her son. "I'll have to return to the UK soon, so you can understand my urgency. I can't bear the thought of leaving without Jeremy. If you're a parent I'm sure you understand." Zorro didn't answer. It was as if something she'd said had triggered an idea. "Hello? Are you still there?" said Ren.

"Uh, could you hold a sec?"

It took a long minute for Zorro to come back to the phone.

"Sorry about that," he said. "Come on over, I'll text you the address."

"Can't you tell me over the phone?"

"I could but I don't know you. You could be anybody. What if it's not your kid? What if you're a weirdo or one of those crazy people who steal babies from the hospital? I need to see you in person."

"I'm not any of those things—" The call ended. Thirty seconds later, her phone buzzed. An address in some place called Lakewood. The GPS on her phone said Lakewood was twenty-five miles away. The trip should take forty minutes. Not long, but she was still impatient. She followed the directions, moving along nicely until she reached Downtown LA and a traffic jam. She fumed. She jogged faster than this. The trip time on her GPS was increasing. It took an hour and fifteen minutes to reach Lakewood, a place so unpicturesque she wanted to leave as soon as she got there.

Many of the houses were small and neglected; sad women sitting on the unpainted stoops, kid playing on the uncut grass. Some of the cars she saw were old, dented fenders and worn paint, but the rims were bright and shiny. Must be an LA thing. She parked in front of the address. It was in worse shape than its neighbors. The gate scraped the cement. The front window was covered with cardboard, the screen door had no screen in it. Are all of Fallon's old friends disreputable? she thought. Doesn't he know anybody that isn't a bum? She started to get out of the car and hesitated. She called Marlowe.

"Don't go in until I get there," Marlowe said. "Use your head this time."

"Marlowe, I'm forty feet away from this Zorro person," she said. "What if he knows something?"

"Then he'll know it until I get there. Come on, Ren. Look at the neighborhood, look at the house. Do you think nice people live there?"

"Okay, I'll wait," she said with a sigh. "How long?"

"Lakewood has one of the highest crime rates in America, not the city. *America*," Marlowe said.

"How long?" Ren repeated.

"How long did it take you?"

"Over an hour."

"See you then."

Ren sat in the car, churning with frustration. Over an hour? Maybe traffic had worsened and he'd be longer than that. She looked at the house. It was shabby, yes, maybe even ominous, but the key to finding Jeremy might be right behind that scratched and battered door. *No, be sensible, Ren.* She would wait for Marlowe. She sat there for what seemed like a long time. She looked at her watch. A little over three minutes had passed. She couldn't stand it and got out of the car.

A woman answered the door. She was young and might have been pretty but her face was taut with worry and lack of sleep. Her hair tied in a messy ponytail, no makeup, bare feet, oversized sweatshirt.

"Hello. I'm Ren Stewart. Is Zorro around?"

"I'm Lee Anne. Come on in." As soon as they got inside, she said, "Could I see some ID? Sorry about this." She was truly apologetic. "It was Zorro's idea, not mine." Ren showed Lee Anne her passport.

"I'm sorry about the mess, sit anywhere," Lee Anne said. She seemed like she said "I'm sorry" a lot. There was fast-food debris, empty liquor bottles, pizza boxes, laundry and magazines scattered around. There were dark stains on a tweedy sofa, the armrests were frayed. Ren took a seat on a wooden chair.

"Sorry. I haven't had time to clean up," Lee Anne said. *Ever?* thought Ren. The predominant smells were weed and alcohol with garbagy undertones.

"Want something to drink?" Lee Anne asked. "We have water and I can make coffee if you want." She was nervous, wringing her hands, forcing a smile.

"No, thank you," Ren said. "I'm sorry for being rude but I'd really like to know about my son. Is Zorro—"

"Hello, Ren, nice to meet you," Zorro said as he entered, wiping his hands on his none-too-clean wifebeater. He came forward and shook her hand a little too forcefully. It was still damp. Zorro was in his thirties, pale, careworn, rodentlike features, a shadow instead of a beard. There was a dark band of skin across his eyes. More like a raccoon than Zorro, she thought.

"Nice to meet you too," Ren said.

"Did you hit any traffic coming here?" Zorro was trying to look affable with no success. He was jittery, anxious. Most troubling was his eagerness, like he was sizing her up for the air fryer. His pupils were dilated.

"No, the traffic was fine," Ren said. "I'm sorry to hurry this along but I'd really like to know about Jeremy."

"I won't lie to you," Zorro said. "I don't know anything about your kid."

She was shocked. "Then why in the world did you—"

"I don't know where Fallon is either, but I know what he's doing." It took a moment for that to register.

"You do? You really do?" Ren exclaimed. "Please tell me!"

Zorro shrugged. "Hey, I'll tell you—"

"Oh, thank you! Thank you so much!"

"But I want you to do something for me."

"Oh, dear God!" Ren shouted at the ceiling. "It's my child! Couldn't you do the decent thing and just tell me?"

"Do I look like the kind of guy who cares about decency?" Zorro said. His mouth was dry, he kept smacking his lips. Ren had been tricked by Cecil the Balls but not this time.

"If Fallon was here, what did he want?" she said.

"Money. He wanted a loan," Zorro said. That sounded right, she thought.

"Did you give it to him?"

"I'm a bad person but I'm not an idiot," he said. Lee Anne was nodding.

"When did you meet Fallon?" Ren asked.

"We were in Pine Grove together. Youth authority, drug charges. Not a lot of white boys in there. We looked out for each other."

Fallon never told her about Pine Grove but he did say he was kicked out of high school for drugs. "Did he have a beard or was he clean-shaven?" Ren said.

"Clean-shaven."

"Tattoos?"

"I don't know. He wasn't naked," Zorro said testily. He looked at Lee Anne.

"None that I could see," Lee Anne said. Her brow furrowed. "I remember he was wearing a hat—no, it was more like a—I don't know what to call it." She brightened. "A beret! That's it! A beret!" Ren's gut tightened. She was talking about Fallon's tam. People often confused the two.

"Can we get on with it?" Zorro said.

"What is it you want of me?" Ren said, wanting to get on with it.

"I want you to deliver a package," Zorro said.

Ren closed her eyes. *Deliver a package?* Was everything in LA a movie? She should be Michael Cera or Zach Galifianakis playing the innocent dupe, not a proper young woman with a graduate degree in English literature.

Before she could speak, Zorro said, "No, I'm not joking. I'm not in the mood for laughing."

"May I ask what's in the package?" Ren said. Zorro hesitated. "Oh, for heaven's sake," Ren said. "You want me to deliver a bloody package but you're not going to tell me what's in it? What if it's plutonium or anthrax?"

"Yeah, that's what I am, an anthrax dealer," said Zorro. "It's heroin."

"Of course it is," Ren said, shaking her head. "What was I thinking, a muffin basket?" It was an outrageous proposal but he had her penned in. She would do anything to rescue Jeremy. Anything.

"We're talking a lot of money here," Zorro said. "Say you buy a kilo wholesale for, say, twenty grand. Even numbers, you add a fifty percent cut. You now have a kilo and a half or fifteen hundred grams. Grams go for around a hundred and fifty, twenty-eight grams in an ounce. You sell your ounces for forty-two hundred apiece, thirty-five ounces in a kilo but you've got a kilo and a half. So that's fifty ounces times forty-two hundred bucks and you've got two hundred thousand K and change, times four kilos, that's eight hundred thousand worth of Mexican Brown."

Stunned, Ren said, *"Eight hundred thousand dollars?"*

"It's right there in that backpack." It was green and made of canvas.

"I'm gobsmacked," she said.

"Gob what? Never mind," Zorro said. His mask got darker. "I'm warning you, Ren. People get killed over deals like this. All you have to do is deliver it and you're done. No stops along the way, no talking to people. Do the job and I'll tell you everything you want to know about Fallon."

"Can't one of your criminal associates do this?" Ren protested. "I'm sure you have plenty."

"Hundreds of 'em. But like you said, they're criminals. I wouldn't trust any of them with something like this. With you, I have leverage, the kind you can't buy."

Ren's brain was inundated with questions. *What if Zorro is lying? What if he isn't? You have to do it, Ren. It's Jeremy. But what if you're arrested? What if you go to prison? Is the risk worth ruining your life forever? What kind of mother would you be then? What kind of mother would you be if you didn't fight for him? No, be sensible. Wait for Marlowe.*

"I have to think it over," Ren said.

"No, no thinking, no time to call somebody," Zorro said. "Do it now or get the fuck out." *Do you mean it or don't you, Ren? Will you do* anything *to find Jeremy?*

"Tell me what to do," she said.

Zorro and Lee Anne watched her through a tear in the cardboard window. Ren was carrying the backpack to her car. She looked like a normal everyday person. She was well dressed. No gang tats, no shaved head, no ink on her neck. She could drive right by a whole battalion of narcs and they wouldn't give her a second look. She was shaken and still crying. Lee Anne felt sorry for her.

"She could back out," Lee Anne said.

"She won't. It's about her kid," Zorro said.

"She could call somebody."

"Call somebody and say what? Hi. I'm holding eight hundred K worth of smack. How about helping me out?"

"What about the cops?"

"Yeah, that's dicey but she's smart. She'll play it out in her head. If the cops come here, we'll say, What heroin? What kid? Did you wipe the backpack down like I told you?"

"Yeah, I did. The bricks too," Lee Anne said. "The only finger-prints on them are hers." They came away from the window. Zorro went into the kitchen and came back with a bag of Doritos and a beer. He sat in front of the TV and zoned out. Lee Anne was worried. They were being evicted. The sheriffs were coming tomorrow.

"Do you think you could help with the packing, Z?" she asked.

"Just take the bare essentials," he said.

"That's all we have." She sat down beside him, ate chips, drank from his beer.

"Do you think Freddie will mess with her?"

"Mess with Ren? Why would he?" Zorro said.

"Because you're two weeks late."

"If she drops off the bag and leaves, she'll be fine," Zorro said.

"How much did you cut the dope?" Lee Anne asked.

Zorro shrugged. "I eyeballed it."

"Oh Z." She sighed. "What did you cut it with?" she asked.

"I don't remember."

"You don't—if the junkies start dying Freddie won't like it."

"Could you get off my case?" Zorro said. "I'm in enough shit as it is." Lee Anne washed the chips down with another swallow of beer.

"What about Freddie's brother?" Lee Anne said.

"You mean Komodo? I don't know. Maybe he won't be there."

"Komodo is always there." They sat staring blankly at the TV.

"If she drops off the bag and leaves, she'll be fine."

It took Marlowe an hour and twenty-two minutes to reach the house in Lakewood. Ren wasn't there. That could mean a number of things. One. She was dead and buried in the backyard. Two. She was on her way to Saudi Arabia to be sold as a slave. Three, and the least likely, she was still in the house. Marlowe got out and went around to the trunk. He kept a lockbox under the spare tire. He did the combination, opened the box and took out a Ruger LCR .38 revolver. It was lightweight, the barrel less than two inches long and hammerless so it wouldn't snag on your clothes. He slipped it in his pocket. He went up the walkway and kicked in the door on his first try. *Thank you, Jahno.* He walked into the room with the gun drawn. A man, presumably Zorro, was slouched on the raggedy sofa, watching TV and eating from a family-size bag of Cool Ranch Doritos.

"Uh—" Zorro said. He started to sit up but Marlowe grabbed him by the throat and held him down. Zorro's mouth was open, a cement mixer of masticated corn chips in there.

"Hoof are voo?" he said, spitting crumbs. "Fludda flu font."

"I want Ren. Where is she?" Zorro swallowed.

"I don't know anybody named—what was that you said? Ken?"

Holding him fast, Marlowe jammed the barrel of the gun into Zorro's ear.

"Hey, man! You're gonna make me deaf!"

"That's what you're worried about? Deafness? Tell me where Ren is!"

"Yeah, yeah, I'll tell. Just get off me." Marlowe stayed where he was. Zorro explained that Ren was delivering heroin to another dealer named Freddie.

"Unbelievable," Marlowe said. "Ren wouldn't do that voluntarily. You know something about Jeremy, don't you? What is it? Tell me now, goddammit!"

"It's no big deal, okay?" Zorro said. "I know what Fallon is doing, that's all. He's—" In his peripheral vision, Marlowe saw someone.

He turned his head. A colorless woman with trembling hands was aiming a pistol at him.

"Let him go," she squeaked. Zorro laughed.

"That's my baby!" He gleefully took Marlowe's gun. "Oh, you're in for it now," Zorro said.

"We don't have time, and don't beat him up," the woman pleaded. "It's an assault charge. That's all you need. Now let's go!" Zorro grumbled, found Marlowe's wallet and took the cash.

"This is for the gun in my ear," he said, and he slugged Marlowe in the stomach.

Marlowe doubled over and fell to his knees. He heard them scrambling around, gathering things, and they left.

Ren was driving. The air conditioning was on full blast but she was perspiring. Her pulse throbbed, she was breathing in short breaths, the pressure was fracturing her psyche. She got off the freeway, pulled over to the curb and put her forehead on the steering wheel. Marlowe called.

Without preamble he said, "Let me see if I have this right. At present, you're driving a load of heroin to someone named Freddie."

"Eight hundred thousand dollars' worth. That's retail, of course."

"May I ask where you're going?"

"To a place called Homeland, of all things," Ren said. "On the map, it looks more like an outpost than a town."

Marlowe checked the map on his phone. "Meet me in Castle Park in Riverside. The parking lot. Not Freddie's crack house. Castle Park, Riverside. Are we clear?"

"I hesitate to say 'crystal' but yes."

"Are you sure?" he said. "When I said to wait at Zorro's you ignored me completely."

"I see that now."

It took Marlowe over an hour to get to Castle Park. Ren was sitting on the hood of her car, arms crossed, fuming. "You took your time getting here," she said.

"I'll take the heroin to Freddie," Marlowe said.

"No, he's expecting me and nobody else." She looked at him, the resolve in her eyes immutable. "It's for Jeremy and I'm doing it."

Marlowe sighed. "Do you have any information about Freddie?"

"I asked Zorro that," Ren said. "He said Freddie is a 'swell guy' but that may have been sarcasm. Lee Anne made a face like she'd found a dead mouse in the fridge."

They drove out of Riverside in Ren's rental car, the Mustang would make the wrong impression. The landscape was unwelcoming. Bleak, pale sky, piles of gray boulders, scraggly brush, tall saguaros standing guard. There was nothing to see in Homeland. Ren followed Zorro's directions. They turned off the highway onto Joppe Avenue, a dirt road that wound through desolate foothills. Everything seemed a harbinger of menace. A dented road sign shot through with bullet holes. A railcar diner enveloped in dust, windows broken, windswept tumbleweed piled against the door. A truck frame burned black; the melted steering wheel left by its long-dead driver.

"What now?" Marlowe said.

"Zorro said to go to the end of the road, about five miles. There's supposed to be a trash dump there. Then north another few miles and we'll run into it." The car bumped along, the road full of potholes and washboard, the suspension creaking, dust eclipsing the windshield, gravel clattering. The trash dump was unofficial. Old tires, appliances, bedsprings, barrels of chemical waste, garbage bags piled high and a desiccated mule filled an arroyo to the brim. Marlowe got out of the car and climbed into the backseat. They turned north, the road winding and gradually ascending. They stopped on a rise. "Oh dear," Ren said.

Freddie's abode reminded Marlowe of Michael Madsen's place in *Kill Bill.* A trailer set on cinder blocks. It was the color of a dirty Band-Aid, aluminum siding dented, splotched with rust and falling off, the window screens opaque with grime, an old-fashioned TV antenna listing on the roof. A pickup truck sat under a sagging carport. There was a dog. A Doberman pinscher, barking savagely.

"At least it's not a pit bull," Ren said.

"Approach slowly," Marlowe said. Ren crept the car forward.

"Stop," Marlowe said. They were forty feet from the house. "Put the car in reverse and keep your foot on the brake," he said. "If I say go, go." Marlowe ducked down. He could see between the front seats and just over the dash.

Ren watched a man come out of the trailer. He looked oddly normal. Like an insurance salesman on his day off or her uncle Malcolm, the pharmacist. Overweight, plaid shirt, chinos, running shoes. He had a benign, chubby face, apple cheeks and an amiable smile. Ren rolled her window down a few inches. The heat wafted over her.

"Hello there. You must be Ren. I'm Freddie," he said, hitching up his pants. It was unsettling, the contrast between the place and the man.

"Hello, Freddie," she shouted over the dog.

The dog had gone berserk, drool flying, the barking overwhelming. Sharply, Freddie said, "*Sitz*, Vlad!" The dog immediately stopped and sat down. A German command, thought Marlowe. Lots of trainers use German. *Wait, did he just call the dog Vlad? As in Vlad the Impaler?*

"Hot day," Freddie said, shading his eyes from the sun. "Why don't you come in, Ren? I made a pitcher of lemonade. It's fresh."

"I'd like to give you the backpack and go."

"It will only take a few minutes. We've got to look the merchandise over, see that everything is shipshape."

"Couldn't you do that after I'm gone?" Ren said.

"We could," Freddie said, as if the burden was untenable. "But we want you there as a witness. If the count is wrong or there's been some sort of mishap. You understand."

In reply, Ren popped the trunk lid.

Freddie pinched his lips together and scowled. He hitched his pants up again and came toward the car. He was a big man, shaped like a butternut squash, fifteen or sixteen stone and taller than Marlowe. Intimidating. *Keep it together, Ren.* She heard Marlowe squirming around, grunting. He'd apparently stuffed himself behind the front seats.

"My, you're quite pretty, aren't you?" the big man said. "Will you please get out of the car?"

"No, I won't," Ren said.

"Please, I insist." The dog started growling.

"I'd like to get this over with," Ren said. "I'm leaving in one minute."

Freddie's smile imploded, as if his throat were sucking in his features, his flesh crinkling into a jagged crack, his eyes like fissures; a beast carved into a cliff face. Ren recoiled, jerking her head away from the window.

"You will regret this, Ren," Freddie snarled. He stomped around to the back of the car.

They heard Freddie rummaging around in the trunk. It was taking a long time, her view blocked by the trunk lid. She called out, "Can't you find it? It's right there in front of you." Finally, Freddie reappeared with the backpack. The smile was there but with a different glint, like you were all-in with three kings and he had a straight flush.

"We'll see you again, Ren."

Under her breath she muttered, "The bloody hell you will." She backed out, turned around and headed back the way they came.

Marlowe sat up. "Freddie was stalling for time. I heard someone underneath the car." They drove, waiting for something to happen.

"The car is getting hard to steer," Ren said.

"They let air out of a tire," Marlowe said. "Keep going, slow down gradually. We want to keep the tire on the rim as long as possible." The car went much farther than Marlowe expected, pitching and yawing, the shocks bottoming out. Ren had to wrestle with the steering wheel. A flapping, grinding noise came from beneath the car.

"The tire's gone, we're on the rim."

"There they are," she said, glancing in the mirror. "About a kilometer back." Marlowe got out his phone and dialed.

"No reception. That's why they waited before coming after us. They knew we couldn't get a signal here." The rim was digging in, the car swerving wildly. Ren could barely hold on to the steering wheel.

"I can't control it, Marlowe!" Ren shouted.

He looked ahead. A sharp bend in the road. He pocketed his phone and lifted the door handle. "Slow down, the slowest you can."

"Why? What are you doing?" Ren said. They rounded the bend, the pickup out of sight for a moment. Marlowe opened his door.

"Where in God's name are you going?" Ren shouted.

Marlowe got out, shoving the door closed as he stumbled off into the brush. He hid behind a boulder and watched the pickup speed past. Ren kept the car on the road for another half mile or so before swerving into a ditch. The pickup was right behind her. Freddie and another man jumped out. The other man broke Ren's window with something, dragged her out screaming, Freddie standing by with a gun. They shoved her into the pickup, made a U-turn and drove past Marlowe again. The engine noises receded and the car was gone. The air was dry and still, the silence so acute it was almost a sound. California is not the beach. California is the desert.

He walked a half mile to Ren's car. There was a bottle of water in the side pocket of the front door. He drank some and saved the rest for later. When Ren called Marlowe from Zorro's house, he was eating frogs' legs and oxtail salad at Papilles Bistro in Hollywood. He was wearing merino wool slacks, a light cashmere sweater and shoes made by Joseph Cheaney & Sons in London. A perfect ensemble for outdoor activities. Should he have stayed in the car with Ren? No, he thought. If he'd been captured too, both of them would have to escape. The men were armed and they'd be tied up. He could head back to town but it was much farther than the hike to Freddie's. But those two assholes had Ren. God knows what they were doing to her. *Focus, Marlowe. Get to Ren as fast as you can.* "Onward," he said. And he started walking.

Ren was surprised when she was shoved into the trailer. It was neat, clean motel furniture, dishes drying in the rack, no dust on the blinds. It smelled like room freshener.

"Tie her up, Komodo," Freddie said.

"Please don't," Ren said. "I just want to get my son back. I won't cause any trouble."

"We're out of duct tape," Komodo said.

"Improvise. Surely you can find something," Freddie said.

Komodo was a small man with a potbelly and a long nose. He waddled when he walked, a red tracksuit zipped up to his chin. He looked like a sulky penguin in a Santa Claus suit. He might have been funny but he wasn't. He seemed emotionless, devoid of something human, like he could break your arms or eat breakfast, it didn't matter to him. He'd smashed the car window with a short crowbar and still had it in his hand. He hefted it, like he was considering whether to use it—on her or Freddie, it was hard to tell. Sulking, Komodo went into the kitchen area. He set the crowbar down and unplugged the toaster oven. Then he got a butcher knife out of a drawer and whacked off the cord.

"Fantastic," Freddie said. "How are we going to make waffles?" Komodo bound Ren's wrists together with the cord and sat her down in a chair. She didn't struggle or cry. *Save your energy, Ren. Wait for your moment.* Danger be damned. Her life and Jeremy's future were at stake. The idea of killing someone had never occurred to her. Could she do it? she wondered. Could she *kill* Freddie and Komodo? Shoot them? Strangle them? Stab them? Yes, she decided. If that was what it took to get her son back, she'd beat them to death with that crowbar.

Freddie had busied himself with the backpack. He put one of the plastic-wrapped bricks on the counter. He made a cut with a pocket-knife and withdrew a amount of white powder. He tasted it, shook his head. He looked at Komodo and shrugged.

"Impossible to say," Freddie said.

"Impossible to say what?" Ren said.

"How much this is cut and with what. Could be baking soda, bleach, rat poison, Rizzy powder."

"Rizzy powder?"

"It's a toxic substance used by florists to dye flowers," Freddie said informatively. "It eats away your skin. Leaves horrible scars."

"Oh," Ren said.

"But it's not Fentanyl I'm worried about. That's the bugaboo."

"Really?" Ren said as if she were really interested. *Engage him. Be appealing.*

"It's in every drug you buy on the street," Freddie said informatively. "It's cheap and a hundred times more potent than morphine. That's why there's so many ODs. It's a shame really. All those dummies have to do is try a sample but no, they shoot up the whole thing and kill themselves."

Be accepting, Ren. She tried to sound worried. "Does that concern you, Freddie? Is there a business reason?"

"Yes, I have a reputation around here," Freddie said, immodestly. "People know me as a straight shooter. Most of those I sell to are return customers. I want to get them high but I don't want to kill them. It's a question of degree. Did Zorro cut it a little or a lot? I have to know."

"That's very conscientious of you, Freddie."

"I've been doing this for fifteen years and law enforcement's never heard of me." There was a note of pride in his voice. "But a cluster of deaths might draw attention and suddenly I'm on their radar. Komodo? Why don't you get started?" Freddie said.

Komodo grumpily donned latex gloves and a surgical mask. He laid what looked like a plastic pegboard down on a card table. He spread two handfuls of empty half capsules on the board and shook it until all the peg holes were full. He poured the excess off. He took one of the bricks of heroin, opened it, and carefully spooned the powder over the tops of the half capsules. He used a kitchen scraper to push the powder back and forth until the half capsules were full. Komodo was efficient, his movements swift and sure.

"We use capsules," Freddie said. "That way, the customers are getting the same amount."

Ren didn't get it. Freddie's worried about Fentanyl but he's selling the heroin anyway? "What will you do if your customers start dying?" she asked.

"I'll warn them, of course," Freddie said. "Some might listen but most won't. Still, it would be nice to know."

Komodo did the same thing with another pegboard, filling the peg holes with the other half of the capsules and spreading the heroin around until they were full. He put an empty pegboard between them, making a kind of sandwich. He used his hands and pressed down on the top one, making sure he'd covered the whole surface. He took off the top one and removed the middle one. He turned it over and several hundred capsules packed with heroin spilled onto the table. "I have to pee," Komodo said, and he waddled away.

"Why do they call him Komodo?" Ren said. "He looks nothing like a Komodo dragon."

"Oh, it's not because of his looks," Freddie replied. "It's because of what he's done."

"Done?"

"I'd rather not get into it."

Ren and Jeremy watched a lot of animal documentaries. She remembered something and felt herself blanch. The Komodo dragon's primary source of food was carrion. *Carrion? You have got to get out of here, Ren.*

According to his vintage Patek Tiffany Rectangular watch, Marlowe had been walking for an hour and ten minutes. He'd trade the watch, the bespoke shoes and the sweater for a ride to Freddie's place. The value of expensive things just got transactional. He could do an hour and ten minutes on a treadmill in Jahno's air-conditioned gym. But this was rocky, sandy, gravelly, uneven ground and it was mostly uphill. Then there was the heat. He took off the sweater and hung it on a saguaro. The shoes were ruined. His T-shirt was soaked through. He took it off and wrapped it around his head. His back would get scorched but his face wouldn't broil. He wanted to stop and give up and share a burrow with a badger or a prairie dog. He finished the bottle of water. He thought about Ren. He thought about the two men. "Onward," he said.

Ren sat, her wrists bound with electrical cord. Freddie and Komodo were talking like conspirators, stealing glances at her. It was alarming but she'd made good with Freddie. *Stay calm, Ren. You're a guest, not a victim.* With sudden intent, the two men turned and came at her, grim but eager. *Oh my God, they're going to rape me!* Freddie got behind her. He put one massive hand on her forehead and tipped her head back. He got the other hand under her chin, his fingers squeezing at the joint where her jaws met. She was forced to open her mouth, the pain excruciating. Komodo was alongside her now. He had something in his fingers. He pushed it back in her throat, then forced a bottle of water into her mouth and made her swallow. They let her go. She choked and gagged; her nose was running.

"What did you do?" She coughed. "What was that?"

"Call it quality control," Freddie said.

Ren froze with shock. *They gave her a capsule.* Maybe more than one! "How could you do this to me, Freddie?"

"What? Did you think we were friends?" he scoffed. "Once you're unconscious we'll cut you loose. There's the possibility you'll vomit and suffocate and we wouldn't want that, would we? Komodo would be very disappointed."

Minutes went by, Ren didn't know how many. She was woozy, her vision darkening, her brain enveloped in warm oil, Jeremy swimming through it, looking for his mom. And then nothing.

It was dark. It was hard to see where he was going. Marlowe stumbled along, the brush snagging his clothes, the temperature dropping. He was sorry he'd ditched the sweater. He'd left the sureness of the road and cut overland, thinking he'd save time and distance. He was good at keeping his bearings but the thirst was making him dizzy and now he wasn't sure. Maybe he'd never get to Freddie's place. Maybe he'd slog on pointlessly forever. He was reminded of Hiroshi Teshigahara's

Woman in the Dunes, a film about a scientist captured by natives in the desert. The scientist was forced to live with a woman whose sole task in life was to endlessly shovel sand. Marlowe identified with the woman.

He reached Freddie's place, light-headed and exhausted. He wanted to sleep. He was on a rise above the property. The main entrance was at one end, where Freddie had emerged. A second entrance was at the other end, both lit by harsh spotlights. Marlowe didn't see Vlad the Doberman but he was there, probably near the main one.

Marlowe made a wide circle and approached the second entrance. Ren was in there. If they hurt her, Freddie and his friend were done. Marlowe got low and crept up to the second door. He stopped and listened, nothing so far. The door lock was simple and as old as the trailer. He found his wallet and slipped out the Visa card.

Ren woke up, face down on the sofa, one limp hand on the floor. It was dark. She was groggy and heavy-headed. Her clothes were intact, she hadn't been raped. She lay there for a while, getting her senses back. Her first thought was Jeremy. *You have to get out of here, Ren.* Polka music was coming from another room. Somehow, it seemed to fit with Freddie. She kept her eyes half closed. She heard Komodo crossing the room. He was humming cheerfully, tunelessly. He sounded barefoot, padding around the linoleum. He'd taken his shoes and socks off. *Oh, dear God.*

Komodo went past her field of vision. He was wearing red boxer shorts, his hairy paunch hanging over the elastic. His impossibly short legs were albino white, his feet more like fins. He was wearing a powerful cologne that smelled of overripe pineapples and a damp basement. Ren was afraid. And angry. Whatever happened, she vowed, this freak was not getting his penis back.

She lay still, Komodo still padding around. She heard him slide something hard off the table, and then he was in front of her. "Hey, you awake?" He had the crowbar, short, rusty, chips in the black paint. He poked her with it. "Hey, you awake?" She didn't move. He poked her harder. "Hey. I said are you awake?"

"What?" she mumbled. She opened her eyes and closed them again. She was far from normal but in control.

Komodo reached down and slapped her. "Wake up, goddammit!"

She groaned, rolled her eyes, pretended to get up but flopped back down.

He grabbed her by an arm, lifted her to her feet and slung her over the coffee table, knocking things off as she sprawled to the floor. The slap stung more than it hurt but it was demeaning.

You'll pay for that, you hideous dwarf.

"Komodo? Could you keep it down?" Freddie yelled from the bedroom. "Take her outside or something."

Marlowe slipped the Visa card between the door and the frame. He bent the card back toward the door lock until they were almost touching. That gave him more room to push the card in farther. His hands were trembling. He bent the card the other way, making it slip under the angled end of the interior latch. Then he put his left shoulder to the door and pushed hard while he moved the card back and forth. His outside foot slipped on the gravel, he grabbed the doorknob for support, the sounds as loud as an avalanche. Silence ticked by. No Vlad. *You're okay, Marlowe.* Then he heard the dog's galloping strides and savage barking. Marlowe ran down the side of the trailer, the dog turning the corner behind him. There was no protection, no trees to climb. The dog was closing the distance.

When Komodo threw Ren over the coffee table, she'd deliberately rolled over onto her back, her legs apart, knees bent, helpless, vulnerable, baiting him. She was far from herself but the adrenaline keyed her up. Komodo stood between her legs, chortling gleefully. He dropped the crowbar. *Big mistake, arsehole.* He reached down both hands, either to throttle her or pull her to her feet. She grabbed his elbows and yanked him into her as she raised both knees and slammed her feet into his gut. He wheezed, fell backward and hit his head on the corner of the table. She got up and let a moment of vertigo pass. Komodo was curled on the floor, bleeding profusely from the gash in his head.

"What are you doing out there?" Freddie shouted. He exploded out of the bedroom, so massive he blacked out the doorframe. He saw Ren, roared and charged headlong. There were numerous techniques for fending off an attacker but they could break down when your opponent outweighed you by a hundred and twenty kilos. *Knock his bloody block off, Ren.* She picked up Komodo's crowbar and hurled it like a tomahawk. There was an ugly metal-against-bone sound as the crowbar smashed into Freddie's face. He cried out, stumbled sideways and slammed into the wall.

The car keys, Ren! Where are his car keys? She raced into the bedroom, rifled through Freddie's clothes and found the keys. As she ran back to the living room Komodo barreled into her. They crashed to the floor, Komodo on top. She looked up at him; blood streaming through his hair, his beak open, red tongue squalling, screaming. He raised the crowbar to strike. *Jeremy, my Jeremy, I love you, my beautiful boy.*

Marlowe burst through the front door, slamming it shut, Vlad crashing into it behind him. Komodo was getting up. Marlowe kicked him in the rib cage and heard something crunch. Vlad was still outside, barking and scratching at the door.

"I have the keys to the truck," she said.

Ren got to her feet. Marlowe picked up the crowbar. He took her hand and led her through the length of the trailer to the second door. "Run for the truck. I'll be behind you." He opened the door and Ren took off. He followed her, walking backward, knowing he'd have to kill the dog. *You don't want to do it, Marlowe, but you have to.* Vlad appeared. The dog didn't charge, he stalked; his head low, eyes black and opaque, growling from deep within, a predator on the hunt. *You don't want to do it but you have to. You don't want to do it but you have to.*

"Hurry, Marlowe! Hurry!" Ren shouted.

He kept backing up. The dog was already in a trot. *Do it, Marlowe. Kill the dog!* He drew in a sharp breath, hand tensed on the crowbar. *Hit him in the head, Marlowe. Crack his skull open!* Vlad was charging, full speed, a black torpedo with fangs.

"Run, Marlowe! For God's sake, run!" Ren screamed.

I don't want to kill the dog, I don't want to kill the dog! Marlowe backed up, backed up, raising the crowbar, turning his hips for power. *What did Freddie say, Marlowe? What the hell did he say?* Vlad was about to launch himself—

Marlowe yelled, "*Sitz*, Vlad!" Miraculously, the dog came to a stop and sat down.

They drove the pickup to Castle Park and switched to Marlowe's Mustang. He drove fast to Zorro's house. There were no lights, no movement, no car in the driveway. Ren leapt out and ran to the door. She rang the bell five times and then banged on the door with her fist. "Zorro? Are you in there?" she yelled. "Open up, you son of a bitch!" Marlowe was in the car, watching. Ren's anguish was so painful, he lowered his eyes and looked at the speedometer. She was crying and cursing, ringing the bell and kicking the door. "Zorro? Lee Anne? Where are you? I know you're in there! Let me in!" She kept it up until she'd exhausted herself. Marlowe helped her back to the car.

The living room was white, curtains fluttering. Marlowe and Ren were on the sofa, his arm around her, her head nestled in his neck. "I don't know what to do, Marlowe. I have no reason to stay but I can't leave Jeremy here."

"Then stay."

"The semester is starting. I have to support myself, I have to pay the bills."

"What if I—" Marlowe began.

"Thank you, but no more charity and I can't stay here indefinitely. Not without a lead. I'll have to go home and earn enough to come back." She burrowed farther into him, tears spilling. They didn't speak, as if conversation would shorten their time together. Marlowe's brain was buzzing, racing, trying to think of something.

"You're an idiot, Marlowe," he said.

"What?" she said.

"I should've thought of it before. There's a way to find Zorro."

"Please, Marlowe, I understand you want to help but—"

"Emmet is a cop," Marlowe said.

"Yes, I *know* that." She was exasperated.

Marlowe dialed Emmet. They talked a moment. Marlowe gave him Zorro's address. He always remembered addresses.

Ren was completely frustrated. "What difference does it make?" she demanded. "Zorro is already gone!"

"Emmet can run it through the system. See if there's a name attached to the lease."

"Do you really think—?"

"Thanks, Dad," Marlowe said. He held out his phone and showed Ren a mug shot.

"Is this him? Is this Zorro?"

She was astonished, even joyful. "Yes! Yes, it is! Oh, thank you, Emmet! The next time I see you, you get a big kiss!"

"Emmet says thanks, but he'd rather you bake him a pie," Marlowe said. He handed her the phone.

"Zorro's real name is Zeke Rowdy," Emmet said.

"He's gone, Emmet. We'll never find him," she said.

"We're not gonna try. We'll find his wife, Lee Anne."

"But if she left with Zorro, how do we—"

"Sorry to interrupt, but I'm a detective, remember?" Emmet said, irritated. "Zorro knows Freddie will shoot Fentanyl into his forehead and Komodo will eat his carcass. If Lee Anne has any sense at all, she wouldn't have gone with him."

"Yes, but—"

"*Excuse me,* but I'm not finished talking!" Emmet barked.

"You can forget about the pie."

"Let me ask you," Emmet said. "Where would you go if you were scared, had no money and your old man left you?"

"Oh my God—"

Lee Anne's mom lived in Studio City. Emmet paid her a visit. When she opened the door, he held up his badge and said he wanted to speak to Lee Anne. The woman resisted, saying he needed a warrant to come in. Emmet said the entry was incident to an arrest and therefore he didn't need a warrant. A lie since Lee Anne wasn't wanted for anything. He also told the woman that if she didn't get out of his way, he'd arrest her for harboring a fugitive. Lee Anne came to the door, a cowering little thing. Emmet didn't like people who cowered, whimpered, sniveled or claimed they didn't do anything.

"I didn't do anything," she said.

"If you know something about Fallon, you better tell me now," Emmet said.

"I'm not supposed to say," she sniveled. "Zorro would kill me."

"I don't know if you've noticed, Lee Anne, but Zorro isn't here, and since Zorro is Zorro and not Superman, he can't hear you either."

"I'm afraid," she whimpered. Emmet could hardly keep from screaming.

"Oh yeah? Well, this is nothing," he said. "There are women in lockup who have tattoos on their tits that say, 'White girls are snacks.'"

Marlowe and Ren were waiting in the car. Emmet got in. "Fallon is working as an extra in the movies," he said.

"What movie?" Ren said.

"Lee Anne didn't know," Emmet said.

"Where's Fallon staying?"

"She didn't know that either."

"Did she know anything about Jeremy?"

"No," Emmet said. Ren closed her eyes.

"Thanks for trying, Emmet," she said. "I really appreciate it but I—" She broke down and cried. "I can't take this." She got out of the car. "I'll get back to the Marriott on my own."

"Fallon is an extra in the movies," Marlowe said, making a call.

"So what?" said Emmet.

Marlowe's call connected. "Hi, it's Marlowe. I'm trying to find someone named Fallon Stewart. He's working as an extra. It's urgent. Yes, that's all I know." He kept his ear on the phone, got out of the car and went after Ren. She was walking fast and he hurried to catch up.

"Wait—"

"No more, Marlowe." He took her arm and held it.

"George wants to speak to you," he said.

"Who's George?"

CHAPTER TWELVE
FLOWBEE

Zoya packed hurriedly, going up and down the stairs, carrying boxes and trash bags full of her stuff. Tato was probably looking for her right now. She was the only one who was close to Andy and "close" was the operative word. She didn't love him and he didn't love her. They understood each other. She used to believe him when he said he had a "fantastic new opportunity!" But Andy was a guy who thought an idea was the same thing as progress and that talking was the same as getting it done.

When he told her about the Russians giving TK Productions $150 million to launder, she said, "Uh-huh, do you want to order Thai food?" But it turned out to be true.

"You know the Russians don't play around, right?" she said.

"It's under control, babe," Andy replied. Always a bad sign. Things were never under control, she thought. It made no difference who you were or what you were doing, something could always go sideways. Her mom used to make ice cream in an ice cream maker. She followed the recipe down to the letter. The rock salt, ice, heavy cream, milk, sugar, tempering the eggs, the strawberry puree, cooling it to room temperature and so on. Her mother was an extremely careful person but sometimes the ice cream wouldn't freeze or it was icy or too loose or didn't resemble ice cream at all. Everything was like that, Zoya thought. You follow the recipe, do everything right and you end up with a bowl of strawberry shit.

When Andy's scheme actually worked, she forgot about the danger. It was actual money coming in, not her depressing, tax-riddled paycheck. *Of course,* Andy scammed the others. They knew he was a ruthless crook but they let him handle the money anyway. They deserved to be robbed for being so stupid.

And there was a lot of stupid to go around. Andy had the money converted to cash. She yelled at him, reasoned with him, pleaded with him to put it back in the account but he wouldn't budge. He said he liked to see it, feel it, smell it. That made it real and not some numbers on a bank statement. He said he kept the money hidden but didn't say where.

One night, they were going out to a party. Andy came over carrying a big suitcase and a bottle of champagne. What is this? she thought. Does he think he's moving in? She was all ready to go out, her suit was too tight, her whisker makeup was smudging and this asshole wasn't even dressed. She started to complain but he went into the bedroom and dumped the suitcase out on the bed. There were stacks and stacks of cash.

"I saw this in the movies!" He jumped on the bed and started rolling around. "Come on, babe, let's fuck!"

She told him hell no. The bills weren't new and a million nasty hands had touched them, and they all had grease, snot, drugs and STDs on them. Andy stopped rolling, called her a buzzkill and went to take a shower. She stared at the money piled upon her bed. She decided she'd better be nicer to him. She took off her clothes, popped open the champagne and got in the shower with him. They soaped each other up and she did everything she could think of. It was one of their understandings. You want something, you pay for it.

Only a few more things left to put in the car. *Hurry, Zoya!*

Cody was sitting on a bus bench across the street from Zoya's place. It was a dismal stucco house with rusty burglar bars and a cement lawn. As she sat there, she remembered something Terry used to say: "Don't expect the next thing, kitten, expect everything," though he never took his own advice. Cody never expected she'd be robbing

Andy's girlfriend at gunpoint. She felt the now-familiar heartbeat of real-life risk and real life and death. *Don't be a wimp, Cody. Think escape. Think freedom.* Zoya's car was in the driveway, the hatch was open, cardboard cartons stuffed in there. Cody nodded with satisfaction. Zoya was leaving town. She had the money, all right. There were gates on both sides of the house. Cody would have to sneak down the neighbor's driveway and climb over the fence into Zoya's yard. Given the amount of gang graffiti on the bus bench, sidewalks, stop signs and every other flat surface, that probably wasn't a good idea. The front door was the only option. She hoped Zoya didn't have a piece.

Cody had been to Zoya's once before. It was a couple of years ago. Andy had broken his ankle and was staying with her. Terry was bringing Andy another one of his hurried, shitty scripts. He said they read better on paper. Cody had an opinion about screenwriting. Write strictly for money and you're guaranteed to produce crap. Why? Because you're trying to anticipate what the studios want. You're thinking, how about *Clueless* meets *King Kong* or *Pretty Woman* meets *Napoleon Dynamite* and what you end up with is none of the above.

Zoya let them in. She looked like a bigger version of Lisbeth Salander, the character in *The Girl with the Dragon Tattoo*. Tall, thick, Gothy makeup, a nose ring, wearing a hoodie indoors. Terry left to find Andy.

"Could you get me some water?" Cody said.

"See that door? It leads to the kitchen," Zoya said. "In the kitchen there's a faucet. Turn the handle and water comes out."

"What's your problem? I just asked for water," Cody said.

"No, you expected *me* to get your water," Zoya countered. "You're an idiot, just like your old man." Cody thought Terry was an idiot too but that didn't mean this bitch could say it.

"Can I ask you something?" Cody said.

"What?" Zoya snapped.

"What kind of stupid, hard-up skank would bend over for Andy?

Don't you have any self-respect? You'd be better off humping a crack-head or a convict. At least you wouldn't catch something." Zoya stared a moment. Then she unzipped her hoodie and shrugged it off.

"I'm gonna kick your ass."

"Maybe," Cody replied. "But you'll know you were in a fight." She had no chance against this thug. Zoya came toward her, Cody backed up.

"Where're you going, bitch?" Zoya sneered. Cody's hard self arose. There was only one option. A dirty trick. She backed up more.

"You're not so badass now, are you?" Zoya said. "Come and take your beating like a man." Cody turned and ran into the kitchen. Had to be something in there.

"You got no place to go," Zoya said with a laugh. Cody saw what she wanted, grabbed it and when Zoya was right behind her, she turned and swung the meat mallet. Wooden handle, heavy metal head. It cracked Zoya across the clavicle. She spun around, hand on her shoulder, screaming.

"Not so badass now, are you?" Cody said, grinning. She hefted the meat mallet. "Come and take your beating like a man."

"Shit, Cody, what the hell are you doing?" Terry said. He was standing in the doorway with Andy.

"Hey, babe. You okay?" Andy said. Zoya was enraged. She snatched a kitchen knife off the counter and lunged for Cody.

"Whoa! Settle down!" Terry said. He stepped in front of Zoya and put his palms out. "Easy. You don't want to hurt anybody."

"I'll kill her!" Zoya shouted.

"Put it down, babe," Andy said. "You could go to jail."

Cody was restless, she'd been sitting on the bus bench for fifteen minutes. At last, Zoya came out with another box marked BLOUSES, TANK TOPS. She put it in the hatch and went back inside. The front door was open. *Go now, Cody.* She hurried across the street. Zoya had left the door open. Cody went inside, her right hand on the gun. She was in the foyer. She could hear Zoya rustling around in another room. Go back there? No. You don't know your way around.

You could look into the wrong room, give Zoya a chance to get away, give her a chance to grab a gun. You want her trapped with her hands full, Cody thought. Zoya would be the most vulnerable when she was carrying a box in both hands. Cody quietly shut the front door. Zoya would try to balance the box on one knee or set it down on the floor. Cody would come up behind her, stick the gun into the back of her head and tell her to lie down on the floor. She'd ad-lib the rest.

Cody stepped into the coat closet. It was musty, close and she smelled like old shoes. She kept the door open two inches. She heard Zoya come down the hall. She entered the foyer carrying a box. She saw that the front door was closed. "I left it open!" she fumed. She started to put the box down, Cody stepped into the foyer raising the gun. SLAM! The front door burst open, knocking Zoya to the floor. *Run, Cody! Move your ass!* She darted into the living room and ran down the hall. The kitchen was ahead, she could just see the back door. BANG! It was kicked open. A man came in. *Holy shit, it's Tato!* Cody did an immediate about-face, went back and peeked into the living room. No one was there. Zoya and the intruders were still in the foyer. Cody was between them. Footsteps coming down the hall. She hurried to the sofa, moved it slightly and squeezed herself between the sofa and the wall. She was lying on her side, her hands folded over her chest.

Tato, another man and the men from the foyer converged in the living room. The sofa's dust skirt ended about two inches from the floor. Cody could see their shoes. Zoya cried out as she was shoved to the floor. An old man was talking to her. He didn't yell, but he was intense, like he was holding back from killing her.

"Where is the money?" the old man said.

Zoya sobbed. "I don't know. Andy had it. I don't know what he did with it!"

The old man gave orders. One man to search the car, Tato and the other men to search the house. Cody felt their clomping footsteps through the floor.

"You had Andy killed, didn't you?" the old man said, a note

of admiration in his voice. "You had him killed and you took the money for yourself."

"No, I didn't!" Zoya cried. "I wouldn't kill anybody and I didn't know where the money was!"

The old man's shoes stepped closer to Zoya. "I know you, young lady, not you personally but young people like you. You think money is everything. Isn't it?" he said.

Cody thought, Yes, asshole, it is.

"Sure, money will buy things," the old man continued, "but not respect. Only envy."

What's the difference? Cody thought.

Tato came in. "I found something."

"That's not mine!" Zoya shouted, terrified. "I never saw it before!"

"Where did you find it?" the old man said.

"Under her bed."

The old man sighed. "Tell me, young lady, are you so rich you keep hundred-dollar bills under your bed?"

Zoya put her hands over her face and cried. "Andy brought the money here, but only one time. He—"

"Stop, go slower. What happened?" the old man said. "Leave out nothing."

Zoya took a breath. "I was really pissed. We were supposed to go to a party but he wasn't dressed and I was wearing a stupid cat suit."

"The money," the old man said.

"Andy had a suitcase, a big one. It was full of cash, like stacks of it. He dumped everything on the bed and said he wanted to have sex."

Tato and the other men were still searching the room. Cody heard things being smashed, kicked over and knocked down.

"What happened then? Did you go to the party?" the old man said.

"No. We celebrated. We had sex in the shower and got drunk."

"What happened to the suitcase?"

"I don't know. When I woke up in the morning, Andy was gone."

"Do you know where Andy took the money?" the old man said.

"I told you! I don't know!"

"You screwed in the shower and you were drunk but Andy told you nothing? I don't believe you. I don't believe anything you said. Who is your partner?"

"Partner? What partner?"

"The one who chopped Andy's head off," the old man said. "Clever. Only a vicious gang would do something like that."

"I don't have a partner," Zoya groaned. "I didn't have anything to do with that. I was Andy's girlfriend!"

"I see you are stubborn," the old man said. "Tato! Finish searching!"

Cody saw Tato's shoes coming toward the sofa. *Oh shit.* Tato grabbed the top of the backrest. She could see his big hand and his hairy arm. He started pulling the sofa away from the wall, wooden legs scraping on the floor. *You're done, Cody!* Someone banged on the front door.

"Open up, it's the police!" he roared. It was Emmet. "I've got a search warrant, open the goddamn door!" One of the men left and came back again.

"Shit! It's a cop! He's got his badge against the window!"

"We can go through the back," Tato said. The banging was louder.

"Police! Open up or we'll knock down the door!" Emmet yelled.

The old man and the others hurried down the hall and Cody heard them exit through the back door. She got up and went into the foyer.

"It's me," she called out. "You can come in, they're gone." Emmet entered, badge in one hand, gun in the other, Marlowe right behind him. Emmet looked around, everything torn up and broken. Zoya on the floor weeping.

"Yeah," Cody said. "It was tense."

They took the freeway south, heading back to Emmet's place. Cody was sitting in the back, seething. "You mean you guys were out there the whole time? Why didn't you come in sooner?"

"Because Zoya didn't have the money," Marlowe said.

"How do you know?"

"If you had two million dollars, would you take the time to

pack your shitty belongings in cardboard boxes?" Emmet said. Cody groaned and cursed and stamped her feet on the floor.

"Well, do you know who has it?" she demanded.

"Yeah, we do," Emmet said. "Roy's gun? Give it to me."

Marlowe drove. Yet another fiasco. It didn't seem possible. He considered stopping the car and throwing Cody off an overpass but that seemed a little extreme. He had to keep reminding himself that she was in serious danger. Tato was still out there and as far as Marlowe knew, the money was still missing. Roy was the attacker at Musso's. The man in the alley was Pav. Cody was right. But Pav's motives remained a question mark. Did he really try to kill Cody because Kendra told him to? That was shaky ground. But there was the tape to consider. Kendra and Pav talking about killing Terry. True, they had caught Cody eavesdropping but that had always bothered Marlowe. Kendra and Pav didn't know Cody had taped them. From their perspective, Cody's eavesdropping was mortifying but not really threatening. Cody's recounting what she'd heard while she was underneath the deck wasn't evidence or even something she could convincingly tell the cops. *That's right, Detective. My stepmother the movie star and her flunky said they killed Terry! I heard them! Honest, I did!* Something was definitely wrong but Marlowe didn't want to think about it anymore. He wanted to turn the car around and be with Ren.

Marlowe drove on. LA was an ugly city. It had no character, no texture, no architecture, nothing to engage you. LA was a hot, endless flatland of streets, telephone poles, strip malls, gas stations and dry cleaners. Some places were brighter and had taller buildings, but you could hardly call that charm, character or even interesting. Emmet didn't seem to mind. Marlowe had lived here all his life and had never once taken the long way home.

When Tato and the Russians escaped from Zoya's house, they ran out the back door, Grigory's men helping the old man along. They reached the rear of the property and a gate, the latch locked with a padlock. One of the Russians rammed it with his shoulder and ripped the latch out of the frame. They went through the gate and into the alley, but Tato stayed behind. He ran across the yard to a fence and clambered over it, landing in the neighbor's garden. He trotted down the side of the house, climbed the gate and reached the street. He looked around, no Russians, no cops. Were the men at the door really cops? Where were their sirens? Where were the cop cars?

Tato walked briskly to the end of the block, made a right, walked another block, made a left and stopped under a tree to rest. The Russians had taken his gun but that was all. He called a taxi, went to Staples and bought a briefcase. Then he went to his bank. He opened his safe-deposit box and found his emergency kit. Gun, ammo, money and a fake ID. He put them in the briefcase, bought a bottle of Patrón and rented a motel room. He took a shower and rested.

Tato had read about Andy's murder in *Asbarez,* the bilingual Armenian newspaper. How they found his body in the hills above Little Armenia. It wasn't Hzoy. It was someone who wanted it to look like Hzoy. Tato thought about it. When they were beating DeSallis he said Cody had the money. But if Cody had the money, why hadn't she left? Why was she with Marlowe? Tato sipped his tequila from a Styrofoam cup. He shook his head and muttered. He should have figured this out before. He had another sip and thought for a minute. He nodded with satisfaction. "Yes," he said.

"Why do you think Racine and Branko have the money?" Cody said. "They're as stupid as a goldfish."

"Andy was living with them," Marlowe said as he drove. "It's a small house, they must have been on top of each other. When I was there before, there was a car under a car cover. The car cover was new, the tires and rims were new. Where did those two find the money to buy a new car? Branko was wearing a new Rolex and he wanted sex all the time. That slug is suddenly a stud? Money can do that to you." They'd brought Cody along so she wouldn't cause another disaster. Emmet said she was like Godzilla, tramping through the city, kicking over buildings and stomping on people, bullets and rocket fire ricocheting off her.

"If they have the money, why haven't they left town?" Cody said.

"Racine is wearing an ankle monitor. She's on probation," Emmet said. "She can't leave town until sometime next week."

"That means Branko cut Andy's head off? I don't see it," Cody said. "I met him once. That slob couldn't chop firewood."

"Before Branko came to the US, he was a war criminal," Marlowe said. "His unit, Arkan's Tigers, fought in the Bosnian War. They killed, tortured and raped thousands of people. Cutting somebody's head off was probably no more difficult than stepping on a cockroach."

"Racine and Branko have the money?" Cody lamented. "That's *my* money. I earned it!"

"That's not your money and you didn't earn it," Emmet said. "You stole it. Earned means you worked for it."

"Right, that's what I'm saying. I worked my ass off."

They were a block away from Racine's house when they ran into a police roadblock. Barriers, flares, an ambulance, police cars with their lights flashing. An officer motioned for them to turn around. Emmet stopped the car, got out, showed the officer his badge. They talked briefly and Emmet came back to the car.

"Racine and Branko are dead. Someone shot them," Emmet said. "Neighbors heard a loud argument and then gunshots. They say a man came out carrying a cooler. He wore a hoodie, no one saw what he looked like. The guy put the cooler in the car and drove away. No one remembers the make of the car or the license plate."

"Had to be Tato," Marlowe said. "No one else who could have known about them."

"Wait a second," Cody said. "*Tato* has my money? What kind of bullshit is that?"

"I think it's great news," Emmet said.

"You earned it, Dad," Marlowe said.

"What are you talking about?" Cody whined.

"If Tato has the money then he's no longer after you," Marlowe said.

"*And,*" Emmet said. "This is the best part. You can go home!"

"No, I can't!" Cody protested. "Pav, remember him?"

"Kendra didn't send Pav to kill you," Marlowe said. "The only reason she'd do that is if you drank all the gin."

"You don't know that," Cody said. "You can't prove Kendra didn't send him."

"You can't prove a negative," Emmet said. "Tell you what. Prove the Flowbee isn't God."

"Okay, then," Cody countered. "What about the tape? You know, the one where Kendra and Pav talk about killing Terry? Did you forget about that?"

"Drive somewhere and pull over, Dad," Marlowe said. They settled on a 7-Eleven parking lot so Cody could get a Slurpee in a two-gallon plastic cup.

"Did I tell you I paid a visit to Nicole Wyatt?" Marlowe said.

"Really? What did that home-wrecker have to say?" Cody said.

"Nicole had a fire at her place," Marlowe said. "It was just after the Oscars. I saw the damage when I was there. The fire was deliberate but fortunately only damaged the deck. No one was hurt, but Nicole's Pomeranian was killed. The arson report says the cause of death wasn't the fire. The dog was hit with something like a rock or a brick."

"*So what?*" Cody said.

"The timing looks bad for you, kid," Emmet said. "Kendra finds out about Nicole's affair with Terry. Then she slugs it out with Nicole at the Oscar party and gets her ass kicked, and then Nicole's house catches on fire."

"I don't know what you're talking about," Cody said. "What does that have to do with the tape?" Marlowe got out his phone and played the tape. He and Emmet had listened to it five or six times.

Kendra: "...and knows..."

Pav: "Those investigators are...take the blame...your idea."

Kendra: "... be a baby... can't find evidence in... had to kill..."
Pav: "... take the blame... your idea."

Then, as before, they listened to Pav hacking and clearing his throat.

Kendra: "Do you have to ..."
Pav: "Yes, I have to!"
Kendra. "... glad you killed... little shit."
Pav: "We could still... trouble."
Kendra "... it's over... they're not going to ..."
Pav: "... How... know? You're not..."
Kendra: "... How do I... because it's nothing."

"You guys must be deaf," Cody said. "Take that to court and they'd be in jail right now."

"Sadly no," Marlowe said. "The first line. Where Kendra says 'fucking bitch.' Is that what she would call Terry, a bitch? In my experience, women very rarely call a man a bitch. That's what women call each other."

"You're reaching," Cody scoffed. Marlowe went on.

"Then Kendra says, 'I hope Terry is'—I hope Terry is what? I hope Terry is dead? I hope Terry is in hell? According to you, both those things have already happened. Kendra is talking in the present tense, as in, I hope Terry is hit by a bus. This recording was made *before* he was killed."

"Bullshit," Cody said. "I was there, okay?"

"And the last part of that line Kendra says, 'and knows,'" Marlowe said. "Emmet? Can you help us out here? The sentence is, 'hope Terry is, blank, blank, and knows.' Could you give us your answer, please." Emmet was smiling. Twenty years ago, he was a contestant on *Wheel of Fortune* and won $14,000. He had Pat Sajak's autograph.

"I hope Terry saw the fire and knows it was me," Emmet said.

"Oh, come on! You've gotta be joking!" Cody said.

"The next line is interesting too," Marlowe continued. "Pav uses the word *investigators.* Wouldn't he say cops or the police? What were you telling me, Dad?"

"The guys in the arson squad are called investigators."

"More bullshit!" Cody said.

Marlowe went on. "Kendra tells Pav not to be a baby, and then she says 'can't find evidence in.' Can't find evidence in what? Find evidence in the sand? The house? The car? What about it, Dad?"

Emmet yawned. "Kendra probably said something like, 'They can't find evidence in that pile of ashes.'"

"Unbelievable," Cody muttered.

"Then Pav has a coughing fit," Marlowe said.

"He had a cold! Or are you going to twist that around too?" Cody said.

"If Pav had a cold, he wouldn't be talking with Kendra," Marlowe replied. "She's a germophobe. Pav is coughing because he inhaled smoke."

Cody shook her head. "Is this what detectives do? Sit around and make shit up?"

"Then Kendra says 'Do you have to' and Pav comes back with 'Yes, I have to!' He shouts it because he's pissed off. He takes a huge chance setting fire to Nicole's house and Kendra complains about his coughing."

Cody was muttering bullshit, bullshit, bullshit.

"Then Kendra says, 'glad you killed ... little shit,'" Emmet said.

"Bingo," said Cody. "It's totally clear."

"Is that what Kendra would call Terry?" Emmet said. "A little shit? I don't think so. I think it's something you'd call a Pomeranian you just killed with a rock."

"This is so messed up," Cody breathed.

"Then Pav says, we could still be in trouble," Marlowe continued. "And Kendra replies, the police have come and gone and the case is over. If this is two days after Terry was killed, why would the case be over? Then Pav says, how do you know, and Kendra says it's nothing. Kendra is one of the most detestable people I've ever met but she wouldn't say Terry's death was nothing."

"But she might if it was petty arson," Emmet added.

Cody didn't reply. She looked out the window. "Can we get out of here, please?"

The following morning, Marlowe picked up Cody at Emmet's. He was taking her home. Emmet didn't feel anything like he thought he would. Like happy or relieved. He felt guilty about sending the girl away, but that made no sense. He'd done his best, stuck his neck out to a ridiculous degree, resolved what needed to be resolved and now she was returning home—not to the hood or the mean streets of Hollywood. She was going back to Malibu. It embarrassed him, but he was sad. He was actually going to miss her. Emmet couldn't believe himself. You're going to miss that spoiled, impulsive, sociopathic ingrate? What's wrong with you? Maybe ease up on the drinking.

Marlowe and Cody arrived in Kendra's driveway. Noah and Chris were there, washing a car. Cody immediately undid her seat belt and got out. She retrieved her backpack from the backseat and strode angrily toward the house, Noah and Chris watching her.

"What are you faggots looking at?" she said.

"Nothing. I'm looking at nothing," Noah said. Cody went in the house and slammed the door. Marlowe thought he should say something to Kendra so he got out of the Mustang.

"Hello, Mr. Marlowe," Noah said.

"Sorry to bring you bad tidings," Marlowe said.

"No worries. We pretend she's not here."

"Nice car. Yours?" Noah smiled and nodded. It was a new Nissan GTR. Glistening white, matte black trim, black wheels, probably five or six hundred horsepower. It was wretched excess but so was the Mustang. Marlowe had never seen this model before. The overall shape was clean and modern but he didn't like the cowcatcher front fascia or the taillights. Two circles, big and small, on either side of the trunk lid. They looked dated.

"Well, I guess we don't have to have our talk, Noah," Marlowe said. "A good thing for both of us."

"I think so too. Are you going in to see Kendra?"

"'Fraid so."

"Be strong," Chris said. "Do you have a weapon?"

Cody entered the foyer and dropped her backpack on the floor. Lucy appeared with her totally fake smile. *"Hola,* Miss Cody. *Esperaba que te comieran los perros salvajes o que Dios te hubiera asfixiado con una almohada."*

"You know I don't speak Mexican. What the hell are you saying?"

"I'm saying I'm very happy to see you," Lucy said, still smiling. "Kendra is on the deck. Guess what she's doing."

"Oh, dear God," Kendra said when she saw Cody. It wasn't an expression of welcome. It was more like something you'd say if you were stuck in a snowbank buck naked.

Kendra was seriously drunk, staring blankly at an empty pitcher of martinis. "Yeah, great to see you too," Cody said. "Don't you want to know if I'm okay?"

"What? Oh that, yeah, how are you, kid?"

"I nearly got killed twice, Marlowe was whipped with a bullwhip, his father had a fight with Roy and they almost shot each other and—oh yeah. An Armenian gang killed Terry."

"Is that so?" Kendra said with mild interest. Pav was leaning on the railing, glaring, all malice and contempt.

"How ya doin', asshole?" Cody said. "Don't you have to guard something? How 'bout the fridge? Lots of good stuff in there."

Kendra gazed mournfully out to sea. "You know I spent all that money on the party and not one call? No, that's not true. I got offered the leading role in a movie called *Lesbians for Sale* and what was that other thing? Oh yes. The part of the wife in a sitcom called *The Stupid Family."*

"Who's the dad?"

"Pee Wee Herman. Look, it's been nice talking to you, kid, but would you mind leaving me alone? Tell Lucy to mix up another batch and leave off the vermouth." Cody gave her the finger and left.

Marlowe came in, smiling broadly. "Nothing like reuniting a family. It's these moments that make it all worthwhile. Hi, Pav. You take care of Cody, okay? You're all she talks about. Well, Kendra, mission accomplished."

"And you know how that turned out," Kendra said. "Good thing I'm not paying you by the hour. I'd have to sell the house."

"I was hoping I could get my last check."

"The likelihood of you getting a check is the same as Mel Gibson playing golf with Shimon Peres. I'm not paying you a head of cabbage, you conniving, head-up-your-bunghole, double-dealing homunculus."

"I'm not a homunculus," Marlowe said. Kendra suddenly turned despondent, the famous blue eyes filling with what looked like real tears. "Kendra?" Marlowe said. "Are you okay or are you rehearsing for a part on *Days of Our Lives*?"

"Don't make fun. It's a real tragedy. You didn't get Cody here in time."

"In time for what?"

"The *Vanity Fair* mother-and-daughter interview," Kendra said. "Every star in the business wanted it. I heard Renée Zellweger was trying to rent a daughter."

Marlowe was flabbergasted. "*That's* why you hired me? To bring Cody back for an interview?"

"Of course. Why else would I want that ungrateful succubus around? Goodness knows she can fend for herself. If Tarzan were hunting for her, she'd trick the gorillas into tearing his head off."

"Once again, you move me beyond words," Marlowe said. "Such a big heart. If you opened it, a moth would fly out."

"I did a movie called *Maid Marian's Boyfriend*," Kendra said. "I got very good with a crossbow. I kept it as a souvenir."

"Interesting. Great story."

"If you ever come back here, you infected pustule, I'll put an arrow in your pee hole."

"What? No gratuity?"

* * *

Her room was the same, except dustier and there was a moldy smell. She opened a couple of windows and wondered why Lucy hadn't cleaned the place. Then she remembered telling Lucy she'd confiscate her green card if she ever caught her in here. Cody shoved the clothes off the bed and lay down. She still couldn't get over it. The whole escapade had come to exactly zero. And Eli still hadn't called. These were the darkest days. They needed each other even if he didn't know it, the asshole.

She slept and woke up late. She searched her room but couldn't find any weed. She needed to clear her head. Maybe some air would help. She took a baseball jacket from Noah's room and went out on the beach. The wind was up, her hair flying around, hands jammed into her pockets. There was chop on the water, the moon was full and bright, the waves nearly iridescent. She was there maybe two minutes when she realized she was shivering. This was a dumb thing to do, she thought. What are you, a poet? She turned to go and there was Pav, a snarl on his face.

"Jesus, Pav!" she yelled. "You scared the hell out of me!"

He was shirtless, cut muscles gleaming, moon-reflected eyes like mirrored sunglasses. He said nothing and held her gaze.

Don't back down, Cody. "What? Have you got a problem with that?" she said. She had to talk loud over the wind. No answer. "Aren't you gonna talk? Okay, fine, don't. Who gives a shit? You don't like me and I don't like you. Stay the hell outta my way and I'll—"

"Shut your mouth," Pav said, the words sizzling through his teeth. He was enraged, fists clenched like wrecking balls. He took a step toward her. She was terrified but held her ground.

"I'm not going to shut up," she said. "You're Kendra's concubine. Why should I—"

"SHUT YOUR MOUTH!" Pav shouted. The beach was deserted. Clouds passed over the moon, veiling and unveiling their faces. Pav took another step forward. She took a step back. She was showing fear but couldn't help it. "Do you know how long I knew Terry?" Pav said. "I met him when you were a skinny girl with a big mouth. Me and Terry were like brothers! I saved his ass and he saved mine. We did everything together! We drank together, we went fishing, soccer games, everywhere. We had fun. We talked all the time."

"That's great, Pav," Cody said, hugging herself, freezing. "I didn't know you and Dad were so—"

"Then you come along, a teenager," Pav spat. He kept coming closer, she had to back up. A wave came in, the water frigid, the white foam hissing around her ankles. "You are always around, like a mosquito," Pav said. "'Daddy, take me with you.' 'Daddy, show me how to do this.' 'Daddy, look at the present I made you.' You never stopped. You and Terry are together, I am left out. No more fishing, no more soccer, no more talking. Terry says, Sorry, Pav, I have to take Cody somewhere. Sorry, Pav, Cody needs me. Cody, always *Cody*!" He backed her farther into the water. Low waves hitting her knees and splashing up her back. Pav was crying. "Terry don't need me no more! My brother, he don't need me! He send me to Kendra! I work for her. She is crazy bitch! She cut my salary. She make me do anything. I am her slave!"

"I'm sorry, Pav, I really am!" she shouted over the waves. "I want to go in now!"

Another level of fury rose in Pav. "*You!* You put him with the Russians with their dirty money! Yes, I know! Terry was like a little boy. He didn't know what he was doing! You took advantage, you forced him!"

"I didn't do anything!" Cody screeched. The waves were more powerful, rolling into the small of her back, white plumes erupting on either side, the force pushing her toward Pav. "Pav, please!" She lost her balance, the water up to her waist. She'd die in a salty oblivion. Pav grabbed the front of the jacket and yanked her close. They were both soaked and dripping, their hair fanned across their faces. *He's gonna drown me!*

"You are a devil!" Pav said, shaking her. "You are evil! You got Terry killed!"

"No! No! I didn't do anything!" she screamed. Pav pulled her even closer. Close enough to feel his breath, close enough to kiss.

"You are lucky," he growled. "Lucky you are not already dead."

He walked away. She stumbled out of the water and fell to her knees on the sand.

The crew was waiting at Dima's apartment, Dima standing in front of the window, Viktor on the zebra-skin couch; Leonid was slouched on an easy chair upholstered in the same animal. They waited. Tato had called a meeting but he didn't say why. He came in carrying a cooler.

"What's this, Tato? Are we going on a picnic?" Dima said. The others chuckled.

Tato put the cooler on the floor, took off the lid and tipped it over. Bundles of cash tumbled out, each bound with blue strips of paper, marked $1,000, $5,000, $10,000. The crew rarely showed emotion unless it was drunken laughter. Eyes wide, dropped jaws, bowled over. Tato grinned.

"Two million," he said.

"The Russian money?" Dima said.

"Yes."

"How did you get it?"

"Doesn't matter. You are my brothers. Did you think I'd forget you?" Tato said proudly. "Come, take your money, two hundred and fifty thousand each. The rest is for me." No one argued. Dima went into the kitchen and brought back plastic shopping bags. The crew scooped up their cash, laughing like little boys. Tato watched, smiling and nodding with pleasure.

"Thank you, Tato," Dima said. "You are a great man." The others grinned and muttered their agreement.

"The Russians are after me, so I must leave," Tato said. "I hope you come up with me. No more arrests, no more prison, no more shooting. We would be free."

"What would we do?" Leonid asked.

"Whatever we want. Open a bar, a restaurant, lie on the beach, drink and get women. It's your choice. If you stay, I wish you luck. But I have one favor to ask before we go. It is a matter of honor."

"Anything, Tato," Dima said, and the others agreed.

*   *   *

The bell rang. Emmet checked the peephole and opened the front door. "What are you doing here?"

"Can I come in?" Cody said. She was scared and bedraggled, her hair damp, makeup smudged, paler than she was before, a network of red vessels in her eyes. "I don't have enough money to pay the cab." Emmet let her inside and paid the driver. When he returned, she was sitting on the arm of the sofa, arms folded across her chest, rocking back and forth.

"You won't believe what happened."

"You're probably right but let's hear it anyway."

They put Marlowe on speaker and she told them about the confrontation with Pav. "I was in the water, up to my armpits. I was freezing to death! I thought he was gonna drown me. He looked insane!" Badly shaken, she went on about Pav's torment, his hatred and his love for Terry. "The last thing that asshole said to me was, you're lucky you're not dead already! *Already*. Like he tried once and missed me!" She stopped, sniffled, waited for a response.

"Well, I'm glad you're not dead," Emmet said.

"You're glad I'm not dead?" She screwed up her face. "Well, do you believe me or not?"

"I don't know yet," Emmet said.

"Same," Marlowe said.

"What's wrong with you two?" Cody yelled. "Do I have to be a corpse before you believe me?"

"You have a checkered past," Emmet said dryly. "We're going to talk about it. Why don't you go to bed?" Cursing, she stomped out of the room and they heard her door slam.

Father and son were thinking the same thing. Cody's recounting wasn't an explanation of events; this happened, then that happened, then something else. This was a description of Pav's state of mind. His jealousy, his anger, his sense of abandonment, his hatred for Kendra and his need to punish. These were hard things to make up.

"If Pav really wanted her dead, why didn't he drown her?" Marlowe said.

"Too many questions," Emmet said. "Cody accidentally drowns on a beach in the middle of the night with her clothes on? Who was home at the time? What was their relationship? I'd have Pav locked up the same day."

"I think you're stuck with her for the time being," Marlowe said.

Emmet hesitated. He didn't want Marlowe thinking he was attached to the girl. "Yeah, I guess so."

The call ended. Emmet sat there, not knowing how he felt. He scratched his head. He kept his brownish-gray hair medium length. It was growing over his ears and touching his collar. He needed a haircut.

"You're joking, right?" Cody said. "*A Flowbee?* I thought they were toys."

"Are you going to help me or not?" Emmet groused. Cody was surprisingly enthusiastic. He hauled the upright Hoover out of the closet and rolled it into the bathroom.

"I don't believe it," Cody said, delighted. "*A vacuum cleaner?* Oh, this is the best!"

Emmet got out the Flowbee. It was an old one, scratched and dusty, the hose patched with plumber's tape. Emmet took off the vacuum hose, put on the adapter and replaced it with the Flowbee hose. Then he plugged the AC adapter into the hose attachment and fit the cutting unit to the other end of the hose. There was a small squeeze bottle of oil and he put a few drops on the cutting blades.

"How convenient!" Cody laughed. "What's next? New tires? A propeller?"

"You take one picture and I'll lock you in the garage," Emmet said. He sat on a stool in front of the mirror. "Put the apron on," he said. Cody unfolded the barber's apron with a flourish and tied it around his neck. She was so excited she was jumping up and down.

"Take it easy, will you?" Emmet said. "I don't want to look like the village idiot." He explained to her how it worked. The cutting unit sucked in the hair, the blades inside cropping it to the exact same length.

"Have you got it?" Emmet said. He was afraid she'd mess it up on purpose.

"Yeah, yeah, I've got it," she said. The bathroom was small. The Hoover, the hose, wires, stool and Cody made it seem like they were locked in a junk closet. Cody turned on the vacuum cleaner and then the Flowbee. The noise was like being inside a leaf blower. Emmet had never noticed it before.

"Holy shit, it's loud!" Cody shouted.

"Do the top first!" Emmet said, shouting back. "Be careful, goddammit!" With the concentration of an eye surgeon, Cody ran the cutting unit from the top of Emmet's head down to his forehead, leaving a stark, shaven path, his white scalp in sharp contrast to his hair.

"That's pretty short, Emmet," Cody said, dismayed. "Is this the way you want it?"

"Oh no! Oh no!" Emmet yelled. "I forgot the extensions!" There were plastic extensions that fit over the cutting unit to control how much was cut off. Emmet stood up, cursing, yanked off the apron and jerked the AC cord out of the wall. He stared at the mirror, appalled and incredulous. Cody was in absolute hysterics.

"That's a great look, Emmet!" she whooped. "It's like a landing strip on a football field!" He stared at himself. And stared at himself. And then he smiled. Then they were both laughing, both in hysterics. When they'd finally stopped and caught their breath, they sat down on the edge of the tub, exhausted.

"What do I do now?" Emmet said.

"Cut the rest. Nothing else to do." She cut the rest. It was laborious. She hurried, it was hot, he closed his eyes.

"All done," she said. "Actually, you look better."

"No, I don't."

"No, you don't," Cody agreed. She kissed the top of his head and left. The kiss lingered. It made him inexpressibly sad.

Emmet went outside and brushed the hair off his neck. He didn't regret hacking the front yard to pieces. Actually, it seemed right, the way it should be, like a rain forest mowed down by a Gatling gun. The air was chilly on his cropped head. It would be a while before it grew back. Addie used to cut his hair. He'd watch her in the mirror; moving the Flowbee around, appraising, seeing if the angles were straight or if she'd missed anything. Or she'd look at him in the mirror and smile. Emmet was marooned on an island of loneliness. He missed Addie every day. Ached for her every day. He was sorry every day.

CHAPTER THIRTEEN
URTLE THE TURTLE

Central Casting was the leading company for casting extras in LA. It wasn't hard to become a client. You submitted a current photo and some background information and waited for something to come up. There were ads on the website like:

> *Producer seeking AFRICAN AMERICAN men and women who appear in their late twenties, portray upscale patrons at a Hollywood bar. No visible tattoos please.*

> *Producer seeking ACTUAL COUPLE to portray MARRIED SENIOR CITIZENS.*

Central Casting sent extras to projects shooting all over Southern California. George Bamford called the CEO of the company and explained the situation with Ren. The CEO called back and said the office had checked and Fallon was one of their clients. Day after tomorrow Fallon would be at Warner Brothers, Studio 4, at five o'clock. They'd have passes waiting for them at the gate. Somebody from the studio would be there to direct them.

Marlowe and Ren had dinner at La Rose Cafe, excellent Filipino food. They ate roast pork, marinated milkfish and salads. The mood was somber. George brought them good news but only of a sort.

True, Fallon would be at the studio, but he wouldn't have Jeremy with him. He would make her beg. He would humiliate her. Marlowe told Ren about Cody's confrontation with Pav.

"Was Pav the man in the alley?" Ren asked.

"It's looking like it. We didn't have a motive before and now we do."

"How would you go about catching him?" Ren asked.

"We can't. The crime's already done. Pav would have to try again and we'd have to catch him in the act. That's not going to happen."

Ren was somber, pushing the food around with her fork. Thoughts of Jeremy, no doubt. She probably felt guilty for being here. She'd tried so hard to find him. It worried Marlowe. If she was desperate enough to deliver heroin to a drug dealer she'd do anything. He wished he could do something right now; cheer her up, get her mind off her troubles, even for an hour or two.

"We're going out," he said.

"Out where?"

"You'll see."

"I'll see? What if I don't like it?"

"If we get there and you want to leave, we'll leave."

He took her to La Descarga, his favorite salsa club, on Western near the Hollywood Freeway. There were plenty of nightclubs in LA but most were places to be and be seen, not dance. La Descarga had a Cuban theme. A warm, butterscotch glow lit the room, dark polished woods, sparkling liquor bottles displayed in rounded arches, a mezzanine floor with a fancy wrought-iron railing. It might have been a private club in Havana, Marlowe thought. There was even a cigar room.

A live band played salsa music; tireless beat, all trumpets, bongos and cowbell, the dancers near frenzied, a blur of swinging hips, swirling turns, waving arms and elbows. The atmosphere was fun, happy, people were having a good time, not straining to strike a pose.

"This is fabulous," Ren said as they came in.

"One of the best things about the place is the dress code," he said. The men had their shirts tucked in, many wearing sport coats. Not a hoodie, T-shirt, cap or pair of sneakers to be seen.

"I just thought I'd mention this," Ren said, "I don't know how to salsa."

"We're not going to salsa. We're dancing the bachata."

Salsa, Marlowe explained, is fast-paced, forward and back, quick turns and patterns. Salsa takes up floor space. Navigating through a crowd of other dancers is a skill unto itself. Bachata is slower, the movements more side to side. You stay more or less where you started. Salsa is fun party music. Bachata is more sensual, more seductive. You hold the woman close, your entire bodies touching— not completely necessary but Ren didn't know that. He showed her the steps and basic turns and she caught on very quickly. There's lots of grinding and bumping groins in bachata, not completely necessary but Ren didn't know that.

"Is this really part of the dance?" Ren said.

"Definitely. It's fundamental."

"And the simulated coitus?"

"Also fundamental."

"Am I supposed to have both my arms around your neck?"

Their foreheads touched. They were enclosed in a curtain of Ren's hair. It seemed to block out the music, their eyes and lips inches apart. She kissed him.

"Also fundamental," she said.

They danced until they were sweating and their hips were exhausted. They came out of the club, Ren refreshed, Marlowe a tad overstimulated.

"That was brilliant, Marlowe. Thank you so much," Ren said.

"You're a great dancer."

"I certainly am not. You, on the other hand, are an obscene dancer."

"That's the way I was taught."

They walked to the car. The air was hot and muggy, but it felt like a spring breeze in the Swiss Alps. She took his arm. They stopped at an intersection and she put her head on his shoulder.

"You've been so good to me, Marlowe. I'd like to do something for you." He swallowed hard.

"Um, that's not necessary." *Oh please, please do something for me.*

"It's a little presumptuous."

"Presume all you want," he croaked. *Are you wearing the boxer shorts Emmet gave you for Christmas that say NUT CANNON?*

"I don't want to interfere with anything," she said. *She's asking if you have a girlfriend.*

"Interfere?" he answered quickly. "No, nope, no interference. Clear sailing all the way."

"If you say no, it's perfectly fine, I understand." *Unless I'm a eunuch and didn't know it, I'm not gonna say no.*

"Uh, yes, I mean affirmative—to, um, whatever you're suggesting… whatever that may be." *Way to be smooth, Marlowe.*

"I'd like to be the bait," Ren said.

"The bait?"

"I think you should set a trap for Pav and I'll be the bait."

It took a moment to recover. "Well, um, that's an interesting idea." He pushed the cross button needlessly. "The light's taking forever to change."

Marlowe drove to the Marriott and stopped the car in front of Ren's room. Neither of them moved, both looked straight ahead, the engine huffing like a waiting train.

She turned to him. "Thank you for a wonderful time. I can't tell you how much I appreciate this. Helping me with Jeremy. It's so all-consuming. Like my life has no meaning unless I get him back." Her face brimmed with yearning and sorrow, and he imagined he looked that way too.

"I'll see you tomorrow," he said.

"Yes, Marlowe. I'll see you tomorrow."

Marlowe called Emmet and told him about Ren's offer.

"She might have something there," Emmet said.

"I thought you'd say it was crazy," Marlowe said. "Catching Pav in the act? It's not possible."

"Let me think about it," Emmet said.

"Forget it, Dad. It's a bad idea. I shouldn't have called."

"I *said*, let me think about it."

Two hours later, Emmet called and explained his plan. Marlowe was appalled. It was clearly too risky, bordering on foolish. They'd be breaking a litany of laws. They could be shot or arrested and Emmet's return to the force would be over. Marlowe argued with Emmet but got nowhere. Marlowe was confused. His father was very safety-conscious, especially when it came to police operations. He wouldn't do something like this even if it were official.

"Dad, this makes no sense," Marlowe said. "We'll take him down some other way."

"I'm doing it," Emmet said, like there would be no argument.

"That's nuts, and it wouldn't work anyway. There's too many moving parts, too many assumptions."

"What if Pav tries to kill Cody next week or a year from now?" Emmet argued. "If there's a chance to take him out now, we should do it—don't argue, son. We'll do it in steps. If step one doesn't work, we'll stop. If it does work, we'll go on to step two. That safe enough for you?"

"No, actually, it's not."

Part one of Emmet's plan, call Kendra. "What is it, Marlowe?" Kendra snapped. "Did you forget to charge me for mileage? Do you want to bring a mime to dinner or use my house for your syphilis support group?"

"I've heard the tabloids are sniffing around," Marlowe said. "Rumor is, you were going to marry your bodyguard, Pav, but he ran off with Cody and they got married in Vegas, *and*, you hired a hit man from Colombia to kill them both. It's getting traction, Kendra."

He heard Kendra choke on her martini. *"What?"*

"Cody's friends haven't seen her, the neighbors haven't seen her," Marlowe went on. "They've seen Pav but, according to the rumor, he only came back to get his things and give you a farewell shtup."

"Bastards!" Kendra said. "I can't believe I'm saying it, but you have to get Cody back! She has to show her face to the press!"

"I figured that," Marlowe said. "I found her. She's with me right now."

"Then bring her home immediately!" Kendra said.

"Here's the problem," Marlowe said. "When Cody was there before, you weren't very nice to her."

"What are you talking about?"

"Apparently, you were your usual offensive, obnoxious, narcissistic self and Cody doesn't want to come home for that."

"I see," Kendra said. "So, I'm offensive, obnoxious and narcissistic and Cody is what? Rebecca of Sunnybrook Farm? She's more like that girl in *The Exorcist* who vomited on the priest."

"Do you want her to come home or not?" Marlowe said.

"Yes, yes, I want her to come home."

"Cody will be there tomorrow if you promise to be nice. Not a lot, just a little. Just so she doesn't feel like she's walking into a meat grinder when she comes through the door."

"All right! Fine!" Kendra shouted. "I'll be the best mom anybody ever had. I'll help her with her homework! I'll wear an apron and make her fudge! How's that? Just bring that horrible little trollop home."

"Give me a second. I'll talk to her." Marlowe held the phone to his chest for a moment and came back. "Okay. Tomorrow for sure. She's staying at the Sunshine Court at Fountain and Ohio, room fifteen."

"Why don't I send Pav right now?" Kendra said.

"Cody said she's going out tonight," Marlowe said. "Won't be back until one or so. Do you want to talk to her?"

"God, no," Kendra said. "Bring her home tomorrow morning, Marlowe, and don't screw this up." The call ended.

"That wasn't easy, was it?" Emmet said. "On to step two."

"This is Ren's part?" Marlowe said.

"Yeah. And she couldn't get hurt if she wanted to."

A little after one a.m., an Uber dropped Ren off at the Sunshine Court Motel. The Sunshine was the worst motel in Hollywood and Hollywood had a lot of terrible motels. It was like a dying sewer rat amid a crowd of healthy sewer rats. Ren was wearing Cody's clothes and her backpack, hair tucked under a cap. They were both slender and were close to each other in height. She went into room fifteen and closed the door behind her.

Everything in the room was decrepit. The lights were off. Emmet was in the armchair, his feet up on the coffee table, dozing. Cody was on the sofa, knees curled under her, doing something with her phone.

"Shit. I was hoping you'd be in an accident," Cody said.

"Me too," Ren said. Emmet woke up, blinked the sleep out of his eyes and said, "Good you got here. You look great." Emmet texted Marlowe. *Step 2 over and done.*

"Off you go, ladies," Emmet said, nodding at the interior door. Earlier in the day, Emmet had rented rooms thirteen through seventeen. Fifteen and fourteen were adjoining.

Ren entered fourteen, Cody behind her. "Don't turn on the light," Ren said.

"I know, okay?"

They did rock-paper-scissors to see who got the bed. Ren won. She looked at the dingy comforter. Put a UV light on it and the whole thing would glow. Maybe there were fewer pathogens on the sheets. Ren pulled the comforter off and lay down, head resting comfortably on the pillow. She thought about Jeremy. Photos against the backs of her eyelids. Jeremy. A tiny newborn nestled in her arms, in a high chair, pudding all over his face, his first tottering steps across the green lawn, wowed by his birthday cake, sleeping with the dog, digging in the sand. Ren's favorite. Jeremy on his mother's lap. They're touching each other's nose, the boy gurgling happily, mom smiling lovingly, as happy as she's ever been. Tomorrow they'd meet Fallon at Warner Brothers. Waiting was agony.

"I should get the bed," Cody sulked.

"You lost. Stop whining."

Cody went to the window, moved the curtain aside a few inches. She couldn't see anything but a narrow strip of the parking lot. Emmet had insisted Cody come along. If she was alone, she might screw up something else.

"Close the curtain, Cody," Ren said. "We're supposed to be sight unseen."

"I'll close the curtain when I'm good and ready."

"You're being ridiculous. If Pav sees you, we'll have done everything for nothing, and by the way, he wants to kill you, remember?" Cody hesitated. "Did you hear me? He wants to *kill* you," Ren said. "Perhaps you might remember the alley, when he almost shot you in the back?"

Cody sulked a moment and shoved the curtain shut. "I still should get the bed."

Emmet had taken care of the details. He put a broken bottle of vodka right outside the door of room fifteen, the cement was still wet. The curtains were parted slightly. The lights were off but the TV was on. You could see a half-empty bottle of vodka and another of Kahlúa, Styrofoam cups and a well-used bong on the coffee table. Cody's handbag hung over a chair, shoes and trash on the floor. A human figure was in bed, covered with the blanket. It was a plastic sex doll with a round mouth as if it were saying *oooh*. Marlowe had borrowed it from Basilio. Marlowe asked no questions and imagined no scenarios.

There were two video cameras in the room, disguised as a water bottle and a clock radio. Both had Wi-Fi, motion sensing, DVR and audio. Marlowe had a collection of them. Emmet was in the bathroom, waiting for a text from Marlowe. The front door was unlocked, the chain undone.

Step three: Pav's arrival. Dicey at best, thought Marlowe. Did Kendra tell Pav that Cody was staying at the Sunshine? Maybe the confrontation in the ocean was enough for Pav. Maybe he didn't care anymore. Maybe he had better things to do.

Step four was a doozy. The scenario Emmet hoped for was this: Pav approaches room fifteen, sees the broken bottle and the spillage. Then he peeks in the window and sees Cody asleep; the liquor and bong indications that Cody has passed out. Pav brings something to get in the door or maybe he kicks it in. Best case, he'd turn the knob. There were a bunch of wet towels behind the door to slow his entry.

Step five was a bigger doozy. While Pav was struggling to get in, Emmet would come out of the bathroom in his LAPD windbreaker and Sig Sauer yelling, "Police! Drop your weapon!" or some variation thereof. Emmet was wearing Level IIIA body armor and his marksmanship was a point of pride. Before he started drinking in earnest, he aced the police qualifying course every year. The course was very demanding, even the instructions were hard.

> *Fire 6 rounds in 8 seconds on the 12-yard line. Start in a two-hand Low Ready. When the targets turn, fire 2 rounds on the right target, 2 rounds on the left target, and 2 rounds on the right target. Perform a tactical reload with the 5-round magazine and holster.*

As soon as Pav went through the door, Marlowe would be right behind him with a gun, also yelling. Step six: They'd put Pav on the ground, cuff him and tell him to shut up. In Emmet's estimation it should take seven seconds without a shot fired. Emmet didn't intend to arrest Pav. If things went as planned, they would have a tape of him slipping into a girl's motel room with a gun. He'd either have to leave Kendra's employ or they'd show the tape to the police and Kendra, not that she'd care.

Marlowe was in a rental car, parked in the motel lot. He was hunched down, watching the scene in his mirrors. The only light was from the orange motel sign and a streetlight at the end of the block. There were two other cars in the lot, the guests had rooms on the second floor. The longer Marlowe sat there, the more foolish he felt. If one little thing went wrong, he'd call it off no matter what Emmet said. He hoped Pav wouldn't show. "Stay home, Pav," he said aloud.

Cody sat on the floor in room fourteen, with her back against the wall. She was tired of looking at her phone, always looking at her phone, always *looking at her goddamn phone*. Whichever way this turned out, she wouldn't get what she wanted. Escape. Freedom. The more she thought about it, the angrier she got. At anybody who'd ever stood in her way, slowed her down or made her feel small.

Cody looked at Ren, comfortable, asleep, lying on her side, head on the pillow, arms curled in front of her. That bitch humiliated you, Cody thought. She slammed you to the ground. She hurt you. And after tonight you'll never see her again. *Make her pay, Cody. Make her pay.* She stood up, crept over to the bed. Ren looked so peaceful. Where would be the best place to hit her, the head? No. She didn't want to cause permanent damage and she didn't want bleeding. What Cody wanted was sustained, incapacitating pain. She thought a moment and remembered something.

Cody was at Bar Sinister with Eli and worried about Afro Girl. She was clinging to his arm. She hated herself for being afraid but she couldn't help it.

"What if she's here?" Cody said.

"What if she is?" Eli said. "One punch and you could take her out completely. No blood and you won't bust your knuckles either."

"How?"

"You hit her right here, bottom of the rib cage, right side." He put his finger on the spot. "The pain is unbelievable and you can't breathe."

"Is there a name for it?" Cody asked.

"Yeah. It's called a liver punch."

The pain was a rusty railroad spike driven into Ren's side. She doubled over and rolled off the bed. She lay curled on the dirty carpet, writhing, convulsing, the oxygen blown out of her lungs, the spike twisting and going ever deeper, a Klaxon horn braying inside her skull. She inhaled in gasps, a molecule of air at a time. She heard a voice, barely audible over the torment.

"How you doin', Ren?" Cody said from above. "You look a little under the weather."

Marlowe saw movement in his side mirror. A man was at the edge of the parking lot, partially hidden by a hedge. He wasn't a passerby; he was too still. Marlowe texted Emmet. *Pav is here.* The man came out of hiding and looked around. He was wearing black and a ski mask. He looked strong and athletic like Pav. He was similar in height and weight. Pav went quickly to the walkway that fronted the rooms. He hunched down and moved underneath the windows. Marlowe texted Emmet. *1 minute.*

Ren was on her knees, her head down, arms around her middle, gasping with her mouth open, the pain slashing her insides.

"What happened to the old jujitsu?" Cody said. "You should have hung in there, gone for the black belt." Ren had never wanted to kill before. It was a liberating feeling. *No rules, no nothing, Ren. It's war.*

Ren looked up at Cody, bleary through the tears. Cody was on the bed, head cupped in her hands, kicking her feet, smiling impishly like a teen star from the fifties.

"I know, I know, you want to kill me," Cody said. "How 'bout we do it tomorrow? We don't want to scare away Pav, do we?" Ren's breathing was returning but she kept gasping. The oxygen was circulating. She felt partially restored. She put one hand on the bed table for support and held the other hand against her chest.

"Help me up," she wheezed.

"The only thing I'd help you do is die," Cody said.

Ren coiled into herself. She was on her knees. The power would come strictly from her core. Throw a punch from the shoulder and you telegraph it.

"I can't...catch...my breath," Ren said.

"Yes, that can be a problem," Cody said. "How about a nice cup of soup? Oh damn. We're all out of soup."

Ren snarled and hit Cody with a short, quick punch to the face, her knuckles crushing cartilage. Cody cried out, "Oh shit! You broke my nose!" She swiveled on her belly and tried to crawl off the bed. Ren lunged onto Cody's back and held her down. She wasn't at full strength. Cody was wriggling free. "Get off me, you cunt!" she shouted. Cody was slipping out of Ren's grasp. Half her body was off the bed, her hands were on the floor. *She's getting away, Ren!*

"I'm not done with you, Cody," Ren growled. She lunged forward, grabbed a handful of Cody's hair and yanked.

Marlowe watched Pav sneak past rooms ten, eleven and twelve. Another text to Emmet. *30 sec.* Marlowe tensed, one hand gripping the car door, the other hand on his gun. Pav reached room fifteen. He was holding a pry bar. Marlowe sent another text. *At the door.* Pav slowly turned the knob—it was open. You could see his surprise. He started to go in, pushing against the towels behind the door. *Emmet's plan is actually working!* Pav put one foot inside. A woman's scream can pierce a traffic jam, a gunfight or a forty-piece orchestra playing "The Star-Spangled Banner." Pav didn't hesitate. He ran.

"Aww hell," Marlowe said. He scrambled out of the car. Pav reached the edge of the lot, glanced back and saw him. He turned the corner onto Ohio and was gone. Marlowe raced after him, turning the same corner. He saw Pav running down the street. *Jesus, he's fast.* Suddenly, Pav stutter-stepped to a stop, turned sharply, ran down a driveway and disappeared into the dark.

Marlowe arrived at the driveway. Going after Pav was foolhardy. The man had a gun. Marlowe made a calculation. Pav probably ran through the yard, got over the fence and into the alley. Where would he go from there? To his car. But where was the car parked? Not farther down Ohio. Pav would have parked it closer to the corner, closer to the Sunshine. *Pav's car is behind you,* thought Marlowe. Between where you're standing and the corner. To get there, Pav would have to go down the alley to Fountain, then circle around to Ohio.

Marlowe jogged to the corner. He stepped into a shadow, drew his gun and waited. He couldn't arrest Pav, but he could put a scare in him and keep him off Cody. Marlowe heard Pav coming. He got in position, holding his gun with two hands, ready to step out in front of him. Pav's footsteps were still some distance...getting louder...closer...and then they stopped. A car door opened and slammed closed and a powerful engine rumbled to life, tires squealing.

"You're a dope, Marlowe," Marlowe said.

Pav hadn't parked on Ohio, he'd parked on Fountain, the next block over from the Sunshine. Marlowe turned the corner in time to see the car's taillights driving away. They were round, fuzzing into a red glow and disappearing.

Emmet came out of the bathroom, crossed the room and swung open the door to fourteen. It looked like feral hogs had been fighting. The TV screen was shattered, the curtains ripped down, the chair and nightstand knocked over, clouds of feathers floating around, blood on everything. Cody was on the floor, screaming into the pillow Ren was mashing into her face. "Will you shut up now?" Ren shouted. *"Will you?"* Emmet picked up Ren by her armpits and dragged her off.

"What the hell is wrong with you two?" Emmet hollered. "You screwed up the whole ball game!"

"That girl is *Satan*!" Ren screamed, spit flying out of her mouth. She took another lunge at Cody but Emmet held her back. Cody sat up, sputtering, feathers in her mouth.

"I'm gonna kill that bitch! She tore my hair out!" she screamed. There was a bald patch on the side of her head and her nose was swollen. She took a swing at Ren. Marlowe appeared. He wrapped an arm around Cody's waist and picked her up. She kicked and flailed, the two women cursing at each other.

"This turned out well, didn't it?" Marlowe said.

The owner of the Sunshine Court, Mr. Kwang, wanted $1,500 for the repairs. Emmet offered him $300.

"You cheat me!" Mr. Kwang hollered.

"For three hundred dollars you could remodel the whole goddamn place!" Emmet hollered back.

"I call the police!"

"You don't have to," Emmet said. "I'm standing right in front of your ugly pie hole. Four hundred. Take it or you get nothing."

Ren was upset and didn't want to talk. She called a cab and went back to the Marriott. Cody and Emmet were outside somewhere. Marlowe surveyed the wreckage in room fourteen. He was puzzled. When Cody screamed, that should have been enough to get Emmet running over here. But judging by the extent of the damage, Emmet was late by at least a couple of minutes. Where had he been?

Marlowe went out to the parking lot. He saw Emmet with his hands on his knees, puking all over the azalea bushes. Marlowe was so disgusted he felt like puking himself. Emmet finished, wiped his mouth on his sleeve.

"Yeah? What about it?" Emmet said. "I didn't mess this up. Those two lunatics did."

"What if Pav had gotten inside?" Marlowe said. "You were too drunk to do anything but take a bullet in your chest." Emmet turned and walked away, Marlowe on his heels, his long-held fury breaking free.

"When Addie had cancer, you were drinking," he said.

"This again?" Emmet scoffed. "Addie never knew."

"Addie knew everything. Did you really think you could fool her with breath mints and vodka? Fool *Addie*?"

Emmet stopped and turned. "Get over it, will you? Cancer killed her, not me!"

"You didn't kill her, Dad, but you sped things along!"

"That's a goddamn lie! I didn't do anything!"

"That's right!" Marlowe shouted. "You didn't do one damn thing! How many times did you come to visit your dying wife, Emmet? Do you remember? In six weeks, you visited her four times! *Four,* Dad! You were married for thirty-three years and that's all you could give her?"

Emmet wilted, his chin dropped to his chest, tears running from his eyes. "I couldn't stand to look at her," he sobbed.

"But she could look at you! You goddamn coward! She asked me over and over again, Where's Emmet? What's he doing? I want to see him. Where's Emmet?"

His father backed away. "Stop, please stop!" Marlowe walked after him, relentless.

"Where were you the night she died, Dad? Huh? Where were you when Addie asked to see her husband one last time?"

"I couldn't go...I couldn't."

"You couldn't go because you were drunk! Because you were at the bar, lying in your own vomit on the men's room floor." Emmet kept backing away. He stumbled and nearly fell down.

"I'm done with you, Dad!" Marlowe yelled. "I don't want to see you, hear your voice or read your goddamn handwriting! You're out of my life!" Marlowe whirled around and headed to his car. Cody was sitting on a parking block.

"Come on. I'll take you to my place," Marlowe said.

"No. I want to stay with Emmet."

As Marlowe drove away, he saw Emmet, standing in the same spot, his hands over his face, Cody with her arms around him. Marlowe got home and took his bourbon and cigarettes up to the roof. He was so pissed off he was panting. It took three cigarettes and three drinks to calm him down. He stared out at the city, as weary and depleted as he was. He thought he might have gone too far with Emmet— no, he didn't. Everyone should hear the truth, even if it knocks you down and flattens your dignity. Again, Marlowe wondered why Emmet had gone through with the plan. What was in his mind? Did he want to be Cody's hero? That was improbable. They despised each other, or so it seemed. Were they closer than Marlowe thought? Also improbable. Neither seemed capable of closeness. What he saw in the parking lot was momentary, a flash of vulnerability and that was all.

Marlowe's anger was irresolvable. People say you should confront the person you're angry with and let your feelings out, as if venting them were the same as getting rid of them. Bullshit, Marlowe thought. Venting articulates your anger. Venting sharpens the needle.

He knew he wouldn't sleep. He sat at his desk and stared through the window.

Marlowe replayed the evening's events, from Ren arriving at the Sunshine until he saw Pav's car driving off, its round taillights fuzzing into one and fading away. Marlowe knew a lot about cars. Some Ferraris, Ford GTs and Lotuses have round taillights. A little pricy for Pav, Marlowe thought. Some older Corvettes and Camaros have them and seventies BMWs do too.

He ran a search. The car registered to Pav was a three-year-old Cadillac CTS that had completely different taillights. Was Pav using someone else's car? "Shit," Marlowe said. Or maybe it wasn't Pav at all. The thought made him suck in a deep breath and motorboat his lips. He couldn't believe it. All this work, uncertainty and hair-raising danger on behalf of a seventeen-year-old reprobate with no more conscience than a praying mantis. It was getting harder and harder to equate her with a human life. But there was Emmet to consider, as stalwart as ever. Despite his anger, Marlowe couldn't wimp out on him. There was enough pain, enough sorrow. He needed to sleep.

It was sunny and oppressively hot. Marlowe made the short drive from East Hollywood to the Warner Brothers studio. Ren was staring straight ahead, tight, drawn into herself, brittle enough to break. Marlowe was anxious. He had to find a way to get leverage on Fallon. Hard to do. Fallon seemed like someone who wouldn't cut you some slack unless you broke a bone or two. Marlowe drove up to the gate on Barham. The woman in the kiosk checked their licenses, matched them with the computer and gave them passes. They were met by a young man in a golf cart who showed them where to park. A lot of classic films were made on the Warners lot, Marlowe thought. Cagney in *Yankee Doodle Dandy*, Elia Kazan's *East of Eden*, Bogart in *The Big Sleep* and *Casablanca*. Emmet would love it here. Ren was rigid, silent and staring.

The golf cart puttered through the grounds, the Warner Brothers water tower looming as they passed. The tower used to be next to the fire department, but a local earthquake nearly toppled it. The studio envisioned a hundred thousand gallons of water falling on the fire engines on their way to put out a fire. They moved the tower to its present location. The golf cart approached the sound stages, big, windowless, barnlike structures. They looked secretive; a good place to park your experimental airplane. They arrived at one identical to the rest. They went inside. The set was lit but the gallery was dark. The young man guided them to their seats and left. The extras were already seated, twenty-five or thirty of them. Ren was intense, ready to spring, her eyes darting back and forth. They were near the top and could only see the backs of their heads.

Marlowe had been on sets before. This one was a small-town storefront. A canopy of lights and wires hung overhead. There were two mobile cameras and another on a dolly. Numerous production staff were moving around, talking on their walkie-talkies or staring at their phones, the chatter low and purposeful. "Over there," Marlowe said. "That's the director. He's looking at a quad, a monitor with four screens. The suits standing next to him are probably studio execs. The woman with the headset is either the script supervisor or the associate director."

"Who are those people over there?" Ren asked.

Six men and a woman were watching another monitor. Occasionally, there was forced laughter, but otherwise they were anxious and intense, like they were watching someone defuse a bomb. They were dressed in an incoherent mishmash of sweatpants, leggings, sagging jeans, oversized hoodies and faded T-shirts with sayings on them.

"Those guys? They're the writers," Marlowe said. Suddenly, Ren leaned forward.

"There he is, there's Fallon!" she hissed. He was sitting near the front, talking to the woman next to him, their heads nearly touching. "I just realized something," Ren said. "The only reason Fallon is doing this is to meet women."

A staff person appeared before the gallery. "Okay, we're done for the day," she said. "Go out the way you came in, please. Thank you for your help." The group exited, walking in a loose herd toward the parking lot. Fallon and the girl were talking, laughing, their shoulders bumping, Ren and Marlowe trailing them.

"I can't believe I married that creep," Ren said.

"Me either."

When they reached the parking lot, the girl gave Fallon her number. She kissed him on the cheek and skipped off, tossing her hair. They followed Fallon to his car; new, black and German. He stopped and saw Ren. His face went slack for an instant, then widened into a cocky, condescending smile. "What a surprise. How are you, Ren?" Fallon said as if they'd met at a cocktail party. There was so much violence in Ren's eyes, Fallon took a step back.

"Where is he, Fallon? I want Jeremy back," she said.

"Can't do it. The boy and I have become quite bonded," he answered casually. "And he likes it here, the sunshine and all. He cried when we first arrived but since then, he's been very happy."

"You're a liar and always have been. Where is he?" Ren demanded.

"Safe at private school," Fallon said. "A very expensive one, I might add. He's made lots of friends. I'm pretty sure he doesn't want to go back to dreary old London." Fallon sang the first few bars of "Hotel California." Marlowe wanted to hit him repeatedly.

"Who is this, Ren? Your goon?" Fallon said. His cologne was too sweet for a man. He smelled like a flower show run over by a truck.

"I'm the one that found you and I'll find you again," Marlowe said.

"I'm Jeremy's legal father," Fallon replied, unruffled. "Any attempt to take him from me will end up in court." That smile again. "I have an excellent lawyer. She reps a number of celebrities."

"Fallon, please don't do this," Ren said. She was all tears, all anguish, all hope. "You know he's better off with me and Jeremy does too." Fallon's expression soured.

"Don't worry," he said derisively. "He'll have excellent care." Marlowe had heard that tone before. Fallon had done something objectionable, something he didn't like doing.

"Please don't take him away, Fallon," Ren begged. "I'll do anything

you say, but please, please, don't take my boy." She was practically
on her knees. Marlowe had seen pain before but not like this, not a
heart wrenched from a mother's love.

Fallon shrugged. "Sorry, can't be helped." Marlowe's need to harm
this man was overcome by his alarm. It was as if Fallon were saying,
"What's done is done." Fallon got in his car. Ren grabbed the door
handle and yanked on it but the locks had locked. "Then let me see
him!" she cried. "Please, Fallon! Just once!" Fallon started the engine.
Ren wouldn't let go of the car, it was starting to roll. Marlowe
wrapped his arms around her and held on. Fallon drove away. Ren's
body felt hollow, empty, like a husk. She turned, buried her face in
his chest and wept.

They drove back to Hollywood, Ren blank and out of reach. If you
try and console her you'll be consoling yourself, Marlowe thought.
Ren will fly home tomorrow without her son. You've let her down
completely. People say that when you fail, you learn something you
can build on. Bullshit, he thought. Failure makes you feel like an
inept asshole and the only thing you learn is that you're incompetent.
Then there's that other doubtful saying, what doesn't kill you makes
you stronger. Perhaps. What doesn't kill you may or may not make
you stronger, but either way, leaves an indelible scar. Marlowe had
found Ren's children's book, *Urtle the Turtle*, online. The prologue
was a poem.

There was a small turtle named Urtle
Who lived in the sea and was fertile
She ventured on land
With a plan in the sand
And proceeded to cross every hurdle

In light from the Dipper
She flapped her four flippers
To digger and digger away
She dispatched with her roe

But it filled her with woe
To leave her small treasures to stray

Despite her devotion
She returned to the ocean
And worried and fretted and frayed
No one went back
To see their eggs crack
But Urtle could not stay away

She returned to the place
Where she'd left in a haste
And hoped she would be there in time
And there from the sand
Wee Urtles began
To digger and digger and climb

She watched them with pleasure
Her many small treasures
Frisky and sunny and gay
She thought she'd done well
And wanted to dwell
To watch the young toddlers at play
Instead, she returned
To the sea and the spray
And the surf and the salt and the swells

She wrote that for Jeremy, Marlowe thought. It must be wonderful
to love like that.

Cody was in her room, furious and frustrated. She was worse off
than ever. Trapped, with no resources, no control, no Eli. She called
Naomi, her ex in San Francisco, a doormat if there ever was one.

"You want me to buy you a plane ticket?" Naomi said in her high,
singsongy voice.

"Yeah, I really miss you," Cody said.

Naomi laughed. "You're so full of shit you stink like an outhouse—and you're lousy in bed too." The call ended. Cody groaned and flopped on the bed. Her life was tits up. Her phone buzzed.

"It's me," Eli said.

"Where've you been?"

"I've been working on something."

"Why didn't you call me? I left a hundred messages."

"I have reasons, they're complicated."

"Complicated? What does that mean?" Cody said. "All you had to do was pick up the phone—"

"Shut up, okay? I have a way out." Eli was angry and scared.

"You do?"

"I can get money too."

"Oh my God. Tell me how!"

"I'm home. Tell you when you get here," Eli said. "Hurry."

"Can't you pick me up?"

"No, I can't pick you up! Get here any way you can. If you're not at my place in an hour I'm leaving without you."

"Leaving without—" He ended the call. Cody was dumbfounded. There's a way out and money too? Oh my God she loved him! She snapped back to the moment. No way she could get to Silver Lake in an hour. It frightened her. Eli loved her but he loved himself more. If he was boxed in, he'd leave without her. She needed a car and it didn't matter whose.

Cody stood in the hallway, peeking into Emmet's bedroom. He always left his car keys and wallet in a candy dish on top of the dresser. Emmet was a lump under the covers, murmuring angrily to someone in a dream. Was he sleeping or half awake? She couldn't wait anymore. She slipped in, took his keys and wallet and slipped out again. *Fifty-one minutes and counting.*

Emmet's garage door was manual. Cody used the key and unlocked the padlock. It took two hands and bent knees to lift the thing, creaking and groaning so loud it made her cringe. There were two cars. One was Emmet's unmarked cruiser. There was police stuff in there. Cody was afraid to take it. The second car was old but it looked new. The paint was fresh, the chrome polished and shining. It was also huge. Longer and wider than Eli's Range Rover. She used the key and got in. The inside light didn't go on. Maybe it didn't have one. The car smelled like plastic and some kind of cleaner. She was stumped a moment. All the cars she'd been in had push-button starters. "Where do you put the key?" she said. *Forty-seven minutes.*

Emmet was dozing. He heard something familiar. It was like the first few notes of your favorite song. Someone had started Addie's car. He got out of bed and saw the empty candy dish. He ran through the house and threw open the front door. Addie's car was driving away.

"You goddamn little sneak!" he shouted. "You hurt that car and I'll throw you in jail."

"I'm sorry this is taking so long," Marlowe said. "I should have taken the streets." They were on the Glendale Freeway, stuck in traffic. The drive back from Warners should have taken twenty minutes but they were way past that. Ren hadn't spoken since they left the studio. He glanced at her. She was staring at him bitterly.

"You said you'd get Jeremy back," she said. "You said he was safe and I could take him home and everything would be all right." Marlowe was pretty sure he hadn't said all that. Ren was crying, her face, a sheet of tears. *"You said you'd get him back."* She sobbed.

"Come on, Ren, you're not being fair," he said, more heatedly than he intended. "It didn't turn out but I've worked hard for you. I tried my best. I really did. You can't be angry at me for that." She stared out the window for a while. She stopped crying.

Almost inaudibly, she said, "Yes, you did work hard. I'm sorry for what I said. Really, you've been wonderful, Marlowe." The traffic broke, they drove, the engine droned. It was cool outside but the car seemed close and warm. He opened a window but it didn't help. Ren was going home tomorrow. He had nothing to say. He couldn't help her. He couldn't touch her. He felt an overwhelming desire to kiss her. He felt her hand on his. She was looking at him. He was looking at her. "Yes," she said.

Marlowe's phone buzzed. A text from Emmet. Marlowe wouldn't have responded but the message said, *911 911.* It was a real emergency.

"Dad is in trouble," he said. The phone buzzed again. Marlowe answered, Emmet yelling through the car speaker.

"Cody stole Addie's car!" Emmet shouted.

Marlowe glanced at Ren.

"Help him," she said.

"What do you want me to do, Dad?"

Emmet had a GPS app on his phone. There was a magnetic unit stuck to a frame rail under Addie's car. "She's on Maple Avenue heading toward the Ten," he said. "She's going to see her boyfriend." Addie's car was a 1975 Chevy Monte Carlo in light saddle with a 454-cubic-inch V8. Addie liked to go fast. The car was huge, nearly eighteen feet long. That goddamn kid would crash it for sure. Emmet kept the spare keys on a hook in the hallway closet. He got his gun and badge from under the bluebird cushion. He ran into the garage and started the cruiser.

Cody drove under the speed limit, afraid to go faster. The car was slow to turn, the gas pedal hesitated before lurching the car forward. The steering wheel was as big as a Hula-Hoop, she could barely see over it. You had to put your foot almost to the floor to stop the stupid thing. A car honked, and then another. She was drifting out of her lane. She got back on course, looked ahead and said, "Oh shit, kill me now." A traffic accident. An eighteen-wheeler had crashed into the center divider. Drivers were slowing to take a look. "Who cares!" she yelled. "Hurry up, you assholes!" *Thirty-eight minutes.* The traffic picked up. She stepped on the gas.

Emmet didn't enjoy driving the Monte Carlo. It was a two-ton tombstone and got eleven miles to the gallon. He'd never get rid of it. The car belonged to Addie, however distant her heartbeat. He looked at his phone. He was five miles behind Cody and closing. She was about to cut off on the 110. That would take her to the Glendale Freeway. The Glendale went right through Little Armenia. Marlowe and Ren were there waiting. Then a few hundred brake lights lit up. A goddamn accident. The highway patrol was diverting traffic to a single lane. "No, don't do this to me!" Emmet shouted. He'd taken his eyes off the GPS. "Goddamn you, Cody!" He called Marlowe. "She's not going to Armenia Town, she got off on Silver Lake Boulevard heading west."

"I'll take Fountain," Marlowe said. "It's almost a straight shot to Silver Lake."

Cody was in a panic. She was twenty-five minutes late. Had Eli left her behind? She turned off Silver Lake onto Berkeley and took the dogleg to Berkeley Court, narrow and serpentine. The speed limit was twenty-five miles per hour. Cody was going forty. She knocked someone's mirror off and barely missed a mailbox. Eli's place was a Spanish stucco built into the hillside, a garage at street level, the residence up a flight of side stairs. A light was on. A spark of hope. She parked, ran across the street and ran up the stairs. The door was unlocked. She went in. "Eli, I'm here," she called out. She heard music. Weezer's "Taking Back Sunday," the Emo version of a Valentine song, a song Eli only played for her. It was coming from the bedroom. *He was waiting for her!* She ran down the hall and burst through the door. "Eli, I'm here!" The room was empty. "Eli?" she said. A big hand that smelled like cigarettes clamped over her mouth, a gun pressed against her temple. "Don't say nothing," the man said.

She was thrown on the bed, which terrified her even more. Two men were there. One looked like an eighties porn star, the other was dumpy and dressed like Stallone in the first *Rocky* movie. Porn Star made a call.

"Come now," he said.

*   *   *

Marlowe arrived at the address on Berkeley Court. Addie's car was across the street. He parked behind it and texted Emmet. *At location. Going in.* "Stay here, Ren. If you hear gunshots, people screaming or anything like it, go. Don't think about it. Just go."

Marlowe opened the trunk and got the Ruger. He was wary. Cody might have walked into a trap. He went quietly up the stairs to the landing. He should have told Ren to drive away. That was stupid. The door was open. He slipped inside, stopped and listened. Even if a place was dead quiet, you could tell if someone was there; the slight displacement of air, residual body heat. He smelled cigarettes but saw no ashtrays. Muffled voices were coming from another room. Cody pleading, men with accents speaking gruffly. Time to call the police, Marlowe thought. Many a TV detective would have avoided a shootout if they'd picked up the damn phone. Marlowe went out onto the landing. He was dialing 911. That's when he saw Tato at the bottom of the stairs, smiling and aiming a big handgun at him. "You know what to do, don't you?" the gang leader said. Marlowe slowly put his phone and gun down on the landing. He hoped Ren was all right.

The one they called Viktor duct-taped Marlowe's wrists together, a cigarette dangling from his lips, his head in a moving cloud of smoke. They went down a flight of interior stairs to the garage. Tato was opening the tailgate of an enormous black Escalade. Ren was already there, lying on her side, her wrists bound with duct tape.

"You okay?"

"Yes, Marlowe, I've never been better," she said, her teeth clenched.

"Leonid, what are you doing?" Tato said. Leonid appeared at the top of the stairs, gripping Cody by her uncooperative arm.

"Sorry, Tato. This girl, I want to kill her." He brought her down the stairs.

"It was Eli, not me," she complained. "I didn't have anything to do with it." She saw Ren and groaned. "Oh great, Jackie Chan is here."

"I'm thrilled about it as well," Ren said.

"Get them in the car," Tato said.

* * *

Emmet arrived at the address. He drew his weapon and went up the stairs. He loved this part, how you were hyperaware, the adrenaline amplifying all your senses. You were more than you. You were the police. The door was open. Emmet cleared the rooms one by one. He called Marlowe. No answer. He texted him. *Your location? Are you injured?* No reply.

Even in the most critical situations, Emmet was rarely afraid. He was afraid now. Cody, Marlowe and Ren could be anywhere in the city. He went back to the cruiser and opened the police laptop secured to the dash. He signed in by fingerprint. The computer could access police databases but otherwise, it was your average PC. Emmet could feel time sprinting past him. His son, his friend and a seventeen-year-old girl on their way to a brutal death. He wanted a drink. He needed a drink.

If you're trying to find a suspect, the first place to look is family. Emmet checked. Tato's siblings lived in New Jersey. His mother lived in Hollywoodland. In the early twenties, a developer put up a hillside sign to advertise the segregated housing development he called Hollywoodland. Later, the Chamber of Commerce changed the sign to Hollywood. The sign was only painted wood and by the 1970s it was badly deteriorated. Donors, including Hugh Hefner, Alice Cooper and the yodeling cowboy, Gene Autry, had the sign replaced with the iconic landmark. It overlooked a residential area that kept the name Hollywoodland.

Tato's mother lived on Ledgewood Drive, a narrow road that wound into the foothills. Her house was at the very end. It was isolated, few neighbors, empty land around it. Emmet took off, the cruiser's tires screeching, a trail of blue smoke behind it.

The Escalade rolled along. Tato and the two thugs were in the front, Marlowe, Ren and Cody in the cargo bay, covered with a canvas drop cloth. It was close and hot. "I'm gonna get you back, Ren," Cody said. "After we get out of this, you're finished."

"Leave it to you to bring up something completely irrelevant," Ren replied. "I know! Let's talk about restaurants or climate change."

"I wouldn't get into it with her, Cody," Marlowe advised.

"Why? I'm not afraid of her."

"And by the way," Ren said. "None of this would have happened if you hadn't stolen Emmet's car."

"I had to see my boyfriend," Cody said.

Ren was astonished. "*You* have a *boyfriend*? My God. Did his powers of perception get hit by lightning? Was his frontal lobe bitten by a bat? Did his moral judgment get a bowel infection?"

"See what I mean?" Marlowe said.

"SHUT UP!" Tato yelled.

They drove. The gangsters talked and joked in Armenian, sometimes laughing boisterously. This wasn't an Armenian phenomenon by any means, but Marlowe couldn't comprehend how some few people could clown around when they were about to commit murder. Even serial killers didn't hum Christmas carols while they were sharpening their knives or choosing a blunt instrument. True, Tato and his men had grown up in a violent world. But in Marlowe's estimation, they'd be hard-pressed to connect even one life circumstance with their indifference to killing. These men weren't the ordinary Germans who murdered Jews by the truckload. They weren't the dupes of herd behavior or praised for societal cruelty or indoctrinated to believe that Jews were evil, that it was us or them, that survival depended on eliminating the alien race. Even among hardened criminals, Tato and his crew were freaks, mutants, cancer cells that didn't metastasize but stayed within themselves, waiting like Moray eels to strike out of the darkness with an evil grin.

Marlowe paid attention to the sounds. The car drove on city streets, then a freeway, more city streets, but slower, more turns, probably residential. Then lots of curves, going uphill, the asphalt getting rougher and bumpier. Gravel clattered against the drive shaft. A dirt road. Not good, Marlowe thought. Wherever they were going, it was isolated. Tato wouldn't kill them right away. There were confessions to make, punishments to mete out. He thought of Ren. He thought of Jeremy. How do you apologize for something like this? *She'll be killed, Marlowe. And she'll never see her son again.*

The car stopped. Tato's men got their prisoners out of the back and stood them up. The place smelled of horse dung and hay. There was a plywood sign, some of the paint worn off. WELCOME TO RIDE ON!! Scattered lights lit mucky corrals, morose horses and a long barn with a corrugated roof. There were a few outbuildings in the darker shadows. Smart, Marlowe thought. Tato probably used a cutout to buy the stables and hired lackeys to run the place. A great place to hide your guns, money and drugs. Who would think to look here?

Tato and the others used their phones as flashlights and led their prisoners around the barn to a trail. It was narrow, rocky and rutted with ATV tracks. They trudged, the air was cool and smelled of sage.

"Where are we going? There's nothing out here," Cody said.

"Shut your mouth," Leonid said. "Don't speak no more." He was a bulky man, breathing hard, his leather jacket slung over his shoulder. He cuffed her on the head.

"Hey!" she cried. "Don't you have better things to do than hit a girl? Why don't you lose some weight?" He cuffed her again.

"Hey!"

They reached their destination: a cinder block building. Gun-slit windows, a yellow lightbulb over the black metal door, darkness all around. A place for detainees, for victims, Marlowe thought, for people who were never going home. The door had two dead bolts. Dima stepped out of a shadow: the grim reaper illumed in yellow, the whip coiled around his neck like a python.

"I'm glad to see you, Marlowe," Dima said, grinning. "You and me will have a nice talk, yes?"

The building was larger than it looked. Harsh fluorescents. Bare cement walls except for the giant TV. There were four long tables, four stools, a number of folding chairs and a badly stained couch, bowed in the middle. Gun racks against the walls. Assault weapons, Uzis, riot guns, TEC-9s, long rifles.

One of the tables was for repair. Tools, parts and partially disassembled guns strewn around. Another held stacks of handgun cases and boxes of ammo. On another were hand weapons still in their packaging. A Browning Automatic Rifle was set on a small tripod. On the coffee table was a crate of M61 fragmentation grenades, ordnance probably left over from Vietnam. If the grenades had been stored properly, they'd still go off.

"Eli!" Cody cried. A young man was sitting in a corner, hands bound behind him. His back was against the wall, his head lolling forward. Hard to tell what he looked like. Bleeding lips, purple bruises, swollen lumps under his eyes. She tried to go to him but Tato held her back.

"What did you do to him?" Cody said savagely.

"This is nothing," Tato sneered. "This piece of shit is a traitor! My own fucking brother!" The prisoners were thrown on the sofa. Viktor bound their ankles with duct tape. Ren said, "If I don't see Jeremy before I die I'll kill you, Marlowe." Tato paced in front of them. He drew a shiny blue titanium .357 from a shoulder holster. He used the barrel to lift Cody's chin.

"You're going to tell me everything, do you hear me? If your story is different from the traitor's you will be whipped!"

Emmet drove slowly along Ledgewood, approaching the end. He stopped a few doors down from Tato's mother's house. He wondered if she was in there, peeking through the blinds, looking for intruders. There was a Camry in the driveway but no other cars around. "Dammit," Emmet said. He'd guessed wrong, and the more he thought about it, the more he felt like an idiot. Who would bring kidnap victims to their mom's house? He sat there, thinking about his next move.

Mom's porch light was on, the light extending past the house. He could see the beginning of a dirt road and a big wooden sign. RIDE ON STABLES. FUN FOR THE WHOLE FAMILY! A chain had once blocked the road. The chain and the padlock were on the ground. Emmet's heart rate went up. He drove past the house and onto the dirt road. He turned off the headlights. On his left side was a steep hill. On his right, a sheer drop-off and a panoramic view of Hollywood and beyond. The city lights reflected off the sky but they barely lit the road. Emmet reached a bend and stopped. If he followed the road he might be spotted. Emmet turned the car around to face the exit and parked.

He was wearing his tactical shoes; thick soles and heavy tread. He wore them all the time, even when he was grocery shopping. Before he'd been put on leave, he worked out in the police gym three days a week. He did five miles on the treadmill, free weights, pull-ups, sit-ups. He was scrawny but he could bench-press more than anyone approaching his age.

Emmet got his duty belt out of the trunk. He removed everything except the Taser, extra magazines, knife, baton and pepper spray. The belt made them easier to access. He put on the belt and checked his weapon. He preferred the Beretta 92/FS over the Glock 17. The Glock was lighter and shorter, but the trigger had a safety mechanism that relied on finger pressure. The Beretta had a thumb safety that clicked on and off. Emmet liked to be sure. He put on his reconnaissance jacket, a dark gray hoodie that went over his hips and covered the belt. He didn't want it catching on anything. He took a few deep breaths and started up the hill.

CHAPTER FOURTEEN
AND THEN EVERYTHING BLEW UP

It started with Eli," Cody began. "He overheard you talking about laundering money for the Russians. He told Andy and they came up with a plan."

"No," Eli said. "I told you and you told Andy and the two of *you* came up with a plan."

"Bullshit. You said—"

"Don't say no more, traitor," Tato said. Eli's eyes were closed. He was leaning back, head against the wall. He's given up, Marlowe thought. He knows it doesn't matter who's blamed. No one will get credit for doing less.

"Keep going, Cody," Tato ordered.

"Andy called a meeting at his office," Cody said. "We were waiting for DeSallis."

Cody, Eli and Andy sat in Andy's office, saying nothing. They had a lot at stake. If DeSallis wasn't in, the plan was toast. The office was ridiculous, Cody observed. Scarface must have done the decorating, everything white, shiny or fringed. There was a sword in an acrylic display case with its own lighting. The sword was long, elegantly curved, a short grip and an ornate pommel. It looked like an antique.

"What is that?" DeSallis said as he came in.

"Impressive, isn't it?" Andy said. "It's called a *shashka,* a replica of Prince Dimitri's sword from the battle of Kulikovo. His army defeated the Mongol hordes in 1380 or '90, something like that. It's in the script. I sent the Russians pictures. They loved it."

Andy reiterated the basics. *The Prince of Moscow* would supposedly be shot in Finland. If the costs were real, they'd be astronomical. The entire production would have to set up there. Housing for the cast and crew, food, wardrobe, equipment, building sets, transportation, costumes, an army of horses, and hiring hundreds of local extras. Spending a hundred and fifty million wouldn't be hard.

"I know all this, Andy," DeSallis said. "Why am I here?"

"You're here to make some money," Andy replied. "There's going to be thousands of invoices from Russian shell companies, here and overseas. Among them will be invoices from my shell companies too."

"You mean you're going to steal—"

"*We're* going to steal," Andy said with a smile. "Millions, DeSallis."

"Why do you have shell companies?" DeSallis asked.

"For my other operations." Eli nudged Cody, both of them wondering what else Andy was up to. "We'll take a cut of every dime the company spends," Andy said, beaming, "and everyone gets an even share."

"Where will Terry be?" DeSallis said.

"Shooting his low-budget movie in Helsinki," Cody said. "Out of everyone's hair. He can't know about this. He'd say it threatens his comeback movie and freak out."

"I don't like it. There are too many loose ends," DeSallis said.

"You seem to forget that I'm the head of finance and I approve the payments," Andy said. "Cody will monitor Terry, and you, my friend, are the Wolfgang Puck of cooking the books. Are you not?"

"Perhaps. But won't the Russians have someone on the ground? An overseer?"

"That's the beauty part," Andy said, his smile widening into a grin. "Tato convinced the Russians that Eli was the man for the job."

Eli had lobbied Tato hard, arguing his little brother would be doing something useful instead of tagging along on things he knew nothing about. Eli also spoke Armenian, a little Russian and perfect English. He could deal with people Tato would scare away. Plus, Eli was family and these days, who else could you trust?

"It'll work, DeSallis," Eli said. "We've got all the bases covered."

Andy said the skim would be wired to an account at the Bank de Bandariba, in Curaçao. The US regulations meant nothing. The manager said they used the manuals as toilet paper.

"That's unacceptable. You'll be holding all the money, Andy," DeSallis said.

"We don't like it either but we have no choice," Eli said.

"Look, no matter what we do there's trust involved," Andy said.

"But you're not a trustworthy person," DeSallis replied. Cody wanted to say you're a sleaze and a crook but restrained herself.

Andy shrugged, his palms up. "Okay, fine. Let's skip the whole thing, DeSallis. You can go back to your shitty office, your dilapidated house, your five-year-old Volvo and that shack you call a mountain hideaway and we'll all go home." DeSallis stewed a moment.

"Where'd you get the sword?"

"EBay."

Tato couldn't stay still, standing up, pacing, sitting down, leaning against a wall, always with the .357 in his hand, glaring at Cody to hurry her up. Leonid and Viktor were looking at their phones. It was stuffy and warm. Everybody was sweating. Dima was smirking at Marlowe and fondling the bullwhip far too intimately. Ren had her head bowed, slumped, silent.

"You okay?" Marlowe said.

"If you ask that again, I'm going to bite you in the face."

Tato gestured with the gun. "Hey, stupid girl, did I tell you to stop?" Cody glanced at Eli. She'd tried to betray him and he returned the favor. That's love for you.

"For a while, everything went fine," Cody continued. "Andy showed us the online bank statements from Curaçao and the money was piling up just like it was supposed to. Only one statement was late. Andy said it was because it was Carnival in Curaçao and everybody takes the week off. I checked. It was true. Can I have a drink of water?" she said.

"No," Tato said. "Keep going."

"And then everything blew up."

Terry was an obsessive insomniac, especially under stress. It was late, he was in his apartment, packing. He was going to Helsinki the next afternoon and he wanted to know if the equipment he ordered would be there. The rental company was closed. He couldn't access the company's files online and Andy wasn't answering his phone.

Terry was furious. He charged down to the office, frantic, his mind in chaos fueled on coke. He went into Andy's office and found the cabinet that held the invoices. He forgot he had no key. He'd never been given one. He kicked the cabinet until he hurt his foot. Apoplectic with rage, he took the *shashka* out of its display case and pried open the cabinet, breaking the sword in half. He pawed through the invoices, throwing them on the floor. He stopped suddenly, stared, in shock. There was an invoice from Hollywood Film Supply. That was one of Andy's shell companies. Over eleven thousand dollars for a list of nonsense. Terry was so sickened he barfed, the mess all over the folders.

"How do you know this?" Tato said.

"The next day, Terry wrote me a twenty-page email," Cody said. "Dad was a flake, but he wasn't stupid. He'd figured it out. Andy couldn't be working this alone. He needed DeSallis and he needed me. He didn't know about Eli."

"Keep going," Tato said.

"The next afternoon, Terry called a meeting of his own," Cody said. "He said he had a 'major announcement.'"

When Cody came in Andy was sitting at his desk, staring off. He looked mournful, defeated, and so did DeSallis. Cody saw the broken *shashka,* the open filing cabinet, the folders on the floor covered with barf. The smell was awful.

"Oh no," she said. Then Terry burst in, red-eyed and raving, hair like a fright wig. He screamed at them. What the hell did they think they were doing? They were jeopardizing his comeback movie as well as his life! Were they crazy? He called them lowlifes, traitors and sellouts.

"As of this moment, you're all fired!" he shouted. Terry saved most of his venom for Cody. How could you! You're my daughter! We love each other! How could you stab your own father in the back? You're family, kitten! She hated it when he called her that.

Terry told the conspirators he had come to a decision. He was going to come clean with the Russians. They would respect his honesty, transparency and good faith. If they let him finish his movie, he'd give them all the profits. One hundred percent. He forgot they were already taking ninety-five.

"The Russians will have no reason to hurt us," Terry said. "We'll all be safe!" Everyone argued with him, told him he was naïve and he'd get them all killed, but Terry was adamant. "From now on you're out of the loop!" he declared, and stormed out.

"Terry was very stupid," Tato said.

"We thought he was insane," Cody went on. "Andy said if the Russians found out about the stealing they'd send you to slaughter us."

"He was right."

"Andy said Terry had to be stopped," Cody continued. "No one knew what to say. Then Andy called us cowards and left. We didn't think he'd actually go through with it."

Tato crossed his big tattooed arms and stared at her. "You're telling me Terry's partner killed him?" he huffed. "You Americans know nothing about brotherhood. What happened when you told the traitor?"

"Eli said we had to leave before you and the Russians found out."

"You said it, not me," Eli said.

"SHUT UP!" Tato bellowed again. He paced aimlessly, muttering epithets, you could feel the pressure inside him, feel its heat. He's going to smack somebody, Marlowe thought.

"Idiots!" he shouted at the ceiling. He stood over Cody. Her head down, defenseless. *He's going to hit her, Marlowe.* He thought he should say something like "You're such a coward!" Or "Hit me instead!" But he didn't. Why get beat up before you die? Instead of punching Cody, Tato picked up a folding chair and threw it at Eli. It spun like a Frisbee, banged into the wall over his head and fell on him. He didn't flinch, he didn't care.

"Couldn't you let me go?" Cody said. "I told you everything!"

"No, you didn't tell me everything," Tato said. He looked at Eli and snorted. "The traitor did."

"Please," she mewled. "Aren't you finished with me?"

"Finished?" Tato scoffed. "For what you did, there is no mercy. You are never going home again."

"What? You mean you're going to *kill* me?" Cody exclaimed. "I'm only seventeen! Kill these other guys, I didn't do anything!" Marlowe imagined himself and Cody crossing a vast wasteland. She'd eat all the food, drink all the water, wait for you to die and roast your body parts over the campfire.

"Don't worry," Tato said magnanimously. "We won't kill you right away. We will have a little fun with you before you go."

Cody closed her eyes and sobbed, snot and tears falling into her lap. Tato looked salaciously at Ren.

"Your girlfriend too, Marlowe," the gang leader said. "She's too skinny but that's okay. My boys are not picky." The boys chuckled.

"I'm sorry, Ren," Marlowe said. He couldn't look at her.

She was glaring straight ahead. "Meeting you is the worst thing that's ever happened to me."

Something unsaid passed between the gangsters. Tato stepped away, put the chairs aside and leaned against a wall. Viktor and Leonid did the same.

"What are they doing?" Cody said.

They're giving Dima room, Marlowe thought. Despite the meds, his shoulder was still painful from that single lash. The prospect of more horrified him.

Dima took center stage, the coiled whip in his hand. He let it drop to the cement floor. With an evil glance at Marlowe, Dima turned slightly sideways, made a lazy swing of his arm, and the whip uncoiled behind him. "This is my favorite. The Indiana Jones model," he said. "It's made from kangaroo!" Marlowe had never been this terrified, this completely helpless before. *Hit Cody, hit Cody, hit Cody, hit Cody.*

Dima thrust his arm forward, snapping his wrist underhanded at the same time. The whip shot out at Marlowe, no time to react, a black mamba flying straight for his face. Dima snapped his wrist down, hard, CRACK! The cracker brushed the tip of Marlowe's nose. He yelled and nearly released the taquitos he had for lunch. Dima drew the whip back again. He was measuring his distance with the first one, Marlowe thought. He closed his eyes. *Hit Cody, hit Cody, hit Cody, hit Cody.*

"Wait, wait, finish the rest outside," Tato said irritably. "I'm not going to clean up the blood. Are you? Take the girl first, then Marlowe."

Leonid grabbed Cody and lifted her off her feet. She twisted away and fell back on the couch. "No, not me! Take somebody else!" she screamed. Leonid leaned down and slapped her. A grinning Dima stood in front of Marlowe.

"If you resist, I'll drag you—on your face." Why resist? Marlowe thought. Why not die with your features intact?

"Help me up," he said.

Tato's phone buzzed. "Everybody shut up!" He looked at the caller ID and held the phone up to Eli. "Our mother," Tato said. "She won't be mad when I tell her why I killed you." He answered the call. "Mayrig, I told you not to—" He listened for a moment, first puzzled and then alarmed. He said something harsh in Armenian and ended the call.

"A car is coming up the road," he said. "The driver and no one else. Dima, Viktor, you know where to go. Leonid, go see who it is. Bring him here."

"Bring him here?" Leonid said. "What if it's not that easy?" Tato gave him the look of death and that was it. They snatched up walkie-talkies, weapons, ammo. They ran outside, the door closing behind them. Marlowe heard keys and the two dead bolts snapping shut.

"Who do you think is out there?" Cody asked. "The police?"

"No, it's Emmet," Marlowe said.

"We're dead for sure."

"Cody?" said Marlowe. "You don't know shit."

CHAPTER FIFTEEN
GO! GO HARD!

Leonid moved cautiously down the dirt road. He stuck close to the hillside, AK at the ready, a Glock in his belt. He reached a bend, edged forward and stuck his neck out. A car was parked on the side of the road, facing the other direction. Ready to escape, Leonid thought. He crept up to the car. It was a police cruiser.

Alarmed, he muttered, "Cops." He was about to radio Tato but thought a moment. If this was a raid, the cops would have come in numbers, especially because gangs and guns were involved. There would be police cars, SWAT vans and armored vehicles lined up to the street and several helicopters in the sky. Tato's mother said she saw the driver and no one else. There was no reason for one cop to be up here, Leonid thought. The cop's gone rogue. He's here to rescue the prisoners.

Leonid hadn't met the cop on the road so he must have gone up the hill. It was steep. He thought about calling Tato but he'd be pissed and say something like, "Go get him, you lazy shit!" Leonid was in poor shape. Too much food, vodka, sleep and playing video games. He started up the steep slope. "*Kunem voret,* Tato," he muttered.

Emmet reached a plateau. He was breathing hard, heart thumping, winded but okay. He got down on the ground, crawled to the southern ledge and peered over. He could see a long barn, a few outbuildings and a couple dozen horses in a corral. They were calm; an occasional huff, blubbering, hooves shifting. He watched a full five minutes. He was used to long stakeouts. A few of the horses lifted their heads in surprise, the huffing and blubbering more animated. Tato's men are waiting for you, Emmet thought. They know you're here, they're protecting their prisoners. But why do that unless Marlowe and the others were locked up in one of those outbuildings. Time to call in the troops. Emmet backed away from the edge and got to his feet.

A wheezing voice said, "Don't...move."

Emmet turned. A man was coming out of the brush aiming an AK. He was stooped and gasping, a whistling sound coming from his lungs. A bucket of sweat had been splashed on his face. "Your gun...and phone," the man heaved. Emmet took his gun and phone out with two fingers and dropped them on the ground. He was afraid the guy might shoot him by accident.

The man was trying to say something but he was still wheezing and gulping air. He didn't take Emmet's duty belt and didn't tell Emmet to get on the ground. Not a pro, an ordinary thug, thought Emmet. The man spoke into a walkie-talkie, someone yelling on the other end. "But it's very steep, Tato," the man complained. "Maybe send someone to help me." More yelling. "Okay, okay. I'm coming down now—from the hill above the horses." If Emmet went with the man he'd be killed. Marlowe and the others would die too, if they weren't already dead.

"This way," the man said, nodding toward the southern edge of the plateau.

"Okay, anything you say," Emmet said with an obedient nod. "I'm cooperating, okay?" Emmet turned his back, put up his hands and walked decisively to the eastern slope, not running, not escaping. Tato would want to talk to him, he thought. This guy wasn't shooting him.

"Hey, that's the wrong—" the man said. "Come back, you idiot!"

Emmet stepped over the edge. It was nearly identical to the south side, steep, loose gravel and rocks all the way down. He descended sideways, one foot at horizontal in front of him, his hands out for balance, his weight shifted to the inside. If he fell, it would be into the hill. The shoes helped. He went into a controlled slide, rocks and gravel moving ahead of him.

"Wait! Wait for me!" the man shouted from above. Stop or I'll shoot you!" Emmet heard the man coming down after him. Emmet imagined the guy, facing forward, sliding on both feet, one hand clutching the assault rifle, his other arm windmilling for balance; a novice skier on a black diamond slope. The man yelled "Whoaaoh!" and a second later, he somersaulted past Emmet, the assault rifle tumbling after him. The rifle clattered against the rocks, the man disappeared into the dark.

Emmet found him, the man's head wedged between two boulders. He might have been looking for his pet badger. Emmet searched him. The side pocket of the jacket was held closed by magnets. Emmet found the man's phone but you needed a passcode. He used the phone as an ineffective flashlight. If the man had a pistol, Emmet couldn't find it. He located the assault rifle but the magazine was bent. His own gun was on the plateau.

"Shitarooski," he said. Marlowe, Cody and Ren were probably in the barn or an outbuilding. Emmet would have to make a wide circle and come from behind. There was a thin trail, more like a deer path. He hiked through the heavy brush. He was still winded. Even without the gun, the duty belt was heavy. Emmet had no hips and the belt kept sliding down. He'd forgotten the "keepers"; little straps that held the duty belt to your inside belt. His steps were slow and plodding. He was thirsty and sweating through his clothes.

Emmet continued stumbling along, tripping once and falling on his bony knees. *Damn, that hurt.* It was a struggle to get up again. He thought about Marlowe, Cody and Ren. Tato would do obscene things to them. They'd be whipped until their bones showed through. Emmet slogged on, hard to measure time in the dark. He stopped to rest and judge his location. He saw a yellow light.

Tato and Dima were standing at the bottom of the southern slope. They were waiting for Leonid to bring down the intruder. "What's taking so long?" Tato demanded. "All he had to do was bring him down the hill!" he yelled into his walkie-talkie. "Hey, you stupid asshole, what are you doing up there?" There was no answer. "Leonid! Say something!"

"Maybe the guy got him, the one your mother saw," Dima said. Tato thought a moment. "He's here to get the prisoners. We have to go back. Call Viktor. Tell him someone is coming."

Emmet crept through the brush toward the cinder block building. He got down on one knee. He could see a guy standing guard, his AK resting against the wall. The guy stamped out his cigarette and immediately lit another. A chain smoker. Emmet wondered how to make his approach. There was no way to do it without being seen. Chain Smoker got a text. He read it and snatched up his AK. He moved away from the building. If he remained in the light, he couldn't see anything. Emmet thought he should move to better cover. He started to stand, but his leg muscles were tight. It hurt. He made an involuntary groan. Chain Smoker heard it. He hunched low, racked the slide on the AK and started toward Emmet.

Marlowe, Ren and Cody were alone in the armory. "Marlowe, could you *do* something?" Cody said. "They're gonna kill me, you know."

"Be quiet," he said. Marlowe had been looking at a table, the one stacked with the hand weapons. There must be something with an edge in there. The table was seven, maybe eight feet away but it looked like a mile and a half. His hands and feet were bound.

"I have to get to that table," he said.

"Forget it. It's impossible," Cody said.

"Way to be encouraging, Cody," Ren said.

"Piss off, Ren."

"Later!" Marlowe barked. He had to get up first. He pulled his feet in close and bent at the waist to get his weight forward. He heaved himself upward, stood, tottered but kept his feet. *Thank you, Jahno.*

"Way to go, Marlowe," Cody said. "You're a bad mofo." Distracted, Marlowe nearly fell over.

"Shut up!"

With visions of the bullwhip spurring him, Marlowe hopped twice more.

"Woo-hoo!" Cody hooted. "Way to go, big man!"

"WILL YOU SHUT THE HELL UP?" Marlowe shouted. Two more hops and he'd be close enough to put his hands on the table. He was greasy with sweat, mouth dry, lungs burning up, searing pain in his legs. He breathed deeply, relaxing his muscles, letting the lactic acid dissipate, trying to get his focus back. *Do it before you fall down, Marlowe. Here...we...go!* He hopped, but it was like the president trying to jump over the podium. He seesawed and swayed, bent his knees. *Keep your balance, Marlowe! Keep your balance!*

"You can do it!" Cody shouted.

Marlowe fell like a full-length statue of himself. He saw the table rising up at him and he closed his eyes. He landed facedown. There was a huge crash, the table legs on one side folded. Marlowe went rolling down the tabletop like a hot dog on a stick. He opened his eyes to see a pile of weapons sliding toward him. He was pelted by the packages. Cans of pepper spray, telescopic batons, ninja stars, hunting slingshots, nunchakus, brass knuckles, fighting sticks, weighted gloves and a variety of knives. He put his hands in front of his face, which protected his face but nothing else. It seemed to go on for a long time.

"Watch out!" Ren shouted. The twenty-pound Browning was sliding off the table. It was like the sight gag you see in every baseball movie ever made. The barrel of the gun hit Marlowe in the crotch. He doubled over and shrieked like Racine's doorbell. He lay there groaning, bruised and buffeted, his reproductive future at serious risk.

"Does it hurt?" Cody said.

Marlowe let the pain pass. He rummaged through the weapons with his taped hands. He found a tactical knife in a sheath. He took the knife by its grip and pried off the safety snap with his teeth. He bit down on the tip of the sheath. He jerked his head back, yanking and pulling until the sheath fell away. The knife was free.

"Bravo, Marlowe," Ren said.

"That was pretty cool," Cody said.

Marlowe cut the tape off his wrists and ankles. He got up, went over to Ren and cut her hands free and gave her the knife. She cut the tape off her ankles.

"Do me! Do me!" Cody said, holding out her wrists. Ren hesitated. She looked at Marlowe.

"Should I?"

"Hey, don't mess around!" Cody said.

Marlowe shook his head. "I don't know, it's a close call."

Chain Smoker was coming. He wasn't using a flashlight. That would make him a target. Emmet was hidden behind a huge agave plant, its fronds like serrated tentacles. Emmet took the Taser out of his belt. Shaped like a fat derringer, it weighed seven ounces, was seven inches long with a laser sight that put a red dot on your chest. Compressed gas propelled two barbed darts attached by ultrathin wires. They hit you with 50,000 volts and shorted out your circuit breakers.

Emmet was crouched, cold and exhausted, his muscles were tight, his knees nearly frozen in place. He would have to wait for Chain Smoker to go by and shoot him in the back. The Taser's max range was fifteen feet. With a sudden jolt, Emmet's left calf cramped up, the pain like a flaming ice pick. He almost screamed and clamped his hand over his mouth.

Chain Smoker had slowed his pace. He was creeping. He knew he was getting close. Away from the city, on a clear night with no sound and no breeze, you could sense a calorie of temperature change, a small breach in the air. Emmet turned away to hide the Taser's laser sight. He pushed the power button. It didn't come on. *The goddamn battery was dead.* The Taser had been sitting in the heat of Emmet's trunk for months. Emmet thought a moment. He stood up under the canopy of fronds. He drew the folding knife.

Marlowe tucked a 9mm into his waistband and loaded the Mossberg 500 pump-action shotgun.

"Where's my gun?" Cody said.

"Have you ever fired one before?" Marlowe said.

"Yeah, I'm really good."

"Then without a doubt you'll shoot me. Take what you want," Marlowe said.

Eli had risen from the grave. Marlowe had cut him loose and now the kid was loading two pistols, expertly, crisp movements, like an assassin in an action movie. He looked like he had another agenda besides getting out of here. Every now and then he'd shoot a poison look at Cody and get one in return. Marlowe wondered if they'd shoot each other.

"Eli? Do you know a shortcut back?" Marlowe said. "I don't want to meet Tato on the trail."

"Yes, I know," Eli said. "It splits off to the right. It's more like a path. Animals use it." Marlowe showed the group how to make improvised earplugs. Shotgun blasts in a cement room would be extremely loud. A half a piece of toilet paper. Get it wet, squeeze out most of the water and roll it onto a ball. Stick it in your ear and it was reasonably effective.

"Okay, here's how it will go," Marlowe said. "I'll take out the locks and kick the door down. Eli goes through firing at anything that moves, I'll step out and cover him. Ren and Cody, you come next. Keep low and split off to the right. Eli will catch up and lead you to the trail. I'll watch our backs. And remember, if you can see them, they can see you. Take cover and shoot." Ren was grim, a thousand-yard stare. She'd chosen another shotgun. She glared at Marlowe.

"I'm getting out of here," she said. "And if I don't? I'm going to kill you."

"Here we go," Marlowe said. Marlowe put the barrel of the Mossberg to the door, angling it down, aiming at the locking mechanism, not the door lock itself. He squeezed the trigger. BOOM. Wood chips flew, the lock was torn away from the frame. BOOM! The second lock was gone. Marlowe kicked the door down, Eli slipped past him, but didn't fire. They were clear. "GO!" Marlowe shouted. "GO HARD."

Chain Smoker was on the other side of the agave plant, waiting, motionless, wary of an ambush. Sweat was getting in Emmet's eyes, a cloud of mosquitos stinging his face and arms. The cramp hadn't gone away. The pain was crippling. Chain Smoker took two nearly soundless steps. He was coming around the agave. Emmet held the knife like he was shaking hands, thumb resting on the spine of the grip, four fingers curled under. You don't stab, you thrust. *He'll be down low and in profile, Emmet. Let him go past you so he can't swing around and fire. Then it's your forearm around his throat, stick him wherever you can and don't stop.*

The pain from the cramp was searing. The muscles in his calf had turned as hard as a steel tie rod. He saw the barrel of Chain Smoker's gun and a sliver of his face. Chain Smoker hesitated, then took a few steps past the agave. Emmet was behind him now. His knees were frozen. The pain was crippling. He started to rise but he was too slow. Chain Smoker heard him, began to turn when two shotgun blasts cracked the silence. BOOM! BOOM! Chain Smoker swiveled and looked back. Emmet stepped through the fronds and stabbed him. The man dropped his rifle, held his guts and shouted something in Armenian. He staggered away and fell into the brush. Emmet dropped the knife. The pain and exhaustion were too much. He grabbed at the agave to stay upright but the thorns cut his hand. He collapsed to his knees and fell sideways into the dirt.

*   *   *

Tato and Dima were running down the main trail toward the armory. They heard the shotgun blasts. They saw Eli, Marlowe and the women emerge from the building and slip off into the dark. Eli had shown them the shortcut. Tato cursed. Another reason to kill him. It was too dark and brushy to cut them off. He and Dima would have to start near the trailhead. Dima was in the best shape.

"Go get them," Tato said. "I'll catch up."

Eli, Ren and Cody were making their way along the deer path. They couldn't go very fast. It was treacherous in the dark. Cody was falling behind. "Wait," she said, but the others had rounded a bend. She stopped to take a breather and heard a voice.

"Over here," it croaked. She peered into the dark.

"Emmet?" She went toward the voice, squinting, squinting, moving her head around to get different angles.

"Help. Please help me." She found him on all fours, gasping, drool dripping from his open mouth, unable to get up. She was going to call the others but hesitated. Why should she do anything? The old man was always shouting at her and putting her down. Why not leave the asshole here? Who would miss him? She looked down at him thinking, *You'd have the house to yourself, Cody.*

The others were gone. Marlowe waited, hidden in some brush. He heard someone coming up the trail. He was moving fast. Probably Dima. Marlowe didn't want to kill anybody and he didn't want a shootout. He stood up.

"Drop the gun, Dima!" Dima skittered to a stop. He was holding an AK. Marlowe saw mostly silhouette. Dima hesitated but Marlowe didn't. He aimed high and fired off two rounds. BLAM! BLAM! In the flashes he saw Dima, head drawn into his shoulders, one hand up in surrender.

"Okay, okay, don't shoot."

"Throw the gun away," Marlowe said. Dima obeyed, the AK landing in the dark somewhere. "Lie down on the ground and put your hands on your head," Marlowe said. Dima started to kneel.

"I'm sorry about the whip," he said. "Don't kill me, okay?" In an instant, Dima leapt sideways into the brush. It happened so fast, Marlowe didn't have time to react. He aimed high and fired off three shots in different directions. None would come close to hitting Dima but it might stall him a little. Marlowe took off down the trail.

Marlowe stumbled along. He could barely see the trail. He hadn't gone far when Dima came rushing out of the blackness. He hit Marlowe like a linebacker, his shoulder ramming Marlowe's hip. Marlowe spun, staggered but he didn't go down. In an instant, Dima was behind him, his powerful forearm around Marlowe's neck, squeezing tight, his other hand pushing hard on the back of his head. A choke hold. Dima was strong, the pressure immediate and huge. Marlowe couldn't breathe, his brain filling up with blood.

"Thought you could get away from Dima, huh?" Dima gloated. "I will choke you to death, my friend."

Emmet had taught Marlowe the move. It was pretty simple. Marlowe clamped one hand on Dima's forearm to hold it steady, swung his other hand back, grabbed Dima's Rocky Mountain oysters, crushing the shells and wrenching them off the reef at the same time. Dima howled and released him, turning in circles and holding his nuts. Marlowe hit him a left-right-left combination and watched him fall.

Tato had a flashlight. He found Dima on the trail, lying on the ground, holding his crotch and groaning. He was in agony.

"What happened?" Tato said.

"Go on, Tato," Dima grunted. "I am coming."

Marlowe caught up with the others. Ren, Eli and Cody were clustered on the trail, winded, breathing out clouds of steam.

"We were worried," Ren said.

"Me too," Marlowe said. "Anyone seen my dad?"

Emmet stepped out from behind Ren. He put his hand on her shoulder for support. "I'm here."

"He was lost. Cody found him," Ren said.

"Thanks, Cody," Marlowe said.

"Yeah, sure," she mumbled.

"I'll stay and cover," Eli said. "You guys go." He said it like there would be no argument. He wants a confrontation with his brother, thought Marlowe. Family. There are always old scores to settle. Cody turned and walked away.

The group was farther up the trail when a gun battle erupted behind them. The boom of Tato's .357, a smaller one than Eli's Glock. The two brothers were going mano a mano. They reached the stables, kept going until they got to Emmet's cruiser.

"Can we go now?" Cody said, impatient.

"We're waiting for your boyfriend," Ren said. There was a rapid exchange of shots. Then silence. Everyone waited, suspended in the dark. One shot rang out. The .357.

They heard sirens in the distance. "*Now* can we go?" Cody said. Ren and Emmet got in the backseat. Marlowe behind the wheel, Cody next to him. He started the engine and the dash lights came on. He saw it for an instant. Cody was smiling. Marlowe knew why. Because she was the last man standing, because there was no one left to rat her out, tell the police, tell anyone. She had all the secrets.

Marlowe took the gun away from Cody. Then he dropped her and Emmet at Emmet's place. He drove Ren to the Marriott. It was a long silent drive. She'd stayed in the backseat by herself. He couldn't see her in the mirror and was glad. He stopped the car in front of her room.

"I'm sorry, Ren," Marlowe said. She got out of the car and went quickly inside.

Tato and Dima drove away from the stables. They said nothing for a long time. Tato smiled and then burst out laughing. "We have the money, my friend! We are rich! We can do what we want!"

Dima laughed too. "You're a genius, boss." Dima's share of the cash was in his apartment. They arrived at the building and drove into the underground garage. Dima steered the car toward his parking space and stopped. The Russians were there.

"Hello, Tato," Grigory said. "Please get out of the car." Dima immediately exited.

Disbelieving, Tato said, "You are my brother." It made sense, he thought sadly. Safer to be with the lions. Safer to be in the cage. He clambered out and stood. That was when he saw the whip bending in the air, unfurling and coming straight for his eyes.

CHAPTER SIXTEEN

OUR FATHER, WHO ART IN HEAVEN

Emmet and Cody slept until noon. Emmet was beat up and exhausted. He'd gone out anyway and brought back burritos. They must have weighed two pounds apiece. They ate at the breakfast table without looking at each other.

"Good," Cody said when they were finished.

"Mm, yeah," Emmet said.

They used paper towels to wipe the cheese, beans, pork, salsa and guacamole off their faces. Emmet read the paper. Cody rinsed the dishes. That's new, Emmet thought. He wondered if he should thank her for saving his life but he knew she wouldn't want him to. When she was finished with the dishes, she wiped her hands on a towel.

"I made a mess of everything, Emmet. I'm sorry." She left. He heard her move down the hall and quietly close the door.

Emmet sat there brooding. He was confused, not a new feeling now. Cody had disappointed him again and again. There was nothing redeemable about her. She was as corrupt and coldhearted as any of the criminals he'd arrested. But he wanted her to stay. Ridiculous, he thought, and yet it nagged him for the rest of the day. He was wondering what to make for dinner when he realized he wanted to save her. The idea was absolutely moronic but he couldn't shake it. He got the vodka out of the freezer.

* * *

Marlowe called Ren but she'd blocked his number. She was leaving today without her Jeremy. He was sitting on the edge of the bed, staring at the blue screen and listening to Diana Krall. He was restless and irritated. Something was wrong but he couldn't identify what. Everything had been resolved. Andy killed Terry. Branko killed Andy. Hzoy killed DeSallis, and Tato had the money. But the feeling of incompleteness wouldn't go away. Marlowe and Emmet had another commonality. They were both unwaveringly tenacious.

Marlowe sat at the picnic table with his laptop, a pot of coffee brewing. He opened Terry's file. Marlowe knew the facts but he read them anyway. Around midnight on October 31, Andy forced Terry out of the house and onto the beach. Andy had an urgent motive, a cutthroat personality, and he'd declared to the others that Terry had to be stopped. He shot Terry twice in the face. Marlowe hesitated. That didn't seem right. Andy wasn't a pro. It would have been a nightmare for him to shoot Terry in the face or anywhere else. Marlowe stared at the date. October 31. Halloween. So what? he thought dismissively. It could have been Valentine's Day for all it mattered. And what was Halloween anyway? Kids wear costumes and go trick-or-treating. Adults wear costumes, go to parties and drink. Marlowe continued reading the file and stopped again. *Costumes.*

He thought back. Zoya was being interrogated by a Russian man. Cody was behind the sofa, eavesdropping. She described to Marlowe and Emmet what was said. Zoya told the Russian man that Andy came to the house late one night. He dumped a suitcase full of cash on the bed and wanted to have sex. Zoya was disappointed. Andy wasn't dressed and she was wearing a cat suit. Why? Because it was Halloween.

"Son of a bitch," Marlowe breathed.

On the same night Andy was supposedly murdering Terry in Malibu, he was in Little Armenia trying to get laid. Marlowe shook his head. He'd been wrong again.

He got a cup of coffee and looked out the window. Someone

else killed Terry. Not Andy and not Hzoy. Hzoy didn't know about the stealing until after Terry was dead. Racine and Branko weren't involved until much later. Who then? DeSallis? DeSallis was a spindly fifty-six-year-old accountant, not the burly guy seen on the surveillance video.

"Damn you, Cody," Marlowe said. She was a loathsome creature but it never occurred to him that she'd shoot her father and leave him dead on the sand. But how did she do it? Presumably, she was at a party on Canaan Road. She didn't come home until after Terry was dead. Detectives questioned her and were satisfied. There was no gun residue on her or her clothes, no sand on the floor of her room.

A PI didn't have to produce evidence that held up in court. A PI speculated, deduced and conjectured until a theory formed that felt right to an experienced investigator. Marlowe could never replicate Cody's thinking or her individual moves. The best he could do was ask himself, *How would you do it, Marlowe?*

Okay, he thought. Terry is going to blow the deal with the Russians. You decide to take him out. You choose Halloween as the date because Kendra and Pav won't be home. The party on Canaan Road is your alibi and Terry will be alone. You get Terry to drop you off at the party. Not something you'd ask someone if you were planning on killing them. You stay at the party until you're sure you're seen. Everybody is wasted so it's easy to slip away. You text Eli and he picks you up. You go to the public access entrance to the beach. Chain link fence, open gate, no cameras. Eli brings you a .45-caliber handgun. Overkill, but that's just the way you are. You change clothes in the car. You put on Noah's catcher's vest. The vest gives you big shoulders and width across the chest. Over the vest, you wear a big black sweatshirt, transforming you into the strong, athletic male seen on video. You don a Jason mask, something a man would choose.

You and Eli trudge up the beach in the wind and the cold. You reach Kendra's place and slip on latex gloves. Eli cuts off the padlock with a bolt cutter. You know the surveillance camera only shows the inside of the gate. Eli is unseen. You change shoes with him. He wears size 10½. That's why you stumble on the stairs. You disarmed the security system before you left for the party. There are no cameras inside the house.

You find Terry, lead him down the stairs and away from the house lights. You know about blood spatter. That's why you wear a KingSeal disposable apron. You have a box of them in your room. Careless to leave them there but there's no way to connect them to the shooting. You shoot Terry, twice in the face because that's the way you are. Then you and Eli hike back to the public access entrance and the car. You change back to your party clothes and Eli drops you off at the party again. Nobody notices your return, everybody's more wasted than before. You drink and smoke so you can be legitimately stoned out of your mind.

You ask that loser Nathan Schwartz to take you home. You can hardly stand up when you get out of the car. He has to help you to the door. You take a long shower. You scrub yourself with Lava soap and wash your hair. The next morning, a detective questions you. You have a plausible story and an alibi. He's convinced and he leaves. A technician sweeps you with a portable sensor. No gun residue. Meanwhile, Eli disposes of everything connected with the shooting and brings back Noah's vest. You wipe it clean and forget about it. You're home free.

Marlowe exchanged the coffee for a bourbon, sat down at the picnic table. He sipped his drink and brooded on his theory. A defense attorney would poke holes until it bled to death. Didn't matter. He was an experienced investigator and he was satisfied. He had a 9mm Sig like Emmet's hidden inside a covered frying pan. He took the gun and removed the magazine. He aimed the gun into the dark and pulled the trigger. *Click. Click. Click. Click.* People always disappointed you. They were so self-serving, greedy and pernicious, it made you want to leave the world, or at the very least, wonder why you stayed. He had to call Emmet.

Emmet was cooking. Cody could smell it from her room. It was awful, like he'd made something out of hot dogs and fish. She took a shower, turning the water up as hot as she could stand it. She felt her skin burn. Her lungs filled with steam. Nothing had gone right, everything had backfired, her great plan was a pile of smoldering garbage. She couldn't ask anybody for help, not even Roy. She wondered if she really loved Eli. Now that he was gone she'd have to say no. Her intense feelings weren't about him. They were about escape. He was the way to freedom.

Freedom. She'd felt caged in all her life. People with their rules and conventions and good behavior. She was in the eighth grade, stuck in English class. Mrs. Harris read a poem every day, standing there in her ugly green sweater set and low heels, warbling like a turkey about love or trees or some bullshit about good fences. She told Terry how bored she was but she never said how much she hated Mrs. Harris and how she longed to strangle her with those stupid pearls she wore every day. She never told Terry that she found his gun on the top shelf of the closet and when no one was around she shot the sea gulls sitting on the sand. She didn't tell him she wanted to kill Gary Marx with that snow globe and how jealous she was of Noah and how someday she'd cut the brake lines on his precious sports car. Once, she actually heard that troglodyte say, "I feel the need—for speed." Oh yeah, hotshot? Wait'll you're driving back to Lancaster, crash through a guardrail and plummet into a canyon, screaming as you realize your sister has done you in.

She remembered in some detail the night she shot Terry. How she trudged up the beach with Eli, hunched over, hands in their pockets, the breakers loud, the wind and grit making their eyes water. They hadn't spoken of their fear. They reached Kendra's house. Cody's hands were damp inside the latex gloves. She was all adrenaline, heart thundering, mouth parched. Eli was better at hiding it but she knew he felt the same. He held her close.

"You sure about this?" he said.

"Yeah, I'm sure." She wanted to do it. She wanted to watch that sap die.

At that moment, she thought she couldn't do this without Eli.

Looking back, she could have done it without anybody. She'd gone up and down the side stairs countless times, but they looked unfamiliar. Eli's shoes were too big and she stumbled a couple of times. Every footstep seemed loud and emphatic.

She went inside. She could hear the TV. Terry was in the den. She walked down the hall. The fear had left her. She was keyed up, superaware and eager. She reached the den. She heard canned laughter. An episode of *Cheers* was on TV; Sam and Diane doing their back-and-forth. Terry loved the old shows. *Dick Van Dyke. All in the Family, M*A*S*H.* He said they were like comfort food.

Terry was sprawled half on, half off the couch, wearing a torn bathrobe, asleep and snoring, an open script on his chest. A half bottle of Scotch and a water glass were on the coffee table. Some people look innocent and peaceful when they're asleep. Terry looked homeless. She walked over and aimed the gun at his face. All hesitation had left her.

"Dad, wake up." Terry didn't stir. "Dad, *wake up.*" She pressed the barrel against his forehead. So this is what it feels like, she thought. Terry groaned and slapped at the gun. She jammed it in hard. His eyes jerked open.

"Hey..." He pushed the barrel away and blinked a few times. "Who are you?" She lifted the Jason mask.

"How ya doin', asshole?" Cody said.

"Kitten?"

"Don't call me that." Terry saw the gun.

"What are you doing? Is that real?"

"Yes it's real. Give me a hard time and I'll shoot you," she said. He started to get up but realized she wasn't kidding. He lay back on his elbows.

"Kitten, I don't—"

"DON'T CALL ME THAT!" she screamed. She hit him with the butt of the gun. He cried out, fell back, an ugly cut on his forehead. Blood dripped down his face. He touched it, looked at his hand.

"This is crazy! This is insane! Why are you—?"

"Get up or I'll shoot you right now!"

He walked ahead of her with his hands up, limping because he was wearing one slipper, tugging at the bathrobe tie because it wouldn't stay closed. He was bewildered, muttering the whole way. *If you could just tell me what's wrong. What did I do? Really, Cody, what did I do? There must be something. Did I say something? Do something?* His voice high and strangled with fear.

"Why? Please tell me why!" he shouted.

"Why? Because you're weak," she said. "Keep walking." They met Eli on the sand.

"Who's this?" Terry said. They shoved him farther away from the house, a few feet from shore. The wind and breakers made it hard to hear, Terry's flop sweat gleaming in the moonlight. She couldn't stand looking at him. Terry was a coward and a leech. He was pitiful. He had no dignity.

"It's about the Russian money, isn't it?" he said. He told her he'd changed his mind, that he was being impulsive, foolish, he'd work it out with the others and everything would be fine. "We'll do it together!" he gushed. Cody aimed the gun at Terry's face. He was sobbing, the wind flapping his bathrobe around, tears streaking across his face, hands clasped like he was saying a prayer. In a way, he was, Cody thought. *Our Father, who art in heaven. Save me from my vicious daughter.* She was oddly hesitant. Not from a pang of conscience. Not from a pang of anything. More a quick calculation. Was this the right thing to do? Surely it was. Terry thought her hesitation was hope. He made an awful grin, his craven eyes black holes of desperation, sucking in every human emotion Cody'd ever had.

"You can't shoot me, I'm your dad, right?" he said. "We can put this behind us! Make a brand-new start! We'll be pals again!"

"You mean like you and Noah?" she said. He didn't hear her and went on, merrily inane.

"Come on, kiddo! Let's work things out like we always do!"

"Don't talk anymore, Dad."

"Just like the old days! Screw the Russians! We'll go off on our own, do something together, just you and me!"

"Be quiet, Dad!" Her anger fattened, festered, a swollen blister

about to burst. Terry was laughing, like he knew he was dead, like he might as well keep going. He kept talking faster and faster.

"Think about the times we've had! Remember when we went to that dude ranch in Arizona? What was it called? Rim Rock, Red Rock—whatever it was, wasn't it the best? We were all wearing freaking cowboy hats, and what was that horse? It was your favorite. You know the one I mean, it was grayish, right? And it had, uh, it had something, uh—spots, right? Yeah, that was a great horse..." His voice trailed off. "Come on, Cody, you love your old man, don't you?" he whimpered. "Please, don't do this. I love you, kitten." That did it. She shot him twice in the face. She'd felt worse when she shot a sea gull. It wasn't very dramatic, Terry a lump in the sand. Eli grabbed her hand and they ran off.

It went fine after that. No hitches, no problems. After she got home from the party, she went to bed and slept fine. Lucy woke her up, screaming and jabbering. Then two detectives came in, a Dudley Do-Right–looking white guy in a checked sport coat and a stringy Black woman with skeptical eyes and an attitude. Dudley was in charge. He wanted to interview the hot teenage girl in the thin cotton pajamas. She'd cut off the top two buttons just for the occasion. The Black woman left the room rolling her eyes.

Cody played it hungover, too wasted to be hysterical, sort of a sloppy, grieving drunk. Dudley asked his questions. She answered truthfully to a point, interspersed with sobbing and arm waving, which gave him an opportunity to look down her top. She excused herself and went into the bathroom. She gargled with the egg whites she'd left in her toothbrush cup and threw up violently. She came out of the bathroom wiping her mouth with a towel. "Well, that about wraps it up," Dudley said. "I'm sorry for your loss."

The smell of Emmet's cooking was stronger. Cody lay in bed, staring at the pebbly ceiling. She would not give up. She would not submit to an ordinary, boring life. There had to be a way out. She cursed herself. There was no point thinking about the future unless she had money. It took a few moments, but she realized she had to stop feeling sorry for herself and think small. Think incremental. She needed a start but she had no access to people with money, or money in any form. She closed her eyes. *Christ, you're a moron, Cody.* What she needed first wasn't money. It was a gun.

Emmet was in the backyard, lying on a chaise and having a beer. It was early evening, his favorite time. Two sparrows were taking a dirt bath, a hornet emerged from the dead plants. The tuna casserole was in the oven. It was Addie's recipe but it didn't smell right. Maybe it was the extra ingredients. He hadn't decided whether to let Cody stay. Kendra wouldn't care but the optics were terrible. The Department would come down on him for sure. A seventeen-year-old girl and non–family member under the watchful gaze of an old man on leave for drinking on the job? That wouldn't fly. Maybe on weekends or something.

Marlowe called. "Cody killed Terry," he said. Emmet didn't say anything. Every sign that Cody was a ruthless sociopath was there. The narcissism, greed, the lack of conscience, her indifference to the pain of others. He'd recognized Cody's corruption but dealt with it incident by incident. In effect, forgiving her for whatever had come before. She was as vicious as anyone Emmet had ever arrested. How did you let this happen? he thought. How was it possible to think you could save her? Were you dreaming about having a granddaughter?

"Do you have enough for an arrest?" Emmet said.

"No. I don't have anything except assumptions and guesswork."

"That's okay, I'll do it," Emmet said.

"She's dangerous, Dad."

"I won't tell her anything until I drop her off," Emmet said. "If she gives me a hard time I'll cuff her." The call ended.

Emmet went inside and took the vodka out of the freezer. He was getting a glass out of the dish rack when a mournful ache fell over him, so crushing and deep he had to sit down. He hadn't been dreaming about a granddaughter. He'd been dreaming about a daughter, the one Addie always wanted. Susan. The whimsical pink figurine who had a shelf all to herself.

Marlowe ordered takeout from Marouch. Lamb shawarma, tabouleh and Lebanese bread. He'd called Ren several times but she'd blocked his number and his email. At least you're done with Cody, he thought. He wanted to feel some sense of resolution but he didn't. *Forget it. You're being obsessive. Eat your goddamn dinner and shut up.* He put the food out on the picnic table, opened a bottle of Allagash and sat down. He picked up his fork and put it back down again. He was pissed. "What, Marlowe?" he said. *"What?"*

Marlowe fired up his laptop again and went back to his notes, dogged, his father's son. He met Kendra for the first time on the fourteenth of this month. She said she was going to a premiere the following night, the fifteenth, the same night Cody and Roy were attacked in the alley. The premiere was held at the El Capitan Theatre across the street from Grauman's. There were paparazzi shots of Kendra getting out of the Bentley, her legs splayed like a new-born giraffe getting to its feet, giving a grateful world a panoramic view of her canary-yellow thong. Pav was driving. You could see him through the windshield. The premiere began at eight. If you counted in cocktails, the movie and schmoozing time it probably let out at eleven or so. Cody and Roy were attacked around nine thirty or ten. Pav had plenty of time to leave the premiere, shoot at them and return to pick up Kendra. Pav also had motive. He blamed Cody for Terry's destruction. Pav and Terry were blood brothers, they loved each other. Love, Marlowe thought. Sooner or later, everything came back to that cave of terrified bats.

But if Pav was the shooter, he was also the man who approached Roy and paid him $1,000 to set up Cody. Marlowe remembered the stack of twenty-dollar bills on Roy's coffee table. That made no sense. Pav blithely stopped at his local ATM and withdrew a grand out of his checking account? Most people had a withdrawal limit of $500 or less but the bank saw fit to double the limit for Pav? No.

Somebody else gave Roy the money. That was another thing Emmet said. Sometimes the answer is in the question you ask.

Who else loved Terry?

Marlowe checked his notes again. The day after the alley attack, he called Noah's coach. He wanted to know if Noah was in Lancaster the previous night, the fifteenth. The coach referred him to Noah's buddy, Chris Patterson. The one who reminded Marlowe of a younger Mahershala Ali. At the time, Marlowe didn't know Chris was Noah's partner. Kendra said they were in love and wanted to get married. Maybe Noah had given Chris an excuse for his absence that night or maybe Chris knew the whole story. But when Chris was asked by a supposed police detective if Noah was in Lancaster the previous night, he knew to say yes. Yes, Noah was there. Then there was the fiasco at the Sunshine Court. Marlowe had seen what he thought was Pav's car driving away. It had round taillights that didn't match the car registered to Pav. Marlowe remembered the day he brought Cody back to Malibu. Chris and Noah were washing Noah's car, a Nissan GTR. Marlowe had never seen one before. He admired its aesthetic but didn't like the taillights. They were round, two on either side.

Noah loved Terry. Noah wants Cody dead.

Marlowe wondered if he'd ever get angry enough to murder someone. He loved Emmet and Addie. It was possible he'd get angry enough to kill their murderer. Marlowe didn't love Ren, or at least not yet, but would he kill her killer? No. He'd beat the guy into melted cheese but wouldn't take his life. Another human foible, he thought. A parsing of feelings could determine if you lived or died.

When Marlowe spoke to Noah and Chris, Chris said they were going to baseball camp in nine days. That was the nineteenth. Nine days from the nineteenth is the twenty-eighth. Today. After the camp, Chris said they were going skiing and then would ad-lib the rest of their itinerary. Marlowe heard an alarm bell clanging. If Noah didn't kill Cody tonight he wouldn't get another chance for weeks, maybe months. Marlowe phoned Kendra. *It can't be. It just can't be!* It rang six times before she answered.

"What do you want, you malevolent fart? I'm in the middle of a crisis here."

"Have Noah and Chris left for baseball camp?"

Kendra took a swallow of something. "Oh God, it was a disaster! Noah and Chris had a terrible fight. I didn't hear most of it because I was yelling at Lucy. It was something about Noah going somewhere and Chris saying it was a huge mistake."

Marlowe cringed and said, "Where was Noah going?"

"I don't know but they broke up!" Kendra said tearfully. "I couldn't believe it! Chris called Noah insane and he left."

"Is Noah there?" Marlowe asked hopefully.

"No, he's not!" Kendra wailed. "He said he was leaving for camp early and—"

Marlowe hung up. He called Emmet and got voice mail. He texted him three times. No answer. Marlowe bounded down the stairs, jumped into the Mustang and roared out of the lot. Traffic was bad. He did his boy racer thing, ran a red light and got to the freeway. The entry ramp was jammed. He drove up on the shoulder and flew past the line of cars. *Please, God, no cops.*

It was a few months before Terry's death. Noah was at training camp. His conversations with his dad were alarming. Terry was always exhausted and complained about working too hard. Noah knew he was drinking. Terry would babble on for five minutes and say he had to go. When camp was over Noah rushed back to LA and went directly to Terry's. He didn't call, he wanted to surprise him, see his old man smile and tear up and give him a big hug. Cody opened the door. She huffed and said,

"Oh look who's here. Caught any ground balls lately?" The apartment was awful, nearly squalid.

"Where's Dad?" Noah said.

"Sleeping," she said. Sleeping? Noah thought. Terry was an early riser and it was nearly two in the afternoon. Terry came shuffling out of the bedroom, unshaven, sallow, huge bags under his eyes, wearing pajama bottoms and an old T-shirt. He looked at Noah, confused at first. As if his son were a stranger.

"Oh. Hey, Noah, it's, uh, good to see you," Terry said. His voice was scratchy. "Do you want some coffee? Make him some coffee, Cody."

"We don't have any," she said as she walked out of the room.

"Uh, um, why don't you sit down, son," Terry said. Noah stayed standing. There were discarded scripts in the overflowing wastebasket, crude storyboards taped crookedly to the walls, along with pictures torn out of magazines. Possible locations, Noah thought.

"Are you making a movie, Dad?"

"Movie?" Terry smiled anxiously. "Naah. This is just, um, you know, messing around." He's lying, Noah thought. Why? What's so wrong about making a movie?

"You told me over the phone you were working too hard," Noah said. "What are you working on?"

"Uh, well, me and Andy have some interest from investors. I mean, nothing set in stone, of course, but we're moving into a real office. Not like this dump. But like I said, nothing's set in stone."

"Dad, you look terrible. What's going on?"

Terry faked a laugh. "Going on? Nothing really. It's, uh, just, uh, whaddayoucallit—a prospect. Or let's call it a possibility. Yeah, that's what it is. A really good possibility. I mean, they can't keep me down forever, right? Right?"

"I don't understand. It's just a possibility but you're moving into an office?"

"Did I say we were?" he said. He tapped on his noggin with his knuckles. "What I meant was, we might. Yeah, we might. Depends on how things turn out but nothing's—"

"Dad, it's me, okay? You're making a movie."

"No, I'm not." That fake laugh again. "I mean I'd know if I was, wouldn't I?"

"I grew up in the business, Pop," Noah replied. "If you're making a movie, where'd you get the money?"

"There is no money. I don't know what you're—"

Noah nodded at an elaborate camera standing in the corner on a twelve-legged tripod. "That's an IMAX camera. They rent for sixteen grand a day, so don't tell me there's no money."

"Okay, there's *some* money but—"

"Tell me, Dad, *what's going on?*" Noah pleaded. Terry was frazzled, shaking, near tears. "You know you can tell me anything," Noah continued. "Remember what we used to say? Straight-up and no bullshit. That was us all the way." Terry nodded, agreeing, seeing the light.

"Right, right, straight-up and no bullshit," he said. "Well, um, there's these Russian guys. They, um, they're investing in my comeback movie. I don't deal with them directly, they have these Armenians work for them."

"And in return?" Noah said.

"I'm supposed to—well, the company is supposed to, um, launder money for them." Terry looked at the floor and spoke quickly. "It's a short-term deal, nothing to worry about, really, I mean it's in and out and we're done, they're good guys when you get to know them and when you think about it, where else can I get funding? I already have the talent, the experience, the—"

"Laundering money? Dad, that's insane!" Noah said.

"Why don't you mind your own business," Cody said as she came in. She handed Terry a cell phone. "It's Tato, about that other thing."

"Sorry, I've got to take this," Terry said. He looked relieved. He took the phone and left the room.

"What have you gotten him into, Cody?" Noah said. "He'd never do this on his own."

"Dad's got a big mouth."

"Who's Tato?" Noah said.

"He delivers the mail. Get out of here, will you?"

Noah got up, went around her and walked down the hall. Terry was in the bedroom talking on the phone.

"Dad?" Noah said.

"Can't now, son," Terry said, with a panicky smile. "Important call. Sorry. We'll have lunch or something." He turned his back and spoke in a low voice. Noah returned to the living room. Cody was on the sofa. She was painting her toenails black.

"Russian gangsters don't mess around, Cody," Noah said. "You're going to get him killed."

"Nobody's gonna kill anybody. And who said they were gangsters?"

"Most ordinary Russians don't launder money. If something happens to Dad, I'll hold you responsible."

"You're in my air space, asshole. Leave, okay?"

"He's our father, Cody. How could you do this?"

"He's a failed movie director," Cody retorted. "He'll never get back in the business again. He's depressed, he's drinking, if it goes on like this he'll kill himself. Is that what you want?" She was still applying the polish in tiny, deft strokes.

"That's why you're doing this?" Noah scoffed. "For his sake? What a joke."

"You're blocking the light."

Noah glowered down at her. "I love Dad, even if you don't, and I'm warning you, Cody. If something happens to him? Something happens to you," then adding as he went out the door, "and it'll be ugly."

Emmet drank his vodka, still reeling from the news. Over the years, he'd arrested a lot of Cody types. Assholes that targeted others but in the end, self-destructed. His favorite sportswriter, Mike Lupica, said, "It's like they take poison and then hope for the other person to die."

"Stay right there, Emmet," Cody said. She was standing in the doorway, pointing his service weapon at him.

"Where'd you get that?"

"From that chair with the stupid bluebird on it. I saw you take it." The night they went to Musso's, Emmet thought. He made her turn around but she'd seen his reflection in the window. "I've been waiting for this," she said. "Why don't you yell at me now, old man?" If he resisted, she'd respond with violence. *Get her to drop her guard, Emmet.* He tried to look fear-stricken, not hard to do under the circumstances.

"Hey, come on, Cody," he said. "I took you in, didn't I? I treated you good." He put a quiver in his voice. "Please, Cody, I didn't mean any harm, I'm sorry I yelled at you." She smiled spitefully.

"Too late, Emmet. We're gonna finish it, you and me." Emmet tried to work up some tears but he couldn't do it. She gestured with the gun. "Let's go."

"Can I have another drink?"

"Let's go, goddammit!"

He got up slowly, drunkenly, moves he knew well. They went down the hall, Emmet shuffling unsteadily, his hand on the wall for support he didn't need.

"Hurry up!" she screeched.

Traffic eased. Marlowe drove fast. What if Cody was already dead? he thought. What if Noah had killed Emmet as a witness? Marlowe called 911.

"Nine-one-one. What is your emergency?" the dispatcher said. Marlowe was going seventy-five miles an hour and didn't know what to say.

"Girl. She might be in danger."

"Might be, sir?" the dispatcher said.

"I think her brother is going to kill her."

"You *think* he is? How do you know that?" she said. Traffic slowed to walking speed. Marlowe changed lanes, cutting off an eighteen-wheeler, the horn blasting.

"Sir? Sir? Are you there?" the dispatcher said.

"Yes, yes, I'm here, I..." *Make something up, Marlowe!* "There's a shooting! A shooting! A girl!"

"Where, sir? What is the address?"

"Seven ninety-five East Adams, right off San Pedro."

"Sir? Are you in your car?"

"What? Yes! I'm in my..." Another swerve, another honking horn.

"If you're in your car, how do you know there's a shooting?" she said.

"Because...because I know!" Three lanes were blocked. "Get out of the way!" he hollered, leaning on his horn.

"Sir? What's going on?"

"Somebody's gonna shoot my dad!" Marlowe cut all the way over to the right lane, accelerated, a motor home drifting in front of him. He jerked the wheel, went up on the shoulder again and floored it, the guardrail a foot from his fender.

"Shoot your dad?" she said. "You said it was a girl."

He reached his off-ramp, sped down it, the light at the intersection turning yellow. He dropped the phone and punched it, engine WAAAH'ing loud. The light turned red. The Mustang hit a dip, bouncing into the intersection, cars coming at him from the left and right. "DAMN YOU MARLOWE!" Marlowe screamed. There was nothing in front of him but an abutment. He hit the brakes hard, swung the wheel and yanked on the emergency brake. The car skidded sideways, tires smoking, banging into the curb, the airbags blowing up. Marlowe knocked the bags out of the way and drove down San Pedro. The car was hobbling, smoke coming from under the hood. He smelled gasoline. The engine died six blocks from Emmet's house. Marlowe got out and started running.

Cody took Emmet into the study. He plunked down in the armchair, breathing through his mouth and lolling his head.

"Who said you could sit down? Get up!" Cody insisted.

"Please, Cody—please."

"Get up or I'll pistol-whip you!" That was what he wanted. For her to get close and make a mistake. He struggled to his feet, stood there woozily.

"Open the safe," she commanded. "And don't say 'what safe.' I saw it when I was in here before. You didn't put the bowling trophy back." Emmet hid his alarm. When Cody realized Addie's jewelry wasn't real, she'd be angrier than she was now. She'd throw everything on the floor and stomp it into nothing. No, thought Emmet, he wouldn't let that happen. But if he refused, she'd think he was hiding something.

"That's all? Open the safe?" he said, sounding relieved. "Fine. No problem." Cody frowned at that. He went to the safe and squinted at the combination lock.

"What's wrong?" Cody said.

"I can't see the numbers. I need my glasses."

"You don't wear glasses, asshole. Quit fucking around!"

"For reading. I wear glasses for reading. I can't see the numbers."

"Liar!"

Cody was so furious she was no longer recognizable as a human being. Emmet had confronted more than a few people who wanted to shoot him, but none of them wanted the aftermath. None would have delighted in seeing his dead body. Cody pressed the barrel against his spine.

"Open up the goddamn safe or I'll cripple you for life! I swear to God I will!" Emmet put his hand on the dial, the combination was Addie's birthday: 5...21...19...*You can't let her do it, Emmet, not to Addie, not to Addie!* He pretended to pass out, holding on to the shelf as he slid to the floor. She kicked him.

"GET UP! GET UP!"

CHAPTER SEVENTEEN
A LEGEND

Noah parked the car a half block from the old man's house. He'd been here before. It was the day Marlowe returned Cody to Kendra's place. He and Chris were washing the GTR. They didn't want to drive all the way back to Lancaster so they stayed the night. Chris had gone to bed. Noah was in the open kitchen having a snack. Cody came in from the beach. She was soaking wet, crying and hysterical. She crossed the great room toward the hall.

"What's wrong?" Noah said.

"Ask Pav!" she shouted. She was in her room for two minutes and returned. Dry clothes, backpack, calling for a cab. She came into the kitchen and shouldered Noah aside. Then she opened a drawer and took the house money.

"Going somewhere?" Noah said.

"Piss off, Noah." She went outside to wait for the cab. Noah followed her in the GTR, all the way across town to a house on Adams Boulevard. An old man let her in, paid the cab and went back inside. This was Cody's hidey-hole, Noah thought. The old man must be her sugar daddy. Noah went to the gate, looked in and went back to his car. He was pleased. He knew where to find her.

Noah sat in the GTR and screwed the silencer into the barrel of the Glock. He scooched the seat back, slid the gun in his pants and covered it with his hoodie. The old man's house was neglected.

Everything peeling, fading, scuffed. The front door looked solid but
the locks were dark and grimy, they'd been there awhile. The plan
was simple. Go around the back and kick in the door. He was a
catcher, his thighs and calves were like pile drivers. Five seconds to
get inside. Nobody wakes up that fast. He'd go through the house,
find Cody, say what he had to say and shoot her in the face. Twice.
If the old man got into it, he'd get a smack.

Noah wanted a closer look. A trial run. He got out of the car
and walked quickly through the rickety front gate. Lights were on.
He didn't use the walkway and slipped through the foliage. Drapes
covered the front window. He crept around to the side of the house
and stopped at another window. It was masked with a screen but you
could see well enough. The living room was like something out of a
Margaret Rutherford movie. He could hear the TV.

Cody came in. Noah inhaled sharply, hate snagging his heart like
a grappling hook, ripping out his entrails, pulsing and slick with
blood. Look at her. The smug little cunt, sneaking around, up to
something like she always was. He would have fired through the
window but he wanted the confrontation. He wanted to see the
terror in Cody's eyes when he shot her. Her back was turned to him.
She was fiddling around with a chair, why he couldn't fathom. She
skulked out of the room and was gone.

Noah knelt, closed his eyes and waited for his heart to slow down.
He saw his father, lying on the sand, darkness around him, calling
for help, calling for his son. Noah's hate blacked out everything
else. Baseball, his future, his life with Chris. Shooting Cody was
justified. Not only for Dad's sake, but he had to kill her before she
killed him.

Noah was fifteen, playing in the semifinals against the Visalia
Wolves, a night game, a huge crowd cheering on their favorites.
He was the only freshman on the team and their best hitter. It
was the top of the twelfth, the score was tied 3–3. A man on
second. Noah was at bat, facing an All City pitcher with a ninety-
mile-an-hour fastball. If you were the pitcher, what would you be

thinking? Noah thought. The hitter is expecting fastballs. Throw him a slider. Noah waited for it. He got his pitch and hit it over the third baseman's head. The man on second scored. Game over. As Noah walked to the dugout, the fans stood and cheered. He looked up in the stands. Terry was waving and hooting and pumping his fist. Cody was giving him the finger. She was ten years old.

They drove home, Terry going on and on about what a great game it was, Noah in the passenger seat, Cody in the back, sitting right in the middle. He wondered why. Did she want him to see her? He glanced at the mirror. Cody was a silhouette, swaying with the motion of the car. They pulled up to an intersection, right next to a Shell station. Noah glanced at the mirror again. A yellow streak lit Cody's young eyes, a lurid red glowing hot on her face. She mouthed the words *Fuck you* and from that moment on, Noah was afraid of his little sister.

Sometime later, Noah was at a pool party Terry's friends had thrown. Noah was bored, restless, there were no other kids his age. He watched TV in the den for a while and decided to go outside. Some of the moms were hot. He was passing the living room when he saw Cody. It was a strange sight. A little girl in a polka-dot bathing suit, so serious and focused, picking things up, inspecting them and putting them back down again. She might have been shopping for a collectible. She settled on a snow globe. She hefted it in her hand and went outside. Noah watched her through the window. Cody got in the water, turned her back on the other kids, holding the snow globe below the surface. Puzzled, Noah went out and watched her from across the pool.

Cody stood there, not doing anything, kids splashing around her. She's waiting for something, Noah thought. A sniggering kid named Gary Marx came from behind her and bounced a beach ball off her head. It was nothing, it was harmless. Noah felt a rising alarm. Cody was turning around, her face clenched with anger. "Wait—" he said. It was too late. Cody cocked her arm and hurled the snow globe into Gary Marx's face. He cried out, blood gushing from his nose, adults leaping to their feet, yelling, kids screaming, charging for the sides of the pool. Terry jumped into the water, shouting at Cody. He grabbed her around the waist and carried her out. For a split second, Noah saw it. Cody was smiling. It scared him. It informed him. He understood her now. Her vitriol wasn't about jealousy or anything else. This was who she was. Born that way, she would stay that way, and he'd be on guard for the rest of his life. Years later, the feeling was still there, getting worse because Cody was growing up, getting more dangerous. Their fights were increasingly bitter, her threats more disturbing. The Hawkeyes had a game in Tucson. Noah went to a gun show, bought a Glock and a silencer. They don't check IDs in Arizona.

Noah went around to the back of the old man's house. Old door, old locks, no problem. He hurried back to his car. As he approached, he saw two men looking it over, using their phones as flashlights. Black guys. Big shorts, big muscles, wifebeaters and chains. *Oh shit. Gangsters. Who else would be out this late?*

"Fellas," Noah said with a friendly nod.

The bigger one smiled. Two of his teeth were gold. "Nice ride, brutha. Never seen one of these before."

"White with black rims," the second man said admiringly. "Das da way to roll, son." Noah stifled a shout. *This guy was taking pictures!* The first man leaned back against the driver's-side door. Noah couldn't get in.

"Sorry, I'd like to talk, guys, but I really have to go," he said, smiling feebly. The second guy came up behind him.

"Whatchoo doin' out here, man? Old man Emmet your family?" Noah didn't know what to say. He couldn't admit to a relationship or his reason for being there. He turned to face the guy.

"Uh, no, I don't know anybody named Emmet."

"Oh yeah? We saw you comin' out his yard," the first man said. "You was walkin' kinda fast too. What was you doin', scopin' the place out? Emmet ain't got nothin' to lift."

"No, no, no, you don't understand. This was a mistake. I went to the wrong house." He had to turn back and forth to keep them both in view.

"Oh yeah?" the second guy said. "What's the right house? You know somebody around here? Who are they? I prob'ly know 'em too."

"Look. No joke," Noah said. "I have to go." A breeze cooled him and he realized he was sweating. The first man was so wide he nearly covered the car door. "Could you get out of the way, please?" Noah said, a little louder. He was starting to panic. What if a cop comes by? What if Emmet comes out of the house? What if somebody else sees me? *Hurry, Noah. Hurry!*

"Emmet's our boy," the first man said. "He looks out for the whole neighborhood. We see you creepin' around his crib, we like, the hell is he doin'? You wouldn't be strappin', would you?"

"No, I'm not strapping!" Noah said desperately. "Look, I-I-I, r-really, *really* have to get out of here. People are expecting me." He knew he sounded lame but he couldn't help himself.

"Emmet's a cop," the second man noted. "What? You got a beef with him? You looking to set him up?"

Noah's panic was morphing into anger. Turning back and forth between one and the other was exasperating and they knew it. They were messing with him. "It's nothing like that, okay?" he said sharply. "Now could you let me pass? I'm serious." Noah stepped closer to the first man. They were inches apart.

"You close, but you ain't personal, white boy," the first man said. "You think you gonna scare me? I ain't been scared since my mama said she'd sell me to the gypsies."

A woman came out of a nearby duplex. She was wearing a housedress, a head scarf and a pissed-off expression. *Oh God, another witness to say she saw a white boy.*

"I thought you was goin' to the liquor store, Robert," she said. "The hell you doin' out there?"

"Go back in the house, Monique," the first man said. "I'll be there soon enough." Monique harrumphed and went back inside.

"You know what? I'm gonna check with Emmet," said the second man. "See what he has to say." *Oh shit oh shit oh shit.*

"No!" Noah blurted out. "I mean, he's sleeping, he'll be pissed off if you wake him up." *Oh shit oh shit oh shit.* His heart was pounding itself to shit, sweat streamed down his temples.

The second man grinned. "If you don't know him, how you know he's asleep?" With a laugh, he turned to go. *Do something, Noah! DO SOMETHING!* Noah stepped away from the car, drew the gun and shot the second guy in the back, the sound no louder than the clap of a mousetrap. The man dropped to his knees and flopped forward, his head slamming into the asphalt. The first man came off the car. "What the—" Noah shot him. The man crumpled sideways, his arm hooked to the side mirror. Then he slipped off and puddled on the ground.

Noah looked around wildly. The houses were closed up, no traffic, no people. He stared at the bodies, lying motionless on the street, blood creeping out from under them. Reality struck him hard and cold. *You just murdered two people.* "Oh no," he whispered. "No-no-no-no-no!" He kept staring at the bodies, hoping they would get up or speak or breathe. He realized, not that his life was over, but that it would never be good again. There would never be a moment's peace, a moment's love, a moment when he wasn't in torment. He started to cry. He could be home with Chris, playing *Dragon Age* and knocking back beers. Chris had warned him over and over that he was losing control, that he was too extreme. *WHAT WERE YOU THINKING, NOAH?*

He should flee, go now. Monique couldn't ID him, she'd seen him for two seconds. There wasn't any evidence. He thought a moment. No, nothing! He'd drive to Malibu and throw the gun in the ocean, take a shower, ditch his clothes, hose down the car. Then he'd go back to Lancaster, see if Chris was there.

Noah opened the car door and stopped. The second man *took pictures.* "Shit!" Where was the guy's phone? Did he drop it when he was shot? Did he have it on him? In a frenzy, Noah scanned every inch of the asphalt, kicking leaves and trash around. He got on his hands and knees and peered under the car. Nothing. *Find that goddamn phone, Noah!* The second man was lying facedown, limbs at weird angles, only his back pockets accessible. Noah knelt beside him. He tried to flip him over but he was deadweight. *Do it, Noah, hurry. If somebody sees you, you're finished.*

"Oh God," he sobbed. He slipped his hands underneath the man's warm body. Blood, blood, blood, like it would never stop. The man's front pockets held nothing but keys. *What are you going to do, Noah? WHAT ARE YOU GOING TO DO!*

"Robert?" Monique said. Noah got to his feet. "Robert?" she said again. She had her hand over her mouth, her face contorted with horror. She looked at Noah, saw the gun, saw the blood. She backed away, backed away and ran screaming into the duplex.

That's it, Noah. You're done. He sat down on the curb, folded his bloody hands and looked down at his bloody shoes. Hate had divorced him from thought, from reason, from consequences. He thought about prison. What they'd do to him when they found out he'd killed two innocent Black men who were trying to do the right thing. He thought about all he would lose, all he would never have again, his mutilated world beyond recognition, no reason to stay.

Noah got up and retrieved the gun. Absurdly, he wondered if he should stay standing or sit down again. How he would look when he was dead. He wondered what Chris would say. He wondered about the funeral and who would come. He put the gun to his head...finger on the trigger...squeezing...the pressure at the threshold...he stopped. There was a rumbling from deep within him. Tectonic movement, massive plates shifting, his white-hot core expanding to the surface. The hate hadn't gone away. It had only stepped aside. *Cody.* If he was going to hell, she was too.

Cody kicked Emmet until he got up. She pushed him face-first into the shelves and put the barrel to the base of his skull. "Do it now or you're dead, Emmet. Did you hear me? Do it now!"

Why die begging for your life? Emmet thought. She's going to kill you anyway. He wished Marlowe were here to see his drunken father go down like a man.

"I'm never going to open the safe, you shit-faced degenerate!"

Emmet shouted. "Why give you the satisfaction? You wanna know what's in there? Addie's antique jewelry and cash I took off drug dealers! A goddamn fortune!"

Cody pushed the barrel in harder, her searing breath in his ear, her voice rising like distant thunder. "Last chance, Emmet. *Open— the—safe.*"

"Go fuck yourself, you goddamn coward," Emmet said. "Stop yapping and shoot me! Shoot me the same way you shot your—"

Cody screamed, "DIE OLD MAN!" She pulled the trigger, Emmet's eardrums shattering as he fell to the floor.

Marlowe raced toward the house, his legs giving way, his lungs in embers. Noah ran out of the darkness and into the house, a gun in his hand. Marlowe followed, seconds behind him. The living room was empty. Marlowe rushed into the hall. He saw Noah, moving away from him, looking in the doorways. They heard Cody scream, "Die old man!" and then a gunshot. BLAM! *Did Cody shoot Emmet!* Marlowe sprang forward but Noah was aiming his gun into the study. "Yeah, it's me, bitch!" He screamed, "You killed my father!"

"Noah, don't!" Marlowe shouted. The shots were simultaneous, Cody fired once, BLAM! Noah's silencer spat twice. And then it was quiet. Blue smoke drifting. Noah stood there staring at what he'd done. Marlowe had never seen anyone so hopeless, so done with life. Noah turned and saw him. He bared his teeth, not in a snarl, but a grimace, as if all he had left were the remnants of hatred.

"Please, Noah. I want to see if my dad's all right," Marlowe said.

Noah said, sneering, "You hid Cody! You kept her away from me!"

"I didn't know what she'd done. I didn't know who she really was. Please, Noah. Let me go see him!"

Noah glanced into the study. "He's not dead, but he will be, he's bleeding all over the place."

"Let me call an ambulance! Please, Noah!" Marlowe pleaded. Noah chuckled grimly.

"You want to save your father?" he snorted. "Nobody saved mine."

"Let me pass!" Marlowe roared. Noah smiled perversely and raised the gun. There was no place to go. Marlowe stood there, waiting to die. Monique brushed past him. She had a pistol and fired twice. BLAM! BLAM! Noah crumpled to the floor. Monique dropped the gun and put her hands over her face. Monique's choking sobs filled the hallway. Marlowe ran into the study. Emmet was lying on the floor, blood on his clothes, his face, coming out of his ear.

Cody was five feet away from him, writhing in pain and moaning, her hands clutching her midriff, blood spurting through her fingers. "Help me," she said.

A uniformed officer escorted Marlowe to the street. It was jammed with patrol cars, ambulances, ablaze with flashing lights, cops talking on their radios, traffic barriers going up. The neighbors were standing on their lawns in robes and pajamas, watching something they'd probably seen before. Marlowe thought they looked more resigned than horrified, wondering perhaps if their children would ever be safe.

"They took your father to MLK," the officer said. "He was conscious. They took the girl too."

"What about her brother?" Marlowe asked.

"DOA."

The paramedics were loading Robert into an ambulance, a sheet over his face. A female officer was holding Monique back. She'll never recover, thought Marlowe. She'll never be herself again, never have fun again and she'll never love another man. He thought of Kendra. Cody would be no great loss, but Noah's death would end her struggle for status and recognition. She'd erect a wall around herself. Nothing in or out. She was a lousy human being but she didn't deserve to be in mourning for the next forty years, sitting on the sand, drinking and staring out at the gray sea. It was shocking how much destruction one person could wreak on those around them, he thought. People like Cody eroded your belief in justice, corrupted the goodness in you, rewarded your suspicions, your anger and your meanest instincts.

The officer drove Marlowe to the hospital. He remembered that night at Sunshine Court, how he shamed Emmet about his drinking and the pain he'd caused his dying wife. Marlowe hoped he got there in time to tell his father he was sorry; that he'd forgiven him and hoped he was forgiven too. As he was getting out of the car, the officer said, "I hope he's okay. Your old man is a legend."

Emmet didn't die because he hadn't been shot. The bullet had grazed his ear. There were powder burns on his face and he'd have to have surgery to repair his ruptured eardrum. The blood spatter was from Cody. Marlowe wondered why she hadn't killed him. She couldn't miss at that range. She might have been bluffing, trying to scare Emmet into opening the safe, or she might have heard Noah and got distracted. Or perhaps, Marlowe mused, Cody had a moment's compassion for the man who believed in her, protected her and wanted nothing in return.

Cody was shot twice in the gut, the worst place to take a bullet. They could have ripped up her stomach, liver, kidneys, intestines, colon or spine. Marlowe knew she'd have health problems for the rest of her life. Cody will be stooped and gray while she's still a kid, he thought, wandering the prison yard with her hate, her bitterness and a colostomy bag.

Marlowe went home, slept a restless few hours and was up at 6 a.m. He had coffee and went up to the roof. He was surprised nothing had changed, that the night's tragedies hadn't made a dent in the City of the Angels. Ren would be leaving in a few hours. Fallon and Jeremy were in Vegas by now. Marlowe had no options, no avenues, no way to bring the kid back. He sank into despondency.

He got a voice message from George Bamford. He wanted help. He'd come out of retirement to executive-produce a movie. It starred Nicole Wyatt.

"Nicole's being stalked, Marlowe," George said. "It's getting out of hand." Interesting, thought Marlowe, and the possibility of seeing Nicole again gave his pulse a bump. He'd call George tomorrow.

He was still morose about Ren. It was one thing to try to help. It was another to hype himself. He remembered assuring her that he'd get Jeremy back. It made him ashamed. He stood there for a minute, kicking himself. Then his pride slapped him in the face. *You're giving up? What kind of nonsense is that? Get off your ass, you idiot. You're the son of a legend.*

He got his notes on Ren and went through them again, his mind working the data like quick fingers on a Rubik's Cube, the pieces clicking and sliding, going faster and faster, Marlowe's breathing matching the pace, the process going on and on until he thought the colored tiles would never come together. He wondered, like he always did, why key resolutions came after everything has happened? *It's because* everything has happened. The case means less, your thinking unobstructed by tension and anxiety.

It was too early for a taxi or an Uber. Marlowe jogged over to the Marriott. The curtains were drawn in Ren's room. Was she still there? He did some deep breathing to prepare himself and knocked on the door.

"It's Marlowe."

"Go away."

"Fallon sold Jeremy to Victoria." The door opened a bit, she had the chain on.

"*Sold him?* Explain and explain right now!"

"We were at Warners, talking to Fallon in the parking lot," said Marlowe. "You were pleading with him not to take Jeremy and he said, 'Sorry, can't be helped.'"

"Yes, that was a peculiar thing to say, but what about it?"

"Fallon had no choice but to deceive you because Jeremy was with Victoria. Did you smell his cologne? It was too sweet, too floral. It was perfume, the same perfume I smelled on Victoria."

Ren undid the chain. "My God, you're right."

"Fallon said he was going to Vegas," Marlowe went on. "Why? To be a dealer? You said he thought dealing was beneath him. He was going there to gamble."

"Of course. He's an addict," Ren said.

"Fallon had money to gamble," Marlowe said. "His car was new, his clothes were new, Jeremy was going to private school and Fallon could afford an expensive attorney. Victoria wasn't doling out checks one at a time. She paid Fallon in full."

Ren opened the door, astonished. "You mean Jeremy is with Victoria *right now*?"

"Yes. Right now."

Emmet's cruiser was parked in front of Victoria's house. Ren and Marlowe watched Emmet go up the walkway and ring the bell.

"It saves a lot of drama if we let him do it," Marlowe said. A housekeeper came to the door. Emmet showed his badge and said something. She let him in and the door closed. Ren couldn't sit still. She squirmed, brought her knees up to hug them, let them down again, drummed her fingers on the doorsill.

"Oh please, please, *please* be there," she breathed. The door opened and Emmet came out holding Jeremy's hand. "Oh my baby!" she shouted. She leapt out of the car, ran to him as the boy ran to her, crying, "Mummy! Mummy!" He flew into her arms and they hugged until they were one, Ren saying, "It's all right, it's all right, I'm here my darling."

It was straight out of a movie, except for Emmet standing there looking away with his hands in his pockets. Father and son were unsentimental but both had tears in their eyes.

Marlowe bought a one-way ticket from LA to London so he could stay with Ren and Jeremy at the gate. Ren was sitting, Jeremy next to her. She explained to the boy that Marlowe was the one who had rescued him. Marlowe stood there, awkward and embarrassed, while Jeremy looked him over, curious, skeptical, no gush of thanks and Ren didn't prompt him.

"Are you my mum's friend?" he asked.

"I like to think so." The answer didn't seem to register, Jeremy looking at his shoes and swinging them back and forth.

"Is that okay with you?" Marlowe asked. Jeremy shrugged.

"I don't know," he said. The boy seemed to lose interest and rested his head on Ren's shoulder. "When's the plane going to come, Mummy?"

"Soon." They sat there, Ren stroking Jeremy's hair. Marlowe had nothing to do but mill around and look graceless. He glanced at Ren. She was looking at him, smiling with such warmth and true affection he felt himself glow.

An incomprehensible voice from the intercom called Ren's flight. They stood in line. Ren with her carry-on in one hand and Jeremy in the other. Marlowe was behind her, just off her left shoulder. He couldn't say anything. The other passengers were close and there was too much noise. All he could see of Ren was the side of her head. Is this it? Marlowe thought. Shuffling along behind a woman he was wild about, unable to do anything but shout in her ear. *She'll be gone in a minute, Marlowe. Say something!*

They were at the front of the line. Ren turned to him, smiled hopelessly and said, "Thank you, Marlowe. Thank you for everything."

"Sure," he said stupidly.

"Do you think you'll come to visit us?" said Jeremy.

"I'd really like that," Marlowe said.

"Okay, I'll see you."

Marlowe smiled. "Yeah, I'll be looking for you, kid."

Marlowe was home. Emmet called and said the Department had made its final ruling. He had to go to rehab or retire. He said he was still deciding. Marlowe couldn't believe it. Emmet's drinking very nearly destroyed his life and he was *still deciding*? Marlowe got a beer and sat in the easy chair. Nothing ever came out completely right. Nothing was over for good, smooth sailing, a piece of cake or a job well done. Why? People. They screwed up everything. They were so random and confused, so—what's the word? *Individual.* Every single one of them was different in ways as complicated as ocean ecology or supernovas. Each had a hundred million synapses sparking at different times in a different part of the brain. No one saw the same thing, interpreted the same data, heard the same music or talked to the same person. How did anything ever come close to being right? His phone buzzed.

"Hello?"

"It's Basilio."

"Oh no," Marlowe moaned.

"Did Ren turn out okay?"

"Yeah."

"I knew it would."

"What do you want, *Basilio.*"

"I want a little less attitude, Marlowe. I have a case for you."

"I'm exhausted. I don't want another case."

"His name is Josiah Heckler. He's eighty-one years old."

"I said I don't want another case."

"A couple of scam artists, Ronnie Z and Flow Chart, ran the pigeon drop on him. Took his savings, house, everything. You know those guys, don't you?"

"You're not listening, Basilio. I don't want another case."

"Did I tell you Josiah is living under the Hollywood Freeway in a cardboard box?"

"No, you never told me that, you called me just now."

"Josiah was wearing pants with no zipper and a big rip in the back," Basilio went on. "He doesn't own any underwear. He had broken glass embedded in his ass cheeks and weeds stuck in his pubes. It was a sight, let me tell you. I took him a bag of pistachios and a Coke and he called it a feast, like Sunday dinner with his family before they were washed away by the tsunami. They were on vacation in Japan." Basilio was chewing so he was at Panda Express. Marlowe could smell the monosodium glutamate.

"Just out of curiosity, what does it say on your T-shirt?" Marlowe asked.

" 'Impeach Shaniqua.' Why do you ask?"

"I don't want another case."

"Josiah has beetles in his hair and he lost one of his hearing aids," Basilio continued. "If you want to talk to him you have to stand to his left. Oh yeah. When you look at him, look at his right eye. The left one is too cloudy."

"Didn't you hear me? I said I don't—"

"Josiah told me a couple of gangsters ripped up his sleeping bag and pushed his shopping cart in front of an Amtrak train. He couldn't defend himself because of the arthritis. His hands look like turkey feet."

"I'm hanging up, Basilio."

"The poor guy's got dental issues too," Basilio continued. "Have you ever smashed a Hershey bar and thrown the pieces in your mouth? Well, you get the picture."

"Josiah's coming to my place, isn't he?" Marlowe said.

"Yeah."

"When?"

"Twenty minutes. He might be late. He doesn't have bus fare."

"Right."

"Could you feed him?" Basilio asked.

"I'll make him dinner."

"Great, Marlowe, thanks."

"Basilio?"

"Yes?"

"The next time I see you I'm going to choke you to death with an orange chicken."

"Goodbye, Marlowe."

"Goodbye, Basilio." Marlowe got up, went to the kitchen and opened the fridge. He had some leftover enchiladas from El Comal. Maybe he'd serve that.

Acknowledgments

"There are no 'classics' of crime and detection. Not one. Within its frame of reference, which is the only way it should be judged, a classic is a piece of writing which exhausts the possibilities of its form and can never be surpassed. No story or novel of mystery has done that yet. Few have come close. Which is one of the principal reasons why otherwise reasonable people continue to assault the citadel."
—Raymond Chandler, 1945

No one ever came closer than Chandler. His books have moved, thrilled and fascinated us for generations. My career, and so many others, were borne from his talent. On behalf of those he inspired and his millions of fans around the world, our thanks.

About the Author

Joe Ide grew up in South Central Los Angeles and currently lives in Santa Monica, California. His IQ series has won the Anthony, Shamus and Macavity Awards, and has been nominated for the Edgar, Barry, CWA New Blood Dagger and Strand Book Critics Awards. It is currently in development as an original TV series.

...and his new novel, *Fixit*

In the sixth installment of Joe Ide's acclaimed IQ series, Isaiah Quintabe's first love, Grace, has been kidnapped by his sworn enemy, the professional hitman Skip Hanson. Skip is savage and psychotic, determined to punish Isaiah for sending him to prison and destroying his life. Isaiah and his sometimes partner, ex-hustler Juanell Dodson—together again—must track scant clues through LA's perilous landscape as Grace's predicament grows more uncertain.

Following is an excerpt from the novel's opening pages.

PROLOGUE

Grace arrived at the food truck midmorning. She put on a hairnet and an apron and set about prepping for the lunch crowd. Deronda's Downhome Buttermilk Fried Chicken would soon be mobbed. Grace was aware, but not aware, of what she was doing, soaking the chicken pieces in buttermilk, dredging them in the dry ingredients and setting them on the rack to dry. She chopped up the collard greens, fried the fatback and onions and put the stock on to boil. Odeal came in, huffing, groaning, the three steps taxing her weight and her wind. Her grandson Lester brought in the casserole dishes. Grace usually looked forward to it, lifting the tinfoil, revealing the world's best mac and cheese, the top crust golden, the molten mix of cheeses still bubbling. The smells were usually comforting, even heartening, but she was far away, staring into the deep fryer, the first bubbles plinking as they emerged through the amber oil.

"You all right, Grace?" Odeal said. "You don't look well, baby. You comin' down with something?"

"No, no, I'm okay," Grace said. "Not enough sleep, that's all."

"I hope you not out there carousin', young lady," Odeal said, only half joking.

"Not me. I'm a homebody."

Grace busied herself, trying and failing not to think. A few days ago, she broke up with Isaiah, the hurt like a stab wound, bleeding into the void left in his wake. She did it on the phone too.

Impersonal, like she was canceling a magazine subscription. Ending their love deserved better than a voice from a cell tower. Isaiah was in Northern California somewhere, unwilling or unable to meet her because he was in another mess. He didn't tell her the specifics; his way of "sparing her" from yet another human goulash of suffering and grief. She couldn't take it, being with a man who invited violence because he couldn't resist risking his life for every victimized person he met. Everyone in the hood knew his rep. The underground PI who helped you find justice when the police wouldn't or couldn't. His cases covered the range of human depravity. He brought down rapists, armed robbers, kidnappers, drug lords, gunrunners, gangsters, con men, thieves, hired killers and pedophiles. Along the way he'd made enemies.

The waiting wore Grace down. For Isaiah to come home, or not come home, wondering what morally compromising, soul-crushing decisions he had to make, or imagining what subhuman cave dweller was swinging at him with a meat cleaver. Grace wasn't naive, she didn't demand tranquility. She wanted to grow as an artist in relative calm, like anyone making their way. If they were a couple, his enemies would be her enemies. She'd be at risk, a target. That was why he didn't ask her to go with him when he left. He wanted her to have peace, be safe. He was Isaiah, after all.

Grace had gone her own way since she was a kid. She was a loner, a misfit, eschewing pop culture for something more meaningful, always with a pencil or a paintbrush in her hand. She didn't know what she wanted in a man until she met Isaiah. Kind, compassionate, loving in his quiet, unobtrusive way, immeasurably competent, and courageous as the three hundred Spartans. But life with him was so dangerous, so fraught with evil, it was, or seemed to be, intolerable.

All she wanted now was something resembling ordinary. There were takers everywhere. Looking for a man? Put on a hairnet, wear no makeup and a shapeless apron, be entirely indifferent to whoever you're talking to and you'll be hit on by every lonely guy in LA. She was saying things to herself like *It's no one's fault, it wasn't meant to be, you're better off without him, things happen for a reason* and a bunch of other fucked-up, nonsensical, bullshit clichés, none of which made one fucking iota of sense.

She missed Isaiah. Every day, all the time. She couldn't have spent more energy thinking about him if he were here. Neither ever said, "I love you," because it didn't matter. Why say something you knew to be true? Why say something that was so obvious it was etched into your retinas? They'd never talked about marriage and they probably never would. Commitment was supposedly a decision. With Isaiah, it was genetic; indelible, like the color of your skin. *Call him, Grace. Call him now. What are you waiting for? Do you think Isaiahs grow on trees?* She resisted. If you were Isaiah, how would you feel? Overjoyed because some fickle artist says she'll cut you a break? Save yourself the effort, Grace. You've lost him once and for all.

She was on edge the whole afternoon; angry at herself and the world that kept her apart from Isaiah. *Be a grown-up, Grace. No tantrums today.*

A bearded man came to the window. Faded T-shirt, pinched face and cadaverous, all ribs, clavicles and elbows. He looked like an unpublished poet.

"What can I get for you?" Grace said.

"Is your chicken non-GMO?" he asked.

"No, it's not," she said. A proselytizer. Cut him short, Grace. "Have you decided? You've got a line behind you."

"If your chicken is not no-GMO you should put it on your sign," he said indignantly. Why do all the assholes end up in this line? she wondered. She felt her temper coming on, like the creaking of a doorknob.

"You mean we should put 'We buy our chicken at Vons' on the sign?" she said. "I'll speak to the management. Could you please order?"

"What kind of oil do you use?" he demanded.

"Pennzoil, 10W-30," she said. "Come on, dude, this is a food truck, not your guru's gluten-free commune. Order or get out of line." The doorknob was turning.

"I'm a consumer. I have the right to say what I think!" the man shouted. He turned to the people in line. "I'd like you all to know, their chicken contains dangerous hormones!" In return he got a chorus of boos and fuck yous. The anger door swung open.

"That's it, asshole!" Grace shouted. She was about to lunge through the window and stab this moron with a plastic fork, but a heavyset Black man in a postal uniform shoved the guy out of line.

"People are hungry, boy. Go home and make your own chicken!"

There was a round of applause and Grace joined in. She went back to work. After serving the postal worker, she realized she felt different. High emotion triggered high emotion, and there was nothing more emotional than her feelings for Isaiah. *What's your problem, Grace? Isaiah's not worth fighting for? You're afraid he'll reject you? The risk is too great? I've got news for you, girl. Love is risk.*

She told Odeal she was leaving early and drove home, anxious and eager, her heart bumping, damp palms choking the life out of the steering wheel. First thing she'd do was fix her hair, put on a little lip gloss and fresh clothes—ridiculous for a phone call but she'd feel better. Where should she be when she made this momentous call? There was the chaise in the backyard or the easy chair in the living room but neither felt right. Maybe in bed. Yes, that was it. Talk to your man while you're in bed.

She parked the battered jeep in the driveway, turned off the engine and lifted the door handle. Skip surprised her as she got out of the car, saying her name like he was spitting, gleeful when he hit her in the gut, the breath ripped out of her throat, the pain erupting, doubling her over. The hitman cackled as she fell to her knees. The last thing she saw before the sky went dark was a dog collar hanging around his neck; chrome-plated, shiny and spiked.

CHAPTER ONE
THE MESSAGE

Isaiah was a patient at the Coronado Springs Hospital, five hundred miles away from East Long Beach and home. He was recovering from injuries he'd sustained during a case—a case he didn't want, need or ask for. To compound his troubles, he was suffering from PTSD. A lifetime of violence, tragedy and suffering had ruined him; his body depleted, his psyche shattered, his emotional self a charred wreck. He was tortured by nightmares and racked with horrifying flashbacks. He couldn't sleep, he couldn't stay awake, every thought a tirade of self-loathing, doubt and pity. The idea of another case repulsed him. He didn't want to be IQ anymore. He didn't want to make a difference. He wanted to be nobody. He wanted Grace.

He was in this condition when he met a young man named Billy Sorenson, an escapee from the local neuropsychiatric ward. Isaiah came back to his cottage one day to find Billy stealing food from his kitchen. He was in a pathetic state; scared, on the run and friendless. Billy believed a serial killer named William Crowe was coming to Coronado Springs. Crowe's presumed intention was to murder someone, identity unknown. According to Billy, Crowe was the infamous AMSAK killer, so called by the press because he disposed of his seventeen victims at the convergence of the American and Sacramento Rivers. Crowe was on a nine-year killing spree and the police had yet to identify him. Billy wanted help bringing him down.

Isaiah soon learned Billy was not a reliable source. He was an alarmist and had a history of making up stories and crying wolf. The whole town knew about him. Isaiah wanted no part of it. This was exactly the kind of thing he'd vowed to stay away from. No more falling into the sewer with the filth and the vermin, covered in the blood and sludge, never to be clean again. He told Billy no.

He told himself he'd take a look. That was all. Isaiah interrogated Billy at length. He laboriously checked the kid's story and went through a raft of police and FBI computer files Billy downloaded from his mother's laptop. She was an assistant district attorney. Isaiah carefully examined the data, reluctantly concluding Billy's story was true. Why is this your business? Isaiah thought. Self-preservation demanded he walk away. But he didn't. Couldn't. The local sheriff didn't believe the story and Crowe would kill another innocent. He had to be found. He had to be caught.

The case was insanely harrowing. Isaiah came close to death several times, closer than he ever had before. He became a fugitive and contemplated suicide. He was kidnapped by outlaws. A gale nearly blew him off a cliff face. He had a knife fight in the middle of a bonfire. He crashed a motorcycle and was nearly crushed by an avalanche, and in the midst of this maelstrom a stinging irony revealed itself. The PTSD symptoms had virtually disappeared. The danger, the adrenaline, the mental machinations and extreme physical demands abated the illness. But when the case ended, the symptoms roared back and flattened him. Now here he was in the hospital contemplating his future. There were only two choices. To be sick again, or to resume the work that made him sick. "I'll be sick," he said as he lay there on the gurney. He'd never return to the cesspool. He would get out of here and go someplace where there was peace, where no one knew him, where there was no IQ. Where there was no I.

A nurse had just left his room. Isaiah was curled in the crisp hospital sheets. He should have asked her for more meds. Something to make him sleep and escape his misery while images of Grace strobed in and out of his mind. They'd lived together briefly. In the late afternoons, she'd set up her easel in the backyard. She said the light was warmer and softer when the sun set and rose. Isaiah observed her from the window. She stood at her easel, perfectly still, like an egret waiting in a tide pool. Long minutes passed. She wasn't restless and she didn't fidget. He admired her humility, knowing the world changed in its own good time. They did small things. Cooked, shopped, went for walks, talked about nothing, sat on the stoop and drank cold beers and read to each other lying in bed; things he immediately forgot but that now in retrospect seemed so meaningful and sweet.

Deronda called and stirred him out of his reverie.

She was breathless, like she'd run up a flight of stairs. "Grace has gone missing," she said.

Isaiah sat up. His pains vanished, his stomach lurched. "Missing? What do you mean?"

"I mean she's missing and nobody knows where she's at. Last time I talked to her was yesterday. I texted her a bunch of times, but she don't answer. I was hoping she was with you."

"No, she's not." He was already out of bed and donning his clothes. Deronda said Grace left her handbag behind. Keys, wallet, everything.

"The police ain't doin' shit. They told me to wait seventy-two hours," Deronda said. "It's some kinda policy."

"Do they know who did it?"

"Dodson said it was somebody named Skip Hanson. I asked him how he knew and he said it was the dog collar."

"Dog collar?"

"It was left in the driveway. It's supposed to be some kinda message." Isaiah froze. The fear was overwhelming. Skip was a hitman, cunning, brutal and erratic. They met on a case. At the time, Skip lived alone in the desert, murdering people for money and raising a pack of lethal canines. They were his family and the only source of love in his life. Isaiah sent Skip to jail and his loved ones were put down. Even five years later, Skip's hatred was palpable, a radiating heat, like standing in front of a blast furnace. "I'm on my way," Isaiah said.

Isaiah was on the road, the headlights carving a tunnel through the darkness. He was driving Grace's car. A 1968 Mustang GT she'd lovingly restored in memory of her father. She'd given him the car before he went away. Isaiah could feel her presence, her small hands on his, turning the wheel, guiding him home. He'd pass through Lake Tahoe soon, take Highway 88 to Interstate 5 and an eighty-mile-an-hour sprint to Long Beach and home. A seven-hour drive. He'd do better than that.

There was a $25,000 bounty on Isaiah's head. A network of gangs across the breadth of SoCal were looking for him, along with drug dealers, junkies, thieves, hustlers, thugs and ex-cons of every sort. Manzo Gutierrez led the posse, the highly intelligent Khan of the Sureños Locos 13. Manzo and Isaiah weren't friends, but they respected each other's strengths, exchanged favors and stayed on their own sides of the street.

Isaiah had betrayed Manzo, not for his own gain, but to save an emotionally disabled young woman from murder charges. The reason was immaterial. Manzo was humiliated and the Locos lost out on a seven-figure arms deal. There was no forgiveness, only restitution and death. The bounty lured ordinary folks into the pursuit. That was a lot of coin for pointing a finger. Looking for Grace under those conditions was impossible, never knowing if the butcher, the baker, the crackheads in the parking lot or the checker at the supermarket would rat you out. Manzo would have to call them off and somehow rescind the reward. Convincing the shrewd gang leader would take ingenuity, conviction and a giant set of brass balls. Isaiah possessed all of the above but little hope he could pull it off. He was a fugitive from street justice.

With every mile, Isaiah felt IQ returning. Keen, relentless, senses wide open, his mind working smoothly, without doubts or indecision, measuring the meager data, considering options, making choices. He felt like a mother whose child is pinned under a car, that nexus of love, urgency and terror giving her the strength to lift the massive weight and save her baby. Maybe the PTSD would return after he found Grace, he thought. But it didn't matter. *Get her back, Isaiah.*

His phone buzzed. A number he didn't recognize.

"What's up, Q Fuck?" Skip said. Isaiah was stunned. His phone was new, a burner. Grace probably gave him the number.

"Skip," Isaiah said, hoping his voice didn't falter.

"Well, well, well, how things change," the killer said. Isaiah knew to avoid accusations and aggression. It gave Skip a reason to hurt Grace.

"Hey, Grace, I've got your boyfriend on the phone," he called out. She's not dead in a ditch, thought Isaiah. That means I can find her. "Funny thing," Skip went on. "We were just talking about you— weren't we, honey? By the way, she's not bad or anything but a guy like you could do way better than this." No, thought Isaiah. No one could do better than this. "She's not so great in the personality department either," Skip continued. "But we're getting along great. Oh, she got out of line a couple of times and I put her in her place. Holding a gun to her head took the starch right out of her, right, Grace?" Isaiah couldn't swallow, couldn't speak, he was trembling. "Are you there, asshole?" Skip said.

"Yes, I'm here." He let it hang. He wasn't going to say Please don't hurt her, or Is she okay? Or, especially, I'm going to kill you, motherfucker. Skip would taunt him all the more.

"Yeah, the strong, silent type," Skip said, contemptuous. "You always were. Do you want to talk to her?"

"You're in charge. I have no say in it," Isaiah said. Skip laughed.

"I like this, I like it when you're humble. Yeah, it suits you, and you know what? It's gonna get worse, Q Fuck. *It's gonna get much worse.* Hey, Grace, get over here!" There were rustling sounds. "Say the wrong thing and you're fucked," Skip said.

"Isaiah? Don't worry, I'm okay," she said. Her voice was soft and throaty, a lance through his soul. Just like her, he thought. Kidnapped and she's reassuring you.

"I'm glad. I'm glad you're okay," he said. *Stay steady, Isaiah.*

"I mean that, I'm really fine," she went on unconvincingly. "I'm not injured or anything and I'm all right. Skip's treating me fine." Isaiah opened his mouth but nothing came out. What could he say? Keep your chin up? You'll come home soon? I'll be there in a jiffy?

"That's good," he said. He didn't want her to talk anymore. He knew they were on speakerphone and he knew Skip was standing over her with a baseball bat. If she said the wrong thing she'd likely get her skull cracked open.

"Skip said he's going to let me go so don't worry," she said.

"You should get off, Grace," Isaiah said. There were more rustling sounds and Skip came on.

"All right, that's it." He was probably upset because Isaiah told her to get off and not him. "Go over there and sit down," Skip said. "Go on!" Skip threw something and Grace yelped.

"Okay! Okay!" she said distantly. Isaiah instigated the deaths of others, but he'd never killed anyone himself. *Oh, you will be punished, Skip.* For every mark that's on her, for every time she cried in pain, for every time you touched her, you will be punished and it won't stop until you're dead.

"You know what's gonna happen now, don't you?" Skip said. Isaiah did know. Skip would use Grace to torment him. "We're gonna play hide-and-seek," Skip said. "I hide Grace and you seek. Think you can do that, Q Fuck?"

"I, uh, I don't know," Isaiah said.

"I'm an impatient guy," said Skip. "If you don't find her and I get tired of waiting, I'll kill her and stuff her body in a dumpster. Better put a move on it, Q Fuck. Oh yeah, I left a message for you." Skip disconnected and Isaiah suddenly realized he was going nearly a hundred miles an hour. Skip said he left a message but didn't say where. It took him one second to figure it out. He called Dodson.

"It's Isaiah," he said.

"Where the hell are you?" Dodson said. "You couldn't send a text or something, let people know what's goin' on? You better be on your way back." Antagonism was Dodson's opening bid whatever the circumstances.

"Just leaving Fresno," Isaiah said. "What's happening?"

"Nothing here. Everybody's on the lookout. I told 'em Skip was long gone but they're still looking. I don't know why but lots of folks round here are fond of your ass."

"I talked to Skip."

"You *talked* to him?" Dodson said. "What's that crazy muthafucka got to say?"

"He has Grace. Wants to play hide-and-seek."

"Uh-huh," said Dodson like he knew it all along. "And you'll be runnin' around all crazy, following clues Skip made up, and you know what's gonna happen then? He'll lead you right into a trap."

"Seems like it," Isaiah said.

"I know what you gonna do too," Dodson replied.

"Oh really? What's that?"

"You'll see it coming like you usually do, then you'll walk right into it."

"Why would I do that?" Isaiah said.

"Because if you find Skip, you find Grace. That, and you think your freakishly large brain will get you out of anything even when it won't."

"I'll meet you at Blue Hill," Isaiah said.

Dodson's voice went falsetto. "Blue Hill? Ain't nothin' out there but—" Isaiah disconnected before Dodson could give him twelve reasons why that made no sense.

Dodson entered the kitchen. Cherise was sitting at the breakfast table with a stack of files and her laptop. She supervised a team of paralegals at a downtown law firm and brought work home all the time. Cherise was a fine-looking woman. She possessed a sweet, sexy side that still air-fried his hormones after six years of marriage. She was also churchgoing, frighteningly intelligent, so honest it was off-putting and a firm believer in earning your daily bread. On the whole, he was glad he married her. He'd still be a no-account, meandering low-life hustler if he'd continued his wayward ways. On the whole.

"I just got off the phone with Isaiah," he said.

"You did?" Cherise said.

"He's coming. Just leaving Fresno."

"That's fantastic news," Cherise said, pushing the laptop away. "I feel so sorry for Isaiah. He's such a good soul. He loves Grace and she loves him. I don't know what I'd do if—"

"What'd you do if—what?" Dodson said. "Somebody kidnapped me? Y'all should worry about the kidnapper."

"I didn't mean you, I meant our son, Micah. Remember him?" Their five-year-old boy, growing like a mushroom cloud.

"Isaiah wants me to meet him at Blue Hill," Dodson said.

"Good, I'm sure he'll need help," Cherise said. He turned away, relieved because they were supposed to have a "serious talk." Cherise said, "I haven't forgotten, Juanell. Sit down. This won't take long." Dodson closed his eyes. That meant it would take forever.

"Not now, baby, I'm upset."

"I'm upset too but that doesn't mean we have to put our life on hold." He sat. Cherise looked at him a moment. It wasn't a nice look. More like a linebacker on fourth and one.

"The last time we talked about your chronic unemployment, you said you were going to be a fixer," Cherise began. "I thought it was a shady idea but okay, I can see how it fits your personality. You said you wanted to help people with their problems, like you did with Deronda. I'm proud of you for that."

It happened months ago. A man named Bobby James tried to blackmail Deronda for half her business. Dodson stepped in. He made a shrewd calculation, squashed Bobby James and sent the asshole on his way. Deronda said he should be a fixer and regretfully, that was what he told Cherise.

"What I want to know is, why aren't you out there fixing things?" Cherise said.

"Because nobody knows about it," Dodson said. "It's hard to flex that kind of thing. What do I say on social media? 'Hello, friends. I'm proud to announce my new career as a professional fixer. My qualifications? I was a street hustler, I sold drugs, I ran a Ponzi scheme and spent time in Vacaville.'" Cherise rolled her eyes. Dodson continued as if she wasn't there. "'It was there I got my degree in duplicity, deception, bribery, double-crossing, double-dealing, short cons, long cons, extortion and graft. Please have a look at my website. W W W dot sneaky muthafucka.'"

"You know how I feel about that language, Juanell, and as a matter of fact, I have a client for you." She looked at him, hesitant. She was never hesitant. He was getting a bad feeling.

"You gonna keep me guessing?" Dodson said.

"Reverend Arnall." Cherise said it like she was confessing something.

"Reverend Arnall? If he needs help, why don't he ask Jesus? Can't the Son of God help him out?"

"I'm angry with you already, Juanell," Cherise said, narrowing her eyes. "Profane Christ and you won't see me naked again until you're playing Chinese checkers at the senior center."

Dodson made a small groaning sound. "What does the Reverend want?"

"He can tell you himself," Cherise said. Dodson's relationship with the church was a puff of air.

"If this is about my chronic unemployment, is the Reverend gonna pay me?" Dodson said. Again, she hesitated.

"He'll pray for you and give you the Lord's blessing."

"Is that like Bitcoin?" Dodson said. "I need a new car."

"You'll be helping others, Juanell. Isn't that the point?" Cherise said.

"That's one of 'em. I believe the other was money."

"Never mind," Cherise said, waving like she was batting away a mosquito. "I've made an appointment for you with the Reverend on Thursday and don't you *dare* blow it off."

The sun was rising when Isaiah reached the desert, brown and barren, piles of gray boulders and low, dusky foothills. It was already in the eighties. The closest civilization to Skip's place was Fergus, a two-block truck stop that sold inedible donuts and bad coffee. Isaiah drove into the parking lot of the Dew Drop Inn and saw Dodson sitting in his car. A fifteen-year-old, gleaming white Lexus RX. Dodson was in the driver's seat, his arm straight out on the steering wheel, bobbing his head to Tupac's "How Do U Want It." Isaiah was glad with his whole heart. He pulled up, driver's side to driver's side. Dodson smiled his cocky, breezy, don't-you-ever-fuck-with-me smile.

"Whassup, Q?" Dodson said.

"Same old," Isaiah said.

"What happened to your hand?" Dodson asked. Isaiah's hand was bandaged. He burned it in the knife fight with William Crowe. Dodson added, "Did your brain get so big you had to punch yourself in the face?"

"Yeah, that's what happened," Isaiah said, smiling. "You ready?"

"Why you always ask me that?" Dodson complained. "When I fell out the womb I was ready."

"Whose car? Yours or mine?"

"Mine," Dodson said decisively. "Goliath's kids might be up there and you drive too slow." Dodson had a pit bull phobia. It had worsened since Goliath nearly ate him for supper.

It was a short drive to the LANDFILL 6 MILES sign and the dirt road. Isaiah was elated to see Dodson again and he knew Dodson felt that way too. Showing it was uncool, embarrassing and confusing. Step outside their unspoken, long-established rules and who knows what would happen.

The road was full of potholes and stretches of washboard, Dodson wincing with every bump. "We shoulda called an Uber," he complained. "Biggie don't like this bullshit."

"Who's Biggie?" Isaiah said.

"My car—hey, man, look at all this goddamn dust! I can hardly see!"

"It washes off, you know."

"Hang on, Biggie," Dodson said, patting the dashboard. "I'll get you outta here soon enough." Dodson was into old-school rap, the nineties was his era. Biggie, Tupac, Nas, Lauryn Hill, Scarface and

Jay-Z. He listened to contemporary rap but said it didn't move him. There were no memories attached to the songs.

The BLUE HILL PIT BULLS sign was where it had been before, grimy and faded and nailed into the same dead tree. They parked and walked across the rocky expanse of dirt that used to be the front yard. The small house was a wreck; broken windows, missing front door, crumbling stucco, a rain gutter hanging loose.

"I got a lotta bad memories about this place," Dodson said.

"Yeah, me too," Isaiah said.

"What are we doing here?"

"Skip said he left me a message, but he didn't say where."

"Then how do you know it's here?"

"Because I know," Isaiah said.

"You don't need to get snippy," Dodson said.

"I'm not snippy," Isaiah said. Another one of their perennial arguments.

"Normal people don't have your psychic powers," Dodson said. "Maybe while we're here you can talk to my dead grandmother and find out where she hid the silverware." It was comforting, Isaiah thought. The banter was something they did no matter what the situation. It kept the edge off the nervousness and covered over the fear.

They went in the house, ducking under the cobwebs, stepping over the broken glass, smashed furniture and assorted junk. Dodson glanced down at the floor. "See them footprints?"

"Yes, I see them," Isaiah said. "Work boots, size ten."

"There you go bein' snippy again," Dodson said.

"I'm not being—forget it."

They went down the hall and stopped at the bedroom. At one point in the Goliath case, Isaiah and Dodson tried to kidnap the dog as a means of coercing Skip into submission. All the dogs were kenneled in the barn—except Goliath. Skip left him loose as a kind of roving security guard. The dog chased Dodson into the house. He wanted to lock himself in the bedroom but there were no interior doors. Skip removed them so Goliath wouldn't have to slow down while he was chomping your ass to shreds. The dog cornered Dodson in the closet and was about to bite his face off when Isaiah shot the beast with a tranquilizer gun. He borrowed it from Harry Halderman.

"Could we move on, please?" Dodson said. "This place will give me nightmares." A rectangle of newspapers and flattened cardboard boxes was on the floor, fast-food debris scattered around.

"Skip spent the night," Isaiah said.

"Why?" Dodson said.

"The message. Whatever it is, it took some time."

The roof of the barn was caved in, grime, crud and cobwebs clinging to every surface, dust motes nearly stationary in the dim light. The kennels were in shambles. Frames broken, gates broken, ancient dog turds embedded in the cement.

"Goliath's kennel is at the end of the row," Isaiah said. It was intact, twice as big as the others, made of heavy chain link. The gate was new. Fresh-cut wood, pine smell, sawdust scattered. The floor was swept.

"Why'd Skip do all this?" Dodson said.

"He's telling me we're starting over," Isaiah said. "He's telling me it's a new day." A dog food can was set on the ground. It was shiny, no label, *Q FUCK* written on it with a red Sharpie. Isaiah did a quick scan for booby traps and stepped over the railing. He held his head back and nudged the can with his foot. No rattlesnake. Inside was a memory stick.

Isaiah and Dodson were in the car, the air-conditioning up high. Isaiah inserted the memory stick into his laptop.

"What do you think is on there?" Dodson said.

"Photos."

"Take it slow, Q," Dodson said protectively.

Isaiah hesitated, gulped in a deep breath and brought up the first photo. At first, he couldn't focus, or maybe he didn't want to. He saw a young woman—but it wasn't Grace! He took in another breath and abruptly held it. No. It was Grace. She was sweaty and bedraggled, hair over her face, her wrists wrapped with duct tape, a strip over her mouth. Isaiah had been bound like that a number of times. It was terrifying. He stared at her, swallowing dry. Skip was standing next to her, a car behind them. The hitman was grinning triumphantly, his arm around her, hand gripping her shoulder. Rage exploded inside Isaiah's chest.

"He's touching her," he said. He growled through his teeth, shivered violently and snapped shut the laptop. He got out of the car and slammed the door.

Dodson watched his friend storm blindly into the brush. He stopped, stood there in the white-hot sun, quaking, veins bulging in his neck, breathing in short huffs, his whole body tight as a clenched fist. Then he lifted his head and screamed, loud and piercing, his voice an axe blade, leveling the tumbleweed and flattening the foothills, pausing only to suck in a breath before hurling more outrage at the sky. His throat was raw but he kept screaming until he choked up and stopped.

Dodson took a bottle of water, got out of the car and walked after him. He was surprised. Everything was the same, the rocks, the brush, the stunted trees and hazy sky. Like they didn't hear a thing. Like Isaiah was never there. Yeah, let that be a lesson to you, thought Dodson. Whatever your troubles, you on your own, son. The universe don't give a shit.

Isaiah was breathing hard, eyes closed, chin on his chest like God condemned him to misery ever after. Dodson handed him the bottle of water.

"Here. If you die of heatstroke I'm gonna leave you out here."

MULHOLLAND BOOKS

You won't be able to put down these Mulholland Books.